A STICK OF BLACKPOOL ROCK

For years Ellen Bamber has suffered the violence of a drunken husband, tolerating his abuse only for the sake of their two young children. When William Bamber falls under a hansom cab after a drinking bout and dies, Ellen feels her silent prayers have been answered. After his funeral, Ellen discovers William had also been unfaithful to her and the knowledge of his illegitimate child tears her apart. Moving her family to Blackpool and setting up in the rock-making industry, she remarries, but still fears that one day the legacy of William's misconduct will destroy the happiness she had found...

A STICK OF BLACKPOOL ROCK

A Stick Of Blackpool Rock

by

Margaret Thornton

Magna Large Print Books
Long Preston, North Yorkshire,
BD23 4ND, England.

British Library Cataloguing in Publication Data.

Thornton, Margaret
A stick of Blackpool rock.

A catalogue record of this book is
available from the British Library

ISBN   0-7505-1545-7

First published in Great Britain by Headline Book Publishing, 1997

Published in Large Print 2000 by arrangement with Headline Book
Publishing

Magna Large Print is an imprint of Library Magna Books Ltd.

Printed and bound in Great Britain by
T.J. (International) Ltd., Cornwall, PL28 8RW

When I speak to people of my generation I often hear the cry, 'Blackpool isn't the place it used to be!' Sadly, this is true. Those of us who were born and reared in the resort cannot help but regret some of the ways in which our town has changed in recent years. I hope that my novels help to recapture some of the essence of Blackpool as it once was and, in many ways, still is – the foremost seaside resort in Great Britain, if not in the world!

ACKNOWLEDGEMENTS

I would like to thank Mrs Margaret Race for permission to use many of the facts from her informative book *The Story of Blackpool Rock* and the additional information she and her husband gave me when I visited their factory in Marton.

Thanks also to Mr Frank Higgins for permission to adapt for my own use some of the details concerning his own family.

The firms Bamber and Tucker and Hobson's Rock used in my story are, of course, wholly fictitious and the characters are purely figments of my imagination.

Chapter One

'Look, Mummy, look – a pig! An' he's smiling, isn't he? Can you see him, Georgie, that great big piggy smiling at us? Isn't he 'normous?'

Many people in the crowd lining Fishergate turned to smile at the excited little girl and her slightly younger brother. The giant pig, part of the elaborate display put on by Myerscough's, the Provision Merchants, was proving to be one of the highlights of this Preston Guild procession of 1902. Fat and pink and – as the little girl had said – smiling, he was mounted on a flower-bedecked float drawn by a glossy black shire horse. At the side and the rear walked a group of men, doubtless Myerscough's assistants, dressed in long white aprons and white wide-brimmed hats.

Ellen Bamber was pleased that, at last, there was something to reawaken the children's attention. They had been excited at first by all the noise and colour and the crowds, more people than they had ever seen before in their short lives, but now, after over an hour of watching the many and varied displays of the Trades' Procession passing in front of them, their interest was beginning to flag. Four-year-old Rachel, and George, aged two and a half, were good children. Ellen didn't think any mother could have better behaved children than hers, but enough was enough. She knew that she couldn't expect them to stand still much longer. She had lifted George up a few times when he complained of feeling tired, but he was a robust, well-built boy, already taking after his father in stature, far too heavy for Ellen to hold for long.

'Yes, he is enormous, isn't he?' Ellen smiled at her daughter. 'He's like the pig in your story book, Rachel. The one that built the house of bricks. I bet the big bad wolf wouldn't get the better of that fellow.'

'Will there be some more, Mummy?' asked George. 'Some more piggies?'

'No, I don't think so, love. No more pigs,' replied Ellen. 'But there'll be all kinds of exciting things. You just watch, there's a good boy.'

'I'm tired, Mummy.' George sighed, sitting down on the pavement and stretching his sturdy little legs out in front of him. 'My legs is hurting.'

'All right, dear. We won't stay much longer. We'll just wait for Daddy's float to go past, then we'll get off home and make a nice cup of tea and have something to eat, how's that?'

George didn't answer, but Rachel nodded stoically. 'Our Georgie's sure to be tired, isn't he, Mummy? He's only a little boy. But we'll have to wait and see Daddy. That's why we've come, isn't it? He'd be ever so disappointed if we didn't wait to see him.'

'Yes … yes, I daresay he would,' replied Ellen, not very convincingly. She doubted that William would even notice their absence.

The floats of the Cordwainers – the ancient name for shoemakers, which also included cobblers – were towards the end of the procession. They had already seen the butchers and bakers, the housepainters, bricklayers and plasterers, the saddlers and harness makers, the plumbers and gas-fitters, to name but a few. Most of the displays had been colourful and eye-catching, a tribute to the combined efforts of employers and employees. Ellen had been impressed by the wire pagoda, decorated with garlands of flowers and hanging baskets, the creation of the wire-working and window-blind manufacturing firm of James Starkie and Son. It was known as the 'Rose Temple' and, according to Ellen's mother, it had been a notable feature of the 1882 procession. And here it was again. The Preston Guild thrived on tradition. The children, until the appearance of the pig, had been most impressed by the display put on by the Fire Brigade. Their uniforms were immaculate, their brass helmets, buckles and equipment all brightly burnished and gleaming in the September sunshine, as were the shiny black coats of their magnificent horses. A huge cheer had gone up for these brave men as they passed, and there were murmurs throughout the crowd of how the Fire Brigade had been a popular feature of the Guild procession since the early nineteenth century – so they had heard – and would be for evermore.

Ellen couldn't remember the last Guild, the one of 1882, as she had been only two years old, the age that Georgie was now, but she had often heard her mother speak of it. And by the time the next one came round in 1922 Ellen would be ... forty-two. She suppressed a shudder at the thought of it. It didn't do to look too far ahead. It was more than enough for her to cope with life as it was at this moment; with her two children and her home and her little job, making and selling sweets on the market … and her husband, who no longer loved or even wanted her, except when he had had too much to drink.

There was a saying around these parts, and further afield as well. Whereas most folk would say, 'Once in a blue moon', Lancashire folk said, 'Once every Preston Guild', because Preston Guild was a festival which took place only once in every twenty years. It was an ancient tradition having its roots way, way back in history, as far back as 1179, when the Guild Merchant was granted to the town of Preston by King Henry II. The core of the celebrations, which took place at the beginning of the week on the balcony of the Town Hall, was the ceremony where the burgher rights were renewed. This was not witnessed by most of the ordinary folk of Preston, but their time for celebration came later in the various events and activities that went on throughout the week – the processions, entertainments, feasts, balls and dances, the sporting events, sideshows and circuses and, to round off the week, a magnificent firework display!

Ellen would not be partaking in many of them, but she was proud to have just a tiny part in the revelry that was taking place in the town of her birth. Pride was what all the townsfolk felt. Wasn't their town always referred to as 'Proud Preston'? From where she stood, Ellen could see the initials 'PP' boldly emblazoned on the crests

14

decorating the triumphal arch at the end of Church Street. There had been several of these arches put up at various points along the processional route. Ellen and her mother had taken the children to see the decorations one Sunday afternoon, whilst William was sleeping off the effects of a late Sunday lunch and a surfeit of beer. They hadn't walked all the route, which was several miles, but they had seen a goodly part of it.

Proud Prestonians had been erecting triumphal arches in celebration of their Guild for 150 years. The one at the end of Fishergate proclaimed 'A Hearty Welcome' – there would be thousands upon thousands of visitors swarming into the town that week – while at other points there were Japanese, Chinese and Moorish arches. Closer to the hearts of Preston folk was the arch in Stanley Street, near to Horrockses mill, constructed entirely of cotton bales. The cotton industry was of such importance in the town that the textile workers had their own procession, distinct from that of the general trades.

'Mummy, Mummy, I think they're coming now,' Rachel tugged at her mother's skirt. 'I can see some men carrying big sticks with shoes on the top of them. D'you think this'll be Daddy's lot?'

'Yes, it must be.' Ellen nudged her son gently with her foot. 'Come on, Georgie love. Stand up now. Daddy'll be coming. Watch out for Daddy, then you can wave to him.'

In front of the floats walked two men in medieval costume with long cloaks and plumed

15

hats. They carried a banner emblazoned with the words, *Preston Guild, Success to the Cordwainers. May the Manufacture of the Sons of Crispin be trampled underfoot by all the World.* St Crispin was the patron saint of the shoemakers. Behind them walked apprentices holding long poles on which were placed ladies' and gentlemen's shoes of different fashions. They were all wearing red morocco-leather aprons bound with light blue ribbons. Then came the two floats, each drawn by two horses. On the first one, which resembled a shoemaker's shop, three men were busy making shoes and three young women doing binding work with leather.

But it was the second float that the Bamber children were eagerly awaiting. For there, in a facsimile of a clogger's shop, sat their father, William, tapping away at a clog iron, fastening it on to a wooden sole. Near him sat Amos, the gangling youth who was his assistant, likewise tapping at the sole of a clog. Amos was a simple soul, 'a few bricks short of a load', as William put it, and Ellen knew that her husband led him a merry dance. Two other men, cloggers from another part of Preston, sat opposite them. William wore a huge leather apron, such as he always wore when he was at work, and a blue collarless shirt which enhanced the bright blue of his eyes. At the excited shout of 'Daddy, Daddy!', he looked up from his work and waved.

'Hello there, rascals. Behaving yourselves?' he said, all there was time to say in the few moments it took for the float to pass by. But in those few moments as he smiled at the children Ellen was able to catch a glimpse of the handsome young man she had married, the young man with whom, at that time, she had thought she was so much in love. Then, as his glance shifted from the children to her, she became aware of a sardonic glint in those intensely blue eyes and a cynical smirk, rather than a smile, playing round his wide, well-shaped lips. He lifted one eyebrow, almost imperceptibly, as he glanced at her, then quickly looked away. It was possible that no one else in the crowd around them would have noticed the look he gave her, but Ellen, who knew only too well his every gesture, every nuance of each smile or frown or comment, read in it that she had angered him again last night, and that he would be waiting to take his revenge. Tonight, more than likely, when he had drunk his fill at the Old Dog Inn. His drinking and his subsequent ill-treatment of her was becoming an almost nightly occurrence.

William's ruddy complexion which many, Ellen knew, put down to healthy living, was a result of these successive drinking bouts. At the time of their marriage he had never tasted alcohol. When old man Bamber was alive he wouldn't have dared to do so because his father, strictly teetotal, had ruled him with a rod of iron. And he had continued to do so even after the lad had married and left home. Ellen knew now that William had realised only too well on which side his bread was buttered. He had only to keep the old man happy, and the lease of the clogger's shop on Church Street and his father's house on Stonygate would one day be all William's. He was the only son of elderly parents and his mother had died a few years before. Should he displease his father, however, old Joseph Bamber would be quite capable of taking his revenge by leaving the whole lot to charity. Sure enough, on his father's death, just after Georgie was born, William had become the sole inheritor of the business and property. He and Ellen had left the two-up, two-down house which they had rented and moved to the larger premises.

Ellen, though she had been fond of the old man, was happy to think that she now had a comfortable home in which to bring up her two children and – who knew? – there might be several more before long. William was an extremely lusty young man. It had come as something of a shock to Ellen on her wedding night to discover the extent of his virility; there were several things that had been a shock to her. Now, as well as his parents' home, he had a thriving business. She and the children would want for nothing, at least as far as material things were concerned, or so Ellen had thought.

His drinking had been only spasmodic at first, and Ellen had seen it as a show of bravado, the dutiful son at last breaking free from the shackles which had bound him for so long. But it had become progressively worse, and now William was seldom sober after eleven o'clock at night. Not so drunk, however, that he didn't want to make love to her, if the frenzied, uncouth coupling which took place in their double bed could be called love. Ellen knew that it couldn't. She had ceased to love William, and she was aware that he no longer cared for her. If he did, if he had an atom of feeling for her, he wouldn't treat her so shamefully. The biggest mistake Ellen had made had been to resist his advances and to make it quite clear that his beer-laden breath and clumsy embraces were repugnant to her. It was then that the beatings had started, although William, befuddled as he was, had the sense to make sure that the bruises and weals which marked his wife's body were in places where they wouldn't show. Last night had been worse than ever. Ellen had felt humiliated beyond belief at his treatment of her, though there had been a certain satisfaction in the knowledge that William had been unable to bring the act to a conclusion. It was the first time that this had happened, but Ellen felt sure that it wouldn't be the last. The 'demon drink' was taking its toll in all sorts of ways, as the proclaimers of abstinence always avowed.

There were not many of Ellen's friends or family who knew about her trouble. For William, quite amazingly, was as right as rain again the following morning. His inebriety didn't seem, so far, to have affected his work; the clogger's shop was always busy and his wares much in demand. Possibly her mother and her sister had an inkling, but they had no idea of the extent of her problem. It wasn't something that you could talk about, not to anyone, and Rachel and Georgie hadn't, as yet, appeared to notice any difference in their father. He still treated them with the same nonchalant affection – almost as though they were pet puppies – as he had always done.

19

There were many, indeed, who envied Ellen her handsome husband, her two delightful children and her seemingly comfortable lifestyle.

The little group attracted many benevolent glances and smiles as they pushed their way out of the crowd lining Fishergate, making their way towards Stonygate and home. What a credit they both were to their mother, the people who had been standing near to them remarked. The pretty little girl was the image of her mother, with the same delicate features, deep brown eyes and fairish hair waving gently beneath the brim of her straw hat. And the little lad in the sailor suit, anyone could see that he was the very spit of his father, that handsome fellow on the clogger's float who had waved to them. She was a lucky young woman to have such a lovely family.

'You watched the procession then, did you, lass?' Lydia Tucker asked her daughter later that afternoon. Ellen had arrived at the market to help her mother on the sweet stall which they ran as a family concern. The name on the hoarding was her mother's – *Tucker's Tasty Toffee,* it proclaimed – and most of the produce had been made by Lydia, although Ellen had contributed a sizeable share just recently.

'Yes, I took our Rachel and Georgie, like I said I would,' Ellen replied. 'They got a bit bored though, Mam, as it was so long. We just waited till we'd seen William's float then we went home. Our Georgie was dropping, nearly falling asleep on his feet he was, poor lamb. But I warmed up some broth then we had some apple pie and custard and they were as right as ninepence again.'

'So they're at our Mary's now, are they? Happen she'll bring 'em round this afternoon to have a look at us.'

'Yes, she said she might. She'll be taking the twins out in their pram, and you know how Rachel and Georgie like to think they're looking after their little cousins.' Ellen's elder sister, Mary, had twin boys, aged nine months. She was no longer able to continue with her job at Horrockses cotton mill, where her husband, Fred, was employed, so she looked after Ellen's two children as well as her own on the days when Lydia and Ellen ran the market stall. 'I hope the crowd has thinned out a bit before our Mary comes out,' Ellen went on. 'You couldn't put a pin between them on Fishergate this morning. I'm sorry you couldn't manage to watch the procession, Mam. You missed a treat.'

'I've seen it all before,' said Lydia casually. 'I watched the last one – with you, when you were only knee-high to a grasshopper.'

Ellen laughed. 'Oh, come on, Mam. That was twenty years ago.'

'Aye, I know.' Lydia sniffed. 'But I doubt if it's much different. I went to watch the religious procession, mind you, the other day. Our lot, I mean, the C of E. It's a pity your Rachel couldn't have been in it. I'd like to have seen her, bless her, in a white frock and flowers an' all. But it would have been too far for her to walk. And next time she'll be too old. And I shall be … God knows where I shall be. Pushing up daisies, more than likely.'

21

'For heaven's sake, Mam, don't talk like that.' Ellen felt the proverbial goose walking over her grave as she had done earlier that day, thinking about the passing of time and what they would all be doing twenty years hence. 'In 1922 you'll only be ... what? Sixty-eight? Not even your threescore years and ten, so we'll have less talk about you pegging out, thank you very much.'

'I didn't mean it, lass,' Lydia laughed. 'It makes you think though, doesn't it, with this lot only taking place, like they say, "Once every Preston Guild". How many are you likely to see in your lifetime? Three ... maybe four, and that 'ud be pushing it a bit. And at each one your circumstances have changed. First you're a child, then a mother, then a grandmother ... and a widow an' all; at least that's what I am. Aye, it makes you think all right...

'One thing I was glad about was that they'd separated the religious processions this time,' Lydia continued. 'I remember at the last lot there was no end of bother when the Catholic procession was attacked by them Orangemen. Silly fools they are, all as bad as one another, if you ask me.'

'Yes, I think it's a great pity, though, that they can't all march together,' Ellen commented. 'I believe the Nonconformists – the Methodists and Baptists and all that lot – had their own procession too. It's a shame folks can't all get on with one another without all this strife.' Not much chance of that, though, she thought to herself, when even families can't get on, even husband and wife.

'It's the way of the world, lass. Always has been and always will be.' Ellen felt her mother looking at her keenly. 'William didn't come home and have his dinner with you?'

'No … he took a snack to have at the shop. He'll have gone back there after the procession. It'll be business as usual this afternoon. He had to close this morning; he couldn't very well leave Amos in charge.'

'No, poor lad, he's not fit to be given much responsibility.' Lydia shook her head sadly. 'It's only the big firms – Horrockses and the like – that have got the whole week off. For the rest of us, family firms and that, it's business as usual, as you say.' She broke off to serve a woman with a quarter of treacle toffee and a bright red lollipop for the little boy at her side.

'You won't have done much this morning though, Mam, with the procession being on?' asked Ellen. Lydia had insisted on opening the market stall as usual, though she had also insisted on Ellen taking the morning off.

'Oh, you'd be surprised. I've been kept busy enough. The old folk, you know, who live round about, the regulars, they can't be bothered pushing their way up Fishergate for all that ballyhoo. And it'll pick up this afternoon, you'll see. We won't be able to turn round soon, when all the visitors find their way to the market.'

Preston Market was popular not only with residents, but with people from outlying towns and villages. The Covered Market, it was always called, as the huge roof, supported by iron pillars, had only been completed a few years before Ellen was born. Her mother often told the tale of how, one windy night in August 1870, the original roof had collapsed. There had been no casualties, but it would have been catastrophic if it had happened earlier in the day when the market was thronged with people. There was no danger, however, of the present structure coming to grief. It had been inspired, so it was said, by the enormous Market Halls in Paris and was a lasting tribute, with its sturdy pillars and intricate wrought-iron work, to the local boatbuilder, Thomas Allsop, who had designed it.

Lydia Tucker lived in Sefton Street, a street of small terraced houses some five minutes' walk from the Covered Market. Because she lived so near she was able to transport her goods – tin trays of toffee, jars of sweets and boxes of assorted novelties – back and forth in a huge pram. Preston Market was held on three days of the week, Wednesday, Friday and Saturday. On two of the other days Lydia travelled further afield, to Chorley and Leyland Markets, and on these journeys she was given a ride in a pony and trap belonging to one of her neighbours. He and his wife had a stall selling 'fents', the name given to remnants from the cotton mills, plus buttons, braid, lace, binding and thread – everything that a home dressmaker might require. Mary, Lydia's elder daughter, lived in the same street with her husband and two baby boys, and it was there that Ellen and William had lived when they were first married. It was a common enough practice for northern families to settle near together, but Ellen had always believed in keeping herself to herself, even when she had lived in close proximity to her mother and sister. She was not one to divulge her innermost thoughts to anyone, or to betray her husband, however bad he might be.

Her mother was giving her some odd looks, though, today. Ellen knew that she was more than usually withdrawn, last night's loathsome scene with William having affected her deeply. This morning, in the company of the children, she had felt a temporary alleviation of her burden, at least until William's float had appeared, but now, as the time for meeting with him again was drawing near, she felt sorely troubled. And Lydia had noticed.

'Is there something the matter, lass?' she asked eventually, when there was a lull in the selling. They were having a busy afternoon, as Lydia had predicted. 'You look down in the dumps – it's not like you.'

'Not really.' Ellen shook her head, but her voice was unconvincing. 'I suppose I'm rather tired, Mam. It's been a long day ... and William came in late last night. We were late getting to bed.' She hadn't intended saying anything at all, but now that she had uttered his name she felt a little easier. Mam, of all people, would understand, although she must never, never know the full extent of Ellen's troubles. Ellen would be ashamed to confess that to anyone.

'He's drinking, isn't he?' Lydia asked flatly.

'Well ... yes, you know he is.' Ellen tried to answer casually. 'He's been taking a drink ever since his father died. You used to say, didn't you,

Mam, that it was unnatural the way he kow-towed to the old man.'

'I mean he's drinking more than he should,' said Lydia, giving her a searching look. 'He's coming home the worse for drink, isn't he? I know what he was like the Sunday we took the bairns to see the decorations. Out like a light, he was, although I know you tried to pretend it was just his Sunday dinner.'

'Yes ... I'm afraid he's having too much,' Ellen sighed. 'I suppose it's because he didn't take any for so long. He doesn't know when to stop.'

'Aye, that was your father's trouble,' remarked Lydia, 'not knowing when to stop. And I hoped and prayed you'd never have to put up with what I did. It was one of the reasons I let you marry William – only seventeen, you were – because he never set foot inside a pub. I thought it was odd, mind you, but I reckoned it was better that way than taking too much. And he was a God-fearing lad an' all, at least I thought he was. That was where you first got to know him, wasn't it, at one of the church dos?'

'He's changed, Mam,' Ellen admitted, although she had no intention of saying how much. 'He's not like he was when we were courting.'

'Are they ever?' Lydia remarked drily. 'Happen you were too young after all. Our Mary now, she had the good sense to wait till she was twenty-three afore she got wed, and she's got herself a good one in Fred. He doesn't seem much different from the day she married him. But most of 'em, you'd hardly recognise 'em once the gilt has worn off the gingerbread. Your father now, he was never out of the Black Horse at the end, and he'd hardly touched a drop when we first got wed. Many's the time I had to go and stand at the pub door on a Friday, to get some money off him. And I wasn't on me own neither. Crowds of women there used to be, standing there. But he'd always cough up, to give him his due, provided I got there in time. If I didn't then he'd likely spend the lot … then it 'ud be the pawn shop for me. I couldn't send you and our Mary to school with nowt on your feet, could I?'

Ellen had little recollection of those days, at least not of the poverty of which her mother was telling. She recalled her father as a cheerful, corpulent, red-faced fellow – which was hardly surprising! – who was forever joking with the two little girls and with his wife as well. They had seemed a happy enough family and it had come as a great shock when he had died suddenly of a seizure when Ellen was ten. She had heard her mother speak before of her father's weakness and, indeed, she remembered seeing it for herself. Drunkenness was rife in their neighbourhood and her father had been only one of the many culprits. But there was one thing of which Ellen was quite, quite sure. Never had Lydia Tucker suffered at her husband's hands the indignities and brutality which Ellen was enduring. She fell silent now at the thought of it, and again she felt her mother's searching glance upon her.

'Is there something else you're not telling me, lass?'

'No, of course not, Mam,' Ellen lied. 'What

could there be?'

'He's not knocking you about, is he?'

'No, don't be silly,' Ellen answered, too quickly. 'He shouts a bit sometimes, throws his weight about ... but I try to shout back.' She gave a careless little laugh which didn't ring true.

Lydia looked at her concernedly, and doubtingly, too, as though the idea of her gentle daughter raising her voice in anger was ludicrous. 'If I thought for one moment that William Bamber was ill-treating you, I'd ... I'd murder him!' Lydia grasped hold of a huge jar of sweets, squeezing the neck hard, as though her fingers were tightening around her son-in-law's throat. 'I would that. I'd swing for him!'

'Steady on, Mam,' said Ellen, as calmly as she was able. 'I'm all right, I've told you. I can handle him.'

But Ellen knew that she couldn't, and never would she be able to do so. William's persecution of her – and looking back, now, she recognised it for what it was, although she hadn't given it that name at the start – had begun even on their honeymoon, the two days they had spent in Southport.

'Don't be such a prissy miss,' William had told her, his bright blue eyes looking over her gloatingly, when she had demurred at some of his more extravagant acts. 'I can see that I shall have to teach you a thing or two. I can't do with being married to a prim prude...' And so Ellen had tried to learn, although she had been an unwilling pupil and some of the things William had endeavoured to teach her had sickened and

28

disgusted her. She had had little idea of what was involved in marriage, beyond a vague inkling as to the rudiments of love-making; but she had thought, in her naivety, that it would include affection and trust, companionship and sharing, not this nightly invasion of her body with acts which seemed to her to be lewd and shameful. She submitted, however, trying, at first, to simulate as much affection as she could. She knew it was her duty as a wife.

Ellen was unable to make a comparison – William had been her first young man – and there was no one she could ask. When her sister, Mary, was married a few years later Ellen wondered if she was going through the same experiences. But Mary's obvious happiness and the loving concern that she and Fred showed for one another seemed to refute this idea. Ellen gradually came to the conclusion that her own husband must be somewhat ... unusual and that not all marriages were like the one in which she was trapped. But it was only after William took a liking to the bottle that her life became really unbearable. She had to admit, however, that on the nights when he was sober he now left her alone, but at other times his excesses were almost too much to bear ... and then the beatings had started.

Ellen had begun to spend more time at the market stall and to contribute more of her own produce to sell. For one thing, William was leaving her short of money and to ask for more would only provoke his wrath. And also there might come a time, Ellen tried to convince herself, when she could break free from William, although it seemed well-nigh impossible at the moment. First and foremost there were the children to consider. They were the one good thing that had come out of her marriage and Ellen never ceased to give thanks for them. In the meantime, though, she could endeavour to put a bit of her own money on one side. The tin box, hidden away at the back of her wardrobe, was growing quite heavy.

It was when her own husband died that Lydia Tucker had begun to build up the business that was now well known in the markets of the area. It was the toffees for which Lydia was renowned – the ordinary toffee, made simply from sugar, water and cream of tartar – and the variations on this theme. Treacle toffee, almond, walnut and ginger toffees, butterscotch, caramel, invalid toffee; all made with just the addition of a different ingredient to the basic recipe.

Ellen, since she had started taking a bigger share in the business and its profits, had been concentrating on the softer sweetmeats; fudges of various flavours, fondants, coconut candy, nougat and marshmallow. This last delicacy was tricky, involving the use of gum arabic, but Ellen hoped that she would soon have a batch ready for sale. At the moment she was experimenting with just small quantities until she had mastered the procedure. Then she hoped to try her hand at Turkish Delight as well.

The two women didn't make all their own sweets, although Lydia would have liked to think that they could be completely independent.

Other items – chocolate bars, lollipops, liquorice novelties and sweets such as pear drops, aniseed balls and dolly mixtures – were bought from the wholesale warehouse on the outskirts of the town. They made a trip there every few weeks, wheeling enormous prams, minus the children.

'Now that's what I call a good afternoon's work,' said Lydia with a satisfied smile at half-past four. The Town Hall clock, with its Westminster chimes, had just struck the half-hour. 'I told you we'd be busy, didn't I? You'd best be making tracks now. Off you go and pick the bairns up and I'll clear away here. I don't think we'll do much more now.' All round them were signs of stallholders packing away their wares and shutting up shop for the day. Morning and early afternoon were the busy times at Preston Market. By five o'clock, most people were back home preparing their evening meal.

Ellen had seen the children only about an hour earlier when their aunt had brought them to the market, but she was glad, as always, to see them again. Their happy smiles and excited chatter soothed her as they walked home although she was only listening with half an ear to what they were saying. Her mind was already on the evening ahead of her and what it might hold.

William, however, didn't go out that evening. He sat and read the paper, then smoked cigarette after cigarette from the tin of Player's Navy Cut which he kept on the mantelpiece. He had recently gone on to this fairly novel invention in preference to his pipe. Ellen, watching him tap the ash on to the hearthrug more often than into

31

the fire, as he stared moodily into its flames, sensed that he had something on his mind. But she refrained from asking him what was the matter. She would be told, no doubt, that it was none of her business, and they rarely conversed after the children were tucked away in bed. Ellen's needles clicked furiously as she turned the heel of the bright blue sock she was knitting to match Georgie's sailor suit. For the moment she was content in the knowledge that, tonight, he would leave her alone. And tomorrow could take care of itself. Ellen knew that all she could do was take one day at a time.

Chapter Two

There was no market on a Thursday so Ellen decided to spend the day, after she had done her usual chores, perfecting her marshmallow. The last lot had been rather too sticky; a little less gum arabic, she thought, should do the trick. Rachel and Georgie, who were never much trouble to her, played together happily in the living room whilst she worked in the kitchen, the door open so that she could keep an eye on them.

It was a great boon, here in Stonygate, to have such a large kitchen. In their previous home in Sefton Street there had been only a combined living room-cum-kitchen-cum-scullery in which everything took place. Cooking, baking, eating, relaxing – when there was time – even washing. Here, Ellen had a brick-built washhouse, so that the steam was kept out of the house, and an indoor bathroom and lavatory as well. She had thought it a great luxury, when they had first moved into her father-in-law's house, not to have to make trips to the privy at the end of the yard. And the zinc bath tub, which had been used every Friday night for the children, and for herself and William, too, when they didn't feel like paying a visit to the nearby Public Baths, was now obsolete.

Ellen had learned, however, during the couple of years they had spent in this superior dwelling, that more rooms and more modern conveniences didn't help to make you any happier. Not that she had been blissfully happy back in the old house, but there had been times when she had been contented, or at least had felt that she could put up with her lot. Now, those times were becoming fewer and fewer.

Her thoughts, as she painstakingly stirred the glutinous mixture in the large copper pan, were not cheerful ones, but at least the marshmallow seemed to have worked out right this time; she could tell by the feel of it on the spatula. Carefully she lifted the heavy pan from the hob and poured the runny marshmallow into the prepared tins waiting on the pine table. The consistency looked perfect, not too thick and not too thin, and had that glistening appearance and the sweet – some would say sickly – smell that Ellen loved. That, at least, was one blessing. Her efforts had at last borne fruit and there need be no more trial and error with this particular sweetmeat. Ellen actually smiled to herself now. Her sweet-making, something she enjoyed and knew she was good at, was bringing her satisfaction, even a quiet joy, especially at the times when she was on the market stall and could temporarily forget her troubles.

'Now then you two,' she said, wiping her sticky hands on her voluminous white apron as she entered the living room. 'I think Mummy's deserved a nice cup of tea, don't you? And what about a drink of lemonade for two good children? Would you like that?'

Rachel and Georgie looked up from the jigsaw

puzzle they were doing and nodded happily. It was Rachel's jigsaw really, a simple wooden one depicting cats dressed up in frocks and bonnets and knickerbockers, but Georgie liked to think he was helping and could already fit in several of the pieces.

'And – guess what?' she said, opening her eyes wide with a hint of a mystery. 'I've finished the marshmallow! And when it's set there might even be a piece to spare for each of you. Only one, mind, that's all.'

'Yes, the rest of it's for the market people, isn't it, Mummy?' said Rachel seriously; while Georgie, beaming all over his round face, began to smack his lips together in an exaggerated way.

'Come on now and have your drink,' said Ellen after a few moments. 'Leave your jigsaw; you can side it away later.' She sank down thankfully in one of the sagging easy chairs, a relic from their past home, but too comfortable to throw away, sipping appreciatively at the strong tea. Opposite her, from the other easy chair, two pairs of eyes, one dark brown like her own and the other a vivid blue, regarded her earnestly, while two tumblers of home-made lemonade disappeared quickly down two little throats. Ellen, for a short while, was experiencing contentment, almost happiness, as she shared this quiet moment with her children.

She was startled to hear the back door open and bang shut again and she glanced nervously at the wooden clock on the mantelshelf. Surely it couldn't be William already? It was only half-past four and he didn't close the shop until half-past five. Her hand flew to her throat as she felt the mounting panic, such an effect did he have on her recently. For it was William; she could hear his heavy footsteps sounding on the flagged kitchen floor. Hurriedly she placed her partially drunk cup of tea on the table at her side, her hand shaking and slopping the liquid over into the saucer.

Then the living-room door was flung open and her husband stood on the threshold, his bulky form and the air of menace he brought in with him seeming to fill the room.

'What the hell's going on?' he bawled. His eyes, glinting dangerously, more grey than blue now, were as cold and as hard as flintstone. 'I come home from work, bloody exhausted, and what do I find? The house full of ... toffee! Blasted toffee!' He spewed the words out with venom as he drew nearer to where Ellen was sitting, and a glob of his spittle flew across the room, landing on her upper lip. As unobtrusively as she could, but with great distaste – she could already feel the bile rising in her throat – she lifted her hand and wiped it away.

'No meal ready. Oh no, thass too much to expect. No smell of cooking ... just stinking toffee, thassall. And my slut of a wife sitting there like Lady Muck, drinking tea! And t'bloody table's not even set.' With one vicious lunge he seized hold of the brown chenille cloth and dragged it to the floor. The cup rolled away, spilling its contents on to the clipped rag hearthrug, and the pieces of Rachel's jigsaw were scattered far and wide.

Ellen glanced at her children, almost afraid to do so lest William's rage should be diverted at them. He had never been overly angry with them before, but there could always be a first time. The stink of beer hung heavy in the air. The two children were both staring at their father, in puzzlement rather than fear, as though they didn't recognise this stranger.

'Be off with you, the pair of you,' William said gruffly, pointing in the direction of the door. Rachel hesitated, stooping to pick up a few pieces of her precious jigsaw. 'Leave that mess! Be off with you, I said. Yer mother'll clear it away later ... when I've finished with her. Go on, get moving!'

'Go along,' said Ellen quietly, 'like Daddy says. Go and play in the parlour. There's no fire, but you should be all right. It's a warm day.'

'Of course they'll be all right,' scoffed William as the children scuttled out of the room. 'You mollycoddle 'em, woman. You'll have 'em as lily-livered as you afore long. Now ... come 'ere.' Roughly he grabbed hold of her arm. His fingers were like a band of iron digging into the soft flesh above her elbow as he dragged her into the kitchen. 'Now ... I'll show you wharr I think of your bloody toffee!' He let go of her so suddenly that she stumbled against the pine table. She grasped hold of the side of it for support as she watched her husband seize the tins of now set marshmallow, one by one, and tip the contents out on to the stone floor.

'Toffee! Nowt but flamin' ... stinkin' ... toffee!' he shouted as he trampled on the confection with his hobnailed boots, grinding it into the flagstones as though his very life depended on it. 'Nowt to eat in this blasted house but soddin' *toffee!*'

This wasn't true as William well knew. There was always an appetising meal awaiting him when he came home from the shop. Today would have been no exception, but he was early, more than an hour so. Ellen was dismayed at the wicked waste of all her work and hurt, too. Nothing that William had ever done had hurt her as much as this but, oddly enough, she didn't feel like crying. To do so would only provoke his wrath even further.

'You were early, William,' she said, her voice sounding devoid of any emotion, although she could feel the righteous anger boiling up inside her. 'More than an hour early. Why was that? I thought you didn't close the shop until half-past five.' She was being foolish, she knew, in questioning his actions, but her anger was adding boldness to her words, quietly spoken though they were.

She might have guessed at his reaction. 'What the hell has it to do with you, woman, what I do and what I don't do? You're here to do as I say, and don't you damn well forget it. To hell with yer fancy sweeties. What've you got for me tea?' He seized hold of her arm again, bringing his face close to hers. 'It'd better be summat good, I'm warning you – or else!'

'Steak and kidney pie,' replied Ellen coldly, daring, even, to stare right at him. 'And cabbage and mashed potatoes. I'm just going to warm it up and peel some fresh potatoes.'

'You'd best gerron with it then, after you've cleaned up this lot.' William gave her a hefty push in the direction of the gooey mess on the floor. 'An' you can have a taste of this to be goin' on with.'

With one hand he pulled off his belt and with the other he pushed her across the table top. She felt the buckle bruising her thighs, her back and her buttocks, but not with the same force as she had known in the past. He was too drunk, she knew, to divest her of her clothing. It was at the times he attacked her bare flesh that she suffered the most. When he flung the belt on the floor after a few desultory swipes at her and stormed from the room, she felt too weary and sick at heart to care. She stumbled across to the sink and started to peel the potatoes.

Ellen couldn't believe her good fortune when William left her alone that night. He went out to the pub, to be sure, but when he returned, well after midnight, he merely staggered across the bedroom and collapsed on the bed fully clothed. He must, however, have awakened at some point during the night and undressed because when she awoke, at half-past five or so, he was clad in his nightshirt, snoring heavily at her side. She lay motionless, listening to the clatter of the knocker-up's clogs on the pavement and the tap, tap, tap of his long pole on the neighbouring windows. Not on their windows, though. They had the advantage of an alarm clock, a luxury in some households. Ellen never needed it. She was awake long before its strident clamour would have broken into her slumber, although William invariably slept until it woke him.

Ellen was thankful for another of life's blessings – and she tried so hard to count them – that of deep, untroubled sleep. For after she had tumbled into bed at night, or after, as was often the case, William had finished abusing her, she was able, miraculously, to cast aside all her care and fall, as some would say, into the arms of Morpheus. Ellen preferred to think that she was resting in the arms of God. She usually remembered, no matter how tired or troubled she was, to have a few words with Him before she went to sleep; and she was sure that He answered her prayers and gave her rest. There were other prayers, however, which she felt that even God, in His infinite power, would be unable to grant. For how could she ever be rid of William?

Ellen didn't move until the grey light of dawn began to creep through the chinks in the curtains, then she arose, washed and dressed quickly and went downstairs to prepare the breakfast. Bacon and eggs for William was a daily ritual, but porridge or toast and marmalade sufficed for her and the children. Then there were the sandwiches – cold meat or cheese – to be packed away in his tin box for William's snack dinner. But before she dealt with these tasks Ellen, this morning, took from off the stone slab in the larder the trays of marshmallow that she had placed there to set the previous evening. She had started, as soon as William had gone off to the pub and the children were in bed, to make another batch. Now, before William came downstairs, she hid the trays away in the old pram she used as a handcart and covered them with a white cloth, then pushed the vehicle back under the stairs. On no account could she risk the ruination of another few hours' work. But William was preoccupied and ate his breakfast in stony silence. He exchanged not a word with either Ellen or the children before he departed for work.

Ellen had loved the market, the sounds and the sights and the smells – the very essence of it all – ever since she had been a tiny girl, and she counted herself very lucky to be actually working there now. When she had left the children with Mary she pushed the pram back along High Street, aware already of the aroma emanating from the Fish Market at the far end. There were the stalls, selling cod, haddock, whiting and plaice, as well as cockles, mussels and whelks, measured out in tin cups. There, too, were the Southport shrimp women in their distinctive white bonnets and aprons, their wares laid out on simple stalls supported by barrels. They sold shrimps and prawns still encased in their scaly coverings, their protuberant eyes seeming to be watching you, and potted shrimps, pale pink like babies' toes, in glistening yellow butter. Further along were more exotic items, like lobsters, crabs and oysters, for the rich people who lived in the vicinity of Winckley Square or Fulwood on the outskirts of the town. There might well be visitors, though, in this Preston Guild week, who would purchase the costlier items that the market had to offer. Ellen had noticed that many of the stalls were better stocked than usual.

There were stalls with golden pats of butter and brown eggs, pots of jam, marmalade and lemon curd, made by the farmers' wives from Broughton or Woodplumpton. Fruit and vegetable stalls with enormous cabbages, swedes and turnips and creamy white cauliflowers that always reminded Ellen of heavy lace. And oranges; never were there such huge oranges as you could buy at the market. These were not grown locally, of course, like much of the fruit. Jaffas, her mother always called them, and Ellen had been quite grown up before she realised that Jaffa was the name of the faraway place that these fruits came from and not just the orange itself.

Ellen wrinkled her nose as she hurried past the pungent-smelling cheeses, then averted her eyes as she passed the meat stalls. The bright red lumps of beef and lamb, the links of speckly sausages and the trays of dark brown liver always turned her stomach, although she enjoyed a tasty joint of meat for Sunday dinner as much as anyone, when she could afford it.

Their own stall was at the end of the row of food products, just before the pots and pans, crockery, toys and fent stalls began. Ellen produced her trays of marshmallow – six of them, three pink and three white – from her pram, with all the pride of a conjuror producing a rabbit from a hat. She felt a grim satisfaction that she had been able to supply the goods against such odds, although her mother must be left in ignorance of what it had cost her in time and heartache and disillusionment.

'By heck, lass, that looks good,' Lydia grinned. 'I knew you'd manage it one of these days. Practice makes perfect, as they say.'

'Yes, Mam. It was a bit tricky,' was all that Ellen replied as she took a sharp knife and started to cut the soft cushiony confection into square-inch-sized pieces. 'Let's hope it all sells, eh? The trouble is it may not keep all that well. It soon goes hard.'

'It'll sell; I'm sure of it.' Lydia popped a piece into her mouth and chewed thoroughly. Then she licked her lips and wiped the back of her hand across her mouth. 'Mmm ... you've got the knack all right, Ellen lass. You'll be as good as yer mam afore long. I tell you what, though. The pieces are going to stick together when we put 'em into t'bags.'

'Hold your horses, Mam. I've thought of everything.' Ellen lifted an admonitory finger as she took a shaker of fine icing sugar from the depths of the pram. 'I'll sprinkle them with a good coating of this and there'll be no problem.'

'Aye, that's not a bad idea.' Lydia was not always fulsome with her praise. 'Wouldn't it've been better, though, if you'd done that at home instead of messing about here?'

'There wasn't time, Mam. I only finished it last night after the children had gone to bed.' Ellen occupied herself now in a space at the far end of the stall. She didn't want her mother asking too many questions. Lydia, at the other end, was busy breaking the toffee in the trays into small pieces, banging the undersides of the tins with a tiny metal hammer, cracking the pristine smoothness of the surface.

Ellen smiled to herself as she watched her mother pop another sweet into her mouth, a piece of treacle toffee this time. It was a wonder that Lydia wasn't as enormous as Fat Alice, the woman in the sideshow on Blackpool Central Beach, she thought. She was constantly munching at the produce, but it seemed to make little difference. Her mother was as thin as Ellen herself and had the same delicate features and fine, fairish hair. Lydia's hair was greying now at the temples, but it was usually pushed under the brim of her brown felt hat that she wore, winter and summer alike, to stand on the markets. Her small stature belied her physical strength; sinewy arms protruded from the sleeves of her blue checked cotton frock and the veins on her hands stood out like knotted cords with the lifting of heavy pans and tins.

Anyone could tell at a glance that these two women in charge of Tucker's Tasty Toffee stall were mother and daughter. It was obvious, also, that the younger woman, Ellen Bamber, didn't have the stamina of her mother, at least as far as physical appearances went. There were times when it seemed as though a puff of wind would blow her over, and some days she looked very tired.

There was little time for talking, hardly time for eating their snack lunch, as the day wore on. Friday turned out to be even busier than Wednesday had been; and when the money was counted at the end of the day Ellen found herself with a goodly pile of silver and copper to store away in her tin box at the back of the wardrobe. Her nest egg for ... for what? she often asked herself. For the day when it all became too much for her? She had found, however, that she was dipping into this reserve fund more and more of late, as William left her increasingly short of money.

She had been dreading his return from the clogger's shop this teatime, but she told herself that, whatever happened, it couldn't be as bad as the previous day when he had ruined her marshmallow. Nor was it, at first. William ate his meal in silence. It had been ready for Ellen to take from the oven when he entered the house at a quarter to six, then he disappeared upstairs to their bedroom. She could hear him stamping about while she helped the children into their little nightshirts and washed their hands and faces at the kitchen sink. What her mother always called 'a lick and a promise', but that had to suffice at night as she must leave the bathroom free for William.

It was when the children were sitting by the fire drinking their cocoa and Ellen was washing up the remainder of the tea things that William stormed into the kitchen. Ellen glanced round and saw, to her dismay, that he was holding her tin box in his hands. His eyes were cold and hard, as they had been the previous night, and an angry flush was creeping up his bull-like neck into his cheeks.

'What the bleedin' 'ell's all this?' He turned the

tin upside down on to the table and the money poured out. Copper and silver and a fair amount of sovereigns rolled around on the table top before coming to rest in a shining heap, some of the coins spilling on to the floor. Ellen automatically bent to pick them up, but she was stopped by a stinging blow on the side of her head.

'Leave it, woman. You don't touch it, d'yer hear? It's mine – the whole bloody lot of it's mine.'

'Oh no, William. This is what I've earned at the market.' A fury, such as she had never felt before, was making Ellen brave. 'It's not yours ... it's *mine*.' She stared fixedly at the man for whom she now felt nothing but contempt and dislike. 'I earned it ... and I keep it.' She paused as he stared back at her with equal hatred. Then, 'You knew I was making a fair bit of money,' she said, more quietly. 'What did you suppose I was doing with it?'

'How should I know, woman? I thought you were spending it on food and on the kids ... and on coal and suchlike. That's what you damn well ought to be doing. I don't know what I thought.' His anger was making him incoherent. 'That's what it's for, not for stashing away to buy yerself some fancy gee-gaws.'

'How can you say that, William?' Ellen was seething now. 'You know very well I never spend a penny piece on myself, except when I have to.'

'Whassit for then?' He took hold of her shoulders, shaking her back and forth like a rag doll. 'What you doin' with it, eh?' He pushed her away then and she fell against the edge of the sink, bruising her back. 'Every penny of it belongs to me, by law. A woman isn't allowed to have any money, d'you know that, eh? You're damned lucky I haven't got it off you before. Can't think why I didn't. Must've been soft in me head to let you keep any of it.'

'Oh no, William, you're wrong.' Ellen had never stood up to him like this before and she knew, even as she spoke, that she would most likely suffer for it. 'A woman's allowed to keep her own money now. The law says so. It was passed in Parliament. Ages ago.' She looked at him defiantly, although she wasn't absolutely sure of her facts. She knew vaguely that there had been a Woman's Property Act, sometime in the 1880s, she thought, but she was somewhat hazy about just what that entailed.

Her words were like a red rag to a bull and, like that proverbial animal, he bellowed and charged at her. 'You lyin' cow!' She felt another glancing blow against her temple which sent her reeling across the room. 'Don't you dare tell me what women are allowed to do! Women are here to look after their menfolk, and don't you forget it. And for summat else an' all – not that you're any bleedin' good at that, are you … *sweetheart?*' He was leering at her now, his red, heavy-jowled face close to hers, pinching her cheek so hard between his coarse thumb and forefinger that it hurt. 'I shall be wanting you tonight, Nellie. You'd best be ready for me, hadn't you?' His voice was a sibilant whisper.

Ellen knew that his anger was arousing him and, to her horror, she could see the tell-tale

47

bulge in his trousers. But surely even William wouldn't be such a brute as to take her here and now, with the children in the next room. They were very quiet. Ellen wondered how much they had heard.

He didn't try. Instead, he scooped up the pile of money and dropped it back into the tin. Then he closed the lid with a decisive click and put it under his arm. *'This ... is ... mine,'* he said, grinning sardonically at her, 'and there's not a damn thing you can do about it, so don't you try.'

And Ellen knew, indeed, that there was no point in her arguing any further. She would be unable to wrest the box from her husband without him causing her great injury. And she was still conscious of Rachel and Georgie in the next room.

But she did dare to ask one question. 'What do you want it for, William?' Although she thought she knew. Drinking at the Old Dog Inn; that was where most of the money went.

'Gambling debts, Nellie. Gambling – that's what it's for.' She hated it when he called her Nellie, a diminutive of her name that she couldn't bear. But she hardly noticed that, so stunned was she at what he had said.

'Gambling?' she faltered. 'But ... I didn't know...'

'There's a lot you don't know, sweetheart. Yes, your husband's been a naughty boy. At least that's what you'd think, you mealy-mouthed little prig. I've been playing cards and I've lost some money, so this'll do very nicely to pay it back. Ta very much, Nellie.' He grabbed his coat from the hook by the back door, then he was gone, leaving Ellen staring after him in amazement. Gambling, as well as drinking... This was the first she had heard of it.

That night his treatment of her was worse than ever. No longer did he seem to care that the bruises he inflicted on her were in places where they would show.

'Open yer legs, you silly cow,' he bawled, as she started to resist him. When he struck her she knew that her eye would be blackened in the morning, but before she had time to worry about that he was astride her, trying, to no avail, to force his way into her. 'You're useless, woman, bloody useless. Lying there ... like a ... sack of ... bleedin' potatoes.' His words, delivered staccato fashion with the effort of his futile exertion, were almost inaudible. At last he rolled away from her, sighing deeply. 'At least there's something I can do, you good-for-nothing cow.' Seizing hold of her, he pushed her face down across the bed. Ellen knew, as the blows rained down on her, that she wouldn't be able to stand it much longer.

'Good grief, our Ellen, what on earth have you done to your eye?' asked her sister Mary the next morning.

Ellen didn't answer. It was too late now to prevaricate, although she still didn't want her mother to learn the truth.

'It's never that swine of a husband of yours?' Mary gasped. 'He's done that to you?'

Ellen nodded numbly. ''Fraid so, Mary. That ... and more. I've tried to keep it from you, but I

49

can't now, not any longer.'

'And why should you keep it from us? We just want to help you, me and Fred, although God knows what we can do. I had an idea he was knocking you about, but I never dreamed it was so bad. Here, sit down, love, and have a cup of tea.' Mary pushed her gently into one of the bentwood chairs at the kitchen table while placing her hand on the brown earthenware pot. 'This 'ere's still warm an' I can make some fresh when Fred comes down. He's havin' a bit of a lie in.'

'No thanks, Mary. I haven't time, honestly. I can't be late this morning. Mam thinks we'll be extra busy today, the last day of the Guild week...' Ellen stopped speaking, looking at her sister pleadingly. 'What am I going to do, Mary? I'm at my wit's end, I am really. And Mam's sure to notice this today.' She touched her eyebrow gingerly. 'She'll be round playing merry hell with William, I know she will. And that'll only make things worse. She said the other day she'd kill him if she found out he was ill-treating me. And she would an' all.'

'Time somebody did, the bastard,' said Mary grimly. 'I see what you mean, though. It's no good adding fuel to the fire. We've got to be realistic. For instance, there'd be no point in me asking Fred to go round and give him a good hiding, would there?'

Ellen gave a weak smile. 'Not a bit of it.' Little Fred Pilkington was only the height of sixpennorth of copper. It would be like a mouse attacking an elephant. 'I'll just have to try to grin

50

and bear it for a bit longer.' The tears which she was trying so hard to contain spilled over now and began to run down her cheeks.

Mary looked at her in concern, shaking her head sadly, then she took a large hanky from her apron pocket and shoved it towards Ellen. 'Here, dry your eyes ... and you're going to have that cup of tea, so don't argue. Mam'll have to manage for a few minutes.' Mary poured out the tea, then drew up a chair and sat down opposite her sister. 'Now...' She folded her strong arms on the edge of the table and leaned forward. 'There must be summat we can do. How about the police? Don't you think this could be a matter for them? I mean to say, that bruise...'

Ellen shrugged. 'I doubt it, Mary. I think they'd regard it as just a family tiff. A husband's entitled to give his wife a good hiding, isn't he?'

'Not in my book, he's not.' Mary's tone was fierce. Indeed, Fred would come off the worse, thought Ellen with a tinge of wry amusement, were he to try. Mary was taller than her husband by a few inches and more solidly built, too, taking after her father, Samuel Tucker, whereas Ellen resembled her mother. 'But happen you're right; the police might think it was nowt to do with them,' Mary added thoughtfully. 'You'll have to do summat though, our Ellen, if it carries on. Why don't you just leave him? Walk out and leave him to it, you and the bairns.'

'How on earth can I do that? Where would I go?'

'Back to our mam's, of course. She'd have you, you know that.'

51

'But there's not room to swing a cat round in Sefton Street,' said Ellen, forgetting for the moment that the house she was sitting in was also in Sefton Street.

'Some of us have to manage,' retorted Mary. 'And Mam managed, too, bringing up you and me. Beggars can't be choosers, you know, and your big posh house hasn't done you much good, has it? Oh, I'm sorry, love,' she added, as her sister's lip began to tremble. 'I didn't mean to upset you. You know me, both feet right in it. But you really will have to do something, won't you?'

'Yes, I know, Mary.' Ellen dabbed at her eyes, trying to compose herself, then drank the last of her somewhat stewed tea. 'But now I shall have to get to the market.' She rose, glancing at herself in the mirror at the back of the sideboard. 'Good heavens! Mam'll have a fit.'

'Come here, let's have a look at you.' Mary pulled a strand of Ellen's fair hair from beneath the brim of her straw hat, arranging it so that it covered most of the bruising which, fortunately, was above her eyebrow. 'There now, that's not too bad. Pull the crown down a bit further ... that's right.'

Ellen tried to smile. 'Thanks, Mary. Sorry to be such a misery this morning.' She went across to the other side of the room where Rachel and Georgie were playing happily with Mary's twin boys, building towers of wooden blocks for their little cousins to knock down again. She doubted that they had heard a word of her conversation with her sister.

'Ta-ra, you two,' she said, stooping down to kiss

52

each of them. 'Be good. See you at teatime.'

'You needn't worry about them,' Mary assured her. 'They'll be as happy as Larry with our Charlie and Tommy. They always are.'

'I know that, Mary,' Ellen nodded. 'Thanks ever so much.'

The children, indeed, were the least of her problems, but as she hurried back along Lawson Street towards the market her mind was beset with them all. She knew she couldn't put up with William's brutality any longer, not another day. Then there was the money, her hard-earned money, thrown away on gambling; and, more imminent, her mother's reaction when she saw her daughter's bruised face. 'Oh, please God, help me,' she muttered, over and over inside her head. 'Please show me how to get away from William, or ... or make him behave better, Lord.' But in her heart of hearts she was very dubious that God could do anything at all.

One small prayer, however, did seem to be answered. Lydia never even noticed the bruise on her daughter's left temple. Ellen endeavoured to keep in the shadows all day or at the other end of the stall away from Lydia. They were extra busy too. The Saturday market was always the busiest of the week and today they had not only their regular customers and the children spending their Saturday pennies, but crowds of visitors who had taken the town by storm. When they counted their takings at the end of the day Ellen knew that she had made enough to start saving again. She would have to find a new hiding place, though.

She was almost sick with apprehension by the time she arrived home with Rachel and Georgie at around five o'clock. William closed the shop early on a Saturday; he might well be home before her. She quickened her steps along Stonygate, the two children frantically trying to keep up with her, anxious to be home, yet fearful at what might await her when she arrived. But William wasn't there, nor did he put in an appearance all evening.

There was to be a torchlight procession on the Saturday evening as a climax to the events of the Guild week, but Ellen felt too dispirited to go and watch it. She would have to take the children, and she decided that the crowds would be too much for them, worse, more likely, than they had been on the Wednesday. She put them to bed, then sat at her fireside, quietly knitting. She was relieved at William's absence, but she knew that it was only a temporary respite. At any moment he could walk through the door, then it would all start again.

William staggered from the door of the Old Dog Inn, then along Church Street in the direction of Fishergate. His drinking cronies – they could hardly be called mates; he had few of these, especially since he had started gambling – followed him at a safe distance. William, in his cups, was not the most pleasant of companions.

'He's three sheets in the wind tonight, he is that,' one of them remarked.

'Aye, talk about one over the eight. He's had more like a dozen.'

'He'll just about make it home. He's only to go round t'next corner.'

'*If* he goes home, that is...' There was a guffaw of lewd laughter, before one of the men yelled, 'Look out, William! For God's sake, man...'

For William had stumbled from the kerb, in an attempt to cross the road, straight into the path of a hansom cab.

'Oh, Christ, no!' They started to run, but by the time the small group had arrived at the scene William was spread-eagled across the road. His sightless eyes were staring up at them as though surprised, as the blood streamed from the corner of his mouth, and across his left temple was a livid scar where the horse's hoof had kicked him.

When a very concerned policeman called, some time later, to break the sad news to the poor fellow's wife, all she could do was stare at him in wonder.

Chapter Three

Ellen was not so naive as to believe that this was God's answer to her prayer. She knew that God didn't act in this way. If He did, then there would be many more women suddenly finding themselves widows. But this accident was fortuitous, to say the least. Ellen floated through the next few days in a kind of trance, full of disbelief and wonderment that this should have happened. She wouldn't truly believe that William had gone until she saw his coffin lowered into the ground and the earth shovelled on top of it.

She knew that for the sake of propriety she had to put on some semblance of mourning; never, though, she told herself, would she be able to show grief, and if her neighbours and friends were to think her callous, then so be it. Few, if any of them, had the faintest idea of how she had suffered during the last couple of years.

St John's Parish Church and the surrounding graveyard were only a short distance from Stonygate where Ellen lived, so she was able to dispense with the customary black-plumed horses to draw the hearse. Instead, William's coffin was borne on the shoulders of two of the undertaker's top-hatted men and two of the dead man's acquaintances who had been pressed into volunteering. Little Fred Pilkington, Mary's husband, was, to his obvious relief, several inches too short to be of service. William had no family to speak of – none, at any rate, that Ellen knew of, and few friends. So it was quite a small band of mourners who followed the coffin along the cobbles of Stonygate and into the churchyard. Ellen and Lydia; Mary and Fred; a few near neighbours; a few former friends of William from St John's Church, from the days before he had fallen by the wayside; and his companions from the Old Dog Inn, the same little group who had seen him fall beneath the wheels of the hansom cab.

Ellen, supported by Lydia's arm, felt little emotion as the vicar went through the simple service, in the church and then at the graveside. But when she saw her husband's coffin disappearing into the deep, deep hole and she heard the clods of earth thudding on to the oak lid, then, to her amazement, she felt the tears begin to flow. Not only that; sobs began to shake her thin shoulders and she found herself leaning against the comforting bulk of her sister, crying as though her heart would break. When, after a few moments, she lifted her head, she was aware of the rest of the mourners looking at her in sympathy and some relief. Her tears had been a long time in coming.

Most of the people assembled round the open grave didn't realise that these tears were not ones of grief. Neither were they entirely ones of relief. Ellen was weeping, rather, for the sheer wastefulness of it all and for the wanton destruction of a life which had once held so much promise. But it was William himself who had destroyed it. She had married him in good faith, believing that she had loved him. So what had gone wrong? Was she in any way to blame, she asked herself now, for the complete metamorphosis of William's personality? She thought not. She had tried, especially at first, God knew how she had tried. William had had a comfortable home, a good job, two lovely children ... and yet it had all gone wrong. If it hadn't been for the drink, she thought now, they might have been all right. It was the drink that had done it.

She felt her mother squeezing her hand and saw compassionate brown eyes smiling into hers. 'All over, love,' her mother was saying quietly. 'It's all over now.' Lydia leaned closer, whispering in her ear. 'You can have a fresh start now, lass. Forget it all. Begin again.'

Ellen nodded, smiling sadly as she wiped the tears from her eyes. Yes, she would try to forget; and she was being given another chance. It was then that she noticed the woman – a stranger – standing some distance away, half-hidden behind one of the gravestones. She was staring fixedly in Ellen's direction, but as Ellen looked at her she turned and walked quickly away towards the gate. It was the same woman, surely, who had been sitting at the back of the church, alone. Ellen had been vaguely aware of her, out of the corner of her eye, as the mourning party had passed. She was not dressed in black, as all the other women were, and her green coat and the green hat with the feather at the side looked incongruous at a funeral gathering. That was why

Ellen had noticed her, because of her manner of dress, and the mass of black hair which hung to her shoulders. But after she had wondered, very briefly, who she was, Ellen put her out of her mind.

At the house in Stonygate the curtains had been drawn back, letting the daylight into the parlour once more after the few days of mourning. It was there, in the parlour at the front of the house, that William's body had rested in its oak coffin. Rachel and Georgie had been looked after by Mary, and Lydia, anxious that her daughter should not be left alone in the house, had moved in with Ellen. But Ellen wouldn't have minded being on her own. William was no longer able to hurt her.

Lydia and Ellen had been up since six o'clock that morning preparing the funeral feast, and two neighbours had volunteered to set it out and boil the kettles whilst the mourners were at church. It wasn't laid out in the parlour, however, as a sickly-sweet smell still hung in the air there, but in the living room that adjoined the kitchen at the back of the house. This was the downstairs room that Ellen had managed to stamp with some of her own personality, and it was homely and cosy, the room that Ellen liked best. Here was the three-piece suite from their last home, covered in rose-patterned cretonne, somewhat shabby but still comfortable, with matching curtains at the windows; the rag rug that Ellen had made as a bride from hundreds of pieces of multi-coloured fabric; and, on the walnut dresser, her small collection of Staffordshire figures, and the blue and white crockery that they used every day.

The parlour, stuffy and over-full of furniture and ornaments, with massive gilt-framed pictures on the walls and heavy dark curtains at the windows, was very much as it had been when William's parents had lived in the house. William had seemed to want it left that way and Ellen had not demurred. They used the room very little anyway, although the red plush chairs from the parlour had been brought into the living room today to accommodate the guests. But now Ellen would be able to make all the changes she wished. She assumed that the house would be hers and the shop, too, even if William had neglected to make a will. She doubted that he had bothered to do so.

Ellen was relieved when the assorted group of mourners invited back to the house because it was the 'done thing', rather than from any true feeling of kinship towards them, had departed. Then, with Lydia and Mary helping her, she cleared away the debris left from the mounds of ham sandwiches, sausage rolls, meat pies, trifle and fruit salad, and proceeded to wash up, whilst Fred quietly read the newspaper and smoked his pipe. The four children during this traumatic day were entrusted to the care of a reliable neighbour in Sefton Street.

'I'll be glad to have our Rachel and Georgie back,' Ellen remarked. 'I feel I've neglected 'em these last few days, poor little mites.'

'What else could you do, lass?' replied Lydia. 'You've had your hands full, right enough, and you'll have to go down to the shop an' all before long, won't you, and see what wants sorting out there. Don't worry about your two bairns. You know that me and our Mary'll cope, won't we, Mary?'

Mary nodded. 'Have you told 'em, Ellen? You know, about William? They haven't said owt to me, in fact they've never mentioned their dad at all, and I didn't like to pry. I've kept well away from the subject, tried to make 'em think of summat else.'

'Yes, I've told them,' said Ellen, guardedly. 'I don't know how much they understand, mind you, especially our Georgie. Like you say, Mary, they've gone very quiet about William; they don't seem to want to talk about him.' Ellen was silent for a moment, recalling that her two children had probably overheard quite a lot in the couple of days before William died, things she would prefer them to forget. 'I just told them that their daddy had gone to heaven.' But Ellen wasn't altogether sure that she believed that.

And from the look that her mother gave her it seemed as though she didn't believe it either. 'Huh!' snorted Lydia. She turned back to the sink, plunging her hands deep into the soapy water, muttering as if to herself. 'Shouldn't speak ill of the dead, I know that, but if he's gone to heaven then there's no justice.' With William's death it had all come out. Lydia had been horrified to hear of his barbaric treatment of Ellen and all she had been suffering for the past two years. To think that the poor lass had borne so much and she had hardly said a word against him.

61

'Leave it, Mam,' Ellen replied tonelessly. 'We don't know, do we, what happens after we die, not really, so it's best not to worry about it too much. All I know is he's gone, and though I suppose I shouldn't say it, I'm glad.' The last two words were almost a whisper. Then she lifted her head high, saying the words again, but shouting them this time. 'I'm glad! Do you hear me? I'm glad.' She stood stock still in the middle of the kitchen, her knuckles gleaming white as she gripped hold of the pot towel. 'God forgive me for saying it, but I'm glad.' She gave a long shuddering sigh, her shoulders slumping and her head bowed as all the tension drained away from her body. Then, after a few seconds, she lifted her head again, looking at her mother. 'As you said, Mam, it's all over. Now I can start again.'

'Good lass,' said Lydia quietly. She dabbed at her eyes with her hanky, then she turned away quickly to the stone sink, pulling out the plug and letting the soapy water drain away. Then she, too, took hold of a pot towel to help her daughters to wipe what seemed like a mountain of cups, saucers, plates and dishes. Altogether there had been eighteen people present at the funeral meal, more than enough to cope with in an average-sized room.

'D'you know what we forgot, our Ellen?' said Lydia, in an attempt to change the subject a little.

'No, what was that, Mam?'

'We didn't offer 'em a drink of sherry or anything, did we, when we got back from church? I was going to suggest it, then I thought I'd better not. It'd only have embarrassed you if you'd forgotten to get any in. I should have thought about it myself, I know, and bought a couple of bottles, but there's been so much else to think about.'

'No, I didn't forget, Mam,' said Ellen. Her tone was emphatic and Lydia gave her a puzzled look. 'I'd no intention of giving them anything ... to drink.'

'What d'you mean?' Lydia frowned.

'What I mean is this, Mam. I shall never have any alcoholic drink in my house, not ever again.' Ellen had, in fact, only just come to this decision, this very minute, although the idea had been simmering in her mind since the news had come to her of William's death, probably even before that – the belief that drink was evil and that it must be avoided at all costs. But only now was she giving voice to her conviction.

'Look what it's done to me. I've been left a widow and my two children have been left without a father, all because William was drunk. He was dead drunk; that's why he fell in front of that cab, because he hadn't a clue what he was doing or where he was going. Yes, I know I said I was glad, and I am – but it started long before that, you know. It started when the old man died, two years ago, and I've never had a minute's happiness with William since that day...' Ellen's voice petered away and she stared into space. There were certain things that she could never tell her mother or Mary, about the demands that William had made of her in their marriage bed even before his father died. But these had been exacerbated a hundredfold since he had started

63

drinking. If it hadn't been for the drink, Ellen was convincing herself now, they might have stood a chance.

'In fact, I'll show you how I feel about it.' Moving quickly and more decisively than she had done since William's death, Ellen went into the adjoining living room and flung open the sideboard door. When she came back into the kitchen she was carrying two bottles, which she placed on the table. 'Brandy,' she said, lifting up one that was almost full and unscrewing the top. 'I've always had brandy in the house, for stomach upsets and that, like you have, Mam. But not any more.' She moved swiftly across to the sink and upended the bottle, watching with satisfaction as the amber liquid gurgled down the plughole.

'Hey, steady on, lass,' Lydia started to rebuke her. 'There's no need to be so hasty. There was nearly a bottleful there. That cost good money, you know. Just because William... It doesn't mean to say that–' Lydia stopped as Mary frowned reprovingly at her, shaking her head. Mary understood, possibly more than their mother, what Ellen had been through and why she was reacting the way she was now.

'And this is sherry,' Ellen continued, as though she hadn't heard. She grabbed hold of the second bottle and that went the same way as the first. 'I used to put it in trifles, if you remember. I thought it gave them a bit of a kick, but never again. Fruit juice'll do just as well.'

'Methodist trifle, eh, lass?' Lydia laughed a little embarrassedly. 'I thought that was what we'd had today – now I know why. Eh well, I daresay you know what you're doing. Far be it from me to try to tell you what to do. You're a grown-up woman now. But listen, our Ellen. Not all fellows are as bad as William, are they? He was a right bastard, God forgive me. But he just couldn't hold his liquor, that was the trouble.'

'Neither could my father, from what you've told me,' Ellen reminded her. Her mother seemed to have forgotten that now, in her anxiety about money being poured down the drain. 'No, Mam, it's caused too much unhappiness for me ... and for you. Other folks can please themselves, of course. There's nothing I can do about that. I don't intend to go round waving any banners. But – in my house – there will be no drinking, not ever again.'

The clogger's shop was on Church Street, not very far from St John's Church and the home of the Bamber family. The shop still bore the name of William's father. *Joseph Bamber and Son, High Class Cloggers* was written in now somewhat faded letters above the door. It was Joseph who had built up the good reputation of the business, and Ellen had no reason to believe that William had not continued with the good work in the two years since his father died. She believed that her husband, despite his many faults, had been a first-class clogger. All her acquaintances had told her so and the shop had always seemed busy. But that had been in the early days of their marriage. She hadn't heard much about the business lately; William had certainly never told her anything.

The shop was empty today, of course, on this

morning in mid-September; but, apart from the absence of customers, it looked pretty much the same as it had always done, Ellen thought, as she stared round at the dingy interior. William had always had the door propped open with a last to let in as much light as possible, but Ellen closed the door behind her now. She didn't want disturbing while she tried to sort out the accounts. It was her intention to sell the shop as a going concern. William had never made a fortune – and she suspected that, of late, much of what he had earned had gone on drink – but she felt that she should be able to ask a fair price for the 'goodwill' of the business and for the existing stock.

William, as she had suspected, had died without making a will, but there would be no problem, the solicitor had informed her, because she was undeniably his next-of-kin. Once probate was granted, everything would come to her. In the meantime she was entitled to do a bit of sorting out. There would, no doubt, be some bills that needed paying by the end of the month.

The shop smelt of leather, wood shavings and iron filings. A general mustiness hung in the air as the place hadn't been in use for over a week and thousands of dust motes danced in the shaft of sunlight that found its way through the window. William's workbench stood in the centre of the floor, still littered with brass nails, tin tacks, wooden plugs and strips of leather – all the paraphernalia needed for the art of clogging – but he hadn't been very good at clearing away, she mused. On the shelves were boxes of nails and tacks, tins of blacking and cobbler's wax, and on two ropes – resembling washing lines – strung the length of the shop were clog irons; large to very small sole irons and horse-shoe-shaped ones for the heels. Piles of leather lay at the end of the workbench, near to the treadle sewing machine, waiting to be made into clog uppers, with wooden soles, already shaped, at the side of them. It was just as though the shop was waiting for William to come in through the door, Ellen thought with a shudder.

Down one side of the shop was a long wooden bench. Many times Ellen had seen it full of boys, both big and small, many of them barefoot, waiting to have their clog irons replaced. William, like his father before him, had run a 'While You Wait' service as few of the children had alternative footwear. It was only the boys who needed this service, because only male persons had irons on their clogs. Women and girls wore clogs without irons on the soles. Both Lydia and Ellen wore clogs to stand in the market, for they were warm in winter and cool in summer, though not at other times; so did the hundreds of cotton mill workers in the vicinity.

Specimens of William's handiwork were to be seen in the window. Viewing them back to front, she could see the de luxe dancing clogs he had made, some red and some blue, decorated with brass studs and with fancy holes punched in the uppers. There were less grand ones as well; a row of 'barfoot' clogs (without irons) such as women wore and the 'duckbills' worn by men. In pride of place in the centre of the window were two miniature pairs of clogs, hardly large enough to fit a baby, such as all apprentice cloggers made as an advertisement for their work.

Ellen paid but scant attention to these items now. She had seen them all before and she must get on with the job in hand. She opened the drawer in the workbench and a jumble of papers sprang out, spilling on to the floor.

It was far, far worse than she had anticipated. Ellen had assumed that there would be a few unpaid bills, but some of these invoices went back several months. They were for leather; for ash, beech and alder wood; for new equipment that William had bought – a zig-zagger to join the back seams, and a skeiver to trim the leather – but, as far as Ellen could see, none of these items had been paid for.

And then she found the IOUs, scores of gambling debts, owed to his cronies at the public house. It was little wonder, she thought grimly, that William had been so anxious to get his hands on her tin box, although its contents wouldn't have gone very far in clearing this lot. Ellen was appalled at what she was discovering; had William lived longer, it could only have got worse. He would have been capable, she felt sure, of gambling away the very roof from over their heads. She realised now that she couldn't possibly sort this out for herself. She would have to put it all in the hands of the solicitor and see what he advised. She doubted that there would be much 'goodwill' left to sell with the business. It was a wonder that the shop had kept open at all.

At least the house was hers and it was paid for. No one could take that away from her ... could they? She was beginning to wonder what other debts William might have left behind that she was, as yet, unaware of. But she had her job at the market which, if she worked harder, could be more lucrative. It was then that an idea occurred to Ellen. This place would be ideal for her and her mother to make into a sweet shop. But how, in that case, would she be able to raise the money for the debts? The house ... why not? Ellen knew that she would far rather part with the house than the shop; she had never been happy there. Maybe she could look for somewhere smaller.

The jangle of the doorbell broke into her reverie, and she glanced up, startled. She smiled when she saw the tall, gangling figure of Amos, William's assistant, shambling towards her, a wide, childlike grin lighting up his pale blue eyes.

''Ello, Mrs Bamber,' he greeted her. 'I seed somebody inside. I thought as how it might be you.' He took off his cloth cap and stood, turning it over and over in his large red hands and shuffling his feet. 'I were real sorry Mrs Bamber, about 'im, bout yer 'usband, I mean.'

'Thank you, Amos,' replied Ellen warmly. 'It was a shock for all of us.' Ellen's brother-in-law Fred had gone round to Amos's home the morning after the accident to break the news to the lad. 'I'm sorry that you lost your job so suddenly. I know it can't be easy for you.' Amos, aged about sixteen, Ellen thought, was the eldest of six children; and though he didn't earn much, the little he did get was badly needed by his mother, who was a widow.

'No … me mam … not easy,' Amos babbled, looking down at the floor. 'Don't know how to say this, Mrs Bamber. Don't know if I should tell you, but 'im … William, yer 'usband…' He lifted his head then, his pale blue eyes looking at her pleadingly. 'He hadn't paid me, y'see, missis … not for two weeks he hadn't. 'Twasn't the first time, neither. Me mam … she said as 'ow I had to come and tell yer.'

'Good gracious, Amos, that's dreadful!' cried Ellen. She didn't doubt for one moment that he was telling her the truth. She opened the clasp on her black handbag and, drawing out her purse, she counted out the shillings, six of them for each week plus a couple more, placing them in Amos's already outstretched hand. She wasn't sure what William had paid him – as little and as seldom as possible, it seemed – but she thought that what she was giving him erred on the generous side.

He seemed well pleased. 'Ta very much, Mrs Bamber,' he muttered, touching his forelock. 'You're a real lady, you are that. I've always said so, and me mam says it an' all.'

'That's all right, Amos,' Ellen said quietly. The lad's blue eyes seemed to be boring right into her and she was beginning to feel a little uncomfortable. But there was no need to be afraid of Amos; she realised, when he next spoke, that he had been plucking up courage to tell her something else.

'I want to show you summat. Look 'ere, Mrs Bamber.' The words were spoken quickly, then just as quickly the lad bent down and rolled up his trouser leg, revealing a skinny white calf covered in bruises; purply-blue and yellowish, now fading, it was true, but still bearing evidence of a severe ... kicking?

'Oh no,' breathed Ellen. 'Did my husband do that to you?'

'Aye, he did, missis, an' it weren't the first time, neither.'

'But why, Amos?'

'Dunno.' Amos shrugged. 'Well, aye, I suppose I do know. I weren't always quick enough for him, y'see. An' I made mistakes, an' I dropped things. He got me in such a flummox, y'see, Mrs Bamber, an' sometimes I didn't rightly know what I was doing.'

Ellen nodded. She knew the feeling. William had reduced her to the same state many a time and, though he had never kicked her, he had abused her in other ways. She knew that the heavy clogs that William had worn in the shop, or even his hobnailed boots, could be vicious weapons. But to think that he had used them on this poor lad. She gave an inward shudder. 'I'm sorry, Amos,' she said quietly. 'I am truly, very sorry. I had no idea.'

'He were a real bugger,' Amos said now, so matter-of-factly that Ellen almost laughed. 'Pardon me, Mrs Bamber, but he were. I said just now as I was sorry... Well, I'm sorry for you, Mrs Bamber, 'cause you're a widow woman now. Me mam's a widow, and I know it's not easy for widows. But I'm not sorry he's gone. I can't be sorry about that, though I know I says it as shouldn't.' He hung his head, staring at the floor.

71

'That's all right, Amos,' said Ellen again. 'I understand. And thank you for telling me.'

She knew that she must try to make it up to the lad, somehow. But what could she do? She could hardly offer him a job on the sweet stall. He wouldn't be able to cope with the money; besides, they couldn't afford to employ anyone else at the moment. There was Mr Jenks at the fish stall, though. She had heard that he needed an assistant, and it might be right up Amos's street, gutting fish. Or helping on one of the fruit and vegetable stalls, maybe. He would be well able to hump sacks of potatoes and cabbages.

'I'm not promising anything,' she told him, 'but I'll see if anyone at the market wants an assistant. Would you like to work there, Amos?'

'Would I?' His eyes shone with delight. 'Not 'alf I would, Mrs Bamber!'

As she closed the door behind him Ellen's smile faded. She wasn't the only one who had suffered at William's hands. That poor boy had gone through it as well. Ellen was coming to the conclusion that nothing she could find out now about her late husband would surprise her. But there were more startling revelations ahead.

She recognised the woman as soon as she entered the shop, holding a small boy by the hand. It was the woman in green, the one who had been in the church and then in the graveyard. Ellen had thought, at her first glimpse of her, that the woman was smartly, if unsuitably dressed. Now, with only the width of the workbench between them, Ellen could see that the loose green coat with its big collar and wide sleeves, which might once have been fashionable, was threadbare and dirty. Equally shabby was the large-brimmed hat on which the ostrich feathers hung limply. Ellen didn't object to shabbiness. How could she, knowing that many of her own clothes were decidedly worse for wear? She had, however, always tried to keep herself clean, whereas one glance at the woman revealed that that was not the case here. Her curly dark hair was greasy and matted. Her face looked as though it could do with a good wash; even so, her lips and cheeks were unnaturally pink.

'You don't know me, do you?' was her opening remark as she looked boldly at Ellen. Ellen noticed, in spite of her wariness and, if she were honest, her slight repugnance at the strange woman, that she had beautiful eyes. They were clear grey and luminous, fringed with long dark lashes, but the expression in them was one of hostility and Ellen felt her distrust increasing.

'No, I don't think we've met before,' Ellen answered as politely as she was able. She tried to smile, although there was no similar response coming from the other woman. 'I've noticed you, though. Didn't I see you in the church, at my husband's funeral?'

'Your husband. Yes, *Mrs Bamber.*' The words were delivered with undue emphasis. 'You saw me at your husband's funeral, you did indeed. And d'you know why I was there? D'you want to know who I am? Or, more to the point, who this little fellow here is?' She rested her hand briefly on the head of the small boy at her side.

'Yes, tell me,' Ellen breathed, although she

thought she already knew. 'Tell me – who you are?'

'I'm Jessie Balderstone,' replied the woman, 'and this is John Henry Balderstone. I gave him my name, y'see, although by rights he should have his father's name. Bamber, that's what he should be called, John Henry Bamber ... 'cause he's William's son.'

And as Ellen looked at the child she didn't doubt that this was the truth. Not that he looked all that much like William. His curly hair was dark brown, almost black, like William's, but that could have been a legacy from his mother; neither were his eyes the same startling blue, more an indeterminate bluish-grey. He looked at Ellen now, smiling uncertainly. Ellen felt her heart give a lurch and she tried to smile back. Poor little lad. It wasn't his fault; whatever the parents did it was never the children who were to blame. He looked untidy and not any too clean, his mouth still bearing traces of jam from breakfast, but quite healthy and well-nourished. His woollen jacket and knee-length serge trousers showed signs of wear, but Ellen noticed that his feet were clad in a shiny, obviously new, pair of clogs.

Ellen felt angry then. William must have been carrying on with this woman for years. The child looked about the same age as Rachel. He must have known her since the early days of their marriage, she thought, with gradually dawning astonishment. Before his father died, before he started drinking. And, if the little boy's feet were anything to judge by, he must still have been seeing her ... and the boy.

'How do I know?' said Ellen now, narrowing her eyes sceptically as she looked at the woman. 'How do I know that what you are telling me is true? What proof do you have? And what do you expect me to do about it, anyway? It was my husband's affair, not mine – if it's true – and now he's dead. It has nothing to do with me.' Ellen's words came out with much more conviction than she was, in truth, feeling. She was confused, dismayed, disillusioned; but, in spite of all these feelings, furious as well and she was determined to put up at least a token resistance.

'Proof?' yelled Jessie Balderstone. 'What more proof do you want? Look at him! Look at him, woman. He's the spitting image of his father.'

'Not really,' replied Ellen evenly. 'He has dark hair, that's all, but so have you. I want more proof than that. A birth certificate, for instance. Have you a birth certificate ... with his father's name on it?'

'No, damn you, I haven't,' shouted the woman. 'It's got my name on it, that's all, 'cause I knew it would be me that had to bring him up. I knew he was married. I knew all along. He came to me for a bit of comfort, summat you weren't all that good at giving him, were you?' She raised one eyebrow eloquently, a cynical smile curving her over-pink lips. Ellen felt her hackles rise, but she didn't answer; she just stared back impassively at her adversary. She knew it was true though, every word of it.

'And he promised he'd always take care of us, me and the lad,' Jessie went on. 'He'll have left me summat, I know that. He always said he would, but until then, until the will's sorted out, me and John Henry here, we've got to live.'

'There is no will,' Ellen replied flatly.

'What! What d'you mean? He said—'

'It doesn't matter what he said,' Ellen went on, more reasonably now. 'William didn't leave a will. He died – what do they call it? – intestate. That means that everything comes to me, as his widow. You see, I don't suppose he thought for one moment that he was going to die. He was only twenty-five.'

Jessie blanched quite visibly. 'But he promised... He always said...' She glanced round uncertainly, then flopped down on the wooden bench. 'He's helped me out all along. I can't manage now. What'll I do?'

So he's helped you out, has he? thought Ellen, her inclination to sympathise being swamped by a burst of righteous indignation. He had helped this woman at the expense of his own wife and children. There had been times when Ellen had found it hard to make ends meet; it would have been well-nigh impossible if not for her own little job.

'I suggest you do the same as I do,' said Ellen drily, 'and go out to work. Isn't there anyone who'll look after your little boy? He looks as though he's nearly ready for school, anyway. How old is he?'

'He's four,' replied Jessie briefly. She didn't go on to say when his birthday was, so Ellen had no means of knowing whether he had been born before, or after, her own little girl. Rachel had

76

been four last June. Had William gone straight from her bed to that of this ... Jessie? Or was it possible that he had known her even before that? Ellen didn't particularly want to find out.

'Me mam looks after him already,' Jessie Balderstone went on, her voice devoid of emotion now. 'An' I do work. I work damned hard, I can tell you. I work at the cotton mill.'

'Horrockses?' enquired Ellen.

'No, not that big 'un. A smaller one, near where we live.'

'And ... where's that?' Some paradoxical impulse, akin to rubbing salt in the wound, was driving Ellen on to ask questions to which she really didn't want to know the answers.

'Maudlands,' answered Jessie, referring to the area centred around the Church of St Walburge's, the one with the impressive spire. 'We live with me mam, me and John Henry. And, like I say, she looks after him. But I shan't be able to work much longer. Me mam's ailing; she's already brought up a big family an' it's getting too much for her.' She looked directly at Ellen now, her grey eyes unflinching. 'So I want some help, Mrs Bamber. I want some money ... an' I want it now.'

Ellen looked back at her, her own glance just as steadfast. 'But your little boy will be at school soon. You've told me he's four. There are lots of women in the same boat, Mrs ... Miss ... Balderstone.'

'Miss'll do,' interrupted that lady. 'That's what I am, an' I don't try to disguise it.'

'So I see no reason why you can't continue with

77

your job at the cotton mill,' Ellen went on, hating herself for seeming so hardhearted. 'I've told you – I have to work. And I shall have to work a darned sight harder now. William has left a load of debts, debts that I knew nothing about, Miss Balderstone.'

'Don't you talk to me about having to work, you stuck-up cow!' Jessie rose to her feet, her fists clenching and her eyes dark with rage. 'You with yer big swanky house an' yer shop an' yer toffee stall! You know nowt. Nowt at all about what it's really like to be on yer uppers. I can't go on working, Mrs flamin' Bamber – and d'you know why? There's summat else I can't disguise, as well as the fact that I'm a Miss. Look 'ere. Now … are you satisfied?' She flung open her loose-fitting green coat and Ellen saw, to her horror that Jessie Balderstone was pregnant, some six or seven months so.

Chapter Four

'She's there again, Ellen.' Lydia nudged her daughter's arm as she nodded in the direction of the neighbouring fruit and vegetable stall. 'And the little lad with her an' all. You'll have to do something before long, you know. Put your foot down and tell her to stop pestering you. I know she's upsetting you. You're like a cat on hot bricks whenever she shows her face.'

Ellen groaned as she glanced across the crowded aisle between the two stalls. Yes, there was Jessie Balderstone again. It wasn't altogether a surprise to see her there now, as it had been the first time she had appeared at the market. That was a month ago and she had turned up every Saturday since then, always at the same time, just after the Town Hall clock had struck three. That was the time when bargains were to be had on the greengrocers' stalls; when most of the shoppers had completed their purchases and the stallholders were anxious to get rid of their overripe fruit, bruised tomatoes or blemished vegetables. The woman was bargaining with Mr Wilkins now over a brown speckled cauliflower and some wizened apples.

The child, John Henry, was there too. Ellen, who was supposed to be concentrating on serving a customer, watched him out of the corner of her eye. While his mother was busy with

79

the stallholder he sneaked away. Ellen saw him cram a few black grapes into his mouth, then, quick as a flash – Ellen felt sure he must have done it before – he grabbed hold of two small oranges and shoved them deep into the pockets of his tweed jacket, one at each side. Then he went back to his mother who was tipping the cauliflower, apples and several overripe pears and bananas into her capacious shopping bag.

'There's not much I can do, is there, Mam?' said Ellen in a hurried whisper, when she had finished serving her customer. She knew that, if she ran true to form, Jessie would soon be making her way over to the sweet stall. 'She's as much right to be at the market as the rest of us, when all's said and done.'

Lydia gave an indignant sniff. 'Not when she's touching you for money, she's not. I'd send her away with a flea in her ear if I were you, the brazen hussy! You're too soft, our Ellen, far too kind-hearted for your own good.'

Ellen didn't answer. It was useless to tell her mother, as she had done when Jessie made her first appearance, that she felt sorry for the woman. That would only exasperate Lydia even further. Ellen hadn't intended being so kind-hearted. She had meant to take a firm line with Jessie Balderstone right from the start, from the very moment, in fact, when she had walked into the clogger's shop and made herself known. She had told her quite emphatically that there was no money for her, that she would have to carry on working just as she, Ellen, was forced to do. But on finding out that the woman was pregnant, for the second time, Ellen had found her resolution wavering. Her hardness of heart had melted, more for the sake of the little boy at her side than for Jessie herself. That first day she had parted with a sovereign, far more than she could really afford. Since then, on Jessie's visits to the market, a couple of half-crowns and a florin had gone the same way. Ellen was now beginning to realise, as her mother had warned her, that this could well be a situation to which there was no end, if she didn't put her foot down.

She looked up from serving a customer with a quarter of butterscotch to see Jessie in front of her, John Henry at her side. It was the sight of the child that always unnerved Ellen, more than the woman herself. John Henry Balderstone, by rights John Henry Bamber, or so his mother had said. William's bastard... Her husband William, who had lied and cheated his way through the travesty of their marriage, who had abused and humiliated her and who now, even after his death, had left her with a multitude of problems. Not least of which was this woman with the swollen stomach, leaning against her sweet stall in such a bold manner, and this scruffy child, whose grubby fingers were now mauling at the sticks of barley sugar at the front of the counter.

'Leave those alone! Don't touch, d'you hear me!' Ellen spoke more sharply than she intended. The boy usually evoked her pity, but that didn't mean that he could go messing about with her goods. He had already pinched some fruit from Mr Wilkins and that had angered her, although she had no intention of splitting on him. The colourful confections on her own stall were always a temptation to youngsters, but usually their mothers managed to keep the childrens' prying little hands away. Jessie wasn't even trying. It was obvious that the boy was a handful, but his mother didn't seem to be making any effort to curb his waywardness. Ellen wondered if she knew about his pinching from the greengrocer's stall and decided that she probably did.

Ellen was surprised when Jessie said mildly, 'Yes, leave 'em alone, John Henry, there's a good boy. You heard what the lady said.' Ellen had expected a torrent of abuse, not against the child, but against herself. 'I daresay the lady'll give you one, anyroad. Which would you like? One of them barley sugars? Or what about a nice red lollipop, or a stick of liquorice?'

The cheek of it, thought Ellen. Lolling against the stall as though she owns it and making free with my merchandise! Always, at their previous visits, Ellen had given the child a few of their farthing lines, but the sight, just now, of him stealing from Mr Wilkins, a hardworking man if ever there was one, had riled her more than she had realised. She was, in fact, coming to the conclusion that his mother had put him up to it and that maybe Jessie Balderstone wasn't quite as poverty-stricken as she made out.

'He'd better have the barley sugar, seeing that he's already had his mucky little hands all over it.' Ellen grabbed hold of the curly orange stick and shoved it into a cone-shaped paper bag. 'And a lollipop; just one.' A streak of malice, something

Ellen didn't often experience, made her choose a green rather than a red lollipop. Red ones were the favourites with children, the green ones often being left at the bottom of the box. 'And that's all he's getting today so he'd better make the most of it. Here … John Henry.' Ellen held the bag out towards the child. 'And what do you say?'

The boy looked at her insolently for a few seconds, his greyish-blue eyes narrowing slightly. Then, as she made to withdraw the bag, 'Ta, missis,' he said quickly, making a grab at it. 'Ta very much.'

As she handed it over Ellen caught a glimpse, just a fleeting one, of William; that gloating expression he had shown when he thought he had got the better of her. She had previously looked in vain for any resemblance to her late husband, although she had never thought to doubt the truth of what Jessie had told her. It stood to reason that a man as lusty as William would not be satisfied with only one woman, especially one as inadequate as he had considered her, Ellen, to be. It explained his late homecomings – sometimes it had been the early hours of the morning before he had returned home – and even why, on the night of his death, he had been attempting to cross Church Street. There would have been no need to cross over if he had been going straight home. But Ellen knew now that he had been on his way to visit Jessie Balderstone, as he had done on so many occasions.

'You don't need to teach him his manners, thank you very much,' Jessie retorted now. 'He's been brought up to say please and thank you. I know what's what, though you may not think I do. Me own mum brought me up proper, an' that's what I intend to do with John Henry here. And the next 'un when it comes. It won't be long now.'

She bent closer to Ellen, leaning across the front of the stall. Ellen found herself recoiling slightly from the aroma that assailed her nostrils, although she tried not to make her revulsion too obvious. It wasn't stale body odour – it did seem that Jessie, though untidy, kept herself fairly clean – but that of cheap scent mingled with the unmistakable smell of liquor. 'Only a few more weeks,' Jessie was saying. 'I've had to give me job up, like I was telling you, Mrs Bamber. The boss didn't want to risk me havin' it on the factory floor. Anyroad, me mam can't go on looking after John Henry any longer. She's badly, y'see. It's her heart, and she's got rheumatics an' all. So if you could just...'

'No!' Ellen's sharp retort cut across Jessie's pathetic ramblings. If Jessie Balderstone had money to spend on booze, then she had no business coming here touching her for more. 'No, I won't!' Ellen's tone was emphatic and she saw her mother, at the other end of the stall, glance across at her. 'You've come to ask me for money again, haven't you?' Ellen lowered her voice slightly, although there were no customers around at the moment. 'Well, the answer is no. You've had all the cash you're having from me. And you can think yourself lucky that there's been any at all. Coming to me with some cock and bull story about my husband! I told you right at the start – you've no proof, none whatsoever.'

'He's all the proof I need.' Jessie put a protective arm round the boy's shoulders, drawing him closer to her. 'And well you know it, Nellie Bamber! And d'you know why yer husband came to me, eh? Because you were no bloody good, neither in bed nor out of it, that's why. I looked after him though. These last five years, and more, I've been seeing to him. You'd be surprised what I've–'

'Be quiet, can't you!' Ellen hissed. She could see that the drink was now making Jessie peevish and maudlin, as well as causing her to wander away from the point of the argument. 'If you don't stop making such an exhibition of yourself I shall get the police. They'll soon move you on. That's right, Mam. You go…' For Lydia was now moving purposefully away from the stall.

'Oh, hark at her! She'll get the police. Miss Hoity-Toity! All right, all right, don't wet your drawers, I'm going.' But Jessie stayed her ground. '*When* I've got what I came for…'

Ellen knew when she was beaten. She had had more than enough for one day. She hated arguments of any kind and a few people were casting curious glances in their direction, as they always did whenever there was a to-do at one of the market stalls. But Ellen was determined not to be as generous as she had been in the past. She rooted through the tin cash box at the back of the stall, well out of reach of the customers, and drew out a half-crown. 'Here – that's all you're getting.' She thrust the coin at Jessie. 'And don't let me see you round here ever again, or I will get the police. I mean it. Now, get moving.'

'You've not heard the last of this, I'm warning you, Nellie Bamber. I shall get even with you if it's the last thing I do.' Jessie's grey eyes were flashing with more hatred than Ellen had ever seen there before.

Ellen didn't answer. The altercation had upset her very much and she could already feel her legs and hands beginning to tremble. She turned her head slightly, wondering where her mother had got to; she was feeling in need of moral support. Then she breathed a sigh of relief, tinged with apprehension. For there was Lydia, not more than twenty yards away, coming towards them, followed closely by a policeman. What a stroke of luck, thought Ellen. He must have been on his beat on Lancaster Road, near to the market.

Jessie turned her head at the same time. Then, 'You bastard!' she shrieked at Ellen, though not too loudly. 'You sneaky devil! You–'

'Not sneaky at all,' replied Ellen, though her voice was shaky. 'I told you I'd get the police.' Her threat, however, had been more a show of bravado. Ellen hadn't expected her mother to act upon it so quickly, or, indeed, to return almost immediately with one of the boys in blue.

'Come on, John Henry. We're getting out of here.' Jessie grabbed hold of the boy's arm and pulled him away. 'You haven't seen the last of us though. I'll get me own back one of these days. You just see if I don't, Nellie Bamber!'

By the time Lydia and the policeman arrived on the scene the two of them had disappeared down one of the crowded aisles. Ellen could just see the top of Jessie's bright green hat as she hurried away.

'Trouble, love?' asked the policeman. 'It looks as though the bird's flown.'

'Yes. I'm sorry, Officer. I'm sorry we've had to bother you,' said Ellen. 'There was a spot of trouble – just a family matter, really. It's nothing much...'

'Nothing much! I don't call it nothing much when my daughter's being insulted in a public place, and being touched for money time and time again.' Lydia's face was as red as the apples on the next stall with her exertions and her rage about her daughter's dilemma. 'Anyroad, it seems she's gone. Good riddance to bad rubbish, that's what I say. We were too late, worse luck. But we're very grateful to you, Officer.'

'All in a day's work, missis,' the policeman grinned. 'We're used to being fetched to sort out a barney or two on a Saturday, 'specially when the pubs turn out. Caused trouble before, has she, the woman in green?'

'You know her then?' asked Ellen.

'No, I can't say I've noticed her before. Just saw she had a green coat. Could hardly miss it, could you? But I daresay I'd know her if I saw her again.'

'I shouldn't imagine she's been in trouble before,' said Ellen slowly, trying to be fair. 'It was ... is ... like I say, just a family matter. I don't think we'll see her again.' But Ellen was not at all convinced of that.

'Very well then. Just as you say. Glad to be of

service.' The policeman touched his helmet, then he was gone.

'Oh Mam, I'm all of a tremble,' gasped Ellen as he walked away. 'Just imagine that! Having to call the police. I never intended...'

'Here, lass, sit down.' Lydia drew out a three-legged stool from beneath the stall. 'Take it easy now. You'll be all right in a minute or two. Anyway, she's gone and she won't be back. You were marvellous, our Ellen, sticking up to her the way you did. I never thought you had it in you.'

'Nor did I, Mam,' Ellen sighed. 'An' I tell you what − I don't feel any too happy about it neither.'

'What d'you mean? The woman's a menace. You were right to send her packing. I've been telling you so ever since she first appeared. What if the lad *is* William's by-blow − and I must admit he probably is. It's nowt to do with you. An' I'll tell you summat else. You don't know that the next one is, do you?'

'No, Mam, I'd already thought of that,' replied Ellen. 'But I can't help feeling, not exactly sorry, and certainly not responsible for her, but ... she's up against it, isn't she? I know you say we've got problems of our own, but they're nothing compared with hers, are they? We've got a roof over our heads, me and the children, and a very sound one it is, too.'

'You very nearly didn't have,' retorted Lydia. 'What with William and his boozing and gambling. All them debts... You've been bloomin' lucky to hang on to that house. As it is, it's damned near empty.'

88

'Yes, that's what I'm trying to tell you, Mam,' said Ellen patiently. 'I'm lucky, I know I am. I'm lucky to have a house to live in, a house that's paid for, one that belongs to me. It's more than a lot of folks have. I know it's nearly empty now I've sold all that old stuff. And I know it's too big for me and Rachel and Georgie. It's a barn of a place to heat and light, but we're looking for somewhere smaller, aren't we? And at least I've been able to keep the shop. I tell you, Mam ... I'm lucky.'

Things hadn't, in fact, been as bad as Ellen had at first anticipated. William's debts had been legion, with no money in his bank account to meet them and Ellen had thought she would be forced to sell the house. It had been the solicitor's idea that she should realise some cash by selling off, not the house itself, but most of the contents. The two display cabinets in the parlour had been veritable treasure houses, packed with solid silver tea services and trinkets; Rockingham, Spode and Royal Crown Derby porcelain; cut glass and crystal bowls and jugs. Sitting atop the elaborately carved mahogany mantelshelf there had been a pair of what Ellen considered to be hideous vases, all gold and glitter and curlicues, and two enormous groups of figures from the Royal Dux factory; a sentimental shepherd and shepherdess and a biblical group which she thought was Isaac, Esau and Jacob. They might have been to the taste of old Joseph Bamber and his sanctimonious wife, but they were most definitely not Ellen's cup of tea. She had been glad to see the back of them at the auction sale only last week, together with the gilt-framed pictures on the walls – some of them fairly valuable – and the heavy red plush chairs and sofa, and, last but not least, the Indian carpet. Ellen couldn't help but think that it would all have gone ages ago, had William realised that his parents' house had held such riches. However, they had now raised enough to clear William's debts and there was quite a bit left over. What did it matter if the Stonygate house was now partially empty? As Ellen was trying to explain to her mother, they did have a roof over their heads, and, maybe in the New Year, when the business with the shop was all sorted out, they would move to a smaller place.

'Yes, I must agree with you that it's worked out very nicely about the shop,' Lydia replied now. 'It'll be just the job, and if the shopfitters get their skates on and get it finished before Christmas, like they've promised, then we'll be laughing, our Ellen. It'll be hard work, though, I've no illusions about that.'

'A darned sight warmer than this place though, Mam, in the middle of winter,' Ellen remarked. Preston Market was a cold place when the ice and snow lay on the ground and the wind whistled between the stalls. The Covered Market, it was proudly called, but the massive roof did little more than keep the rain and snow off. Even now, at the end of October, it could feel decidedly chilly at times.

'But we'll be keeping the stall on, lass, won't we?' Lydia reminded her daughter. 'We can't go biting off the hand that feeds us, not yet awhile.

Aye, we'll be glad of the market stall. We might even be able to pay somebody to look after it for us. We'll have to see how things go. But I don't suppose I shall go traipsing off to Leyland and Chorley much longer. Anyroad, Ellen, you just think of the hard work ahead of you and let's have less talk about how lucky you are. You know what I always say: every tub has to stand on its own bottom. Nobody helped me out very much when your father died. It was up to me to get this lot going.' She waved her hand across the stall and its contents. 'So don't waste your sympathy on that Jessie Balderstone. I know her sort – as crafty as a cartload of monkeys. She'll get by, don't you worry.'

But Ellen couldn't help but worry. In spite of what her mother said, she felt that she had so much ... and Jessie had so little.

Lydia had been very enthusiastic about the idea of turning the clogger's shop into a sweet shop, as Ellen had thought she would be. The way things had worked out it was by far the best solution. Though the business had appeared, on the surface, to be thriving, it was discovered, on closer examination, that there was very little stock; the materials, by and large, had not been paid for, and William's order book was almost empty. It seemed that he had let the business dwindle sadly over the last couple of years so that there was, by now, precious little 'goodwill' to sell to any prospective buyer. Ellen had decided to cut her losses. She would hang on to the lease of the shop, then, after selling off the residue of the stock and equipment to any interested cloggers in the vicinity, she would see about having the premises converted for her and her mother's use.

She had been sorry about Amos Hardy, William's young assistant, especially when she had found out about her husband's cruel abuse of him; but she had been as good as her word and had managed to find him a job on the market. On the next stall, in fact, that of Mr Wilkins, the greengrocer. Mr Wilkins, who suffered agonies with his back, especially in the damp weather, had been only too pleased to find a strong willing lad to hump sacks of potatoes and crates of fruit, to sweep up the rubbish and swill the place down at the end of the day. Amos declared to Ellen that he had never been so happy in all his life. He accompanied Mr Wilkins on his trips to other nearby markets and sometimes helped Mrs Wilkins at their little shop at the far end of Church Street. He wasn't much good at handling the money, but Mr Wilkins declared that his wife had the patience of a saint and that she had been pleased to take Amos under her wing. The elderly couple seemed to be finding this amiable – though certainly slow-witted – young man a refreshing change after some of the brash, 'know-it-all' youngsters they had employed in the past. Ellen guessed that they didn't pay very much and were not very go-ahead in outlook, which was probably why so many assistants had left their employment; but it was suiting Amos down to the ground. Ellen, seeing him make sheep's eyes at her from the neighbouring stall, knew that she had an admirer for life. She was glad that she had been able to help one of William's victims.

She continued to worry, however, about Jessie Balderstone. Not that she considered that young woman to have been victimised by William; far from it. Ellen tried not to think about what had gone on between the pair of them, but she couldn't help but wonder whether Jessie might have cared for him in a way that she, Ellen, had been unable to do. She had undoubtedly been able to look after his bodily needs far more successfully. Could this, Ellen pondered, have amounted to love? Jessie might well have seen a different side to William; she might even have been able to evoke tender feelings in her lover, such as his wife had been unable to arouse. At all events, his death had come as a shock to the woman, a far more unpleasant shock than it had been to his wife.

Ellen knew that she didn't like Jessie, nor ever could. The woman was loud-mouthed and coarse, and Ellen, though she was a child of a working-class family, had always tried to be ladylike. Jessie was, no doubt, devious as well, but Ellen could tell that she was fond of her son and that, in Ellen's view, was a point in her favour. She must be finding it hard to make ends meet now that she was no longer able to work. Ellen had been relieved, but also somewhat surprised, when Jessie didn't reappear at the market, not the next week, nor the week after that. She had been warned off, of course, but women like Jessie as a rule paid little heed to warnings. Towards the end of November, when she still had neither heard nor seen anything of the woman, Ellen was, though not exactly anxious, very curious to know what had become of her. She had more sense, however, than to tell her mother of her concern. Lydia's reaction would be that she wanted her head looking at!

Instead, she confided in her sister, Mary, and her brother-in-law, Fred Pilkington. 'I'd just like to know if she's had the baby,' she told them. 'She surely must have done by now. I know it's stupid of me to even think about it, but that little lad, John Henry, keeps coming into my mind. He's a villain, I know – I told you, didn't I, that I saw him pinching fruit – but I can't help feeling sorry for him. He hasn't got the secure background that our children have, yours and mine.'

'You don't really know that, our Ellen,' Mary argued. 'You've said that you think his mother's fond of him, and he's got a gran, hasn't he? The trouble with you is you're too soft-hearted, like our mam says. I'm not surprised you haven't told Mam what's on your mind. If I were you I'd let 'em stew in their own juice, causing you all that bother!'

Fred was deep in thought. He felt that he would like, if possible, to help his sister-in-law. She had had a shocking time with that devil of a husband of hers. Many's the time he had felt like going and sorting him out, but he would only have got beaten to a pulp if he had tried, and that wouldn't have helped anyone. Fred thought that Ellen was daft, of course, mithering about William's fancy piece, but he would see if he could find out what she wanted to know.

'Where does this Jessie live?' he asked.

'I'm not sure,' replied Ellen. 'I know it's in the Maudland's area, but that's not much to go on, is it? Why do you ask?'

'Happen I could go and make a few enquiries,' said Fred. 'Casual like, you know.' He paid no heed to his wife's cautionary glance. 'The landlords in the pubs usually know what's going on, to say nothing of the regulars. I could have a nose around. And the woman's got an unusual name, so that should help.'

'You watch yerself, Fred Pilkington,' said Mary, looking none too pleased. 'It's a bit of a rum area, from what I've heard. I don't want you getting bashed about in a pub brawl.'

'As if I would!' Fred gave his wife a withering look. 'If I ever do it'll be t'first time and well you know it. Anyroad, I'm not asking owt wrong, am I? Only if the lass has had her baby. An' if it'll help our Ellen...'

'Blessed if I can see how it'll help her,' muttered Mary. 'It'll more likely land her with another load of trouble. It's best left alone, I tell you.'

But Ellen knew from Fred's confidential wink that this time he wasn't going to be browbeaten by his wife.

'It seems that the young woman's disappeared,' he reported to Ellen when she called round the following week. 'And the child as well, John Henry, you said he was called?'

Ellen nodded. 'And ... the baby? Did you find out if she'd...?'

'She lost it,' replied Fred. 'It were stillborn,

95

about a month ago, it were. Another little lad, apparently.'

'Then it must've been just after ... after that last time,' said Ellen. 'The time we got the police. Oh dear...'

Fred told her how he had visited a couple of public houses in the vicinity of St Walburge's Church, and in the second one the landlord, had indeed heard of the Balderstone family. Fortunately he turned out to be a garrulous person. He hadn't even been curious as to why Fred was asking. Ellen was rather surprised to learn that the Balderstones were respectable folk, well thought of in the neighbourhood, though it had to be admitted that the youngest, Jessie, was something of a tearaway, Fred related, in the words of the landlord. The girl had got herself 'in the family way' not once, but twice. She had been carrying on with the fellow – a married man, it was said – quite openly, right under the poor old mother's nose. Mrs Balderstone was more or less bedridden, but it was her other sons and daughters, the married ones, who were caring for her now. Jessie, after losing her baby and, apparently, being quite ill, had upped and left. There had been a blazing row with her mother – what it was about the landlord didn't know – but the upshot of it was that she had gone.

'And they don't know where?' asked Ellen.

'No, they've not seen hide nor hair of her these last three weeks. That's not long, of course,' Fred went on. 'But the fellow I was talking to seems to think she's slung her hook good and proper. Now, don't you worry any more, Ellen.' He patted his sister-in-law's arm consolingly. 'You've a heart of gold, I know, but there's nowt else you can do. The lass has vanished. If she was anywhere near she'd have paid you a visit, you can be sure of that.'

'And you don't know where the old lady lives?' asked Ellen. 'It must have been true, what Jessie said. Her mother *was* ill.'

'No, I've no idea,' answered Fred. It was a lie, albeit a white one. He knew old Mrs Balderstone's address, the street at any rate, but it wouldn't do their Ellen any good to know. 'Forget about 'em, Ellen. You've seen the last of that Jessie Balderstone, I feel sure you have.'

'Yes, maybe.' Ellen nodded slowly. 'Thanks, Fred. It was good of you to go.'

'Yes, you just foreget about 'em, Ellen,' Mary added. Mary added. 'You just concentrate on your new shop. Only another few weeks. By heck! Not only a market stall, but a High Street shop an' all. My goodness, some folks'll be so uppity soon that there'll be no speaking to 'em.'

Ellen took her sister's remark in the good-natured way that it was intended. Mary, though brusque, had never been jealous of her younger sister, either for her more attractive looks or her slightly larger share of this world's goods. It was only recently, of course, that her comparative bounty was doing Ellen any good, for no one could have envied her being married to a brute like William Bamber, even if he had inherited a big house.

Ellen knew, too, that Mary was trying to change the subject and she decided to fall in with the

97

idea. It would be far better all round if she put Jessie Balderstone, and John Henry, right out of her mind.

'Don't worry, I think we'll be able to spare your Tommy and Charlie a few dolly mixtures if you bring them to see us,' she laughed now. 'No, it won't be long. The shopfitters are getting on like a house on fire now. We should be open for Christmas with a bit of luck.' Ellen held up her crossed fingers. 'Our Rachel and Georgie are that excited, there's no holding 'em. I'm glad Rachel's starting school in January. I can tell you. She's nearly driving me barmy with her chatter...'

Chapter Five

The shop opened, as they had hoped, the week before Christmas, 1902, although there was still quite a lot of work to be done behind the scenes. The main thing, of course, was that they were able to start trading and to take advantage of the seasonal rush of dilatory folk who had not yet completed their Christmas shopping. The sign above the door read *Bamber and Tucker, High Class Sweets and Chocolates.* Lydia had insisted that their previous slogan, 'Tucker's Tasty Toffee', used at the market stall, would not now suffice as it was Ellen who virtually owned the premises and who was now contributing a good half of the produce. An advertisement in the *Lancashire Evening Post,* however, left no one in any doubt that this new establishment on Church Street, formerly the clogger's shop, was in the same capable hands as the popular stall on the market.

It was extremely hard work, as Lydia and Ellen had anticipated, especially during the first week of opening. Lydia was manning the market stall single-handed, leaving Ellen to cope with all the business at the new premises. Mary came in one day to help her sister at the shop, but as they also had the four children to look after it was decided, before many hours had passed, that this was not a very good idea and that it might be as well not to repeat the experiment. Admittedly, there was

99

the storeroom opening off the shop where the children could play, but Ellen and Mary had been on pins most of the day, trying to see to the childrens' needs and also to concentrate on the customers.

'They've been real good, though, bless 'em,' said Mary, when half-past five eventually arrived and they were able to bolt the door and turn the sign round to *Closed*. 'It's not their fault that we've hardly had time to see to 'em. I think they deserve a lollipop each, don't you, our Ellen, or one of these little chocolate bars?'

'It'll spoil their tea,' Ellen replied automatically, before adding, smilingly, 'All right, just this once.' She took four Fry's chocolate cream tablets from a wooden display box, open on the counter, and handed them to the children. 'I've got to admit they've been as good as gold. What a temptation, eh? To play in the middle of this lot and to be told not to touch,' she laughed. 'I remember when I was a little girl I used to think how wonderful it would be to work in a sweet shop ... then I could eat as many as I liked and not have to pay! I never thought I'd actually end up owning one.'

'It's no more than you deserve, Ellen,' said Mary quietly. 'You've had it rough these last few years, I know that. And if this works out for you then there'll be nobody more pleased than Fred and me. It's early days yet, I suppose, to say how things are going?'

'Very early,' agreed Ellen. 'We've not been open a full week yet. We've been real busy today, though, haven't we; run off our feet most of the

100

time. I'm grateful to you, Mary, for coming in, but I think we agree, don't we, that it's a bit much trying to look after the kiddies as well? It's not really being fair to them.'

Mary nodded. 'Ah well, you never know till you try, do you? You'll have Mam back with you tomorrow. She's given up the Leyland and Chorley markets now, hasn't she?'

'Yes, we've enough on our plate with this and our own market stall. Mam's still full of big ideas though, I can tell you. You know she's always hankered after being entirely self-supporting? Making all our own produce, I mean; but I persuaded her that you just have to be practical. We'd be foolish, wouldn't we, not to take advantage of the first-class products that Cadbury's and Fry's are turning out. All those lovely chocolate boxes.' Ellen pointed to a colourful display on a shelf behind the counter, fancy boxes trimmed with ribbons and with pretty pictures on the lids. 'I must have sold half a dozen of those today.'

'Yes, and that other chocolate firm, the one that makes the fruit gums,' said Mary. 'What are they called?'

'Rowntree's, the York firm,' Ellen replied. 'Yes, they're all in a much bigger way than we are, of course. They've got all the latest machinery and they can do things so much more quickly.'

'I daresay they started in a small way,' said Mary. 'You've got to walk before you can run. Happen you'll catch up with 'em yourself before long.'

Ellen laughed. 'At the moment I'm quite happy

the way I am. There's something to be said for stuff that's home-made, and that looks as though it is. These fudges, and the toffees that Mam makes, for instance. I think it would detract from them if they were made by a machine, all uniform shapes and sizes.'

'It's been a good idea to put it into these boxes, though,' said Mary, 'instead of just ordinary bags. I daresay quite a lot of Preston folk'll be getting a box of fudge as a present on Christmas morning.'

'And perhaps not just Preston folk, eh?' said Ellen eagerly. 'Maybe some of it'll have found its way to other parts of the country. I think we'll have some boxes printed with our names on, instead of just plain white ones. I'll have to see what we can do, come the New Year.'

'Talk about Mam being full of big ideas,' grinned Mary. 'You're not doing too badly yourself. Anyway, what else was it you were thinking of making? You've got all the range of toffees that Mam makes, then there's all your fancy fudges, and the coconut ice and marshmallow ... and now you've even mastered the Turkish Delight. I shouldn't think there's much else left to try, is there?'

'Oh, Mam had got it into her head that we could make our own fruit drops,' Ellen told her. 'Barley sugars, acid drops, lemon drops ... all that sort of thing. But I told her, "It's not worth the effort, Mam." All that kneading and rolling and snipping into pieces by hand. What's the point when we can get those big jars of pear drops and humbugs and all that at the wholesalers? They're turned out in their thousands at the factories. Of course, I know they're not like home-made, but we've got to have a few lines for the kiddies to spend their Saturday pennies on.'

'It must be a boon for you not to have to cart the stuff home every night,' Mary commented, nodding towards the stockroom where large jars of sweets and boxes of chocolate bars and novelties were stacked on the shelves. 'It must've been a real headache getting that lot backwards and forwards.'

'Yes, Mam's still doing it for the stall,' Ellen replied, 'but we've decided that she'll concentrate on just the home-made stuff, and I'll sell a bit of everything here. It'll be even better when we're able to do some of our sweet-making on the premises. They should be coming soon after the New Year to fit a big gas stove up there.' Ellen glanced towards the ceiling, above which there was, at the moment, nothing but a ramshackle storeroom which hadn't been in use for ages. 'That's all we'll need; a gas stove and some shelves to put our pans and tins on. There's a sink up there already, and cold water. We can boil a kettle for washing up.'

'And you'll need a table, a good big one, I should think,' Mary pointed out. 'Don't forget that.'

'I'll be able to pick up one at the second-hand shop up the street,' said Ellen, 'and any other bits and pieces we find we need.' She frowned thoughtfully. 'But what I need most at the moment is another pair of hands. I hadn't

103

realised just how hard it was going to be, manning this place and the stall as well. Goodness knows how I'd have managed without you today, Mary. But I think it might be best if you just saw to the children for me, like you did before. It'll only be Georgie come January, 'cause Rachel'll be at school.'

'She'll want taking and fetching home, though, dinner time and tea time,' Mary reminded her. 'Don't forget that. I'm glad you had the sense to get her in at the school near us. At least it'll save me traipsing across Fishergate four times a day. She might even be able to come and go on her own, once I've taken her a few times. Anyroad, I'd best be making tracks now. Fred'll be home soon wanting his tea, and there's these two bairns to see to. Come on, lads, let's be having you.' Mary picked up the two toddlers, first Charlie, then Tommy, and dumped them unceremoniously one at each end of the huge black pram that stood in the corner of the storeroom.

Ellen glanced warily at her sister. Mary sounded tired and more than a little on edge, as well she might be after standing nearly all day in the shop. She had been paid for her labours – Ellen wouldn't have dreamed of letting her do it for nothing – but now she had to go home and start all over again. It was no more, of course, than she, Ellen, had to do; but when all was said and done it was her shop. Ellen felt, sometimes, that she didn't show her appreciation for her sister as much as she should. She tried to do so now, but it was difficult. Mary wasn't one for flowery speeches.

'You know how grateful I am, don't you?' she began. 'I just can't tell you–'

'Then don't try,' said Mary gruffly. 'That's what sisters are for, aren't they?' She grinned, her temporary weariness and irritability seeming to have vanished. She manoeuvred the cumbersome pram into the shop; there was hardly room to squeeze between the mahogany counter and the door. 'You'll have to get some help though, our Ellen, or you'll be worn to a frazzle before long. Amos would have come like a shot, wouldn't he, if you hadn't got him fixed up with Mr Jenkins?'

'I hardly think...' Ellen frowned. 'A girl might be better.' She couldn't envisage the gangling Amos in the sweet shop. He would be forever knocking things off the shelves – she gathered that was one of the reasons that William had got so angry with him – and he wouldn't be able to manage the money. Anyway, he was happy where he was.

'Any port in a storm, I'd say, and you know you can't afford to pay very much,' Mary pointed out rationally. 'Hasn't Amos got a sister?'

'Any amount of them.'

'There's one just leaving school at Christmas, isn't there? I heard Mrs Hardy saying in the butcher's the other day that their Phyllis hadn't got a job yet.'

'Mmm ... that's an idea. But d'you think she'd be all right?' Ellen sounded doubtful. 'If she's anything like her brother...'

'From what I hear this one's got all her chairs at home,' observed Mary drily. 'And say what you like about Amos; he's willing and he's used to pulling his weight. I daresay the lot of them are, having no father. At least you could give the girl a try, couldn't you?'

'Yes,' Ellen nodded. 'I think I might, provided she's willing to come, of course.'

Phyllis Hardy jumped at the chance of being employed at Mrs Bamber's new sweet shop. She had heard a good deal from her brother, Amos, about the virtues of that young woman, although she knew that his regard was tinged with more than a shade of hero worship. The lad blushed to the roots of his ginger hair when his family teased him, as they often did, about his attachment to Ellen Bamber; but before many weeks had passed Phyllis, too, was happy and eager to be the young woman's slave. Not that Ellen ever treated her as such. She was the most considerate of employers, always insisting on taking her fair share of the chores.

Phyllis's work was interesting and varied. Sometimes she served in the shop whilst Ellen was busy in the upstairs kitchen – this had been completed by the middle of January – making another batch of fudge or marshmallow. Sometimes she washed the piles of sticky pans and utensils, or she filled the white cardboard boxes with the sweetmeats, ready to be sold in the shop. And sometimes, on a Wednesday, Friday or Saturday, she helped out on the market stall. Phyllis loved the excitement of never knowing just what she might be doing next.

Mrs Bamber hadn't yet entrusted her with the job of actually making the sweets, but she was

106

watching, gradually learning, and patiently waiting, hoping that someday soon she might be asked to assist in this highly skilled job. For Phyllis knew that it was a delicate procedure, not just a question of guesswork – throwing in a bit of this and a bit of that and hoping it would turn out all right, like her mother did when she was making a cake. No; every ingredient had to be carefully weighed and then heated to exactly the right temperature, or else the mixture might all be spoiled. She had learned already that you had to boil the sugar to the 'small ball' stage – 237 degrees Fahrenheit was the magic figure – for the fudges that Ellen made; whereas the toffees that were the province of Lydia Tucker had to be boiled to the 'small crack' stage, 280 degrees Fahrenheit. Lydia sometimes worked in the new kitchen, and Phyllis would try to snatch a few minutes to watch her, but she still did a lot of the boiling in her own home. Fresh batches of the toffees had to be made every day as the pieces stuck together when broken and couldn't be stored for very long. Not that they required much storing; Tucker's Tasty Toffee was so popular that the trays were usually empty at the end of the day.

It was Phyllis, however, who had the idea of wrapping the pieces individually in waxed paper and packing them into boxes, as they already did with the fudges, marshmallow, and Turkish Delight.

'Good heavens, girl, it'll take ages doing it all by hand,' Lydia had declared at first. 'I daresay in the factories they have machines that'll do it for 'em, but we're not at that stage. Not yet,' she added. 'Besides, all the pieces'll be different shapes and sizes. When you buy a quarter of them factory-made caramels they're all the same size ... not that I ever do buy 'em, mind you.'

At Ellen's persuasion, however, Lydia admitted that it might be worth a try, and she did agree that they had to encourage their new assistant in her ideas. Phyllis was proving to be a godsend, so different from her brother that it was hard to believe they were from the same family. She resembled him in looks, at least as far as the straight ginger hair and pale blue eyes were concerned, although the light that shone from Phyllis's eyes was that of common sense and good humour, not a look of bewilderment such as her brother's eyes often revealed. And whereas Amos was lanky and awkward in his movements with large hands and feet, Phyllis was small, no more than five feet tall, with the tiniest hands Ellen had ever seen, no bigger than a child's. She was more than capable, however, of doing everything that Ellen asked of her and after a few weeks had passed both she and her mother were wondering how they had ever managed without her.

'Yes, it was a good idea of that lass's, I must say,' Lydia remarked to her daughter one Thursday afternoon in April. Thursday was traditionally 'half-day closing' in Preston and it was therefore Phyllis's half-day, but for Ellen and Lydia it was a time for them to catch up with their stocktaking and packaging. 'Having a stack of boxes all filled in reserve means that I don't have to be toiling over the stove every hour that God sends. And she's wrapped 'em up very nicely. Quite professional, they are.'

'Yes, she's getting very quick at it,' Ellen replied. 'It helps, of course, when the toffees are all more or less the same size.' For Lydia had realised that if she marked the toffee into squares with a sharp knife when it was partially set, it broke easily into almost uniform shapes.

'And I tell you what else we could do, our Ellen,' said Lydia, chewing thoughtfully at a piece of treacle toffee. She still, to Ellen's amusement, hadn't cured herself of the habit of sampling the goods whilst she was working.

'What's that, Mam?' Ellen smiled.

'Well, instead of having all t'same sort in one box – you know, a half-pound of treacle, or a half-pound of butterscotch – we could have all t'different sorts mixed up together. A selection, like. All sorts, in one box. I only thought of it 'cause I just put a bit of treacle in with that caramel, by mistake.'

'That's how Liquorice Allsorts began, Mam,' Ellen observed.

'What d'you mean?' asked Lydia, still chewing.

'You know Bassetts, the Liquorice Allsorts firm?'

'Of course I know! We sell 'em, don't we? Well, what about 'em?'

'There's a story told that about four years ago – 1899, I think it was – there was a traveller from Bassetts doing the rounds, trying to sell his wares. And apparently he wasn't doing very well. The wholesaler was not at all impressed – not until the fellow, quite by accident, knocked his sample boxes on to the floor, spilling all the sweets. The customer hadn't liked the look of the individual selections, but he did like the look of the mixture! And so Liquorice Allsorts were invented.'

'And where've you heard that?' asked Lydia, laughing. 'That's a tall story if ever there was one, our Ellen.'

'Perfectly true, Mam. I read it in one of the trade journals. And you must admit Bassetts are coming on by leaps and bounds. Yes, I think it would be a great idea to try some mixtures. There's nothing more popular than dolly mixtures, when all's said and done.'

And so the Bamber and Tucker selections, both of assorted toffees and assorted fudges, were started. Ellen decided it would be cheaper and probably more efficient to have their names printed on labels, with which they could seal the boxes, rather than on the boxes themselves. Before very long Bamber and Tucker were a twosome to be talked about up and down Fishergate and Friargate, in the same way as Huntley and Palmer, Meredith and Drew, Bryant and May...

'Burke and Hare,' quipped Lydia, when Ellen mentioned this to her.

'Or Marshall and Snelgrove,' grinned Ellen.

'Who are they when they're at home?'

'Oh Mam, you must have heard of them. Posh shops, aren't they? You know, big emporiums where the rich folk go. There's one in London and I daresay there'll be one in Manchester.

110

D'you know, I've never been to Manchester, and it can't be fifty miles away. The biggest city in the north and I've never even been there.'

'No more have I, lass,' replied Lydia peremptorily. 'And why should we want to go to Manchester when we can get all we need here in Preston? Never mind,' she added, more gently. 'The way things are working out you might be able to trot off to the big city before long. Buy yerself some new clothes – you'll be able to afford it. I'm sick of seeing you in that black, our Ellen, and I think it's about time you came out of it now. It's more than nine months and it isn't as if you were really grieving for him.'

'No, but we've got to observe the conventions, haven't we?' said Ellen quietly. 'Anyway, I may be able to afford a new outfit – it'd be very nice – but it's a question of finding time, isn't it? I certainly can't spare the time to go tripping off to Manchester, or anywhere else for that matter. We're too busy here.'

'D'you know what I think, Ellen?' Lydia stopped in her task of folding a flat piece of cardboard into a box shape and leaned her elbows on the edge of the large pine table. 'You're ready for a holiday, you and the bairns. It's ages since you went anywhere, even for a day. Why don't you take 'em away for a week, to the seaside, maybe?'

Ellen smiled. 'Sounds tempting, Mam, but we're too busy.'

'Nonsense!' Lydia spoke sharply. 'We're only as busy as we make ourselves, and that goes for me an' all. Oh aye, I know I've no room to talk. I've worked hard all me life; I'm a glutton for punishment as they say, and no doubt I'll go on doing it till the day I die. But I could ease off a bit if I wanted to. And so could you, Ellen. Have a holiday.'

'Oh, I don't know about that, Mam. I don't see how I can...'

'Of course you can! We've just agreed that we're doing quite nicely here, and the market stall's going as well as it ever did. I thought business might have slackened off there when we opened the shop, but it hasn't. So why don't you take a week off? Me and Phyllis'll manage between us. If I know that lass she'll jump at being given a bit more responsibility.'

Ellen stared into space. The idea was tempting and she certainly was tired. It was only when she stopped for a few minutes that she realised just how tired she was. As her mother said, it was ages since she had been anywhere. She and William hadn't taken any holidays, not since their honeymoon in Southport. Somehow it had never occurred to them to do so, although they had taken the children occasionally on day trips on the train, to Southport and once to Blackpool. 'I might,' she said hesitantly. 'I've no doubts about Phyllis. I know I can trust her. But what about you, Mam? You need a holiday just as much as I do.'

'Never mind about me, lass,' said Lydia kindly. 'I've only meself to see to, and when I get home of an evening I quite often get me feet up and have a read of the paper, before I think about getting summat to eat. Me time's me own, and there's a lot to be said for that. Not like you; you've always got the kiddies to see to, and I think you could do with a break.'

'Perhaps you're right,' Ellen nodded. 'But so could our Mary. She needs a holiday if anybody does. She has my two kiddies nearly every day as well as her own, and Fred.'

'He's not much bother,' Lydia commented. 'She's got a good 'un there. But I'm blessed if I can see how she could afford a holiday.'

'But I can!' Ellen said eagerly. 'I know what I'll do. I'll pay for her, and Charlie and Tommy as well. You say we need a holiday – well then, they can come with us. Now, Mam, what d'you think about that?' Ellen sounded more excited than she had done for ages.

'I think it would be grand, Ellen,' replied Lydia, though somewhat cautiously. 'But what would Mary say? She's that independent, you know, and she can be touchy an' all. She wouldn't like the idea of charity.'

'Charity be blowed!' exclaimed Ellen. 'As a matter of fact, Mam, I've a bit of money put away from an insurance policy I had on William. It wasn't much, only a copper or two a week, but I paid it myself – that's one thing he never knew anything about! – and there'll be enough to pay for a holiday for us. Me and Rachel and Georgie, our Mary, Charlie and Tommy. I think the twins are old enough, aren't they, to take on holiday? They've turned eighteen months now.'

'Of course they are,' replied Lydia. 'If you can get Mary to agree. Come to think of it, she might be highly delighted at the thought of getting a bit

113

of benefit from William's demise. She never could stick him. Shouldn't say that, should I, lass?' she added more soberly. 'Speaking ill of the dead an' all that.'

'It's all right, Mam. Life goes on ... and you're quite right; it *is* time I got out of these widow's weeds. It's the middle of June now. I think we'd have to wait till August before we went away. I don't want Rachel to miss any schooling. That'll be, let me see...' She counted on her fingers. 'About six or seven weeks.'

'And where have you thought of going?'

'I haven't!' Ellen laughed. 'I've only just thought of going away at all – and it was your idea at the beginning, not mine. Oh, I don't know – Blackpool, I suppose. It's the obvious place, isn't it? It's only eighteen miles away and we can get a train straight there.'

'D'you remember Bella?' said Lydia thoughtfully. 'No, of course you won't. You were only a baby when they moved to Blackpool.'

'No, I don't remember her, Mam, but I've heard you speak about her. She lived in Sefton Street near us, then she took a boarding house in Blackpool, didn't she?'

'Yes, that's right, her and her mother. But old Mrs Forshaw passed on a few years back and now Bella runs it on her own. Happen she could put you up. I'll drop her a line; we still keep in touch at Christmas, and I've been saying for ages I'd get over and see her, but I never do.'

'It'll be grand if she has room for us all, but I wish you could come with us, Mam,' said Ellen wistfully.

114

'Someday, perhaps.' Lydia smiled reflectively. 'Just bring me back one of those little ornaments – A Present from Blackpool. It'd look a treat on the mantelpiece. But the main thing now is to see what our Mary says.'

Mary, strangely enough, raised no objections; on the contrary, she was delighted at the idea of a carefree week in Blackpool. Fred, too, was amenable, laughingly saying that it would be grand to have some peace and quiet, and Lydia offered to see to his meals if he couldn't manage. Phyllis was overjoyed at the thought of being in charge for a week, so when Ellen, with the rest of her family, set off from the station in Fishergate on the second Saturday in August, she had every confidence that her flourishing business was being left in safe hands.

A peek in the wardrobe mirror before she left home had made her feel justifiably pleased with her appearance, but also more than a little self-conscious; she was unused to wearing such finery. Her pale grey travelling costume was, to Ellen, the very height of elegance. Beneath it she was wearing a white silk blouse with the high stand-up collar showing at the neck and her hat of natural straw with the wide brim was trimmed with mauve flowers and ribbons. Mauve, she had thought, was a sensible compromise as she was just coming out of mourning. A mauve cotton blouse with leg of mutton sleeves was packed away in her suitcase, together with the cotton knickerbockers, sunhats and shirts she had bought for Rachel and Georgie.

115

She was hoping that the weather would be warm enough for the children to paddle in the sea. Summers were unpredictable – it was dull and overcast this morning – and Blackpool was renowned for its chilly sea breezes. At all events, she and Mary would not be bathing in the sea. Neither of them had the required costumes, but she would be able to remove her suit jacket if the weather was warm and she had her big black umbrella which could double as a parasol should the sun be too hot.

Never before had she been on such a shopping spree and now, glancing at Mary in the seat opposite, clad in her usual faded brown jacket and limp skirt, Ellen felt a little guilty. Mary, when she did manage to buy clothes, usually had to get them at the second-hand shop. She was very clean and tidy though, as always, and she had trimmed up her last year's straw hat with a riot of pink roses and ribbons which highlighted her fresh complexion.

Nor was there any hint of envy as Mary smiled at her sister. 'You look a real bobby-dazzler, our Ellen. I'll bet Queen Alexandra never looks any smarter than what you do. That high-necked blouse you've got on just reminds me of her. Mam said you were talking about going to Manchester to do some shopping. Looks as though you've been, an' all.'

'Not on your life,' replied Ellen. 'I got it all at Mrs Hamilton's – you know, that little draper's and silk mercer's on Market Street. She's got a nice selection of ready-made clothes in now, and they don't cost too much either,' she added. She

116

didn't want Mary thinking she was extravagant.

Mary laughed. 'It doesn't matter two hoots to me if it cost twenty pounds! You've every right to spend your money how you want. I've been splashing out meself anyroad. There's a new blouse in there – well, new second-hand, I mean.' She pointed to the battered leather suitcase on the luggage rack. 'And some new outfits for the lads. Isn't it exciting, eh, Ellen? Going on holiday! I can hardly believe it. It's been worth all the effort, but at eight o'clock this morning I thought we'd never make it, I can tell you.'

It had been a struggle, indeed, getting to the station with a heavy suitcase and a large pram, plus two excited toddlers. Charlie and Tommy hadn't known what it was they were excited about, but they had been caught up in the general commotion of packing and getting ready. Fred had seen them to the station, his arms nearly pulled from their sockets by the weight of the case, and now the pram was safely stored away in the guard's van and the twins were comparatively quiet, one on Mary's knee and one on Ellen's.

For her part, Ellen had hired a hansom cab to take them to the station. An extravagance, she knew, but a necessary one this morning as she had no man to assist her. Now Rachel and Georgie were sitting in the window seats, one at each side, their eyes eagerly scanning the scenery of fields, neat hedgerows, cows, and occasional farmsteads. Now and again one or the other of them would turn to Ellen and say, 'Can't see it, Mummy. When will we see it? Wish it would hurry up.'

Ellen smiled across at Mary. 'I'm beginning to feel sorry I told them to look out for Blackpool Tower. I thought it would keep them quiet, but just listen to them.'

'You can't blame them, they're that excited, bless 'em,' replied Mary. 'I think it'll be a little while yet,' she said to the children. 'Wait till we've gone through Kirkham. You'll be able to read that on the sign, won't you, Rachel? It begins with a K – you know, a kicking K – and when we've gone through Kirkham there'll be a few little hills, and then you'll see Blackpool Tower! That's right, isn't it?' she added, turning to Ellen. 'I remember looking out for it the last time we came, but goodness knows how long ago that is. Must be donkey's years.'

'It can't be all that long,' observed Ellen. 'Blackpool Tower's only been up since 1894 – nine years ago. You went to Blackpool for your honeymoon, didn't you? You must have seen it then.'

'Oh aye, so we did,' nodded Mary. 'It was only a weekend though. And it poured all the time. Not that it mattered,' she said hastily, smiling reminiscently.

Ellen, glancing at her sister's serenely happy face, thought to herself how contented Mary and her husband seemed to be. An incongruous couple, but so happy with one another.

Lydia had told her daughters to make sure they boarded a train that was going to North and not Central Station, not because of the view of Blackpool Tower – it could be seen from the other route as well – but because Bella Broad-

118

bent's boarding house was on High Street, only a hop, skip and a jump away from North Station. Blackpool Tower was eventually sighted, along with excited cheers from Rachel and Georgie, and two other children in the compartment. Then, some twenty minutes later, the train slowed to a crawl, then stopped with a sudden jolt.

'We're there, we're there!' shouted the children, jumping to their feet. 'Come on, Mummy. Get the case down.'

'Hold your horses,' said Ellen, restraining them. 'As far as I can make out we're in a queue. I'll bet it's half a mile long.'

Indeed it was. The railways of the Fylde Coast were proving inadequate to deal with the increase in rail traffic to Blackpool, often involving a wait of half an hour or so for a vacant platform where the train could pull in. And so it was now, to the growing frustration of Mary and Ellen and the impatience of the children.

'Well, we've got here at last,' said Mary eventually, hauling the suitcases off the rack. 'And we're certainly not going to let a little upset like that spoil our holiday. I'm glad Mrs Broadbent provides all the meals, or else we'd've had to lug all the food along with us as well. Come on, let's go and find the pram.'

So Ellen, Rachel, Georgie and the twins waited on the crowded platform while Mary went to the guard's van. ''Struth!' she gasped on returning. 'How the heck are we going to manage?' She scratched her head. 'We look as though we've dropped off a flitting.'

But manage they did, with the twins squashed together at one end of the pram and a suitcase balanced at the other end. Mary, by far the stronger of the two women, carried the other case whilst Ellen, walking ahead, pushed the pram with Rachel and Georgie clinging one to each side of the handle. It was Ellen who was supposed to know the way. She led them out on to the station forecourt, then stopped and stared around as if mesmerised at the scene around her.

'What a lot of people, Mummy,' said Rachel, echoing her thoughts.

They had seen crowds back home in Preston, especially on market days, but seldom anything to compare with the multitude here today. They were mostly holidaymakers, like themselves, newly arrived and bewildered as to which way to go; and a small army of 'touters', representatives of the local landladies proclaiming vociferously that their lodgings were the best and cheapest in town. Many visitors arrived 'on spec', but Ellen and family, having booked in advance, had no need to listen to such persuasive tactics. With difficulty Ellen pushed her way through the swarm of humanity – the pram helped – with Mary following along behind her. There were hansom cabs waiting at the station entrance, stately landaus and a horse-drawn bus, but Lydia had told them that it wasn't far to Bella's so they could easily walk there.

Rachel and Georgie suddenly turned their heads, staring in amazement at the huge cream and green monster that was clanging its way up the road, issuing warning 'toot toots' at the

120

hordes of people crossing in front of it.

'Mummy, look … look! What is it?'

'Is it an omnibus, Mummy?' This was a new word that Rachel had learned.

'No dear, it's a tram.'

'But how does it go? There's no horses.'

'Er … electricity,' said Ellen vaguely, not being entirely sure herself. 'Look – there are overhead wires.' She pointed to the tramtrack and the wires leading up Dickson Road. She had heard that they would soon be having trams running in Preston, too, but they hadn't appeared yet. 'Come on now, we haven't time to be standing around staring, and Aunty Mary'll be getting tired, carrying that case. Perhaps one day we can all go for a ride on a tram, how's that?'

'Goody goody!' Rachel did a little dance on the spot and Georgie followed suit.

'First right up Queen Street, then second left,' called Ellen to her sister. 'We'll soon be there…'

Chapter Six

'Bella Vista, eh?' said Mary, when they stopped outside the boarding-house in High Street. 'I don't know what it means, but it sounds very "bay windows". If her cooking's as good as the name of her house we shouldn't go far wrong, what do you say, Ellen?'

'Yes, it certainly sounds very posh,' smiled Ellen. 'I expect Bella thought it was a good idea to use her name, that's all, but I'm sure she'll make us welcome, no matter what her house is called.'

Ellen knew that the fancy-sounding words really meant 'beautiful view' or something of the sort, but she was loath to air her knowledge in front of Mary; it would sound as though she were showing off. At all events, the name seemed to be a misnomer, if ever there was one. The only view was of a row of identical houses across the street.

Bella Vista, however, was an attractive-looking house, from the outside at any rate, and Ellen felt sure that the interior would match up to the first impression. It was three storeys high, appearing taller because of its narrowness, solidly built of shiny red Accrington brick, with the woodwork painted green and the stone windowsills and steps edged in cream with a donkey stone. A glass-fronted notice by the door proclaimed that the proprietress of Bella Vista was Mrs Bella

Broadbent, late of Preston. This was a way of telling visitors from that town and its environs that they would be extra specially welcome.

The door opened and there was Bella on the threshold. At least Ellen presumed it was Bella because the woman was beaming broadly and she fitted Lydia's description; small and dark and energetic. Ellen, searching far back in the recesses of her memory, recalled now that she had seen Bella Broadbent before – Bella Forshaw as she had been then – when she was just a tiny girl. Bella, hurrying down the path to greet them, took the words out of her mouth.

'Well, I can guess who you are, easy as winking, I can!' She nodded decidedly at Ellen. 'Even though I haven't seen you since you were so high.' She indicated a height somewhere in the region of her waist. 'And d'you know how I can tell? You're the living image of your mam, you are that. She was just like you are now, the last time I saw her. And this little one here...' She smiled warmly at Rachel. 'Well, it's just like seeing you all over again. There's no mistaking the Tucker clan.'

'Bamber now,' Ellen reminded her, holding out her hand. 'Pleased to meet you, Mrs Broadbent ... or to meet you again, I should say. I do remember you, vaguely, although it's ages ago. And this is my sister, Mary.'

Mary had been standing to one side. Ellen wasn't sure why, unless it was because she, Ellen, had made all the arrangements and would be doing all the paying, although not much emphasis had been put upon that. But now Mary

123

stepped forward. 'Yes, I remember you as clearly as anything, Mrs Broadbent, but then I'm four years older than our Ellen. How do you do?'

'And you're just the same as well, Mary. Older, of course, but aren't we all? You always took after your dad, didn't you, rather than your mam? And these two – well, bless me! Identical twins and the spitting image of their mam as well. And we mustn't forget this little fellow here. You must be Georgie, am I right?' Bella placed her hand on top of Georgie's head, ruffling his dark curls, and the little boy nodded solemnly, clearly overawed. 'Well, this is grand! Come on, come on in, all of you. I'll give you a hand with the pram, Mary. Lift the lads out, then it'll be easier. It's a bit of a job, manoeuvring these steps.'

'Oh dear, I hadn't thought about that. And we'd best mind the paintwork,' Mary sounded apologetic.

'Never mind that,' Bella grinned. 'We're used to kiddies here, and what do a few scratches matter? It might be better to leave the pram in the yard, though, and take it out through the back entry when you need it. That's what we usually do when we've a family with a baby... Now, I'll show you your room, then I daresay you'll be ready for a spot of dinner.'

The room on the first floor was enormous, compared with most boarding-house bedrooms. It needed to be, to hold the double bed (with brass bedstead) for Mary and Ellen, a three-quarter-sized bed for Rachel and Georgie to share, and two cots for the small boys. Plus a huge oak wardrobe, a chest of drawers and a dressing table, all somewhat scratched, but polished to a high gloss, and a marble washstand with a flower-patterned jug and bowl and a pair of dazzlingly white towels hanging on the towel rail.

'There's a chamber pot under the bed,' Bella told them. 'I don't always provide them – there's a WC down the landing, you know – but I thought it might be better with there being so many of you. Anyroad, get yourselves sorted out and come down when you're ready.'

'Mmm, I think we've landed on our feet here, don't you, Mary?' said Ellen, unpinning her straw hat and placing it on the bed. 'I'd say we were honoured, having a first-floor room.'

'At the front an' all,' agreed Mary, walking over to the window. 'Not that there's much of a view, only houses...' She craned her neck. 'Can't see the Tower from here. Must be too far that way. Still, it's better than looking at back yards and washing lines. I've got a bit of a headache, our Ellen.' Mary, too, eased off her hat and put her hands to her temples. 'Must be the travelling, and all that dashing about beforehand, I daresay.'

'Yes, my head's aching as well,' replied Ellen, frowning slightly. She was feeling a little strange and dizzy. 'It's always a bit funny at first, I suppose, settling in to a different place. Never mind, I expect we'll feel better when we've had something to eat, and after dinner the Blackpool breezes'll soon blow the cobwebs away. Come on now, Rachel and Georgie, wash your hands in this bowl. It'll only be cold water, but I expect Mrs Broadbent'll provide hot in the mornings.'

Bella informed them later that that, indeed, was what she did. 'We carry up buckets of hot water each morning, me and the girls,' she told them, the 'girls' being the two live-in waitresses-cum-chambermaids from Blackburn whom she had employed for the season. 'It's my ambition to have running water in all the rooms, like most of the big posh places do, but I'll have to see how funds go. Perhaps by next year... Anyroad, there's a bathroom along your landing if you need it; if you pick a quiet time, say early evening, there might not be too much of a queue. And for heaven's sake, call me Bella. I can't do with standing on ceremony, not with folks that are as good as family, anyway.'

Ellen knew that they were privileged to have been admitted to Bella's private sitting room for an after-dinner cup of tea, a place where run-of-the-mill visitors were not normally invited. The midday dinner, too, of tasty meat and potato pie followed by stewed plums and custard, was not normally served to guests on a Saturday. A special concession had been made for Lydia Tucker's family. Saturday, Bella explained, being 'change-over' day – one lot of visitors departing and another arriving – was more than usually hectic so dinner was not served on that day. The week's 'all in' arrangement commenced with high tea at five-thirty.

'I decided to do "all found" a couple of seasons back,' said Bella. 'Until then it was a nightmare, I can tell you, cooking a bit of this for one lot and a bit of that for another. And you should have heard the arguments. "That's not my meat," they'd say – the cheek of it! "Mine didn't have so much fat on it." When my mother was here, bless her, she didn't seem to mind, but I decided to move with the times. I don't pack 'em in neither, not like some folks round here. I never take more than I can comfortably manage. I've heard tell of nine young fellows all in one bedroom, three to a bed! And another place where they have their breakfast in shifts. Some landladies think that visitors'll put up with anything, just so long as they're in Blackpool, but I think folks have a right to a bit of … well, not exactly luxury – I know I can't provide that – but comfort.'

'You're certainly providing that, Bella,' replied Ellen, smiling happily. All trace of her headache and her earlier feeling of disorientation – of not quite belonging – had now vanished completely in the warmth of Bella's hospitality. 'What about your husband? Does he work in the boarding-house as well?'

'Good gracious no!' replied Bella laughing. 'You wouldn't catch him peeling spuds or washing up till twelve o'clock at night. That's what some poor husbands have to do, although most of them leave the boarding-house business to their wives and do another job. No, my Arthur, he's a tram-driver. Drives one of those new Dreadnoughts. Have you seen them?'

'Yes, I think we saw one on Dickson Road when we arrived.'

'Marvellous they are. They can hold more than a hundred passengers. Some folk are quibbling, mind you, because it's a minimum fare of twopence; but you can ride ever such a long way along the prom for that. You'll take the kiddies on one, won't you? It'll be half-fare for Rachel, and nothing for the others, I shouldn't wonder. Anyroad, I mustn't keep you talking any longer. You'll be wanting to take them on the sands, I daresay. That's if the tide's out – I don't know how it is just now...'

The tide was out, to the delight of the children, leaving an expanse of golden sand stretching north and south as far as the eye could see. In parts, however, the sand could scarcely be seen between the deckchairs, donkeys, ice-cream stalls, Punch and Judy shows, bathing huts ... and people. Multitudes of people, paddling in the shallows of the outgoing tide or, braver souls, swimming further out in the sea. Some were riding on donkeys, others crowding around the various stalls, but most people just strolled or reclined on deckchairs, some of them under huge black parasols. The sun had come out now although there was still a stiff breeze.

The children had not yet acquired buckets and spades, those most necessary items for a holiday at the seaside, but both Mary and Ellen knew that it would be cruel to expect them to walk on the promenade and not the beach. And so they trod carefully down the slope, a safer alternative to the perilous wooden steps which were coated in parts with slimy green seaweed, especially as Mary was carrying one twin and Ellen the other. They had left the pram at Bella Vista, deciding that it might be more trouble than it was worth.

'Hurray, hurray!' shouted Rachel, swiftly echoed by Georgie, as their feet touched the golden sand for the very first time of the holiday. Here, near to the sea wall, the sand was soft and malleable, churned up by hundreds of feet and cartwheels and furiously digging spades; and very soon there was a broad band of the stuff on the bottom of Ellen and Mary's long skirts.

'Oooh!' exclaimed Rachel, frowning a little and shaking one foot, then the other, in some irritation. 'It's all over me shoes. I can't walk properly, Mummy. I keep sinking in… Look!'

'Never mind, dear,' said Ellen laughing. 'We'll buy you some buckets and spades, then the next time we come down you can take your shoes and socks off. How about that? We're only staying down here a little while today, then Aunty Mary and I want to have a look round the town, see if we can find our way around. We're lucky the tide's going out. I thought it might have been in, then there wouldn't have been any sands at all.'

'How d'you know it's going out, Mummy?' asked Rachel. 'It might be coming in, mightn't it?' Her gran had been telling her about the sea at Blackpool, how the tide went out and came in again twice a day.

'Because of the rock pools,' explained Ellen. 'The outgoing tide leaves little pools behind it – look.' She pointed to a pool at the bottom of a flight of steps where a few children were paddling, one fishing, hopefully, with a net on the end of a long stick and another scooping a red bucket into the water. 'They're fishing, for crabs I think,' said Ellen. 'Would you like to do that, Rachel? Perhaps we could get you a fishing net as well as a bucket and spade, if you promise to be very careful.'

Rachel shook her head doubtfully. She didn't seem any too sure about that. But she was quite sure about what she wanted now as she gazed longingly at the crowd gathering round a nearby stall. 'Can I have an ice cream, Mummy ... please?'

'Yes, we'll all have one. Why not?' Ellen was feeling as excited as a child herself. 'We're on our holidays, aren't we? An ice cream'll make us feel as though it's really started.'

The ice cream, though delicious, was soft and runny and soon everyone's fingers and lips, grown-ups and children alike, were coated with the sticky stuff. 'Oh dear,' remarked Ellen. 'We're not a bit organised today, are we? We'll have to remember to bring a towel the next time we come. Never mind; let's just dabble our hands in this pool, then I think I've got a big hanky in my bag. Perhaps Aunty Mary's got one as well.'

'We're short of nothing we've got,' said Mary good-humouredly, searching in the depths of her capacious black handbag.

'I think you could get a sheet in there, never mind a handkerchief,' laughed Ellen, and Mary joined in.

Already it seemed that the sea air and the sunshine, fitful though it might be, was having a favourable effect upon Mary. There was no sign now of the tetchiness which Ellen noticed occasionally in her sister's manner. Ellen hoped that this holiday would prove to be a real tonic for Mary; she deserved it if anyone did.

The ice-cream sellers were by no means the

only vendors on the beach. There were oyster sellers, not only selling from the stalls, but hawking their wares by walking between the crowds of people, armed with big round baskets and bottles of vinegar. There were tea stalls, too, and stalls with lemonade and ginger beer, a Punch and Judy show, just finishing, and further along Ellen could see that a Pierrot show seemed about ready to commence. She decided not to draw the childrens' attention to this, not today. She and Mary wanted to have a quick look round the shops, though it might prove impossible with the twins. They were getting tired now and had insisted on being carried again. Charlie felt like a ton of bricks on Ellen's arm; Mary, however, never seemed to notice the weight. She had stopped a few yards ahead with Tommy, watching the antics of a fellow in a top hat, corduroy trousers, and clogs – of all things! – who seemed to be selling something from a big basket hooked over his arm. Ellen went to join her siste, Rachel and Georgie at her side.

'One for you … and one for you … and one for you,' yelled the character in the top hat, flinging far and wide amongst the rapidly growing crowd some small articles from his basket.

'What's he doing?' asked Ellen, puzzled. 'What's he selling?'

'Not selling; looks as though he's giving it away,' answered Mary.

'It's Blackpool rock,' said a woman in front of them, turning round to grin at Mary and Ellen. Turning back, she deftly caught one of the flying objects in her outstretched hand. 'See, Blackpool rock.' She waved it in front of the sisters. 'Be sharp and catch hold of one while the going's good. He'll stop doing it in a minute, then you'll have to pay for it.'

'Hmmm, I thought there'd be a catch in it,' observed Mary. 'You know what our mam always says, Ellen. You never get owt for nowt in this life, and it's true enough.'

The fellow had stopped his introductory patter now and was selling in earnest, pink sticks of rock at sixpence a time.

'Told you so,' said Mary, starting to walk away. 'Come on, we're not going to waste our time here.'

'Can't we buy some, Mummy?' pleaded Rachel. 'That must be what Gran was talking about – Blackpool rock. She said to me, "Bring me back a stick of Blackpool rock," but I didn't really know what she was talking about. Can't we buy her some, please, Mummy?'

'Of course we will, dear,' replied Ellen, adding in a low voice, 'But not from this man. I don't think I trust him. There's a stall just across the road on the promenade. I noticed it before we came down here. We'll go and have a look there.'

'Yes, let's go now,' agreed Mary, trying to shake the sand from the hem of her skirt. 'I'm getting fed up of traipsing through this stuff. It gets everywhere. Next time we come we'll find a nice spot and stay put, then the kiddies can play to their hearts' content.'

The stall that Ellen had noticed was at the northern end of Central Beach, at the start of what was now becoming known as the 'Golden

Mile'; that mile or so of stalls, sideshows, fortune-tellers, 'Quack' doctors and mock auctions stretching southwards from the Central Station area. *Roger Redman's Rock, the Finest in Blackpool* read the inscription over the stall and the young man there certainly seemed to be doing a brisk trade. Where would we be without alliteration? smiled Ellen to herself, thinking of their own original name, 'Tucker's Tasty Toffee'. A product always sold, of course, if it was of good quality, no matter what the name might be, but it always helped to have a catchy slogan that the customers would remember.

The young man, probably not Roger Redman himself, finished serving the woman in front of her then he smiled at Ellen. 'Yes, madam, what can I do for you? Blackpool rock for the kiddies, mint, pineapple or lemon. Choose which you like. Or some of each; that would be even better, wouldn't it? Just take your time.'

Ellen smiled back at him, knowing instinctively that here was a good salesman, friendly and welcoming without being too pushy. His voice was low and pleasant, unlike the raucous tones so often heard along this part of the promenade. He was about her own age, she guessed, or possibly a year or two older, thin-featured and clean-shaven with golden-brown hair flopping over his brow beneath his straw boater. But it was his eyes that she couldn't help noticing. They were golden brown, too, but of a deeper, richer shade than his hair. Exactly the colour of the caramel toffee that her mother made, thought Ellen, almost laughing at herself. Trust a sweet-maker to come up with a comparison like that, but that was just what his eyes reminded her of as he smiled at her; two glowing pools of rich brown toffee.

She picked up a medium-sized stick of rock; there were various sizes, but just three colours. They were all wrapped in waxed paper, but the vivid colours could be seen through the semi-transparent wrapping.

'The pink's mint-flavoured,' said the young man. 'That's the one you've got hold of. Always the most popular, I must say. And the orange colour is pineapple rock, and the yellow is lemon-flavoured.'

'Oh, I don't know,' said Ellen undecidedly. She turned to her sister. 'What do you think, Mary? Which do you think Mam would like?'

Mary grinned. 'I'll tell you what I think. Let's buy some for the kiddies today – and ourselves an' all if you like, and get some for Mam at the end of the week. It'll only go sticky. Best to buy it fresh, and you'll be here every day, won't you?' she said, turning to the salesman.

'That's right – we're here every day, madam. I'm not always on the stall, but there's always someone here.'

Ellen was looking curiously at an extra-large stick of rock which lay in the centre of the stall. It was obviously not for sale as it was unwrapped, its pink colour glowing much more brightly when viewed without its covering. At one end, in red, the words BLACKPOOL ROCK were clearly visible. Ellen moved her eyes to the other end of the stick of rock. Yes, the words were there as well, BLACKPOOL ROCK.

The young man noticed her interest and he grinned. 'Yes, the letters go all the way through, madam, in all the sticks, not just that one. Incredible, isn't it? Magic, you might say. Go on, ask me how it's done! That's what they usually ask. And do you know what I say? I say, "Ah-hah! That'd be telling, wouldn't it?".'

Ellen nodded, somewhat seriously. 'Yes, it doesn't always do to give away trade secrets, does it? And there's no point in me asking you, is there, if you're not going to tell me.' Her serious expression vanished and she smiled at him. 'But I think I can guess. Let me see ... I've an idea it's something to do with the rolling. Those letters must be quite big to start with, then they're all bundled together and rolled and rolled and rolled until they're quite tiny, like they are there ... Something like that, anyway,' she added, hoping that she wasn't being guilty of showing off.

But the young man didn't seem to think so. He was staring at her in obvious admiration. 'Full marks,' he said. 'You're absolutely right! At least, that's the general idea. As you say, it's all in the assembling and rolling process. But I don't think all that many folk really want to know about it, even though they ask. All they're bothered about is buying a stick of Blackpool rock to take home.'

'My sister's a sweet-maker, you see,' said Mary, with obvious pride. 'That's why she's interested and why she was able to guess how you do it.'

'A sweet-maker?' The young man was looking at her even more attentively now. 'You mean ... for a living? You have a shop?'

'Yes, in Preston,' replied Ellen. 'My mother and I run it, and we've a stall on the market as well. We sell toffees and fudges and that sort of thing, mostly home-made. But no rock,' she laughed. 'I don't think we're clever enough for that, Mr ... I don't suppose you're Mr Redman, by any chance, are you?'

'No; Roger Redman's my uncle. I work for him.' The young man held out his hand. 'How do you do? I'm Benjamin Hobson, usually known as Ben. I'm pleased to meet you. And you are...?'

'I'm Ellen Bamber,' replied Ellen, noting that his handshake was firm and his palm was pleasantly cool. 'And this is my sister, Mary. Mary Pilkington.'

'How d'you do, Mrs Pilkington?' Ben Hobson shook hands with her as well, his smile no less agreeable. But it was Ellen that he turned back to. 'I can't get over this. Fancy you guessing how Blackpool rock is made. You'll have seen it before, of course?'

'Mmm, I think so.' Ellen pursed her lips. 'I seem to remember seeing it the last time I was in Blackpool, a few years ago, but I must admit I didn't take much notice of it. I've heard about it – rock's becoming very popular at the seaside, isn't it? – but there's not much call for it in Preston, you see. And I've never given much thought before to how it's actually made.'

'Would you like to watch it being made at the factory?' Ben Hobson asked eagerly.

'Well, of course I would. That would be wonderful. But I don't see how...'

'No sooner said than done.' Ben Hobson

clasped his hands together decidedly. 'You come to the factory on – shall we say Monday? I shall be working there on Monday, Mrs ... it is Mrs Bamber, isn't it?'

Ellen nodded. 'Yes. These are my two children, Rachel and George.'

'Yes, I see.' The young man hesitated for a moment and his smile seemed to fade. Then, just as quickly, it was back again. 'And if I'm any judge they'll be getting fed up with us talking. Here, Rachel – one for you.' He handed the little girl a small stick of pink rock. 'And one for your brother. And we mustn't forget the other two nippers. Can they have rock, Mrs Pilkington?'

'I don't see why not,' said Mary easily. 'They might get in a mess, but never mind. We're on our holidays, aren't we? Here, Charlie and Tommy.' She pulled back the waxed wrapping paper round the rock. 'Suck it, mind you, don't bite it, then it'll last longer. You as well, Rachel and Georgie.' She turned to Ellen. 'Go ahead and make your arrangements with Mr Hobson here.' She gave a discreet wink which Ellen hoped Ben Hobson hadn't noticed. 'I'll look after the kiddies while you go to the factory. A deckchair for me and some sand for them and we'll be as right as ninepence.'

It transpired that the factory was on Exchange Street, just behind the railway sidings, the very next street to where Ellen and Mary were staying. Ben Hobson refused to take payment for the sticks of rock he had given the children, so Ellen bought another two larger bars which she and Mary, with the children's help, would no

137

doubt eat before the week was out. And she arranged to meet her new acquaintance at the factory at ten o'clock on Monday morning.

'So what d'you think about that then?' teased Mary, as they left the Central Beach area. 'We're not in the place more than five minutes and already there's a nice young man making eyes at you.'

'Don't be silly, Mary,' said Ellen sharply, although she was smiling to herself and could feel a faint blush colouring her cheeks. 'He wasn't making eyes at me. The very idea! If he hadn't found out I was in the same business as he is – well, almost the same – he'd never even have looked at me.'

'That's as maybe,' said Mary darkly. 'Anyroad, we got some free rock, didn't we, and we'll go back and buy some for Mam; it's the least we can do when he's been so kind to us. Did you really want to go and look round the factory?' she asked, turning to look keenly at her sister. 'You weren't just being polite? I was only teasing, you know, just now. You don't think it'll be too much like – what do they say? – taking coals to Newcastle. You are supposed to be on your holidays.'

'Yes, of course I want to go,' replied Ellen. 'It should be very interesting. And thanks for saying you'll look after the children, Mary. I only hope the tide's out on Monday morning – we never thought of that, did we? Or that it doesn't rain.'

'Let's not make problems,' said Mary cheerfully. 'If it rains there's always the Tower. I believe there's all sorts in there – an aquarium and a menagerie and a circus, and goodness knows what else.' They were just passing by that building with its elaborate wrought-iron and glass-canopied entrance. 'I don't know whether I fancy going up to the top, though, do you?' added Mary, peering upwards.

'No fear!' Ellen gave a mock shudder. 'We can't anyway, not with all this lot.' The children were useful to hide behind at times, when there was something that you didn't really want to do. 'I'm sure we'll find plenty to occupy us in Blackpool without going to the top of the Tower. I don't know about you, Mary, but I think I'm too tired to look at the shops just now, and I know the kiddies must be weary. It's seemed a long day.'

'I couldn't agree more,' said Mary. 'Let's find a nice little café, shall we, and have a cuppa, and the youngsters can have some ginger beer.'

'Ice cream and rock and ginger beer,' laughed Ellen. 'They'll probably be sick.'

'I doubt it,' replied Mary, adding for the umpteenth time that day, 'anyway, we're on our holidays, aren't we? And that's what Blackpool's all about. Enjoying yourself...'

Chapter Seven

Ben Hobson welcomed Ellen cordially when she arrived at Roger Redman's rock factory in Exchange Street, promptly at ten o'clock on Monday morning. He was standing at the door waiting for her and she was glad of that; she never found it easy to venture alone into unfamiliar places. He was wearing again the white coat overall he had worn on the promenade stall, but today he was minus his straw boater and Ellen could see that his golden-brown hair was soft and shining with just the trace of a wave.

The factory was not as big as Ellen had anticipated. She hadn't known what to expect at all, but it was nothing more than a large shed – converted stables, Ben told her. The 'office' into which he ushered her was only a small cubicle, separated from the rest of the factory by a flimsy wooden partition. He explained that it was his uncle's firm and that he, Ben, was what might be termed a 'Jack of all trades'. He had served his time as a sugar boiler, but as there were three such hands, they took it in turn to serve on the Central Beach stall. There was another stall at the Pleasure Beach at South Shore, which his Aunt Myrtle ran, but his uncle hadn't seen fit to employ permanent staff for the one at Central Beach. Ellen gathered, from Ben Hobson's tone, that Roger Redman was too mean to do so; but

140

he didn't actually say so and Ellen didn't pursue the matter.

'We've been in production here for just over a year,' he said. 'Blackpool rock has only been made in the town since last year, that's when the first lot was made, and we pride ourselves that we were one of the first firms to make it. Not the very first, mind you, but as near as makes no difference.'

Ellen felt puzzled. 'But I remember seeing it the last time I came to Blackpool,' she said, frowning a little. 'I'm sure I did, and that was before the turn of the century. Of course, I know you must be right. You know much more about it than I do. Please don't think I'm arguing...'

'You're right, you did see it,' replied Ben, leaning eagerly across the table between them. It was littered with papers and pamphlets and, at the end, a typewriting machine. Ellen wondered, in passing, who took care of the accounts, as there was no sign of any typist, neither of the boss of the firm, Roger Redman. Ben's eyes were glowing with enthusiasm. 'Yes, Mrs Bamber, you saw Blackpool rock here at the end of the last century. If you'd been here as early as 1887 you'd have seen it – that's when it was first sold here. But it wasn't made here, you see. That's the strange thing about it; the first Blackpool rock wasn't made in Blackpool at all.'

'Well, fancy that!' exclaimed Ellen. 'I'd no idea. Where was it made then?'

'The first Blackpool rock was made in Dewsbury – in Yorkshire – by a man called Ben Bullock. So the story goes anyway, and I've never

141

heard anybody dispute it. It's already becoming part of the lore amongst the rock-making folk, about this chap, Ben Bullock. Apparently he'd been making rock for quite a while at his toffee works in Dewsbury – he started off with a market stall, like you have, Mrs Bamber. Anyway, he was here on a holiday in 1887 when the idea suddenly came to him that it would be a brilliant plan to put the words BLACKPOOL ROCK through his product. So he went back home and did just that. He made the first batch of Blackpool rock ever, in his Dewsbury factory, and sent it here. Of course, it was an immediate success, and as far as I know he's still supplying it to some shops.'

'Yes, I see,' said Ellen, nodding. 'Quite an entrepreneur – is that the word? – this Ben Bullock. But now there are lots of other firms making rock as well, aren't there, yours included?'

'Yes, indeed,' replied Ben Hobson. 'But as I was telling you, it wasn't actually made in Blackpool until 1902 – last year.'

'And who was the first to make it here?' asked Ellen.

'Ah, now that's a ticklish question,' said Ben, opening his golden-brown eyes even wider. 'Some say one, some say another – there were quite a few firms jumping on the bandwagon at the same time, you see, and there have been countless arguments already about who was actually the first. It was most probably one of Ben Bullock's sugar boilers who left the firm and decided to go it alone. There's been more than

142

one of those, I can tell you.'

'That's quite usual, is it?'

'Why not?' Ben spread his hands wide and shrugged his shoulders. 'It's business, isn't it? If you've learned your trade and think you can make a go of it yourself then it's up to you to try. I wouldn't blame anybody for doing that.'

'So, going back to Ben Bullock,' said Ellen; she was finding this story fascinating. 'Until 1887, rock didn't have any letters running through it at all?'

'Indeed it did,' replied Ben. 'But not the names of towns, like it has now. It's said that the first words to be put through rock – Ben Bullock again – were those of a popular song of the time, *Whoa Emma*. Don't ask me why though,' he laughed. 'I've no idea. Again, the story's becoming part of what you might call the rock tradition.'

'You've got the right name then, haven't you?' said Ellen smiling. 'Ben...' It was the first time she had used the young man's name.

'So I have,' he answered. 'I must admit I'd never really thought about it like that. It's a common enough name. And we rock-makers are becoming fairly common too, although we tried to keep the secrets to ourselves at first. But the whole thing has snowballed. There must be about a dozen firms, at a guess, making rock in Blackpool now.'

'Good gracious,' said Ellen, surprised. 'Are there enough outlets for so many of you?'

'Good heavens, yes,' replied Ben. 'We don't just make for the Blackpool shops and stalls, you see.

Is that what you thought?'

'I suppose so ... I don't know.' Ellen was beginning to realise that although she prided herself upon being a businesswoman, albeit in a small way, there was a great deal that she didn't about the retail trade. 'You mean you supply Blackpool rock to other places as well!'

'Not *Blackpool* rock,' said Ben, grinning at her. 'You could hardly sell Blackpool rock in Morecambe, now could you? But I know what you mean. Yes, we sell rock to all sorts of other resorts, with the appropriate names running through, of course. Morecambe, Southport, Rhyl, Filey, Llandudno, Scarborough...'

'I should think those last two are quite a challenge,' Ellen remarked. 'Isn't it difficult getting the words SCARBOROUGH ROCK through the sticks?'

'Not as bad as you might think.' Ben put his head to one side. 'It's easy enough to cope with up to twenty letters.' He counted on his fingers. 'Scarborough Rock – there's fifteen letters there, against thirteen in Blackpool Rock. I know *that* one without counting.' He laughed. 'Anyway, that's enough talking about it. Come on, and I'll show you round the factory. I think it will be best if we watch the process from the beginning, right up to the end, then it'll give you a clear picture of how it's made. Starting with the mixing and boiling, of course. Be careful when we watch this process, Mrs Bamber. Don't get too near. Boiling sugar and glucose is dangerous stuff – but then you don't really need me to tell you that, do you? I was forgetting for the moment.'

'Yes, I've learned to be careful,' Ellen nodded. 'I don't let the children anywhere near when I'm boiling.' She followed Ben Hobson out of the office cubicle into the main part of the factory. It was, as she had noticed at a first glance when she entered, just a large shed with all the processes taking place in the one area.

She sniffed appreciatively, already feeling quite at home. There was that familiar aroma, sweet and sugary, never sickly to Ellen, although some might think so. Now it was overlaid with another smell, not often used in Ellen's kitchen but nevertheless unmistakable; that of peppermint. 'Mmm, lovely!' she proclaimed, wrinkling her nose before taking another deep breath.

'Yes, I agree with you,' said Ben Hobson. 'Wonderful smell, isn't it? Mint rock today. The most popular of all our lines, so the chances are it'll be peppermint you smell when you come in here. Now, let's begin at the beginning, shall we?'

A clear creamy-coloured liquid was boiling fiercely over a gas jet, in a huge, two-handled copper pan, the largest utensil Ellen had ever seen. 'Sugar, glucose and water,' said Ben. 'Those are the only ingredients needed for rock-making, apart from the colourings and flavourings, of course, which are added later.'

'I see what you mean about being careful,' observed Ellen. 'It's certainly hot stuff in that pan. Have there ever been any accidents?'

'One or two, I must admit,' replied Ben. 'But sugar boilers are trained to be careful.'

Two men dressed in white coat overalls, like Ben Hobson, and with white caps covering their

145

hair – Ben, too, had donned one on entering the workroom – slowly and steadily lifted the heavy pan from the heat and poured the liquid on to a metal-topped table near by. Ellen noticed that the large flat surface was coated with a fine white powder.

'That's called talc,' Ben told her. 'It's to prevent the mixture from sticking. All it is really is a very fine flour. The mixture is very, very hot, as you can see, but it'll soon cool down enough for it to be handled. Now the colour is going to be added.'

Ellen watched fascinated as one of the men poured on to the shimmering silvery mass a portion of red liquid dye. This he worked in quickly with a spatula until the now-cooling liquid took on a glowing red colour. Then he cut away this red portion with a large pair of scissors and put it to one side.

'Red – for the letters,' explained Ben. 'Now this part will have to be kept warm so that it doesn't get brittle before the lump is ready.'

'The lump?' queried Ellen.

'Yes, that's what we call the main part of the mixture. See, he's colouring some of it pink now, using a little less red dye, and that's for the casing, the outside covering of the rock.'

That portion, too, was transferred to a heated table to be kept pliable. Then started the process which Ellen found captivating, although she was finding the whole business of rock-making much more appealing than she had expected. The two men, working together, kneaded the mass still lying on the table into a malleable lump. Then

146

they carried it to the side of the room and slung it over a large metal hook fixed into the wall. One of them stood back while the other pulled and pulled and pulled at the mass of rapidly cooling rock – the 'lump' – doubling it over and pulling, doubling it over and pulling again. Then the other man had a turn; and in front of Ellen's fascinated gaze the mixture gradually lost its silvery transparency, becoming creamy white and opaque. The lump, then ready for use, was carried to the heated table. Ellen could tell from the stance of the men that it was extremely heavy.

'Not a job for a woman, then?' she commented to Ben, although she was not sure why she asked the question. It could have been that a glimmer of an idea was already taking shape in her mind.

'No, indeed; I should think not,' said Ben. 'Sugar boilers are always men. Always have been and always will be. Women just wouldn't have the physique to cope with the heavy lump. Begging your pardon, Mrs Bamber.' He turned and smiled at her almost apologetically. 'Now, at this stage the flavouring is added. Only a little, mind you, or it would be too strong.'

Ben gave a deep sniff as one of the men poured the strong-smelling mint essence on to the lump, then, with his partner, started kneading again. 'That's what you could smell when you came in, Mrs Bamber. They've already done two boilings, haven't you, lads?' The two men, one of them several years younger than the other – sixteen or so, Ellen guessed – looked up from their work briefly to smile and nod their agreement. 'And they'll probably get through three or four more before the day's out. It's essential to keep the lump pliable, you see, to keep working it, so that it doesn't set too soon. Now, watch carefully; this is the really intriguing part – putting the letters into the rock. Could you explain it, do you think, Fred, while you're working?'

"Course,' said the elder of the two hands, grinning widely. 'Now – watch, lady. This is how we made a C, the easiest letter of all, I might tell you.'

Ellen watched as Fred, with a large pair of scissors, cut away a portion of the white mixture which he then rolled into a 'sausage' about a foot in length and an inch across. Then, using a rolling pin, he rolled out some of the red mixture to form a flat strip and wrapped it halfway round the white roll. 'There,' he said proudly. 'Look at it end on, lady, and you'll see that it's a letter C.'

'Good gracious, yes,' said Ellen, smiling at him. 'That's amazing.'

She watched as he and his mate made the other letters in the same way, by adept rolling and assembling, until all thirteen had been made. They were then placed in the correct order with strips of wood between them so that they didn't stick.

'I should imagine you need to be able to spell to do this job,' Ellen observed drily. 'Wouldn't it be dreadful if you got the letters in the wrong order ... or missed one out?'

'Has been known,' grinned Fred. 'That's when we have to sell them as rejects, don't we, Ben?'

Ben laughed easily. 'It doesn't often happen though. Now, look ... he's making the casing.'

The outer covering of the rock was a large flat pink mass. Working quickly the men wrapped it around the letters and the main white part of the rock until the whole lump was formed into an enormous sausage.

'Now ... the rolling.' Ben worked with them this time and, under the three pairs of hands, rolling and rolling and rolling on a thirty-foot-long table, the thick sausage-like lump gradually became a long, thin strip, just the thickness of the Blackpool rock that Ellen had bought on Saturday. And rock hard, too, ready to be cut into small sticks and wrapped.

Ellen was pleased to see that this was where the women came in; two girls deftly cutting and wrapping the bright pink bars, then stacking them away in cardboard boxes ready for distributing to the various shops and stalls around Blackpool.

'And not only to the Blackpool shops, as I've told you,' said Ben Hobson, back in the office once more. 'If you came tomorrow we might well be making Southport rock, or Filey rock ... and you might smell lemon flavouring and not mint.'

'I'm almost at a loss for words,' said Ellen. 'It's been much more interesting than I ever imagined, and yet so simple, when you come to think of it.'

'Like everything else, simple when you know how,' said Ben Hobson. 'Rock-making is an art, a skilled trade, Mrs Bamber, but simple enough to learn. Are you thinking of having a go, back home in Preston?'

Ellen shook her head evasively, although she

149

didn't actually say no. 'We haven't the facilities, Mr Hobson. Only a small shop and a small kitchen. I think we'll be keeping to the toffees and fudges.' For the moment, she added to herself. The germ of an idea, which had occurred to her when she was watching the rock-making, wouldn't let her alone. Impractical, almost impossible – wasn't it? – and yet it was there, not thought out properly yet, but beginning to take root and grow.

'Well, I really mustn't take up any more of your time,' said Ellen, gathering together her handbag, gloves and umbrella. The weather had looked inclement when she set out earlier that morning, although she was hoping it would stay fine long enough for Mary to spend time on the sands with the children. She had promised to meet them later at a pre-arranged spot near North Pier. 'I must go and relieve my sister – she'll have her hands full with the four of them – and I'm sure you have work to do, haven't you?'

'Yes.' Ben Hobson nodded gravely. 'I'll go and relieve Fred now; it's time he had a break. And then this afternoon I've said I'll do another stint on the stall.'

'Who's looking after it now?' asked Ellen. The three sugar boilers, whom Ben had said took turns at this, were all in the factory. It seemed, to her, a very haphazard arrangement.

'My uncle, if he's turned up,' said Ben briefly. 'Between you and me, he doesn't pull his weight, Mrs Bamber.' He lowered his voice. 'Although it's supposed to be his firm.'

'It seems to me that it's you who's keeping it

150

going,' Ellen ventured.

'I do my best.' Ben smiled, a trifle wrily. 'But I suppose you could say it's my Aunt Myrtle who's the brains behind the business. She'll be in later to see to the accounts.' He gestured towards the typewriting machine. 'The problem is he won't employ enough staff. Tries to keep the whole thing going on a shoe-string. Anyhow, that's my problem, not yours.'

He stood now, as Ellen stood, looking at her questioningly for a few seconds, his golden-brown eyes clouded with uncertainty. 'I was wondering – er – you said your sister had the children. Your husband ... is he at home in Preston?'

'No, Mr Hobson, I'm a widow,' said Ellen calmly. 'My husband died last year.'

'Oh, I see. I'm sorry. I shouldn't have mentioned it. Please forgive me.' But Ben Hobson, though unsmiling, didn't look the least bit sorry, and the uncertain look had vanished from his eyes.

'It's all right; you weren't to know,' Ellen told him. 'My sister Mary's husband is at home in Preston. He works at the cotton mill. They've always been good to me, especially since ... since William died, so I asked Mary to come to Blackpool with me. And now I'd better go and find her.' She smiled warmly at Ben; that was how she was thinking of him now, although she didn't address him as such. She held out her hand. 'Thank you once again, Mr Hobson. It's been wonderful. I can't tell you how much I've enjoyed it all. And I'll come to the stall later in the week to buy some more rock.' She laughed. 'I know the children won't give me any peace if I don't.'

'If you make it Friday afternoon, then I'm sure to be there,' said Ben Hobson eagerly. 'It's been a pleasure meeting you, Mrs Bamber, and I'll look forward to seeing you again.' Ellen, returning his smile, realised that he was still holding on to her hand.

The rest of the week was devoted to the children and their wants. Ellen felt that she had already neglected them enough by stealing a couple of hours to herself on the Monday morning. They took walks out across the Irish Sea on two of the three piers, North and Central, South Pier being rather too far distant. They paid for a trip on a paddle-steamer, just up the coast and back, but exciting enough with the squally waves lashing against the side of the ship and the blustery wind whipping through their hair and stinging their cheeks. They had a ride on a Dreadnought tram as far as Bispham and back. They sampled the delights of the Tower building; the aquarium, the menagerie, even a visit to the circus, although they drew the line at actually making the Tower ascent or taking a ride on the Big Wheel. And always, every day when the weather was fine enough, there was the sand and the sea. Sand to make into castles and pies, each with a paper flag on the top, sand to dig into channels and moats. It was Rachel who discovered that by connecting the moat with a nearby rock pool they could have a real river running round their castle. They had tried before to fill the moat with bucket after bucket of water, only to find that it was swiftly swallowed away by the sand.

Ellen, delightedly watching them at play, remembered making the selfsame discovery on a rare visit to the seaside, but she had almost forgotten that faraway time, submerged as it was by all that had happened since. Such trips had been rarities for herself and Mary. She was glad that their own children were able to enjoy more fully the benefits of the bracing sea air. What a blessing it would be to live here all the time, she found herself thinking idly, away from the smoke and grime. She loved Preston, in the way that one always loved one's home town, but clothes never stayed clean for long and it wasn't very often that they were able to get away to the peace and cleanliness of the surrounding countryside.

Ellen's reverie was broken by a shout from Rachel. Tommy had stumbled and sat down heavily in a rock pool. He started bawling loudly though he wasn't hurt, just wet through. His striped jersey and his knickerbockers were soaked.

Mary laughed good-humouredly as she and Ellen rushed to haul him to his feet. 'Ne'er mind, it's nearly dinnertime and we'd have been making a move soon anyway. Come on, there's a good lad; you'll be right as rain now Mummy's wrapped you in this big towel. Now – into the pram. I must say it's a godsend at times. Come on, Rachel and Georgie, pick up them buckets and spades and pile 'em into the pram. We'll have a sort-out once we get home.'

Home, Mary had said unthinkingly, and Bella Vista was certainly turning out to be a home from home. Bella Broadbent, though she kept her house clean and tidy, didn't worry about unimportant little things like trickles of sand or pools of seawater in the hall. Tommy was none the worse for his ducking, but both he and Charlie were very tired after dinner and went to sleep immediately in their cots, something that they had needed a lot of coaxing to do on the previous days.

'Why don't you make hay while the sun shines?' said Bella to Mary, on learning that the twins were dead to the world and likely to remain so for a couple of hours. 'I'll see to them if they wake up – they know me well enough by now, don't they? Off you go, you and Ellen, and have a look round the shops. I know you haven't had a proper chance to do so all week. I think you'll have to take Rachel and Georgie though. I've got the teas to see to…'

'Goodness me, yes,' agreed Mary. 'That would be too much of a good thing. It's really kind of you to offer to have the other two terrors, and I'm not going to say no. Thanks ever so much, Bella.'

'Only one more full day, Ellen,' Mary remarked as the four of them made their way down Talbot Road towards the town centre shops. 'It's flying past, isn't it? Thursday already. Now, what are we going to do? Let's make the most of it.'

'Let's go and have a look round Donnelly's, that big department store,' said Ellen. 'I know we may not be able to afford to buy anything, but it's nice to look, isn't it? I think there's a restaurant up on the top floor. We could have afternoon tea and cream cakes, all posh, with serviettes. How about that, eh?'

And so they partook of tea in Donnelly's elegant restaurant, with Rachel and Georgie, on their best behaviour, sitting up to the white-clothed table eating ice cream, smothered in raspberry juice, from fancy glass dishes. Then Ellen treated herself to a pair of pale grey kid gloves, to match her costume, from the haberdashery department. She insisted on buying a pair for Mary as well, but her sister chose brown which she considered to be a much more serviceable colour.

'And now something for the kiddies,' said Mary, 'but this'll be my treat. No – I insist! You've already spent a mint of money on this holiday, our Ellen.'

For Rachel there was satin hair ribbons, one length of red and another of bright blue, and a little sailing boat for each of the three boys. 'I know there's not much of the holiday left,' said Mary, 'but they can sail 'em in the bath tub when they get back home.'

'I do believe there's a market near here,' said Ellen when they came out of Donnelly's store, turning into Market Street. 'Shall we go and have a look, just a quick one? Up here, I think – there's a short cut.'

'I should've thought you'd seen enough of markets,' laughed Mary. 'I doubt if it'll be as good as Preston, anyroad.' Nevertheless, she followed her sister as she led the way up Euston

Street, a cobbled thoroughfare where small shops, warehouses and stables abounded, the latter not being in such frequent demand, as horses, slowly but surely, were being replaced by petrol-engined vehicles.

One or two stables were already empty, and at the Lytham Street end there was a vacant warehouse. Next to it was a small shop, likewise empty. The sign on the window, in large letters, stated that the premises were To Let, as was the warehouse. It seemed that the two went together and had most likely been a saddler's business. Ellen stopped in her tracks, staring at the notice.

'Come on,' said Mary, nudging her sister. 'Why are we standing here gawping in the middle of the road?'

'I was just looking at that.' Ellen gestured towards the vacant buildings, her face thoughtful. 'I was just wondering...'

'Wondering what?' As light suddenly dawned, Mary's mouth dropped open. 'You're never thinking of...? Good grief, Ellen, don't you think you've got enough on your plate? That is, if you're thinking what I think you're thinking!'

Ellen giggled. 'There's a lot of thinking going on, that's for sure. Shhh! Little piggies have big ears, especially this one.' Fondly she patted her daughter's head, although Rachel didn't appear to be taking much notice. She was playing a game of hopping on and off the kerb on one leg, little Georgie, as usual, imitating her. 'I'll tell you later, Mary, honestly I will. I haven't thought it all through yet, not properly, but it might not be as crazy an idea as you're thinking. At least, as I think you're thinking.'

Ellen gave another little laugh, and Mary, looking keenly at her sister, thought it was a long time since she had seen her with such a healthy colour on her normally pale cheeks, or looking so excited and happy.

Chapter Eight

'I see now why you never got round to selling your house in Stonygate,' said Mary to Ellen later that evening, when the two sisters were sitting with Bella in her private room. 'You had the idea to start up a business in Blackpool. Is that why you wanted to come here this week, to find a place?'

'No, no – not at all. Of course it wasn't,' replied Ellen, a trifle edgily. Mary already seemed to be throwing cold water on her plans, tentative though they were at the moment. But Mary hadn't heard the half of it yet! 'I wanted us all to have a holiday; it's as simple as that. I'd never even thought of coming to live here. But that little shop and the warehouse, they're in an ideal position, right in the town centre, only a few minutes from the prom.'

'But you wouldn't need a great big place like that warehouse, just for making toffees and fudges,' argued Mary. 'And you wouldn't be thinking of living there, I take it, not above that little shop? You'd need a house an' all. And what about Mam? Have you thought about what she'd do?'

Ellen sighed. 'No, I must confess I haven't thought it all out yet, not properly. But it's an idea that came to me on Monday, when I watched the rock being made at Ben Hobson's place, and then, when I saw the empty warehouse...' Ellen looked at her sister pleadingly. 'Hear me out, please, Mary. Don't start putting obstacles in the way. What I'd really like to do, you see, is to have a go at making ... Blackpool Rock!'

'*Blackpool Rock?*' repeated Mary, her eyes nearly popping out of her head.

'Hmmm ... Blackpool rock, eh?' said Bella Broadbent, rather less incredulously. 'Well, it's an up-and-coming trade from what I can see, and there'd be plenty of scope for you.'

'But what in heaven's name do you know about making rock?' said Mary. 'Oh, I know you watched 'em making it the other day, but you can't go opening a factory and start doing it yourself, just like that. You'd need experienced folk, and from what you told me it'd be men you'd need as well as women.'

'Yes, I know,' said Ellen. 'I'd need at least one experienced sugar boiler, and a pan man. And girls, possibly two for cutting and wrapping ... I'd have to advertise.'

'Oh, you've already got it worked out, I see,' said Mary, somewhat sarcastically. 'Put an advert in the paper and they'll all come flocking, will they, wanting to work for you?'

'They might,' said Ellen, staring back confidently at her sister. 'I won't know till I try, will I? Oh come on, Mary, stop looking all po-faced at me. I feel that the children and I need a change. We need to get right away from that Stonygate house and all its bad memories. The only reason I haven't got round to selling it is because I haven't had time, not with starting the new shop and everything.'

'And that's another thing,' argued Mary. 'The shop in Church Street has only been open since last December – it's not a year yet. Don't you think you're trying to run before you can walk? I'm not trying to be difficult, honestly I'm not,' she went on more kindly. 'I think it'd be a grand idea for you to move away from that bloomin' big house – it's half-empty, anyroad – but why move to Blackpool? And why give up a good business when you've got it going so nicely? It's getting to be a little gold mine, that toffee shop of yours.'

'I know,' Ellen smiled. 'I wasn't actually thinking of letting it go… But I can make toffee anywhere, you know, and why not in Blackpool, just as easily as Preston? I probably wouldn't start with the rock straight away, not till we got going.'

'But you don't make the toffee, Ellen,' said Mary, quite reasonably. 'It's Mam that does that. You make the softer stuff, fudges and that. Are you thinking of doing the whole lot here at this Blackpool place, all by yourself?'

'If I have to, but I did think that Mam might come with me,' said Ellen, very tentatively.

'Oh you did, did you? It'd be as well to ask her first, wouldn't it?' Mary's tone was gruff and she was beginning to look disapproving again. 'And what about the Church Street shop, like I said before? That's going to look after itself, is it?'

'I was wondering…' Ellen looked steadily at her sister, right into the deep brown eyes which were the only feature that the two of them had in common. She hoped that by staring un-flinchingly at Mary she might change the still critical look on her face to one that was more agreeable. 'I was wondering if *you* might take it over for me.'

'*What!?*' cried Mary.

At that, Bella Broadbent tactfully arose, heading for the kitchen. 'I'll go and make us all a nice cup of tea,' she said, 'before I see to the visitors' suppers.'

Mary and Ellen, as they had done on the previous evenings, were spending an hour or two in Bella's company in her private little parlour. Most of the other visitors, those who had not gone out 'on the town', usually gathered around the old upright piano in the visitors' sitting room – really the far end of the dining room – having a sing-song, or sat around in small groups playing cards or simply chatting. Mary and Ellen had joined in with the other guests once or twice, but they were more than happy as a rule to sit with Bella, and sometimes Alf, in their private quarters. A day filled with sea and sand and salty air, to say nothing of four boisterous children, always proved tiring. The sisters had no desire to seek the delights of the Music Hall or the ballroom floor – they couldn't do the latter, anyway, without gentlemen escorts – and to enter a public house was strictly taboo for two unaccompanied, well-brought-up ladies. Besides, since William's untimely death, Ellen had been unwaveringly teetotal.

'And what the heck am I supposed to know about making toffee?' said Mary, as Bella disappeared into the kitchen. 'You know I've never had any part in it; it was always just you and Mam. I was in the cotton mill, then I had the twins...' But Ellen was pleased to see that her sister was looking a little less belligerent. 'And I've still got the twins. They take some watching, those two, believe me. Well, you've seen 'em yourself this week, haven't you, what live wires they are? I don't see how I could mind a shop and them two rascals.'

But she was coming round to the idea. Ellen could tell that she was; hidden down the side of the easy chair Ellen crossed her fingers.

'There's Phyllis, you know,' she pointed out, trying to keep her voice casual. 'Phyllis Hardy. She's come on by leaps and bounds since we took her on. She's quite capable of looking after the shop on her own even though she's only fifteen or so. Otherwise, I wouldn't have dreamed of coming away and leaving her. And she's keen to try her hand at the sweet-making, too. She watches Mam and me every chance she gets and I think she's about ready.'

'It's to be hoped she is, 'cause I couldn't do it all on my own, that's for sure.' Mary gave her sister a sly look, a hint of a smile pulling at the corners of her mouth.

'You mean ... you will?' cried Ellen. 'You'll take over the shop? Oh, Mary, that'd be wonderful. And you'd soon learn to make toffee! You're a marvellous cook–'

'Hey, hold your horses.' Mary held up her hand. 'I'm not promising anything. All I'm saying is that I might. I'll think about it. Anyway, there's

162

nowt we can do, is there, until we've talked it all over with Mam. She might be dead against the idea.'

'She might,' agreed Ellen, although she knew that her mother was usually quite amenable about falling in with sensible suggestions, and that she was very keen, just as keen as Ellen was, to make a success of their little business. It had often been Lydia who had had big ideas when Ellen had pleaded caution.

'I must admit that the idea of making a bit of money for myself appeals to me,' said Mary reflectively. 'I don't mean just for myself, of course, but to help at home. Fred's not making much at Horrockses; he never seems to be in line for promotion. The trouble is he won't push himself, not much "get-up-and-go" if you know what I mean.'

'I shouldn't condemn him for that, if I were you,' said Ellen quietly. 'I had one who had too much of that, remember?'

'Aye, I know, and you've made a damned good go of things since he popped his clogs,' said Mary emphatically.

'Very apt,' commented Ellen, finding she was able to smile about it all now.

'What? Oh yes, I see ... clogs.' Mary looked a little embarrassed. 'Anyroad, I believe in giving credit where it's due, and you've pulled yerself up by yer bootlaces all right – and that's something else that's apt. Yes – why not? If you want to have a go at making Blackpool rock, why the heck shouldn't you? You just took the wind out of my sails at first, our Ellen, and I still think it needs careful thought.'

When Bella returned with the laden tea tray the sisters were deep in conversation, their heads bent close together. 'Everything in the garden's lovely then, is it?' Bella said, grinning at them. 'We can't have any falling out, you know, not on holiday.'

'The next time we fall out it'll be the first,' said Mary. 'Isn't that right, Ellen? Serious falling out, I mean. We've had our bits of tiffs, who hasn't? She's managing to talk me round, Bella.' Mary smiled at their landlady who was fast becoming a friend.

'The property you mentioned, on Euston Street, belongs to Adam Birtwistle,' Bella told Ellen as they drank their tea. 'He has an office on Birley Street, quite close to there. That property's been To Let for ages, from what I can remember – I usually cut through there to the market – so I shouldn't imagine there's any immediate rush. But if I were you I'd call in and see him in the morning, just to find out how the land lies. And it isn't as if Blackpool's a million miles away from Preston, is it? If you do decide to go ahead you can always pop over for a weekend, can't you? I'll always make room for you. Like Mary says, you'll have to find somewhere to live, somewhere handy for the shop... Oh, I say, isn't it exciting? There'll be nobody more thrilled than me if Lydia says yes.'

'Hold your horses,' Mary told her, just as she had told Ellen. 'Let's not count our chickens, eh? It depends on a lot of things, not least on Mam.'

Ellen, however, was quite pleased at the way

things were going; and tomorrow she not only had to see the owner of the property, she had to call at the Central Beach stall to buy some more rock from Ben Hobson.

The arrangement she made with Adam Birtwistle was a tentative one; it couldn't, at the moment, be otherwise. He advised her not to delay too long. There were other parties interested, he said, but Ellen knew that this was just a salesman's patter. When she came out of his office she felt confident that the property could be hers to rent if she wanted it.

'What about Ben Hobson?' asked Mary, who met her outside the office with the children in tow. They were on their way to see that young man now.

'What about him?' Ellen answered casually.

'Well, aren't you going to tell him what you've got in mind?'

'Hardly,' smiled Ellen. 'It wouldn't be quite the thing, would it, to tell him I've watched how to make rock, and now I'm going to set up in opposition! Besides, it's early days yet. We can't say anything to anybody till we've discussed it with Mam.' But Ellen had some ideas concerning Mr Benjamin Hobson that she didn't intend divulging to anyone, at least not yet.

He was delighted to see them all again and when they bought six large sticks of rock, two of each colour – some for Lydia and some for themselves – he was more than pleased. He gave Ellen his address, asking her to be sure to let him know if ever she came to Blackpool again. As she reciprocated with her own Preston address,

165

knowing that she might not be there very much longer, Ellen was feeling secretly overjoyed at the way things were progressing.

Lydia listened carefully to her younger daughter as she told of her plans, nodding approvingly, frowning only occasionally and raising no objections. As a consequence, things moved swiftly. By the April of the next year, 1904, well in time for the start of the summer holiday season, Ellen, Lydia and the two children were settled in their new home in King Street, less than half a mile from their business premises. Ellen had suggested that her mother should live with them, if she was agreeable to the idea. Lydia was; she and Ellen had always got on well together and the house was large enough for her to have her own private sitting room, should she ever feel like a bit of peace and quiet. Lydia had lived on her own for a long time and Ellen knew that her mother might want to escape, now and again, from the hubbub caused by two active children.

The little shop in Euston Street was open for Easter. It was almost a facsimile of the shop in Preston, the window attractively arranged with boxes of chocolates, trays of toffee, fudges, nougats and candies, and large jars of the highly coloured sweets that appealed to the younger customers. Above the door was the same slogan *Bamber and Tucker, High Class Sweets and Chocolates* – as graced the shop in Church Street, Preston. That business was now being run very competently by Mary Pilkington, with Phyllis a very able second-in-command. A young girl had been engaged to help out where required and to assist at the market stall. Mary's twins, now aged two and a half, were not nearly so much of a problem as she had feared. She had good neighbours who were always willing to earn themselves a shilling or two when her hours at the shop or in the kitchen prevented her from giving the children the attention they needed.

Likewise, in Blackpool, Ellen's children were not neglected. The school that Rachel attended was near to both the shop and their home on King Street, and it was to one of these two places that she went for her midday dinner, fitting in with whatever her mother and grandmother were doing that day. Georgie was now turned four; he would soon be at school like his sister, then Ellen would feel that the last of her fears concerning her children's welfare had been removed. Since William died Ellen had endeavoured to be both mother and father to the pair of them, which was why she was always extra-sensitive to any neglect they might be feeling. William had been a poor sort of father, but they had been used to having both a mummy and a daddy. That was the norm, what most of their friends had. Perhaps that was why they both showed more than a little excitement whenever Uncle Ben came to visit.

And they were not the only ones, thought Ellen, smiling to herself as she walked along Church Street to her place of work one morning in late April. For the moment, though, she was trying to keep the wraps on her emotions. She was sure that Ben Hobson returned her feelings.

She couldn't have been mistaken about the admiration she had seen shining so often from his golden-brown eyes. But the nature of their relationship at work precluded any ideas he might have had regarding a closer bond between the two of them. Ben showed the utmost propriety in his dealings with Ellen. She knew, indeed, that any suggestion of further intimacy must come from Ellen herself, and this was difficult for a young lady who had been brought up to behave correctly. To make any move now might be too soon and she was anxious that he should not think her brazen. Even so, Ellen smiled, contented enough that the time would come. In the meantime their relationship at work couldn't be a more amiable one.

She hadn't intended it to work out the way it had done when she had called to see him at his home, on that cold January Sunday afternoon, about four months ago. She had gone along in some trepidation. After all, what did she know about Benjamin Hobson apart from his name and address and the fact that he worked for his uncle, Roger Redman, one of Blackpool's rock-makers? He might even be married – a young father to a whole tribe of children – although Ellen didn't think so. The address, Park Road, didn't mean much to her, except that she knew it was in a rather select area on the fringes of what was once the site of the Raikes Hall Pleasure Gardens. The house was impressive-looking – as big, if not bigger, than her old home on Stonygate, and Ellen was already having visions of a pert uniformed maid opening the door and a refined middle-aged couple (Ben's parents) looking down their aristocratic noses at her. She almost had second thoughts and turned away, then she noticed that the green-painted door was not nearly as bright and shiny as it might have been. The woodwork was chipped and faded, the brass letterbox tarnished and the stone steps were in dire need of washing. They certainly were not edged in white with a donkey stone like the steps of most of Ellen's acquaintances, however humble. And at the side of the door was a row of bells with names below them. This elegant house had obviously known better days; now it was divided into 'rooms' and let out to lodgers, one of whom must be Ben Hobson.

As Ellen stood peering at the faded labels, the door opened and a young woman dressed in outdoor clothes emerged. 'Oh, you startled me! You're wanting somebody, are you?' She was polite enough, but seemed in a hurry to be off.

'Yes, please. Mr Benjamin Hobson?' said Ellen, somewhat falteringly. She was beginning to wish she had written instead of turning up on the doorstep like this. Whatever had she been thinking of?

'There you are.' The young woman prodded at the name below the second bell. 'Give it a ring, then go on up.' She grinned. 'Here, I'll do it for you.' She gave the bell a push and Ellen heard a faint buzz inside the house. 'Ben'll be in, likely as not. He's not one for gadding about.'

'Oh, d'you think I should? Go up, I mean?'

'Yes, why ever not? You either want to see him or you don't. Make up yer mind.' The young woman gave a laugh. 'I can't stand here chatting, that's for sure. I'm a bit late already. First floor, door at the end of the passage. His name's on it. Well, go on, if you're going.'

Ellen stepped past her into the hall beyond, and the young woman in a hurry closed the door behind her. Suddenly it all went very gloomy. Ellen was aware of dark-brown paint, dingy wallpaper, also brown, and an aroma of stale cabbage and onions as she hesitantly made her way up the uncarpeted stairs, all the while cursing herself for being such an idiot as to come at all. What a crazy idea it had been!

As she reached the top step a door opened – there were three such doors in a row – and, to her relief, there was Ben. He was wearing a white shirt with a stiff collar, a dark tie and a waistcoat, but no jacket. He peered at her uncertainly through the gloom, then gave a gasp of surprise.

'Good gracious me! It can't be … but it is. It's Mrs Bamber, isn't it?'

Ellen smiled nervously. 'Yes, it's me,' she said, aware that it sounded rather foolish. 'I'm sorry. I should have let you know.'

'Not at all, not at all. It was just a surprise seeing you there, but a very pleasant one, I might add. Do come in, Mrs Bamber. I was just going to make myself a cup of tea.'

Ellen followed him into the room, hardly believing that she'd had the audacity to come unannounced. Even now, she was unsure what she might find. A wife … a ladyfriend? But no – he said 'make myself a cup of tea', and there was nobody else in the room.

'Sit down, sit down, Mrs Bamber.' Ben Hobson fussed around, moving a couple of newspapers from an easy chair, plumping up a cushion, picking up his suit jacket from the sofa and hanging it on a hook behind the door, although the room did look reasonably tidy. There was a small sink and a wooden draining board at the end of the room with a neatly folded pot towel hanging over a wire, next to a little gas ring. The room was large and the sofa on which Ben then sat down looked as though it might convert into a bed. Seemingly, Ben lived in just the one room and Ellen found herself wondering, though it was really none of her business, whether he cooked his own meals as well. There was no smell of cooking in here as there had been in the hall, just a pleasantly faint aroma of lavender polish.

Ben leaned forward, his hands on his knees. 'Now ... what can I do for you, Mrs Bamber?' he said, his toffee-coloured eyes – that was how she still thought of them – alive with interest.

Ellen was somewhat taken aback. Oh dear! What could he do for her? Supposing it had been only a social call; would he, then, not have wanted to see her? But it was not a social call. She opened her mouth to answer.

Ben noticed her hesitancy and he gave an apologetic laugh. 'I'm sorry; that was a silly thing to say, wasn't it? Very tactless – it sounded as though you're not welcome, and you are, I assure you. But you can't be on holiday, not in January?' He put his head on one side, regarding her quizzically.

'No, I'm not on holiday. I'm staying at the same

place, on High Street with Mrs Broadbent, but I'm on my own this time. I'm here on business.'

Ben nodded understandingly. 'Yes, I see. And there's something you wanted to ask me, is there? About … the business?'

'Yes. Oh, I should have written – I know I should!' Ellen shook her head confusedly. 'My mother said it would be better to write, but I'm not very good at expressing myself in letters, and it's something that needs a lot of talking about, so…'

'So why don't I go and make us that cup of tea, then you can talk to your heart's content?' Ben rose and went over to the gas ring, busying himself with kettle, teapot and willow-pattern cups and saucers which he took from a small cupboard below the sink. 'It is lovely to see you again, Mrs Bamber, business or not,' he called out to her. 'And I think we could dispense with the formalities, don't you? Queen Victoria's dead now. I'm Ben, and I know that you are Ellen,' he said, placing a laden tray on a little table at her side.

'Yes, I see no reason why we can't be a bit more … familiar.' Oh dear, thought Ellen, that's not what I meant to say at all! 'I mean a bit more friendly, like,' she corrected herself. 'I think of you as Ben,' she added, smiling shyly at him. 'I still feel it's been very presumptuous of me to call, just like this, out of the blue.' She took the cup and saucer from him, adding a spoonful of sugar and stirring thoughtfully. 'But I knew that if I didn't take the bull by the horns, so to speak, then I might never pluck up courage at all.' She opened her mouth to continue, regarding him seriously. 'Er, you see...'

'Fire away, Ellen,' said Ben, smiling reassuringly at her. 'I'm all ears.'

And so she told him, hesitantly at first, then gradually gaining in confidence, how she had noticed the empty properties last summer, when they were on holiday, and how the idea had come to her to open a business in Blackpool. Her own house in Preston was now on the market, with one or two interested parties, and she had, only this weekend, found a house which she considered ideal, in King Street. Work on the shop in Euston Street was progressing nicely, with the sign-writers due to move in the following week. That was why, Ellen explained, she had decided she must tell Ben now, before the names Bamber and Tucker were painted up for all the world and his wife to see. She didn't want him to think she had behaved in a devious manner.

'Not at all,' said Ben. 'I doubt if you could be devious if you tried. I don't know you very well, Ellen, but that's the impression that I get. And I think it's a wonderful idea for you to open a shop in Blackpool. I wish you all the luck in the world. And coming to live here, too – well, that's marvellous!' He certainly looked pleased, but somewhat mystified as well. 'But, surely...' He frowned slightly now. 'That wasn't all you wanted to tell me, was it?'

Under his questioning gaze her eyes dropped to her lap. 'No, there was something else...' She went on to tell him how the warehouse was

173

empty at the moment, but that, if things worked out according to plan, she hoped to have it converted into a factory where she could make ... Blackpool rock!

'I see! Yes, I thought that might be it.' But Ben didn't look or sound the least bit annoyed, as he might well have done. On the contrary, his eyes were positively gleaming. 'And you're wondering if I can give you some idea how to get started. Well, of course, any help I can give you...' He leaned forward eagerly again.

'No, no!' Ellen shook her head a trifle impatiently. 'You surely don't think I just want to pinch your ideas? That'd be most unfair. No, I was wondering if...' She hesitated a moment before going on. 'When I met you in August I got the impression that you wouldn't mind starting up on your own. Well, what you actually said was that you wouldn't blame anybody for doing just that. I rather got the impression that you were not too happy with the way your uncle was running the firm. So I wondered if you might possibly consider...'

'Leaving him and coming to work for you?' said Ben, giving a chuckle.

'No, not really.' Ellen shook her head again. 'In fact, not at all. I wouldn't presume to ask you to work for me. You know so much more about it all than I do. No, what I wondered was, would you consider going into partnership with me, Ben? I have a feeling that you might set up on your own soon anyway, so I thought that the two of us...' She stopped as she could see Ben Hobson shaking his head, slowly and rather sadly.

'No, I'm afraid that just isn't possible, Ellen.' His eyes were serious now, no longer twinkling with amusement as they so often did. 'You see … well, look around you – you can tell.' He flung wide his arms. 'I have no money.'

'Oh, I see,' said Ellen, more than a little embarrassed. 'But surely that wouldn't matter. I've already got the property – well, what I mean is, I've rented it. It's your help I want, your know-how.' She was floundering somewhat, not being experienced in business deals and partnerships. The one with her mother had always been just a very amiable, family sort of thing, amounting to little more than splitting the profits between them. Since Mary joined them it had become rather more complicated and a solicitor had helped to sort out the details for them.

'And you can have my help, Ellen. All the help you need. I'll come and work for you. I'll be in charge of the rock-making, if that is what you want, but as far as a partnership goes … it was a great thought, but I haven't a bean.' He shrugged resignedly. 'No, I suppose that's not strictly true. I *do* have a bob or two,' he gave a wry smile, 'but not enough to ever think of buying a business of my own.'

'But I can't expect you to come and work for me, Ben. To leave your uncle,' said Ellen, in some distress. She felt she had made a real mess of things. 'It wouldn't be right.'

'Let me decide that,' said Ben. 'I've been thinking of making a move anyway. Let me just tell you, in case you're thinking I'm a spendthrift or a gambler or something, how I come to be

175

here, living in rooms. I had to leave home because of my father. He and I ... well, we don't see eye to eye, and that's putting it mildly.' He stopped, focusing his eyes on the tiny fire that was burning in the grate.

Ellen nodded. 'Mmm ... yes, I see,' she murmured, not knowing what else to say. Ben rose and, picking up the poker, he jabbed fiercely at a large piece of coal. It fell apart, bursting into flames. 'That's better,' he said. 'It takes a while to get going. I only lit it when I got back from chapel.' Ellen surmised that what he was doing was gathering his thoughts.

He sat down again, looking at her steadily. 'You can have no idea, Ellen, a respectable young woman like you, just what it can be like living with ... a drunkard.'

Ellen drew in her breath sharply. Then, 'I think I might,' she said gently. 'Have an idea, I mean.'

Ben didn't answer this, no doubt thinking that she was merely trying to show empathy towards him. 'My father...' he began. 'I couldn't bear to be in the same house with him any longer, watching him hitting the bottle night after night, staggering home from the pub, knocking my mother about and my younger sisters...'

As she listened, saying very little, Ellen might almost have been hearing a catalogue of William's misdeeds; his ill-temper, his swaggering boastfulness, his excessive demands of his wife. Ben didn't dwell too much on this, but Ellen, having experienced it herself, could guess at what he was hinting. Ben and his brother, two years his junior, had stood up to their father on several occasions, suffering badly themselves as a result of their intervention. Ben had left two years ago, unable to stand any more of it. The sight of his eldest son had, apparently, become like a red rag to a bull to Mr Hobson senior. But he had been warned. Ben and his brother, Alec, had on two occasions fetched the police. All they had done, as yet, was to issue a warning to the miscreant, but Alec was there to look after their mother as much as he was able, and Ben frequently called to make sure that matters were not getting any worse.

'And I'm still giving Mam a goodly share of my wages,' said Ben, though not at all boastfully. 'That's been the way of it ever since I left school when I was fourteen. He never gave her much and there are five of us, the two youngest still at school. I'm the eldest.'

Ellen learned that going on to the High School or any form of 'fancy book learning', as his father had put it, had been out of the question for Ben and his siblings, intelligent though they were. Dora, aged eighteen, worked in a seafront hotel, living in during the busy season, and Alec worked in a grocer's shop.

'And ... your father?' asked Ellen.

'Oh, he's a brickie. One thing in his favour is that he's usually in work, but he gets through most of his pay packet himself. No, I'm afraid Mam still needs a lot of help from me. She argues, of course, says I shouldn't be doing it, that I should be saving up to get married. But so far I haven't wanted... There hasn't been anyone...' Ben stopped, looking pensively at

Ellen. 'So – here I am.' He leaned back against the shabby, but clean, cushions of the sofa. 'Twenty-three years of age, living in digs, and about tuppence ha'penny in the bank. Not what you might call a good business proposition, Ellen.' He grinned ruefully at her.

So he was twenty-three, the same age as herself; she had thought he might be a year or two older. 'Have you always been a sugar boiler?' Ellen asked now. 'Is that your trade?'

'It is now, and though I say it myself I know I'm a very good one. I worked in a butcher's shop when I left school, then I joined a sweet-making firm in Blackpool and I decided that that was something I really enjoyed doing. So when my uncle – he's my mother's brother – decided to have a go at making Blackpool rock I thought it might be a good idea to join him.'

'But it's not worked out just as you'd hoped?'

'No, not really,' replied Ben. 'Which is why I'm offering to come and work for you, Ellen. Not as a partner – you can see that's out of the question – but as your first-hand sugar boiler. Call me the manager, if you like, but I'd be a working one, doing the same as the other chaps. You saw for yourself, didn't you, that it wasn't a job for a woman, pulling the rock around? What do you think? I'm ready, willing and able,' he added, smiling.

She met his steadfast gaze with her own, looking deep into his eyes and knowing, with a certainty she hadn't experienced with any man before, that she could trust him. She answered him lightly at first, in the manner of his last remark. 'How can I refuse an offer like that?' she laughed.

'You will then? You'll agree that it would be a good idea for me to work for you?'

'Ye-es. But it will all want going into very carefully – to be fair to you, Ben, I mean. It isn't everyone who would like having a woman for a boss, not that I would ever be a ... well, a bossy sort of boss.'

'I know that, Ellen,' Ben answered quietly. There was a moment's silence as they regarded one another.

'We can work out the details later.' Ellen had another matter on her mind at the moment. 'Ben, there's something I want to tell you, not about the job, something else. You know when you were telling me about your father, getting drunk and all that, and I said I understood? Well, I wasn't just being sympathetic. I do understand – I really do – because I know what it's like. I went through the same thing myself, you see. With William ... my husband.'

She found herself telling her new friend – that was how she was thinking of Ben now, as a friend – about how she had suffered at William's hands. A slightly edited version when it came to his physical abuse of her, as Ben's story about his parents had been, but she told him in some detail about the events leading up to William's death; his destruction of the sweets she had made, his purloining of her secret savings and her discovery, just before he died, that he was a gambler as well as a drunkard.

'My poor Ellen,' breathed Ben, gazing at her in

horrified astonishment. 'I'd no idea...'

'No, how could you have? And I'll tell you something else, Ben. When the policeman came to tell me that he had ... gone, I just stared at him. And I'm sure I must have smiled. It was the relief, you see. Does that sound dreadful?'

'No, of course it doesn't. Perfectly understandable, I would say. There have been many, many times that my mother has wished that my father just wouldn't come back at all. And it could only have got worse for you, Ellen.'

'Yes.' She went on to tell him about Jessie Balderstone and her child and about William's cruel treatment of Amos Hardy. 'You must be wondering why I married him,' she said finally. 'And, believe me, I've asked myself that same question time and time again. All I can say is ... I thought I loved him.'

'As good a reason as any,' Ben smiled sympathetically. 'And that's the reason my mam gave when I asked her. "I thought I loved him," she said. He was a Methodist, too, my father – supposed to be, anyroad, same as Mam; signed the pledge as well in his younger days, but that's all gone by the board now. Ever since a friend from work invited him into the pub for a drink. "It'll do no harm," he said, this friend. "Just give it a try, just once." Well...' Ben spread his arms wide and shrugged his shoulders. 'What was the result? My father got the taste for it, then it became a nightly thing, till in the end he was hardly ever sober. And all because a pal persuaded him to take an odd drink.'

'You believe in total abstinence then, do you,

Ben?' asked Ellen.

He nodded earnestly. 'Yes, I do. That's one of the reasons – the main one, I suppose – that my father and I are now daggers drawn. I'd started going to the Band of Hope before I left home, and that infuriated him. Now I'm one of the leaders at the chapel I attend.'

'The Band of Hope?'

'Yes, you've heard of it, haven't you? It's a temperance society, started by the Methodists.'

'Yes, of course I've heard of it, but I've never known much about it. We're Church of England, you see. I'm inclined to agree with you, Ben, about the evils of drink. Well, I would, wouldn't I?' Ellen went on to tell Ben how she had poured the deadly liquor down the sink on the day of William's funeral. 'But my mother thinks I'm taking an extreme view. I don't think she agrees with me at all, though she hasn't actually said so. A favourite saying of Mam's is that every tub should stand on its own bottom. You have to be responsible for your own actions, in her book, and you shouldn't go around telling other folk what they must or mustn't do.' Ellen frowned perplexedly. It was good to know that Ben agreed with her – they seemed to be finding more and more things they had in common – but she did wonder if his way, the Methodist way of looking at things might be a little extreme. Her mother would certainly say so.

'Don't look so worried, Ellen,' Ben grinned at her. 'I think people are sometimes a bit overawed by me when I march down the street with my Bible under my arm on meeting nights, but I'm a pretty ordinary sort of chap really.'

Ellen smiled. 'Yes, the young lady who let me in seemed to think so.'

Ben threw back his head and laughed. 'Oh, yes, Lucy. She's my landlady's daughter. It's a bit of a joke between us really. She's C of E like you. In fact that's where she'd be going, to her young ladies' class. But they're not in the habit of carrying their Bibles around, not like us Non-conformists.'

'My mam sometimes calls them ranters,' said Ellen boldly. 'The Methodists.'

'Yes, a lot do – rant, I mean. But I can assure that I don't, Ellen. If you can't get your point over without shouting, then you're not very sure of yourself, that's what I think. Anyway, enough of that. What about this job? You've decided, have you, Mrs Bamber? You're going to let me come and work for you?'

Ellen nodded. 'Yes, and thank you very much, for everything.'

He insisted on walking her back to North Shore a little while later, through the cold, almost deserted Sunday-afternoon streets. When they arrived at Bella Vista, dusk was already beginning to fall.

'You're not dashing off back to Preston tonight, are you?' he asked, preparing to leave her at the gate.

'No, in the morning,' she told him. 'As early as possible. I can't neglect my business there. But I'll be over again in a few weeks' time. Thank you again, Ben.' Ellen, on that cold January day, was very content.

She was no less so as she walked to work on that April morning some four months later, a morning that made one feel that spring had come at last. The factory was ready to go into production next week with its first batch of Blackpool rock. Ben had proved to be an invaluable asset to the firm, advising her about equipment and raw materials and also with engaging staff. A few weeks ago he had left his uncle's firm and thrown in his lot with her.

To Ellen's delight they were fast becoming close friends as well as colleagues and her two children were becoming very fond of him. There was little of the employer-employee restraint about their association. Always she listened to his advice and followed his undoubted lead. As she had told him at the start, he knew so much more about the rock business than she did. Nevertheless, there was a certain diffidence, on Ben's part, in their more personal relationship. He had, as yet, not even held her hand. Touched it, of course, but not held it, in the way she longed for him to do.

Chapter Nine

It was a great day for Ellen as she watched the first load of sugar and glucose boiling away in the huge copper pans, the very first stage in the making of her very first batch of Blackpool rock. She intended to watch this first boiling right through to the end, as she had done that day last summer in Roger Redman's factory, the day that the idea had first come to her. She would help out, too, when required, but that would be towards the end of the process when the rock must be rolled and rolled and rolled until it was cool enough to stay round on its own and not lose its shape.

The young man who was working with Ben now, Bertie Shaw, seemed quietly efficient and Ellen felt sure he would be an asset to the firm. Ellen sometimes found it hard to believe that she and her mother, and Mary in Preston, now controlled their own family business. Ben had declined, again, Ellen's suggestion that he should be a partner in the firm, along with the three of them, insisting that he preferred to work for a weekly wage.

Already he was proving invaluable and Ellen knew that she couldn't possibly have managed without him in the weeks leading up to the opening of the factory, ordering the equipment and raw materials required for starting up the enterprise and helping Ellen to engage the staff. Ben, being the honourable young man that he was, would not even consider 'poaching' staff away from a rival firm – most certainly not his uncle's – with promises of higher rates of pay and better prospects, although he knew that this sort of thing went on, frequently. Bertie Shaw had answered the advert in the local paper for an experienced sugar boiler. He had worked for one of the other Blackpool firms, but as Ben hadn't tempted the young man, personally, to leave, Ben's own code of ethics was satisfied. Of the two young women engaged as rock rollers and wrappers, one had previous experience and the other one was new to the work. Ellen, also, who intended to help out when and where required, was new to the art of rock-making, but she felt sure that they would all work very well together. Her spirits were high that Monday morning in May as she watched the process continuing.

Mixing and boiling, adding the colour, then the pulling. She watched, fascinated, as she had that first time, as Ben and Bertie took turns to pull at the silvery substance hanging over the hook on the wall, until it turned opaque and creamy white. Peppermint flavouring was then added, the traditional Blackpool rock flavour for this first batch, to go with the pink colouring that had already been added to part of the mass. Then, the lettering. Ben, the expert, was responsible for forming the letters of BLACKPOOL ROCK for this all-important first batch. As he worked he occasionally glanced up and caught Ellen's eye. He didn't smile at her, but his look echoed her

185

own thoughts. *Well, we've done it! And isn't it grand?*

Then – rolling the lump. This is certainly taking some elbow grease, thought Ellen, as she watched Ben and Bertie transform the huge, pink-encased sausage shape into manageable strings of rock, some thirty feet in length. It was then that Ellen and the two girls, who, until then, had had little to do but watch and wait, joined in the process. Working in unison, spaced out equidistantly along the thirty-foot table, they rolled and rolled and rolled, feeling the still slightly warm rock becoming cold and hard beneath their hands. Forward and back, forward and back, rolling and rolling and rolling, the rhythm of their movements seemed to Ellen to be like a dance routine, each one dependent on the other.

There was a specially designed cutter which was able to measure and cut the rock simultaneously, so it fell to Daisy, the girl who had previous experience, to be the first to handle this gadget, while Ellen and Lizzie, the other young girl, watched intently. Wrapping the rock, also, was not as easy as it seemed. There was a knack to it, Daisy told them importantly, as they watched her fingers deftly wrapping a stick of rock in its oblong of waxed paper. But Ellen and Lizzie soon mastered the operation and in due course all the sticks of rock made from this first boiling had been cut, wrapped and packed in cardboard boxes, ready for distribution.

Meanwhile, the sugar boilers, Ben and Bertie, were already repeating the process with their second boiling. And so it would go on, day in and day out, once the routine was mastered. Ben hoped to achieve seven or eight boilings a day, possibly more as time went on and they grew more used to working together as a team. For this second boiling, however, different colouring and flavouring were to be added; pale green colouring and, to go with it, a lime flavouring. Ben called to Ellen to come over and give her opinion when they reached that stage in the operation.

'I'm trying to get just the right shade,' he told her. 'Lime green – obviously – to go with the lime flavouring.' She watched in total absorption as he poured the colours on to the mass, first blue, just a little, then considerably more of the yellow, mixing them together with a wooden spatula.

'Primary colours – red, yellow and blue – that's all you need, is it, Ben?' asked Ellen. 'It's just like a paint-box, isn't it? I remember mixing colours together, just like that, when I was a little girl, trying to get the right shade.'

Ellen sounded like an excited little girl now and Ben looked up and grinned at her. 'Exactly the same process,' he said. 'And, as you say, it's all done with primary colours, apart from black. We'll need black for the lettering in the aniseed rock and the banana rock.' He had already told her that these were two lines he intended to introduce in the near future. He turned back to the task of colour mixing. 'Just a touch more blue, I think. That was a shade too yellowy. There … what do you think, Ellen?'

'I think that's just perfect,' said Ellen happily. 'And what about the lettering for this batch? Will that be green to match the outside? Or a darker green, maybe...'

'Traditionally it should be red,' Ben told her. 'You remember the rocks you bought from me last year – they all had red letters running through them. But there's nothing to stop us making our own traditions, is there? If you want dark green lettering, then that's what we shall have. After all, this is Bamber and Tucker's rock, isn't it? We can make our own rules.'

'I'll leave it to you, Ben,' replied Ellen, thinking that it should, by rights, be called Hobson's rock, not Bamber and Tucker's. But Ben was still adamant that he would not become a partner in the firm. 'Whatever you think best.'

'It had better be red lettering this time then,' said Ben. 'I've already mixed it, you see. But perhaps we'll change it another time. Our rock's going to make Blackpool sit up and take notice, I'm telling you, Ellen.'

Ellen hoped that, before long, it wouldn't be just Blackpool either.

As well as selling the rock in their own shop in Euston Street, Ben also managed to procure, in the first month, orders from several other sweet shops and stalls in the town. By this time he had not only the traditional pink rock to show to prospective customers, but lime rock, banana rock (cleverly striped in yellow and brown) and brown aniseed rock. He had insisted that if he was to secure orders from shops that were already dealing with his uncle, he must have something entirely different to offer. Roger

188

Redman had, so far, stuck uncompromisingly to mint, pineapple and lemon rocks, but Ben intended to be far more adventurous than that.

He was already thinking about an idea for Christmas. Rock with a Christmas tree running through it, green branches and a black trunk, and the outer casing could be any bright colour, he told Ellen. They might make a batch of each of several colours because by that time Ben hoped that their order book would be filling up nicely. It was summertime now and Ben was making use of the long daylight hours to advertise the firm for which he now worked. He travelled along the Fylde coast obtaining orders from neighbouring resorts – Lytham St Annes and, to the north, Fleetwood – for rock with the name of their own town running through it. He intended to go further afield eventually, as far as Yorkshire and North Wales, maybe, but Ellen knew that before this happened she would have to engage some more staff. Ben Hobson, willing though he was, couldn't be expected to do everything all on his own.

They needed at least one more pan man and another girl to assist in general duties. At the moment, however, Ellen was carefully balancing the budget. Both she and Lydia were more than satisfied with the good start they had made, but they still had to exercise caution. As her sister, Mary, had told her, you had to learn to walk before you could run. It would be ideal, Ellen thought, if they had someone to take sole charge of the accounts. For now, Ellen was doing it herself and, not being much of a mathematician, she wasn't finding it easy. Also, someone to do what Ben was so nobly trying to do, along with his other jobs, to travel the country making known the names of Bamber and Tucker; a commercial traveller – yes, that was what they needed. Ellen was always conscious, at the back of her mind, of Ben's criticism of his uncle's firm, that Roger Redman was too mean to employ enough staff, so that the firm was not flourishing as it should. Ellen knew that she must do all she could to improve the development of their own firm, but at the same time, try to curb extravagance. Running a business certainly wasn't going to be easy, but then she had never imagined that it would be.

Ben was still finding time to attend chapel on a Sunday and to run his Band of Hope meeting on a Tuesday evening. It was towards the end of June when he asked Ellen if she would like to accompany him. She delightedly agreed to do so, more because it was Ben who had invited her than because of any interest in the Band of Hope; it mattered little to her where they were going.

So far, she had met him only at work and at her home, where he was quite a frequent visitor at mealtimes. This, however, was more Lydia's doing than Ellen's. It was Lydia's belief that Ben's landlady, Mrs Banks, didn't feed him properly and that the poor lad – as skinny as a yard of pump water, she maintained – was in need of building up. And Ellen was always happy to concur with her mother's plans, while keeping her fondness for Ben well under control. So far,

Lydia didn't seem to have noticed her daughter's partiality towards the young man ... or so Ellen thought.

. She dressed carefully in her grey suit which had stood her in good stead for the last year or so, and with it she wore a new pink blouse with a high stand-up collar. As it was getting on for two years since William died, she was completely out of mourning and the brim of her straw hat was a riot of pink roses and ribbons. Too flamboyant? she wondered, eyeing herself critically in the hall mirror as she waited for Ben. Too frivolous, maybe, for the staid and soberly-dressed Methodists. But it wasn't as if she were joining their ranks, she told herself. She was only going to a meeting and the hat echoed her mood; she felt light-hearted and happy.

There was little that was light-hearted, however, about the meeting, and Ellen was glad when it was over.

Ben hardly mentioned the meeting as they walked home, talking instead about all sorts of matters. Motor cars, Ellen already knew, held a growing fascination for him, although he would not be able to afford one for a good while. A few were appearing now on the streets of the town, and jolly uncomfortable they looked, too, thought Ellen. The tram was still the most popular mode of travel in Blackpool, that or good old 'Shanks's pony'. Ellen was somewhat lost with Ben's chatter about Daimler and Ford, two-cylinder engines, horse power and miles per hour, but she couldn't help but ponder on how different he seemed away from the earnest atmosphere of the chapel. She had been quietly delighted when he had proffered his arm for her to hold as they walked back along Church Street.

It was almost as though he had read her thoughts when he quickly changed the subject away from motor cars. 'Do you know any Gilbert and Sullivan, Ellen?' he asked.

Ellen said that she did, but not as much as she would like to. She had heard selections played by the park band in Preston, and she had seen two of their works – *HMS Pinafore* and *The Mikado* – performed by amateur companies.

'*Iolanthe* is on next week at the Grand Theatre,' Ben said. 'And just to show you that I'm not always such an old sobersides, will you come with me?'

Ellen was ecstatic, and even more so when, saying good night to her at her gate, he gently kissed her on the cheek.

When Ellen answered the knock at the door one Sunday afternoon in August she was surprised to see a tall lanky figure standing there. She didn't, at first, recognise him, possibly because – to her subsequent chagrin – he hadn't been much in her thoughts of late. But when, after a few seconds, she identified the puzzled look in those mild blue eyes she gave a start of surprise.

'Good gracious! Amos, whatever are you doing here? I mean ... how nice to see you. Do come in. Yes, come along, Amos,' Ellen added as he hesitated on the doorstep. She pushed the door wide open, ushering him inside. 'My mother will be so pleased to see you, and Rachel and

Georgie. We're just finishing our dinner.'

They had, in fact, eaten their roast beef dinner, with apple pie to follow, and Lydia had gone into the kitchen to make a pot of tea. Not that it would have made any difference, Ellen smiled to herself, if they had been in the middle of their meal. It would never have occurred to Amos that to call at such a time might not be very convenient. Any embarrassment that he showed was because of his proximity to his idol, Ellen, rather than because he felt he was in the wrong place at the wrong time.

He shook his head when Ellen asked if he had had anything to eat, and didn't need any persuading to sit down at the dining table – still partially laid – and partake in the remnants of the roast beef, potatoes, cabbage and carrots, hastily warmed up by Lydia in the fireside oven. It wasn't until he had also eaten a huge wedge of apple pie and custard – part of tomorrow's dinner, thought Ellen, but what did it matter? – that they found out why he was there.

He wiped his mouth with the back of his hand, then, 'Lost me job,' he said, looking plaintively at Ellen.

'You mean ... Mr Wilkins, at the market stall?' asked Ellen.

'Aye, him and his missis, they've gone and given up the stall and the shop.' Amos went on to tell, quite coherently, how the greengrocer, who had long been troubled with his back, had finally decided to call it a day. 'They're getting on, of course; you can't blame 'em,' said Amos. 'But now I've got no job. The new folks didn't want

193

me. They've got three sons, y'see.'

Ellen knew she couldn't be so ill-mannered as to say, 'What do you expect me to do?' She thought she knew, anyway, what Amos wanted. He was not quite so 'green as he was cabbage-looking', to quote an expression of her mother's. 'And so you thought you'd come and see if you could find a job here, is that it, Amos?' said Ellen gently.

'Aye, if you'll have me, Mrs Bamber. I know you've got a rock factory. Our Phyllis has told me. Or if you don't want me, p'raps you know somebody as will. You know I'm a good worker, don't you? Anyroad, I had to come and see you.' He gave her a sidelong glance, full of the devotion she well remembered. 'I've missed you, you know, Mrs Bamber, and the nippers.'

Ellen found it amazing that he had managed to get himself on the train at Preston and then walk here from the Central Station, but Phyllis had written the address for him in block capitals and he had asked directions at the station. She made a snap decision.

'Yes, of course I can find you a job, Amos. As a matter of fact, we were needing another pan man. That's a sugar boiler,' she explained. 'You'll be learning how to make rock.' Ellen was aware of her mother's doubtful glance, but she gave her an admonitory frown which said quite clearly, *Leave it to me, Mam.* 'And it will mean that Ben – he's my, er, manager, you see, Amos, Ben Hobson will have more time to concentrate on other matters, orders and all that.'

'Eeh, thanks, Mrs Bamber. That 'ud be grand.

I knew you wouldn't let me down. I said to me mam, "Mrs Bamber'll find me a job, I know she will." And y'know me mam's always said–'

Ellen cut him short, mention of his mother reminding her that his home, at the moment, was in Preston, and that if he came to Blackpool he would have to find somewhere to live. 'You'll be wanting to get back home and tell her then, won't you? Perhaps you could start at the factory in the middle of next week, when you've found somewhere to live. You'll have to find digs, won't you, Amos?'

The lad stared at her in bewilderment. 'I wasn't reckoning on going back to Preston, Mrs Bamber. I've come to Blackpool. I've come to stay.' Ellen recalled now that he had been carrying a shabby hold-all when she opened the door. He must have left it in the hall.

'But where did you think you were going to sleep tonight?' Ellen was trying hard to be patient.

'Dunno.' Amos shrugged his shoulders. 'I s'pose as how I thought you'd find me somewhere.'

Ellen heard her mother's tut, then a sigh of exasperation, only a small one though, so it was doubtful that Amos had heard it. But if he had, it wouldn't have made any difference. He was looking at her with such trust that Ellen, though slightly vexed at the way he had landed on them like this, knew that she hadn't the heart to let him down.

'There's no room here, of course,' she told him very firmly, nipping in the bud any ideas he

195

might have about becoming one of the family. Enough was enough.

'No, I know that, Mrs Bamber. I know you've got your hands full, what with the kiddies and your mam an' all.'

Ellen suppressed a smile at the suggestion that her mother might be a liability and, venturing a glance at Lydia, was relieved to see that she was now chuckling quietly to herself. 'But I might be able to find you somewhere,' she said, trying to keep a straight face. 'My friend, Ben, he's in lodgings in Park Road, and I'm sure he said that his landlady had a room to let.'

'That's a good idea, our Ellen,' her mother joined in. 'Why don't you take Amos round there now and see what Mrs Banks says about it? And you might see Ben an' all. Is he coming for his tea today?'

'No, not today, Mother.' Ellen only addressed her as Mother, rather than Mam, when she was feeling peeved, and, judging by her raised eyebrows it hadn't escaped Lydia's notice now. 'I don't see him every Sunday, you know. He does have other things to do ... and so have I.'

'All right, love; I only asked,' said Lydia resignedly. 'But you'd best be off now with Amos. I'll see to the washing up, then I'll get the kiddies to Sunday School.'

'Thanks, Mam. I didn't mean ... well, thanks, anyway.' Ellen gave her mother an apologetic smile. 'I don't know what I'd do without you.'

'Hmm. Let's hope you don't have to, then,' answered Lydia brusquely. 'Come on now, you two,' she called to Rachel and Georgie who were

196

playing on the hearthrug with Georgie's toy farm. 'Help Gran to side these pots, there's good children.'

I shouldn't have snapped at Mam like that, thought Ellen, as she walked along Park Road with Amos at her side. It isn't her fault if Ben is … if Ben is … *what?* He couldn't be said to be cooling off, because he had never been all that warm in the first place. The visit to *Iolanthe* had been successful, inasmuch as they had both enjoyed the superb singing and acting; and that had been followed by a visit to the Music Hall, then to a concert of light classical music at the Tower Ballroom. Ben's interests, it seemed, were quite varied and he wasn't the fuddy-duddy that some might think him to be if they saw him in his Sunday, go-to-chapel suit with his Bible under his arm. Their relationship, however, had progressed no further than a kiss on the cheek and a touch of the hand; and Ellen was beginning to wonder if, after all, she might have been mistaken about his feelings for her.

Amos was quiet on the way to Mrs Banks's house and Ellen, deep in her own thoughts, was glad of that. It was Mrs Banks's bell that she rang when they arrived, not Ben's, and that lady was pleased to show Amos the one room she had to spare, especially as he was a friend of Ellen's. It was an attic room with a sloping roof and couldn't be called luxurious, but it was spacious enough and had all the necessary – though somewhat shabby – furniture, even a gas ring in the corner, as Ben's room had. From the look of delight on Amos's face Ellen gathered it would be the first time he had had any space to call his own. Arrangements were soon made and Ellen was surprised to see that Amos had enough money with him to pay for the room in advance, although Mrs Banks said that the end of the week would do. The young man had certainly matured in some respects since Ellen had left Preston. She remembered now how Mrs Wilkins had taken him in hand regarding money matters, and her tuition must have been successful.

They left him in the attic room delightedly sorting out his few belongings; and Mrs Banks, quickly weighing up the situation, promised Ellen she would keep a special eye on him. While they stood at the front door, Ellen explaining how Amos was to start work at the rock factory the next day, Ben appeared on the stairs. He gave a start when he saw Ellen; that was reasonable enough, Ellen supposed, because he hadn't been expecting to see her there, and he did, very quickly, smile a greeting and move towards her.

Mrs Banks disappeared into her own quarters at the back of the house while Ellen explained about Amos, how he had just arrived, out of the blue, and was now to be a fellow lodger with Ben.

'Oh yes ... the lad from Preston, from the clogger's shop,' Ben nodded. 'Yes, you told me about him. It's good of you to take him on, Ellen,' he said, when she told him about the job at the factory, but he sounded a little dubious. 'There's no reason why he shouldn't train as a sugar boiler – goodness knows, we could do with another pair of hands – but we'll have to watch him with the lettering.'

'Yes, I've thought of that,' replied Ellen, a little curtly. She was aware that Ben, dressed in his Sunday suit, with his bowler hat in his hands, kept glancing over his shoulder. The next minute she knew why, for along the passage came Lucy Banks, also dressed for going out, in a smart blue costume and straw hat trimmed with daisies and cornflowers. Their deep blue exactly matched the blue of her eyes, thought Ellen with a sudden stab of what could only be jealousy.

The young lady smiled charmingly at Ben. 'Sorry I've kept you waiting, Ben. Oh, hello, Ellen,' she added, as if she had only just noticed her standing there. Lucy's smile faded. 'I didn't realise...'

'Ellen's just brought us a new lodger,' Ben began to explain. Ellen had to admit to herself, when she thought about it later, that he didn't seem to be at all flustered. It was Lucy's proprietory air that disturbed her.

'We're going for a walk on the prom, aren't we, Ben?' she said, with a meaningful glance at Ellen. It was a glance that Ellen had noticed before on the few occasions that she had encountered Lucy.

'Yes, while it's a nice sunny day,' replied Ben easily.

'There's no young ladies' class this afternoon, then?' asked Ellen, trying to sound nonchalant.

'No, not in August. Too many folks on holiday, y'see, or else busy in their boarding houses. The children carry on meeting, but we don't. Come on, Ben.' Lucy touched his arm. 'Let's be going.'

Ellen walked with them along Park Road and

199

down Church Street. She could do no other as she was going the same way, but she politely refused Ben's guileless invitation to accompany them to the promenade. An invitation that didn't please Lucy one bit; the look in her blue eyes seemed to be challenging Ellen to accept if she dare! As Ellen turned the corner into King Street she glanced at the two figures crossing the road. Lucy, her black curls bobbing prettily beneath her straw hat, was clinging on to Ben's arm now. He was a good head taller than she was. Lucy, in fact, was short and dumpy – her figure could soon run to fat, like her mother's – and Ellen thought they looked silly together. Don't be spiteful, she quickly admonished herself. You're just jealous, that's all that's the matter with you, Ellen Bamber.

But she decided there and then that if she wanted to make sure of Ben Hobson, she would have to make a move – and quickly, too. Lucy Banks seemed like a very determined young lady. Ellen made a shrewd guess that it was Lucy who was making most of the running ... or could that be wishful thinking? At all events, Lucy would find that in Ellen she had more than met her match.

Chapter Ten

An added bonus for Lydia in coming to live in Blackpool had been the resumption of her friendship with Bella Broadbent. The two of them had been close friends as young women when they were neighbours in Sefton Street, but when Bella and her mother had moved to the seaside the friendship had waned. It had, however, not entirely died and the two women, now both fiftyish, found that they still had a lot in common.

Ellen, too, quite often visited Bella. She had taken to her at their first acquaintance when she had stayed at Bella Vista, and the older woman, who had never had any children, was beginning to look upon her as the daughter she had always wanted. Ellen hadn't made any close friends of her own age since moving to Blackpool, apart from Ben. He was, she supposed, the closest friend she had. She missed her sister, for Mary, though brusque, was someone in whom she had been able to confide. Now, in Mary's absence, Ellen was drawn more and more to the company of Bella. She was finding, increasingly, that she was able to talk to Bella much more freely than she could to her own mother. There was no one like Mam, of course, and there never would be, but Lydia had seemed withdrawn and uncommunicative of late, disinclined to chatter

201

as she had always loved to do. At all events, Ellen had never been able to confide in her mother about her feelings for Ben.

'It seems to me, my lass, that you're going to have to take the bull by the horns, so to speak,' said Bella to Ellen, on the Wednesday afternoon following the arrival of Amos. Wednesday afternoon was 'half-day closing' for the Blackpool shops and it was a time when Ellen tried to make sure she had an hour or two to herself. The children were playing with a schoolfriend of Rachel's, so now, ensconced in Bella's comfortable little parlour, she was able to talk freely. 'Put your cards on the table,' Bella went on, 'and tell him just how you feel.'

'But surely, if he had wanted me in any other way – apart from friendship – he'd have said something by now,' argued Ellen. Although she wasn't really arguing. She knew that what Bella said made sense. It was just a matter of plucking up courage.

'Not necessarily,' Bella replied. 'See here – you're his boss, aren't you? And he refused right at the start, to go into partnership with you. All credit to him for that, I say. But he happen thinks that it'll look as though he's after your money if he ... well, if he asks you to marry him. And that's what you want, isn't it?'

'Yes,' replied Ellen simply. 'Yes, that's what I want. But as for money, I haven't much of it, Bella. I've got the business – the factory and the shop and the stall now on the prom – and that's where most of the money has gone.'

'Well, there you are then. The money'll come

later, it's sure to. That's what I found with this place. Ben's in a tricky position, my love.'

'Yes, I can see that. But if I don't do something soon, Miss Lucy Banks certainly will. She's not what you'd call backward at coming forward.'

Bella grinned. 'Have you looked at the calendar, by any chance?'

Ellen frowned. 'What do you mean?'

'Aye, the calendar, lass. It's 1904. It's a leap year. Now do you see what I mean?'

Ellen gave a thoughtful smile. 'But February the twenty-ninth has gone, long ago, and I never gave it a thought at the time I must admit; it was too soon then, anyway. And that's the date you have to ask, isn't it?'

'Oh, I don't know about that. Any time'll do, won't it, if you're determined enough. And I think you are. I know one thing, Ellen – it would make your mother happy if you and Ben made a match of it.'

'Mam?' Ellen looked startled. 'Why, has she said...?'

'Oh yes.' Bella nodded sagely. 'She's very fond of Ben and she thinks he would be just right for you, especially after what you went through with William.'

'So you've been talking about me, have you?' Ellen raised her eyebrows, but she wasn't really annoyed. She had guessed that her mother would have spoken to Bella about her unhappy marriage.

'Only because we're concerned about you, lass,' answered Bella. 'And Lydia has said, more than once, how she would be able to die contented if

203

she knew you had a good husband.'

'Die!' shouted Ellen. 'Who's talking about dying? Good gracious, Mam's only just turned fifty.'

'Yes, yes, I know.' Bella held up a cautionary hand. 'It's just a figure of speech, that's all. But I rather think your mother's not been feeling any too well just lately. And that might have started her thinking.'

'What's the matter with her?' asked Ellen in alarm. 'She hasn't said anything to me.'

'Nor to me,' said Bella. 'She's a close one when it comes to her own ailments, is Lydia, and I won't pry. But I shouldn't imagine it's anything more serious than feeling tired. From what I can gather, she's worked harder than ever since coming to Blackpool. I did advise her to have a drink of Guinness now and again to buck her up. It works wonders, as far as I'm concerned. I don't know whether she's taken any notice though... Sorry, Ellen,' she added. 'I know you don't approve, but it's what I would do.'

Ellen gave a wry smile. 'Each to his own, I suppose. Yes, she may well have done, in her own room. She does like to be on her own sometimes and I respect her privacy. And if it'll make her feel better, then who am I to object?' Ellen looked thoughtfully at the older woman, her brown eyes anxious.

'Now don't you go worrying unduly,' Bella soothed. 'Like I said, she's probably just tired, and I daresay you've been too busy yourself to notice. I was thinking of asking her to have a night out with me soon, to the Music Hall, maybe.'

'Yes, that's a great idea,' said Ellen. 'It would do her a world of good. She doesn't get out enough. Maybe I have been expecting too much of her,' she added pensively. 'She's still making just as much toffee as she ever did, and working in the shop as well. Oh dear, I feel awful now. I did notice she was a bit ... well, quiet like, but nothing else.'

'I've told you, lass, don't fret. Lydia'll have the good sense to call a halt when it gets too much for her. Now, I think it's about time I started seeing to the visitors' teas. We're full up this week. That's good, isn't it, Ellen?'

'It is indeed,' smiled Ellen, rising from her chair. 'I saw the No Vacancies sign in the window. Thanks for the tea, Bella, and for listening to me. It's good to have somebody to talk to.'

'Take heed of what I've said then.' Bella wagged a reproving finger at her. 'Get things sorted out with that nice young man. It's about time I bought myself a new hat,' she added, chuckling.

Ellen decided to waste no more time. Bella, as she had promised, quickly made arrangements with Lydia to go to the Music Hall the following Saturday, and so, on the same evening, Ellen invited Ben to come to the house for supper.

It was one thing, however, to be quietly confident in his absence, but Ellen found, when she was alone with Ben, that her courage began to wane. Ben ate heartily from the spread of cold meats and pickles, sausage rolls and meat pies that Ellen had prepared, while she was scarcely able to pick at the food. She had already eaten at teatime with her mother and the children, but that was not the reason for her lack of appetite. She was just plain scared. And when she had cleared away the pots, to wash up later, and was settled in the sitting room with Ben, both of them with a cup of tea on their laps, she felt even worse. To her dismay, she found her hand shaking as she lifted the cup and the tea slopped over into the saucer. Quickly she put it down on the table at her side, but not before Ben had noticed her discomfiture.

'Is there something the matter Ellen?' he asked, likewise putting down his cup of tea and leaning forward in his easy chair. 'You seem ... I don't know, ill at ease, somehow.'

'No ... I mean, yes. Yes, I suppose I am. There's nothing the matter, not really, Ben, but...'

'Come on, Ellen,' he said gently. 'What is it? You can tell me.'

'I don't know if I can, Ben.' Ellen shook her head. 'You see, I asked you to come here tonight because ... because I wanted to tell you something. No ... to ask you something, I mean, and now I don't think I can.'

'Yes, I thought that might be why you'd asked me.' Ben nodded seriously. 'Because you'd something important to say. And I think I've a pretty good idea what it is...'

'What! What d'you mean? How can you have?' Ellen stared at him in astonishment. 'Why, what do you think?'

Ben smiled ruefully. 'I don't know exactly what's in your mind, Ellen, but it must be something fairly drastic or you wouldn't be so agitated. What is it, love?' It was the first time he had ever used that endearment, and though she knew it was most probably just a casual turn of phrase, such as many people used in the North, Ellen felt heartened by it. 'Are you worried about the business?' Ben continued. 'Or are you trying to tell me that you want to ... to appoint a different manager? Dispense with my services, maybe.'

'What!' cried Ellen for the second time, but this time she burst out laughing. Suddenly, her nervousness seemed to be on the wane, dispelled by the concern on Ben's face. Surely he couldn't have thought... 'Oh no, nothing like that, Ben. How could you think such a thing? You know I'd have been in a hopeless mess without you. No, it was just the opposite.' Ellen summoned up all her courage, reassured by Ben's kindly questioning smile. It was now or never. 'I wanted to ask you, Ben...' she looked straight into his warm brown eyes, 'if you would...' her voice faltered a little, 'if you would ... marry me?'

'*What!*' Now it was Ben's turn to shout the exclamation. 'Oh, Ellen, my Ellen.' He rose from his chair and knelt on the floor at her feet, taking both her hands in his own. 'I just don't know what to say. I'm overwhelmed. To think that you—'

'You mean that you...?' Ellen faltered.

'I mean that I will, my darling. Of course I will marry you. Come here.' Very tenderly he cupped her face in his hands and, leaning forward, his lips met hers for the very first time. It was just a gentle kiss at first, increasing in ardour as he felt her response; then their arms were round one another as they laughed – Ellen with relief as well as delight – then kissed, then laughed again.

'Ben...' 'Ellen...' They both spoke at once, before they joyously kissed again.

'I'm only sorry, my darling, that it was you who had to ask me,' said Ben, loosing his hold of her and gently taking her hand. 'No, I'm not sorry, I'm glad, so very glad. What I mean is, I was going to ask you, but I felt that I couldn't, not yet, for one or two reasons.'

'Because I'm your boss?' Ellen's eyes twinkled into Ben's. 'I never wanted to be, you know. How many times have I asked you to be a partner, along with me and my mother? Well, now you can't refuse, can you? I only hope you don't think I was being too forward,' she added quietly. 'It took some courage, I can tell you.'

'And that's something you're not short of, my love,' said Ben. 'I knew that the first time I met you. A quiet courage, that doesn't make a song and dance about things, and that's the best sort. Of course I don't think you're forward. As I said, I only wish now that I'd asked you myself, that I hadn't waited so long.

'It wasn't just because you're my employer. Partly that, I suppose, but I've been saving up, Ellen, and I set myself a target. Fifty pounds. I made up my mind that when I'd saved up fifty pounds I would ask you to marry me. Not a fortune, but it would be a start at least, I thought. And I'm nearly there.'

'Then ... ask me now, Ben,' said Ellen in a whisper. Her eyes, brown like Ben's, but of a darker hue, looked deep into his.

'Oh Ellen, my darling.' Ben once more knelt on the floor at her feet. 'Will you marry me?'

'Yes, I will be honoured to marry you, Ben,' replied Ellen. Then, a few moments later: 'What about Lucy?'

'What about her?' repeated Ben, his eyes laughing into Ellen's. 'Is that why you asked me, all in a hurry, because you saw us together?'

'No,' replied Ellen, too quickly, then, 'Well ... yes, I suppose so.' She knew she would never be able to lie to Ben, not even a white lie. 'I think she fancies you, Ben, doesn't she?'

He chuckled. 'Perhaps she imagines she does. She's only young, you know. She can't be more than eighteen.' Plenty old enough, Ellen reflected, remembering that she had been only seventeen when she married William. 'I bumped into her last Sunday on the way back from chapel, and she started dropping hints about what a nice day it was, just right for a stroll on the prom. So I thought, what's the harm, she's a pleasant sort of lass. Don't worry about Lucy, my darling. I'll tell her – about you and me.'

'Break it to her gently, please Ben.'

'Of course I will.' His arms encircled her again. 'That's one of the things I love about you. You're so concerned about everyone's feelings. And, do you know, I don't believe I've told you yet that I love you. I love you, Ellen ... so very much.'

'And I love you too, Ben.'

They were still there an hour later when Lydia returned from her evening out. She knocked at the sitting-room door before entering. 'Hello,

Ben,' she said. 'Nice to see you, lad,' then she looked questioningly at the couple, a broad smile spreading across her face.

'Mam.' Ellen sprang to her feet. 'Ben and I ... we've got something to tell you.'

'And no prizes neither for guessing what it is,' said Lydia. 'I can tell by looking at you, the pair of you; it's written all over your faces.'

'Yes, Mrs Tucker,' Ben grinned. 'I expect you've guessed right. I've asked Ellen to marry me, and she's said yes.'

'Then I'm delighted for both of you.' A tear was glistening in the corner of Lydia's eye and she hastily brushed it away. 'When's it going to be? Not long, I hope.'

The happy couple looked at one another. 'We hadn't decided, had we, love?' said Ben. 'But soon, I expect. What do you think, Ellen?'

'Yes, soon,' she nodded. 'There's no point in waiting too long, is there?'

'Yes, make it soon, lass,' said Lydia, and as she looked imploringly at her daughter a shadow seemed to fall across her face. Ellen felt a stab of fear.

'I'll go and make myself a cup of tea,' said Lydia hastily, disappearing in the direction of the kitchen.

'Is she all right?' mouthed Ben.

'I think so,' Ellen whispered back. 'Just a bit overcome, I daresay.'

Lydia's voice reached them a moment later. 'Well, would you believe it? They've not even done the washing up.'

Ellen clasped her hand to her mouth as her

mother re-entered the room. 'Oh, Ben, I forgot! How dreadful of me. I'm sorry, Mam!'

'I reckon you've had other things to occupy you.' Lydia, all smiles, seemed to be her cheerful self again. 'Ne'er mind the mucky pots. We'll have a cup of tea together, then me and our Ellen'll tackle 'em. Not you, Ben, not tonight, but I daresay you'll be sharing the workload, won't you, when the pair of you get wed? You seem the sort as will, especially with you working together at the factory.'

'Mam!' admonished Ellen. 'Really!'

But Ben didn't seem a mite put out. 'There's nothing more sure than that, Mrs Tucker,' he laughed. 'I'll never expect Ellen to fetch and carry for me. I've seen too much of that with my own father, expecting my mother to wait on him hand and foot.'

'That's all right then,' nodded Lydia. 'Now don't you think it's time you called me Mam? Or Lydia. Either'll do; I don't mind. I'll go and see to that cup of tea.' She paused in the doorway and looked back at them, a twinkle in her eye. 'I don't suppose it's any use expecting something a bit ... er, stronger to drink your health in, is it? Not with you two.'

'Not a bit of it, *Mam*,' laughed Ben. 'A cup of tea'll do as well as anything.'

It was a late October wedding and Ellen, as she entered the Methodist chapel on the arm of her brother-in-law, Fred, knew that this was the happiest day of her life. The happiest day so far, that is, because there would be many more happy

211

days ahead with dear Ben as her husband.

She felt quite at home now in Ben's place of worship, which was why she had opted to get married there in preference to the Church of England. She loved the homely feel of it all. The solid oak pews; the rich colours of the stained glass – not too much of it, though; many of the windows were of frosted glass, designed to let the light in on their worship, the simple wooden cross on the Communion table; and the telling words, written in black and gold, on the wall behind it: *Jesus Christ, the same yesterday and today and forever.* There was a gallery round three sides of the building, a feature, again, that Ellen was unused to, but which the Methodists seemed to favour; and sometimes on a Sunday morning the gallery, as well as the lower pews, were filled to capacity. And never in her life had Ellen heard such singing as issued from the throats of hundreds of ardent worshippers praising their Lord. It was a wonder that the roof didn't lift off.

They were singing now as Ellen walked down the aisle with Fred, her matron-of-honour, Mary, following behind them. The chapel was not full today, of course, but there was a goodly number there, mainly chapel members come to share in their happiness, enough to make a creditable sound.

'*Praise my soul, the King of Heaven...*' They were singing the hymn chosen down through the years by hundreds of brides. But Ellen, as she reached the chancel steps and her husband-to-be stepped forward to meet her, was aware of nothing but the love shining from Ben's eyes. She thought again how happy she was and how very lucky to have found Ben. No; lucky was not the right word. She glanced up at the black-suited minister standing in front of them, the representative of God. She was blessed; that was what she was, blessed and favoured to have found a husband such as Ben.

'You look beautiful, my darling,' he whispered to her later, as they made their way into the nearby hall where the ladies of the chapel had prepared a wedding breakfast for them. Ellen was too overcome, just at that moment, by the beauty of the service and the sheer wonder of what had happened – she and Ben were now man and wife – to trust herself to speak. She squeezed his hand, which already had hers firmly in his grasp, as she smiled her thanks at him.

She knew that she looked well in the outfit that she, with Lydia's help, had chosen, and she felt that it was fitting, too, for someone who had been married before. Her mother had insisted that she must be a 'real bride' in a dress that was as near as possible to a wedding dress, although they were both agreed that white or even a pale cream, would not be seemly. Together they had scoured the rails of Donnelly's gown department until they had found just what they were looking for. There were so many beautiful gowns to choose from, but pink, Lydia had declared, was too skittish, green was unlucky, blue was not Ellen's colour (not with her brown eyes), mauve was a mourning colour and she had, thank God, put all that behind her, and brown and maroon were too heavy... The poor sales assistant had looked as though her patience was at a very low ebb when they had finally chosen the outfit that Ellen was now wearing on her wedding day.

It was what was termed a 'visiting costume' – a princess-line dress in a dull yellow silk, high-necked with a collarless bolero jacket and elbow-length sleeves gathered into wide cuffs. She wore a circlet of deeper yellow artificial flowers on her fair hair and carried a spray of tiny roses and chrysanthemums in gold, orange and russet – the colours of autumn – with her new cream leather-backed Bible, a present from Ben. Mary's outfit, in deep gold, and her mother's, in a similar shade, complemented her own. Many folk said what a fashionable trio they looked as they posed in the hall for photographs, together with Ben and Fred, and Ben's brother, Alec, who was acting as best man. Ben's parents, of course, were on the group photograph as well, his father on his best behaviour today, and his mother unusually smart in her new brown coat which Ben had insisted on buying for her.

Ellen wouldn't have made nearly so much fuss over her wedding dress as Lydia had insisted upon; it was enough, for her, to be marrying Ben. But she had felt that she must indulge her mother this once. Lydia, it seemed, was set on living life to the full just lately. Ellen and Bella were having a job to keep up with her enthusiasm and her desire to be here, there and everywhere. The visit to the Music Hall, back in August, had been followed by several such outings; in the shop, too, she was brimful of new ideas. Mary, on a short visit to Blackpool for the wedding, had noticed her mother's bouts of chaotic activity. She had noticed, too, because she hadn't seen her for a while, Lydia's slight loss of weight, her pinched cheeks and the feverish, almost frenzied look which was sometimes discernible in her still bright brown eyes. But Lydia had avowed to Mary, as she had continually done to Ellen, that she was perfectly all right, just working hard and 'not getting any younger'.

Ellen hadn't needed much persuading to leave her two children in her mother's care whilst she and Ben had a honeymoon. They all lived in the same house anyway, and Rachel and Georgie had always been reasonably well-behaved children. Georgie, as well as Rachel, was now at school as he would be five in a few months' time, so Ellen had no fears that her mother would not be able to cope.

It had been a morning wedding with an early lunchtime meal, so arranged because the happy couple were embarking on a lengthy train journey; all the way across country from the west coast to the east coast, to the rival seaside resort of Scarborough. Ellen had found her tongue again by the time they embarked from Central Station; she had been unusually quiet through-out the wedding celebrations, a quietness that stemmed from serenity rather than reticence. Now she chattered happily to Ben about the events of the day; their respective families and friends, how pleasant and kindly the minister had been, what a grand spread the chapel ladies had put on for them, and about how she was looking forward so much to seeing Scarborough for the first time. It was a place she had never visited and Ben had been only once. Towards the end of the journey, however, Ellen was tired and she nodded against Ben's shoulder, his arm protectively surrounding her. From York, onwards to the coast, they had the carriage to themselves.

Dusk had fallen by the time they arrived. They hired a cab to take them from the station to their small hotel on the north bay, just where the road inclined steeply towards the castle. Shyness, fear almost, threatened to overcome Ellen as they unpacked their belongings in the bedroom overlooking the sea and had a quick wash in the hot water thoughtfully provided by their landlord. Thoughts of William and of what she had suffered at his hands, though they did not loom large, were, nevertheless, niggling at the back of her mind as her wedding night drew ever nearer. But they were dispelled by Ben's cheerful smile and easy chatter, then by his tender kiss – several kisses – before they went downstairs to enjoy the meal that Mrs Boothroyd had prepared for them; a tasty steak and kidney pie which she had kept warm for them in the oven. The other guests, who had arrived earlier, had already dined and departed. There were only two other couples, Mrs Boothroyd informed them, as it was so late in the year. Many of the other hotels and boarding houses in the town had already closed down, but she liked to keep open for late-season visitors. Ben and Ellen had chosen the small hotel at random from the list in the guide book, but they knew at once that they had been fortunate in their choice.

Ben remembered the way around, though only vaguely, from his previous visit. Hand in hand they walked through the almost deserted streets, round the back of the castle, past the magnificent bulk of the Grand Hotel, then across the Spa Bridge. As they looked back from the cliff path towards the harbour Ellen thought it was like viewing a scene from a picture book. The sea was almost black, with just a few white-capped waves, the horizon where the night sky met the ocean almost invisible; but here and there were shimmers of gold as the lights around the bay, like shining jewels on a necklace, were reflected in the inky depths of the sea. And above it all, black against the sky, the silhouette of the castle ruins.

'Oh, it's enchanting,' breathed Ellen. 'Isn't it, Ben? Just like something from a fairy story. I don't think I've ever seen anywhere as beautiful.'

'Glad you like it, love.' Ben leaned towards her and kissed her cheek. His lips were warm against the coldness of her face; there was a chilly wind blowing here, as there so often was in their home town. 'I thought you'd like Scarborough; that's why I suggested it.'

'Mmm... Much more beautiful than Blackpool, isn't it?' said Ellen wistfully.

'Yes, I suppose so.' Ben's reply was somewhat grudging. 'But you know what they always say – "There's no place like home." And I happen to be sand grown, not like some folks I could mention who have emigrated from foreign parts like Preston.'

Ellen laughed up at him, then she gave a shiver.

'Come on, Ben. Let's get back, shall we? It's a bit nippy, to say the least. I think Scarborough's even colder than Blackpool, but I can't wait to see what it all looks like in the daylight.'

'I can't wait either,' whispered Ben, drawing her closer to him, and she knew that he was not referring to the daytime view of Scarborough. Her heart gave a lurch and, once again, that prickle of anxiety returned.

A couple of hours later, as she lay in Ben's arms, with the moonlight streaming through the window, across their bed and on to their naked arms and shoulders, Ellen knew that she need not have feared. Ben had drawn back the curtains to let the light in upon their love-making, and, as soon as he touched her, her fears had vanished. This time it was so very, very different; so tender and loving, the meeting together of not only two bodies, but two minds, two souls. And Ellen realised, as she had suspected it might be, that for Ben it was the very first time. Indeed it was she who, now and again, found that she was taking the lead, and she did so willingly and joyously.

'I love you, Ellen,' said Ben. 'More than ever now. I never dreamed…'

'Nor did I, my love,' replied Ellen. 'Nor did I. Thank you, Ben, for making it all so perfect.'

It was a memorable week in which they enjoyed the many delights of Scarborough. The cliff-path walks; the elegant shops, the colourful harbour and the stalls selling sea food – the salty, fishy tang which always hung in the air there seemed, to Ellen, to epitomise this resort which relied so much on fishing for its livelihood; the trees in the wooded valleys in all the glory of their autumn foliage, and the comical ducks and water geese which waddled from the mere just outside the town to snatch at the bounty freely distributed by visitors.

These things alone would have provided them with memories to last a lifetime, but as if that were not enough, Ben decided that, as they were so near, they must visit the city of York. Ellen was entranced all over again. Firstly, by the magnificence of the railway station; she stared in wonder at the sweeping curve of the high glass roof, supported by wrought-iron pillars, and at the huge snorting monsters of engines, hauling dozens of carriages from places as far away as London, Glasgow or Edinburgh.

'Come on, we can't stay here all day,' Ben teased, pulling at her arm as she gazed, mesmerised, at the bustle and activity going on around them. 'But we're in for a treat if York's half as grand as its railway station.'

It proved to be every bit as grand. It was Ben's first visit as well as Ellen's, and they knew that they could have done with a week or even a month, not a day, to appreciate the city. They loved it all. The Shambles, where the jettied buildings hung so far across the cobbled street as to almost touch; the medieval gates (called bars); the wide River Ouse flowing through the heart of the town; and, above all, the awesome Minster, its Gothic majesty towering over the narrow streets and old city walls. Enough memories, again, to last a whole lifetime.

It was a profitable week too. Ellen had laughed

out loud, shouting with mock disbelief, when Ben had drawn from his suitcase ... samples of rock, in a variety of colours and flavours with which they had been experimenting recently.

'You'll see I'm right, my girl, when the orders start rolling in,' Ben grinned at her. And, of course, he was right as Ben invariably was. He obtained two firm orders that week from shops in the resort, and half-promises of several more. Ellen was confident that the staff they had left behind in Blackpool would cope admirably in their absence. All the same, she knew that when their idyllic week came to an end, Ben would have no regrets about taking up his place at the helm once again. And she knew that she was coming to rely on him more and more.

Ellen's fears regarding her mother's health were not groundless, although it wasn't until the January of the following year, 1905, that Lydia finally admitted that she ought to see a doctor. By that time, alas, it was too late. The growth which Lydia had discovered – and tried to ignore – had taken too firm a hold of her. The operation was not successful and she died at home three months later, at the beginning of April.

'But why, why?' Ellen cried, as she had done so many times over the past few months, when the sad, sad events were at last over and Lydia had been laid to rest in the cemetery at Layton. 'Why did she leave it so late? If only she had done something earlier she might still be here. It seems so unfair. Mam was only fifty-one. It's too young, Ben, too young to die. When William died...' she didn't often mention him, but it seemed apposite now '...it was his own fault. He was drunk. But this ... I find it hard to accept, Ben.'

'I know, my love.' Ben put his arms around her as they sat gazing into the embers of the fire. It had been a bitterly cold April day, when spring seemed as far away as ever. 'It's hard for us to understand. But your mother would never accept illness, would she? I hadn't known her for very long, just a little more than a year, but I never knew her to have a day in bed, or ever to complain of feeling poorly. Perhaps it's as well it happened so quickly. She wouldn't have liked being an invalid.'

'No.' Ellen shook her head sadly. 'She had no patience with illness. I remember, as a little girl, we were never encouraged to feel sorry for ourselves, Mary and I.'

'You'll miss her, love.' Ben stroked Ellen's hair as she leaned against his shoulder. 'Not just because she was your mam. We'll both miss her, in the shop ... and everything.'

Ellen knew that Ben was thinking of the toffee-making which, inevitably, had suffered over the last few months. Ellen had done her utmost to keep up with both the fudges and the toffees, whilst Ben concentrated on the rock, but it had been hard going. They had employed a few more staff, but there was no one as yet to compare with Lydia as far as the making of sweets was concerned. It was becoming more and more of a family concern, but Ben's family now, not Ellen's. His sister, Dora, was now serving in the shop and his younger brother, Sam, who had recently left school, was a trainee pan man along with Amos Hardy. Which left only Millie, still at school, who also hoped to join the firm eventually.

Ellen was thinking of them now. Good workers, all of them, but none of them with the same flair or initiative as Ben possessed. Sometimes, though, the most unlikely people could rise to a challenge. Look at her own sister, Mary, now running the business in Preston so competently; and it was Mary who had once said she would never be able to master the art of toffee-making.

'Ben,' said Ellen thoughtfully, 'what about your mother?' Thoughts of her own mother had led her, automatically, to think of Ben's, a very different sort of person, however, from Lydia. But maybe... 'Has she never thought of getting herself a little job? We could do with an extra pair of hands in the factory, and it might do her good to get out a bit more. Don't you think so?'

Ellen, in fact, often found herself becoming impatient with Gertie Hobson, a downtrodden little woman if ever there was one. She couldn't help but like her. Ben's mother had the same loving nature as her son, as well as the same toffee-coloured eyes and golden-brown hair, now somewhat faded, but she possessed none of his personality or drive. Her husband was a drunken bully, admittedly, but, as Ellen knew from experience, that didn't mean that you had to allow your own identity to be submerged. Gertie Hobson could help herself a lot more, if she would.

'Ellen, my love!' Ben was staring at her in

222

delighted surprise. 'I never cease to be amazed at the way you take the words right out of my mouth. What do they say? Great minds think alike. Yes, I think it would be a splendid idea for my mother to come and work along with us. We might even get her interested in toffee-making. She's a good cook, you know. The reason I hadn't suggested it...' He hesitated. 'Well, I didn't want you to think that the Hobsons were taking over. There are three of us involved already. After all, it was your business, yours and your mother's.'

'Four of us, Ben,' said Ellen firmly.

'What d'you mean, love?'

'Four Hobsons, Ben. Don't you forget that I'm a Hobson now, and very proud to be one, too.' She leaned forward and kissed him soundly on the lips. 'And, what is more, I think it's high time we changed our name. Bamber and Tucker ... it doesn't apply any longer, does it?' She looked pensive for a moment. 'Well, does it?'

'It's served us very well, love. It's a name that a lot of people know. Besides, what's in a name?'

'A great deal, Ben. And I know that we've got to change it. Hobson's Rock – that's what we're going to be from now on. Come on, admit it. You've no choice.'

Ben laughed. 'That's good, Ellen, although you probably haven't realised what you said. You've heard of Hobson's choice, haven't you?'

Ellen smiled, a little unsurely. 'Yes, I think so. Doesn't it mean that you've really no choice at all?'

'Precisely.' Ben clasped his hands together in a confident gesture. 'And once folks have tasted our rock they know that there's none to compare with it. In fact, no choice at all.'

Ellen pursed her lips. 'How about "Hobson's Rock", and then our very own slogan: "The only choice"?'

'Hobson's Rock – The only choice,' repeated Ben. 'Yes, I like it.' He hugged Ellen and kissed her decisively. 'Yes, I like it very much indeed.'

Chapter Eleven

'But surely it can't mean that we're going to be involved in it as well,' argued Ellen. 'Not Great Britain. It doesn't make sense.'

Ben smiled ruefully. 'War never does make sense, my love, not in my book, but it's beginning to look that way, I'm afraid.'

It was the end of July 1914, and rumours of war were becoming too insistent to be ignored. Ellen, engrossed in the fast-growing business of Hobson's Rock (The Only Choice) and in her happy home life had, like most women, paid little heed to the events that were taking place in Europe and even farther afield. It would all be sorted out by the politicians, she had believed. Why else were they there, if not to get their heads together and prevent a war? But now it seemed that that was not possible.

'Explain it to me, will you, Ben?' Ellen put down her knitting – another pair of socks for fourteen-year-old George, whose over-large feet were constantly pushing through the toes – and leaned back in her easy chair. 'Tell me what it's all about because I'm blessed if I know. Yes, I suppose I should read the newspapers more and try to keep up with what's happening, but it's all so complicated. And I suppose I've been burying my head in the sand,' she added, 'thinking that it could never happen.'

'Haven't we all?' agreed Ben. He leaned his head back against the cushion and sighed, thoughtfully drumming his fingers on the chair arm. 'It all boils down to the fact that the countries of Europe – some of them, at any rate – seem to hate each other so much. Look at France and Germany, for instance. There was a war between them in the last century – about 1870, I think; that's more than forty years ago – but feelings are still running high. Germany won, you see, and took the provinces of Alsace and Lorraine away from France. So I suppose France is bound to feel bitter.'

'Yes, I think I can understand that,' said Ellen. 'I daresay we'd feel bitter, wouldn't we, if Lancashire and Yorkshire, for instance, were taken away from us?'

'Quite,' Ben smiled. 'So France is waiting for a chance to get her provinces back, and Germany is determined to stop her.'

'But there are other problems as well, aren't there? Other countries at loggerheads?'

'Oh yes. There's Turkey – she once had a large empire, but she's lost it. And there's Russia wanting to get her hands on the land near the Black Sea, and Austria-Hungary determined to stop her. They're old enemies, you see, Russia and the Austro-Hungarian Empire.'

'But what about allies?' asked Ellen. 'They can't all hate one another, surely.'

'No, of course not. Germany and Austria-Hungary are allies. So are Russia and France. So you see, my love, that means that if any of them start a war the others are honour-bound to join in.'

Ellen shook her head bemusedly. 'I still don't see what it's got to do with us, Great Britain.'

'Two things, I suppose,' replied Ben. 'We've always promised to defend Belgium, and if the Germans attack her – they have to go through Belgium, you see, to get to France – then we'll have to declare war on them. And it seems as if they're going to do just that. Also, apart from the Belgium issue, I'm afraid we'll have to defend ourselves against Germany. She's becoming too much of a threat. Kaiser William is very jealous of our empire.'

'But he's the King's cousin, isn't he?' argued Ellen. 'He'll hardly want to go to war against his cousin!'

'That's what we might think,' said Ben, 'but he's busy building a powerful navy, strong enough to challenge ours. The way I see it, Europe's like a huge firework. The assassination of Franz Frederick last month – you remember? – was just the first spark that was needed to set it all alight. Austria-Hungary said it was a plot hatched in Serbia, so they attacked her. Russia defended her, then France joined in, and so...'

'And so Bob's your uncle,' said Ellen, smiling grimly.

'Exactly, my love. What began as a little war looks like spreading all over Europe.'

'But if it does, if we do have to join in...' Ellen was suddenly fearful '...you wouldn't have to go, would you, Ben?' The thought of losing her beloved husband to the horrors of war was unbearable.

'I wouldn't want to, but I'm afraid it would be

a question of needs must, Ellen. It wouldn't be what we want to do – any of us – but it would be our duty.'

Ellen looked at her husband pleadingly. 'I don't think there's anyone in the world I know better than I know you, and I would have sworn, if I'd been asked, that you would refuse to join up, that you would want nothing to do with anything as horrible as war.'

'You thought I would be a pacifist, you mean?' Ben shook his head sadly. 'Conscientious objectors, that's what they're calling them now. No, my darling. You're right, of course, in saying that I would find it horrible. But the way I see it, Great Britain does have a cause to answer; we can't let other nations ride roughshod over us. And you must know that I've always been fiercely patriotic.'

Ellen smiled in spite of herself. 'Yes, I remember the red, white and blue rock for King George's Coronation.' That innovative idea of Ben's had proved very popular, as did most of his ideas. 'But there will be a lot of men much younger than you, love. You're thirty-four; not old, I know, but certainly no spring chicken. Don't you think you should let the younger lads go first?'

'Let's not cross our bridges, Ellen,' replied Ben. 'We'd better just wait and see what happens. I've heard it said that if it does come to war it may not last long. It may be all over before I have a chance to get involved.'

'Let's hope so,' Ellen sighed. 'I'm only thankful that our Georgie is too young. He's only fourteen so there'll be no danger of him having to go.'

'No, my love, but he'll soon be old enough to join the firm, won't he?' Ben pointed out. 'And he seems keen enough to do so. Let's think about pleasant things, Ellen, and let the future take care of itself. There's little we can do about it anyway.'

'And it might never happen,' said Ellen, trying to be optimistic again.

But her hopes were soon dashed. Only a few days later, on 4 August, Great Britain joined the conflict. Ellen read in the newspaper the pessimistic words of Sir Edward Grey, the Foreign Secretary. 'The lights are going out all over Europe; we shall not see them lit again in our lifetime,' he had declared on the evening of 3 August, after watching a lamp-lighter at work in Green Park. Ellen couldn't help but share in his sense of foreboding; after all, he should know. But the vast majority of his countrymen didn't seem so dispirited. 'It'll all be over by Christmas,' was the cry on many lips.

It wasn't until January 1915 that Ben Hobson felt compelled to answer the call of the recruiting posters which were appearing on walls and advertisement hoardings all over Blackpool, and, no doubt, in every town and city in the land.

Have you a reason or only an excuse for not enlisting? one of the posters demanded. *100,000 men are needed at once to add to the ranks of the new armies... Age on enlistment – 19–38 years.*

Ben knew only too well that that included him. Most compelling of all was the poster depicting Lord Kitchener with his pointing, accusing finger. *Your country needs YOU.*

Ellen knew that it would be futile – wrong, indeed – for her to argue, and so Ben signed up to join the ranks of the Loyal Regiment which was stationed at Preston, her own home town. The thought of him going away filled Ellen with dread. They were, after nine years of marriage, just as much in love as ever – more, in fact, Ellen often thought, and they sought little company apart from their own two selves. And Rachel and Georgie, of course; the two children had been fond of Ben right from the start and had very quickly made the adjustment from 'Uncle' to 'Daddy'. Or 'Dad' now, as they were both growing up. Rachel, aged sixteen, was quite a young lady and a very attractive one, too. Ben and Ellen had got over their initial disappointment at not having any children of their own. Why this had not come to pass they had no idea, but as it had left Ellen free to concentrate on the business and as Ben had acquired a readymade family, it had ceased to worry them.

A couple of nights before Ben left for the barracks in Fulwood they decided to have a night out at the Empire Theatre in Church Street, a mere stone's throw from their home. This was quite a rare occurrence for Ellen and Ben. Apart from Sunday attendance at chapel, and occasional midweek chapel functions such as concerts and socials – and the Band of Hope meetings which Ben was still enthusiastically leading – they didn't go out a great deal. On most evenings, especially in the winter, they preferred the comfort of their own fireside. Ben had thought that an evening at the Music Hall would be a pleasant diversion, one which would take their minds off their imminent separation, for a short time at least.

Ellen, however, as she sat in the red plush seat in the front stalls, felt very dispirited, not in the mood at all for the over-hilarious comedians, the acrobats, jugglers, dancers and performing poodles. This theatre in its hey-day had seen such performers as Marie Lloyd, Dan Leno and Nellie Wallace, but there was no one of such renown performing that evening. In the darkness she held tightly to Ben's hand, trying to smile at him from time to time as he felt his glance upon her, and fighting to stem the tears that were pricking at her eyelids. Whatever would she do without her beloved Ben? How she would miss him!

The young girl soprano who took the stage near the end of the show didn't look more than seventeen or so. Ellen found herself taking more interest – the performance so far had left her unmoved – because the girl in the pale blue crinoline dress, reminiscent of a style worn some sixty years ago and her wide-brimmed matching bonnet looked something like Rachel. A little like herself, too, Ellen supposed – Ellen and her daughter were very much alike – though much younger, of course. This girl had the same fair hair curling gently round her heart-shaped face, was of the same slim build, and her mannerism of tilting her head to one side was just like Rachel's.

Ben thought so too, because, leaning towards Ellen, he whispered, 'She looks like you – not as pretty though!'

Ellen smiled broadly, for the first time that evening, as she whispered back, 'I think you need your eyes testing, luv! She's like Rachel, though, don't you think?' She glanced at her programme. 'Miss Dolly Davenport. Very good, isn't she? Lovely voice...'

Miss Dolly Davenport, in melodious tones, sweet, but by no means loud, was captivating her audience with a selection of favourite songs. *Sweet Rosie O'Grady, By the Light of the Silvery Moon, I'll be Your Sweetheart...* With her arms outstretched, 'Come on, you know this one, don't you?' she soon had most of the audience joining in the choruses with gusto.

'And now, a song for lovers everywhere, especially for those who may soon be parted. Ladies and gentlemen, I would like to sing for you, *The Sunshine of Your Smile.*' Dolly Davenport's pretty face was not smiling at that moment though; it was serious, almost sad.

There was a few seconds' pause before the orchestra, consisting of a piano and a few stringed instruments, began to play softly. The tune and the words were familiar to Ellen. She had heard the song on a previous visit to the Music Hall and since then it had been sung occasionally at chapel concerts, but never before had the words, especially those of the second verse, come over to her with such heartrending poignancy.

'Shadows may fall across the land and sea,
Sunshine from all the world may hidden be,
But I shall see no clouds across the sun,

232

Your smile shall light my life, till life is done.'

The tears were streaming down Ellen's face as Dolly Davenport began to sing the chorus again. She was too choked to join in the singing; she just clung tightly to Ben's hand and let her tears fall unchecked.

'Give me a smile, the lovelight in your eyes,
Life could not hold a sweeter paradise.
Give me the right to love you all the while.
My world for ever the sunshine of your smile.'

How very true those words were. Ben, over the last nine years, had become Ellen's world, her whole life, and she couldn't imagine what life would be like without him.

'Don't worry, my darling, it won't be for long,' he whispered to her now, aware that she was not singing. 'Anyway, I'm only going to Preston, aren't I?' Through her tears she tried to smile back at him.

Those were the words he repeated to her a few days later as they clung together on the platform at Central Station. 'It's only Preston, my love. Ridiculous really, isn't it? I'll only be eighteen miles away.'

But for how long? thought Ellen. She knew, as Ben surely must know, that before long he would, in all probability, be sent to France, to take his chance, along with thousands of other soldiers, in the trenches. Four hundred miles of them, Ellen had read in the newspaper, stretching from the Swiss border to the Belgian coast.

'Come on, give me a smile,' whispered Ben, and she tried to do so before he kissed her for the last time.

'Give me a smile, the lovelight in your eyes...' The bitter-sweet words echoed in Ellen's mind as, blinded by tears, she walked back home to King Street.

'Life could not hold a sweeter paradise...'

Ben, oh dear, dear Ben. She loved him so much.

But life had to go on, as thousands of women, like Ellen, left without their menfolk, soon began to find. Ellen knew that she was more fortunately placed than many of them. She had a business to run, and though it would not be easy to do so without Ben, she had no doubts about her ability to carry on. It helped to take her mind away from the growing lists of casualties in the newspapers, and from the grim news which came from time to time that first one, then another, of her acquaintances would never be returning.

Ben's two brothers, Alec and Sam, had also joined up. Alec had never been in the firm – he was a grocer's assistant – but Sam was an experienced sugar boiler and his departure, soon after Ben's, left another noticeable gap, especially as Bertie Shaw, his co-worker, had also gone. Amos Hardy, however, Ellen's protégé from Preston, had proved to be a steady and reliable worker. He couldn't be given full responsibility, certainly not with the lettering – he could just about write his own name – but he was strong and willing, over-anxious, in fact, to please. He had been declared medically unfit for the Army, and for that Ellen uttered a thankful prayer. Not just for Amos – the poor lad would have found Army life dreadfully confusing – but because here, at least, was a touch of continuity in the firm. It was odd how she still referred to Amos as a lad. He was now in his late twenties, still residing quite happily at Mrs Banks's lodging house in Park Road.

George, Ellen's son, joined the firm in January 1915, round about the time of Ben's departure; with him came another schoolleaver, a lad of fourteen, so the rock-making side of the firm was able to progress more or less satisfactorily. Raw materials were in short supply as the war went on, but not so much as to seriously hamper production.

It had been a wise move, Ellen often thought, to change the name of the firm to Hobson's Rock after Lydia's untimely death; especially as Gertie Hobson, Ben's mother, to Ellen's secret amazement, had very quickly filled in the void left by her own mother.

'It's been a godsend to me, all this toffee-making,' she remarked, time and again, to Ellen. 'You'll never know what you've done for me, you and our Ben.'

Gertie had become much more of a person in her own right, instead of an insubstantial shadow, meekly submitting to the abuse of her husband. Dick Hobson, too, had changed. Recognising that his wife was not the cringing wretch that she had once been, his drunkenness and bullying had diminished; or it could have

235

been that he was getting older and appreciating, for the first time, the comforts that his long-suffering wife had always tried to give him.

Dora and Millie, Ben's younger sisters, were still working for Hobson's, manning the two shops – there was now another shop on Dickson Road, at the north end of the town – and taking their turn at the two stalls on Central Beach and at the South Shore Pleasure Beach. Visitors were still continuing to come to Blackpool, not in such vast numbers as in peacetime; but the holiday trade was not suffering unduly, and neither was Hobson's Rock. Both of Ben's sisters were married with a growing family, but they organised their lives to fit in with their jobs. That was what more and more women were doing as the war, which many had vainly hoped would be 'all over by Christmas', dragged its way through 1915, into 1916...

'Are you meeting Henry tonight?' asked Ellen of her daughter, one summer evening in 1916. It was just a casual enquiry, made because the girl, peering into the hall mirror, was obviously dressed for going out.

Ellen couldn't help but notice that she was wearing her best outfit, recently purchased from Donnelly's; a lilac and white broadly striped cotton dress with a white piqué collar, and a small straw hat with a turned-down brim. By no means an inexpensive outfit, but Rachel, now in charge of the office and accounts at Hobson's, didn't need to stint herself. Fashions had changed drastically from ten years ago. Gone were the high stand-up collars, tight bodices, large-brimmed hats and skirts sweeping the floor. Rachel's dress was loose-fitting, the square-cut neckline showing far more bare flesh than girls of Ellen's era would have dared to reveal – during the daytime at least – and her skirt, a few inches above ground level, afforded a glimpse of her dainty feet and ankles.

It was obvious from Rachel's smile as, her head tilted to one side, she surveyed herself in the mirror, that she was by no means displeased with what she saw there. Rachel was an undeniably pretty girl. Ellen felt, when looking at her daughter, that she was seeing herself at the same age. She knew that she, too, had been considered pretty – Ben assured her she still was – but Ellen knew that she hadn't at that age possessed the same confidence and self-assurance. Nor the same flirtatious personality! Ellen, at eighteen, the age that Rachel was now, had already been married with a child on the way, to the man who had been her only suitor; whereas Ellen couldn't count the number of young men that Rachel had so far been out with. She had stopped asking too many questions about them. She didn't want her daughter to think she was prying. Besides, Rachel was a well-brought-up girl and Ellen trusted her.

'Yes, I'm seeing Henry – but everyone calls him Harry,' Rachel answered happily now. 'I'm meeting him at the station and we'll go for a walk on the prom, probably on to one of the piers as it's such a lovely evening.' The girl's face clouded over momentarily as she added, 'I may not be seeing him much more, Mum. He's thinking of joining up, before he's forced to go.'

Compulsory service had now been started, to add more thousands of young men to the rapidly diminishing armies. Ellen, with an inward shudder, thought again of Georgie, now aged sixteen. *Surely* it would all be over before he was forced to go?

'Yes, you make the most of your time together, dear,' Ellen answered her. 'And bring Henry, I mean Harry, back for a cup of tea, won't you, if he'd like to come?'

'Yes, I might, Mum.' Rachel picked up her neat little handbag from the hallstand. 'Must dash, I'm a bit late.'

Ellen smiled fondly at her daughter's retreating back. From the front door she watched her stepping out briskly, the louis heels of her patent-leather shoes making a decisive tap-tap-tap on the pavement. Ellen felt sure that this young man was only one of a long succession of admirers, and when Rachel said goodbye to him – however sadly – there would soon be another one to take his place.

This current one seemed a nice enough lad. Ellen had met him a couple of times and had been interested to hear that he came from Preston. Rachel had always brought her friends home, both boys and girls, and Ellen made them welcome. She hadn't taken particular notice of Harry; she didn't even know his second name. When she did discover it, about a fortnight later, she had the shock of her life.

The letter lay there on the sideboard waiting for a stamp, ready to be posted. It was the name of the town that caught Ellen's eye first; Preston, printed in Rachel's confident black capitals. She must be writing to her young man, thought Ellen. Rachel had told her that very soon, in just a few days, he would be joining the Army. Her eyes wandered upwards to the name. Then her heart missed a beat; she felt shockwaves reverberating up to her throat then down to the pit of her stomach. She shouted out loud, 'Oh no!' – an involuntary exclamation of horror, as she read the words written there. *Mr Henry Balderstone*.

Balderstone! No, it couldn't be... It just wasn't possible. Ellen stared at the words in disbelief. Balderstone was an uncommon name, and it was the name of Jessie, the woman who had borne William's child. The woman who had threatened her, vowing to get her own back. But Ellen hadn't thought about her for ages. And the boy; what was his name? Ellen's mind flashed back across the years. She recalled the woman saying, 'This is John Henry... He's William's son.' John Henry – or, as Rachel called him, *Harry*.

Ellen covered her face with her hands as she rocked back and forth in shock and dismay. What on earth was she to do? She was frightened, too, and so very, very confused and unsure. If Ben were here she would be able to ask his advice, as she had always done, but Ben was far away in France. She hadn't seen him for almost a year. There was no one else in the house at that moment. Georgie was out with a friend and

239

Rachel was with ... Harry! Yes, she was with him, even now.

Then why on earth was she writing to him? Ellen picked up the envelope, scrutinising the black letters. The address – Springfield Street – meant little to her. It was a long time since she had lived in Preston; besides, she hadn't known every street in the town. This street might be in the area known as Maudlands, where Jessie had lived. But Jessie had moved away. Had she come back, and John Henry with her? John Henry who was now Harry – who was at this very moment most likely kissing Rachel ... his sister!

Ellen tried to bring his face to mind. She recalled that the young man she had seen, only the other night, had dark curly hair and ... blue eyes? Yes, she thought they were blue, although she hadn't taken much notice. It certainly hadn't occurred to her that he looked anything like William; but then neither had that boy, John Henry. His mother had said that he was the image of William, but he hadn't been, not really, only as far as colouring went. All the same, he and Rachel were brother and sister; Ellen felt sure of it.

'Oh, dear God, what am I to do?' she whispered. And why was Rachel writing to him? It was probably a fond letter of goodbye, she reasoned, telling him that she ... loved him? Oh, dear God, no! Ellen peered closely at the envelope, but she knew that never, never could she open it. Resolutely she put it down.

She collapsed into an easy chair, aware that her legs were trembling. She closed her eyes, and after a few moments she felt calmer. She would do nothing, she decided, nothing at all. Knowing Rachel, this young man, in all probability, would soon be replaced by another, then another. But if not, if Rachel continued to write to him ... well, it was wartime, wasn't it? Thousands upon thousands of young men, already, would not be returning.

'God forgive me for thinking such a thing,' breathed Ellen. 'It isn't what I want. You know, God, that it isn't what I want.'

Nevertheless, Ellen was aware that it would be a solution, and one which regrettably, might very well come to pass.

Chapter Twelve

My Dearest Ellen,

Your photograph is in front of me as I write, one I took of you in Scarborough, standing on the Spa Bridge. Do you remember, darling, how we both loved the place so much when we spent our honeymoon there? So we went back the next summer with Rachel and Georgie. And what a happy holiday that was too. The children are not in this picture, though. Just you, my love, in your pretty lace blouse and floppy hat. I don't know much about fashion, but I always loved you in that outfit. But then I love you whatever you wear, whatever you do, and I always will.

Thinking of Rachel and George, try not to worry too much about Georgie joining up. No, that's a silly thing to say – of course you will worry, but try to see it from his point of view. He has matured a lot recently and I, for one, feel very proud of him. There are some lads with me just the same age as him. They cheer one another up with their joking and fooling about. I can tell you they make me feel quite old at times, my love. And I'm sure Georgie will make lots of new friends of his own age. There's nothing like the Army for camaraderie. That's a long word, isn't it? I hope I've spelled it right.

You haven't said much about Rachel lately, or

about that young man of hers. Is she still writing to him? Letters mean such a lot, my darling. I look forward to yours more than I can say.

You will see from the enclosed photograph that I have been promoted – again! Sergeant, of all things! What do you think of that? There's not much to tell you of life out here. One day is pretty much the same as another. But I miss your cooking, my love. What wouldn't I give right now for a plate of your Lancashire hot-pot, followed by apple pie and custard. Just the thought of it is making my mouth water. All we get is bully beef and Maconochies (that's a sort of tinned Irish stew). And biscuits – they look like dog biscuits, but they're much bigger and sometimes they put jam on them. We have to be thankful for small mercies.

But there is beauty to be found even on the battlefields of France if you look for it. Bright red poppies in the fields, and wild roses struggling to live amongst the nettles and thorns of deserted hedgerows. And sometimes we see the most beautiful sunrise across the vast stretch of field in front of us. It reminds me, my darling, of how we once got up very early, in Scarborough, to watch the sun rise over the bay. And of how we sometimes used to watch the sunset over the sea in our dear old Blackpool. Not very often though – we always seemed to be too busy. When I come home, my darling, we must make more time for things like that – time to stand and stare, as it says in a poem I once read.

Keep on smiling, my love. The words of that song we both liked so much often run through my mind. *Give me a smile, the lovelight in your eyes* … how I would love to see your smiling face right now, but I keep telling myself that it won't be long. So keep smiling, my darling, and keep on praying, as I do, that this dreadful war will soon be over. Then we can be together again, for always.

You are my world, my whole life, my dearest Ellen.

God bless you.

Your everloving husband, Ben.

It was mainly reminiscences, thought Ben, as he read over what he had written. His letters always were, but what else could they be? How could you begin to tell the truth, to give an inkling of the unspeakable horrors of this war? He had been going to write 'blood red poppies', but had changed it to bright red. He had seen far too much blood; blood and rotting flesh of both men and horses, decomposing in a sea of mud.

There was so much that he had omitted from this letter to his beloved Ellen, as he always did, as all the lads did in their letters home. He couldn't tell her that the beautiful sunrise was viewed across 'no man's land', when they strained their eyes, peering into the half-light for the enemy to appear, a line of grey figures on the horizon. Dawn was always a good time for an attack. Nor could he tell Ellen how, on one of those mornings, one young lad, not much older than Georgie, had suddenly gone mad – lost his nerve and turned and run away. And the officer in charge had taken out his gun and shot him.

Ben had started forward in protest, but his mate, Albert, a man a few years his senior who had been with him from the start, had grabbed hold of his arm to restrain him. 'Hold it, Ben, lad,' he said in a gruff whisper. 'You'll only make it worse. They're frightened he'll create a panic – a mutiny – don't you see? Besides, how long d'you think he'd last, poor sod, in a blue funk like that?'

Nor had he told Ellen that promotion had come quickly – too quickly – because so many men had been lost, men he had grown to care about, to regard as pals. He hadn't told her about the shells whistling through the sky above the trenches, about the battery of machine-gun fire, about picking your way through a tangle of barbed wire under a hail of bullets, wondering if the next one would have your name on it.

He had told his wife, as jokingly as he could, about the food ration. But he hadn't told her about the rum ration; nor about how – if he hadn't signed the pledge all those years ago, if he hadn't made a solemn promise to himself, and to God, that he would never let a drop of liquor pass his lips – he would be very, very tempted now. In order to alleviate the pain, the misery and brutality, the sheer horror of it all.

George, some sixty miles away, with a different company, had come to the conclusion that his stepfather, over the years, had been talking a lot of nonsense. Both he and Rachel had gone along with that business of signing the pledge and attending Band of Hope meetings. He, George, had still been going regularly, almost every week, until he had joined up. His tongue had been in his cheek a lot of the time, but he had gone because it pleased his mother and because Ben was such a decent sort of chap.

George remembered being thrilled to bits when his mother had told him that she and Uncle Ben were to be married, that Ben was to be his new father. He had started to call him Daddy – or Dad, of late – although he thought of him as Ben. Dear old Ben. Nobody could have been more of a father to him and Rachel, or a more loving husband to their mother. Goodness, it made you almost squirm at times, the lovey dovey way Ben fussed around her, and that was after twelve years of marriage.

But Ben wasn't always right. The one thing – the only thing, in fact – that George was unable to countenance about his stepfather was his un-compromising attitude to drink. Drink! There was foreboding in the very way Ben uttered the word, as though it were the greatest evil under the sun. Apart from that he was a great bloke. A bit on the religious side – he never used a swear word, even a mild one – but he enjoyed a good laugh. Ben's father had been a heavy drinker, Ben had told George, and because of this he had ill-treated his wife. But Grandma Gertie, as George and Rachel had always called her, seemed all right now, very happy, in fact, working away at her sweet-making. George had an idea, also, that his real father, William, had been something of a tippler. His mother had never openly told him so – it was very rarely that she spoke of William – but George had heard hints here and there. He recalled, too, at the very edge of his memory, his father's loud voice and blustering manner – there had been one occasion when it seemed that the whole kitchen had been turned upside-down – and his mother's fear and unhappiness. But Mum, too, was fine now, apart from missing Ben … and missing him, George, as well, no doubt.

The first time a mate had plonked a pint of beer down in front of George, when he was still doing his training in Bolton, he had refused. But the guffaws of derision had disturbed him a little. He was only seventeen, but he wanted to appear as much of a man as any of them. So the next time he had thought, What the heck! and had struggled to drink it. The time after that it was not such a struggle – he found it quite palatable, in fact – and before long George had been having his pint every night along with the others. And when they got to France, at the beginning of 1918, it was the only thing to do. You just drank anything that came your way – ale, wine, brandy, whisky, rum. It was supposed to be illegal to supply the troops with spirits; you couldn't buy it in the bars, but you soon found out in which private houses you could get a drink of cognac, served in an egg-cup.

There was a legal rum ration, of course, two tablespoons for each soldier, and George soon realised that only a bloody fool would turn that down. He would defy anyone, even his stepfather, Ben, to try and manage without it. It was a lifesaver in winter when you were up to your knees in mud and couldn't feel your hands or feet, when you just stayed there and got wet or dried out according to the weather, like animals in a field. Besides, it made you feel quite merry; made it all seem a bit unreal when you had to go 'over the top'.

There was supposed to be only enough rum for each man's ration, but there were so many casualties that sometimes there would be only half a dozen men left in the section; then the surplus liquor went into the water bottles. This was forbidden, naturally, but it was what happened. George soon acquired a liking for the stuff; he didn't know, indeed, how he would be able to manage without it.

They were all waiting for a 'Blighty one', as they called it, a wound that wasn't too bad, but bad enough to get you sent back to England. However the wounds, when they came, often sent blokes much further than that. Several young chaps, already, with whom George had served had died. One of the worst things was being on burial duty and finding, amongst the carnage, bodies of pals with whom you had shared a laugh and a drink. That was when the rum ration helped; and when the rats, as big as cats, ran from amongst the rotting carcasses. George was convinced he would have nightmares about that as long as he lived.

He often thought what a damn fool he had been to enlist at all. It wasn't as if he had been forced to do so. Compulsory service had started in 1916, but he had still been underage. He didn't look it though, that was the trouble.

George Hobson – he and Rachel had taken their stepfather's name at the time of the marriage – at sixteen was already almost six feet in height, strong and well built, with the dark curly hair and blue eyes he had inherited from his father. He knew that the girls considered him handsome, although he hadn't, as yet, taken much notice of girls. Truth to tell, in spite of his confident appearance, George was somewhat shy of the opposite sex. As a little boy he had followed along in the wake of his sister, and he knew that, of the two of them, it was Rachel who was the leader, who had the stronger personality.

George had noticed, as he turned seventeen and as the war dragged into its third year, that the glances of the girls, once totally admiring, were no longer quite so full of approval. He had seen the raised eyebrows, the sideways looks and, once or twice, heard covert whispers, which he felt he was fully intended to hear.

'Why isn't he in uniform?'

'Big strapping lad like that ... should be ashamed of himself...' Then the final taunt, a white feather in a letter sent to his home.

He had kept this hidden from his mother. She had pleaded with him, not understanding at all why he felt he must go.

'Just wait till next year,' she had said. 'Wait until you're eighteen. I promise I won't stand in your way then.'

But Georgie hadn't listened. His eighteenth birthday, in the March of 1918, was spent in the trenches somewhere near Rheims. After only six weeks he felt as though he had been there for a lifetime. And they were all beginning to think that the war would go on for ever.

'...I love you, my darling Rachel, and I can't wait for the day when I shall see you again. Let's hope it won't be long now. It surely must be the last year, at any rate. We hear a few rumours flying about, but I can't say any more than that.

I hope you're wearing my ring. It was only a little thing, but I'll buy you a proper one with bigger stones when I can afford it. I want us to get married as soon as possible, my darling. I've been thinking about my job at the mill, and I don't really want to go back to Horrockses. Do you think your dad – your stepfather, really, isn't he – would find me a job at the rock factory? Then we could live in Blackpool. I've always thought I'd like to live there, specially since I met you, of course. Ben sounds a good sort, though I haven't met him. I hope he's keeping his chin up, wherever he is, like I'm trying to do. And your Georgie – I thought it was real brave of him to join up at seventeen and I wasn't surprised to hear he was over here in France like the rest of us.

Anyway, let's hope we'll soon be home, all of us. Keep your chin up, darling, and remember I love you.

Your Harry.

Rachel pushed this latest letter into the bottom drawer of her dressing table along with her underwear and stockings. There was a thick wad of letters there now. Her mother had no idea how many there were. She was bound to know, of course, that Harry was writing to her daughter, but Rachel usually tried to intercept the post so that Ellen was kept in ignorance of just how frequently these missives arrived.

At one time, Rachel would never have dreamed of keeping a secret from her mother, but now she felt that she must. Mum had been so ... odd, so ... abrupt – Rachel couldn't find a word to describe just how her mother had been – about Harry, round about the time he joined the Army. It had been a complete change of direction; until then Ellen had seemed to be getting on quite well with him. Not that she had fussed around him overmuch. She hadn't done that with any of Rachel's young men, and Rachel knew that her mother considered her to be a bit of a flirt. That was what Ellen had said, or as good as, when Rachel had asked her, point blank, what she had against Harry.

'Nothing.' Ellen had shrugged evasively, an uncharacteristic gesture. 'But you must admit that he's only one of many. I can't count the number of young men you've brought home already. Besides, you're far too young to be thinking seriously about one particular fellow.' Her mother had looked at her poignantly, her deep brown eyes clouded with anxiety. 'I don't want you to get hurt, my dear,' she said. 'It's wartime... You don't know when you're going to see him again.'

Rachel had begun to explain that it was different with Harry, that already, after knowing him only a couple of months, she felt sure that he was the one and only man for her. Her mother had stared at her for a moment or two as though pondering deeply about something, then she sighed and shook her head. 'Don't tell me any more. It's like I said, love. I don't want to see you hurt.'

So Rachel hadn't spoken of Harry again. She thought that maybe her mother had been recalling her own unhappy marriage and was anxious that her daughter should not suffer as she had done. Rachel remembered the angry scenes that had taken place. But Harry would never behave like William. He was kind and gentle and considerate. His feelings had overwhelmed him, though, that last time, just before he went away, as Rachel's had done. But he had sworn he would love her for ever and had asked her to wear a ring. It wasn't a real engagement ring, just a love token, with tiny chips of precious stones – diamond, emerald, amethyst and ruby, spelling out the word 'dear' – set in gold. Rachel was wearing it on a fine chain round her neck until such time as she and Harry could make it known to everyone that they loved one another. Surely, when the war was over, her mother could have no more objections?

Mam was preoccupied at the moment, understandably, with Ben due home in a few days' time. Neither she nor Rachel had mentioned Harry for ages.

When Ellen first received the card from France, in April 1918, stating that Ben had been wounded, she had burst into tears. Then her anguish at the thought of his injury had turned to relief. Maybe this would mean that he could come home, that he would have to fight no more. The Field Card had held only the barest facts. Sergeant Hobson had been wounded in the shoulder and taken to a military hospital. The details filled in on this official communication – Ellen guessed that thousands of them must have been sent out – were not in Ben's handwriting, neither was the letter which arrived a week later from a hospital near Verdun.

It was from the nurse who was caring for him. The wound in his right shoulder had been quite a nasty one, she informed Ellen, but the bullet had been removed and Ben was now recuperating. His life was in no danger, but there was every chance that he would soon be shipped back to England. She added that Ben sent his love – nothing more than that.

Ellen's mind was in a turmoil. She passed on the news to Ben's mother that he was safe and doing well and might soon be home. Tears of relief welled up in the older woman's eyes. Ben's brother, Sam, the one who had worked at the factory, had been killed on the Somme, and Ellen knew that she couldn't possibly burden her with her own fears regarding Ben. Instead, she went to talk to Bella Broadbent.

'I can't see what you're worrying about, Ellen love,' said Bella. 'The letter seems perfectly straightforward to me. I should've thought you'd be glad that he's coming home. And he must be all right – they wouldn't go saying that in a letter if it wasn't true.'

'I know, I know.' Ellen nodded her head in agreement, but also in bewilderment. 'I can't honestly tell you why I'm worried, Bella, but I am. This letter's almost *too* straightforward. And why didn't Ben write himself? Why did he get this nurse to write for him?'

'Because he's been injured, you silly chump!' Bella gave a little laugh, as though trying to make light of the issue. 'It's his right shoulder, isn't it, so it's sure to have affected his hand an' all.'

'He's got two hands, hasn't he?'

'Oh, come on, Ellen. Have you ever tried writing with your left hand? It's well-nigh impossible when you've used the other hand all your life.'

'But Ben was always a trier,' Ellen persisted. 'You know how he would never let anything beat him. He used to try and try again till he got the pattern in the rock just so. I remember all the trial and error we went through when we started the strawberry design, and that Union Jack when King George was crowned. Now that was a poser and no mistake, but he did it.' Ellen's eyes grew misty and she smiled a little as she looked back on the happy, happy days – they seemed so long ago now – when she and Ben had been working so harmoniously together.

'Besides, if he couldn't write himself, why didn't he get the nurse to write as though it was really him doing it? You know, dictate the words to her, tell her just what to say.'

'I think you know the answer to that just as well as I do,' replied Bella quietly. 'Ben's a very private sort of person, isn't he? He wouldn't want to share a love letter to you with anyone. I'm sure you've had some lovely letters from him, haven't you?'

'Yes, beautiful ones,' breathed Ellen. 'I never knew Ben could express himself like that. Really poetic, some of them are.'

'Well, there you are then,' said Bella. 'He wouldn't want to share his deepest feelings with a nurse, only with you. Don't worry – he'll write as soon as he's able, probably to tell you he's coming home. Back to Blighty, that's what they say, isn't it?'

'But why should he be coming home?' argued Ellen. 'I can't wait for him to come home, but from what I've heard they send them back to the action as soon as possible, and that nurse said that the wound was healing. There must be something else wrong with him. I can feel it, Bella. I *know* there's something else. I'm so close to Ben – sometimes I've felt we're just like one person – that I know it's not just the shoulder wound. He's ill, Bella, I know he is.'

Bella looked at her steadily. 'Yes, it's possible he may be. I'm too good a friend to you, Ellen love, to go on pretending. It may well be that he's suffering from something else as well as the wound. Some of the lads that have been at the Front, I've heard they've got shell shock. That's what they're calling it. The noise of the shells and the machine guns ... they get so they just can't stand it any more.'

Ellen looked at her pitifully. 'And ... do you think...?'

'I don't know, lass. I'm only guessing. But I

255

think it's possible. And if it is, that means he'll be coming home. You'll soon get him back to normal, won't you?'

Bella's smile was reassuring. This little parlour, overflowing with ornaments and photographs, with brightly burnished brassware gleaming on the mantelpiece, had a homely feel to it. Ellen had sat there, in that very chair with the cheerful red cushions, many times over the past years and had never failed to come away refreshed in mind.

'Try not to worry, love,' Bella said now. 'At least you know he's out of danger, and we must thank God for that.'

Try not to worry, try not to worry… The words repeated themselves over and over in Ellen's mind as she walked home. That was what they said to one another constantly these days, knowing that it was futile advice. That was what they had said to her when George joined up; Ben had said it in a letter. *Try not to worry…* Even though she said her prayers for them every night, committing her loved ones, Ben and Georgie, to God's care, Ellen never ceased to worry. Nor would she until this loathsome war was over and they were safe home again.

When Ellen alighted from the train at York Station her mind flitted back to the time when she and Ben had arrived there for a day's visit, during their honeymoon week. How impressed she had been by the grandeur of it all. Now her only thought was to get to Ben, her dear, dear Ben, as quickly as possible. She would only have an hour or so to spend with him before getting the train back to Blackpool, but she would have made the long journey for just five minutes with him. She intended to have a talk with the doctor and maybe at her next visit she could take him home.

The cab dropped her at the gates of the hospital. It was really a large house, a very large one, belonging to a wealthy family, which had been commandeered by the Government. Ellen walked between the velvet-green lawns and flowerbeds, bright with begonias and early flowering roses, towards the porticoed front door. It was a pleasant June day and here and there, dotted about the grass, were wicker chairs in which were seated blue-clad figures. This bright blue uniform, worn by wounded soldiers, had become an all-too frequent sight in the streets of towns and cities. Most of these men that Ellen could see now were bandaged; an arm or a leg, and one like a mummy, the bandaging almost covering his face.

Somewhat timorously she entered the spacious hall. She had just time to glimpse a magnificent parquet floor, a long oak table – it must have been twenty feet in length – and the biggest marble fireplace she had ever seen, before a smiling nurse came forward to greet her.

'Can I help you, madam?'

'Yes, I've come to see my husband, Sergeant Hobson – Ben Hobson. I think he's expecting me.'

'Ah yes. Sergeant Hobson.' The nurse nodded. Was Ellen only imagining that her smile faded a little and that she didn't look at Ellen as she spoke the next words? 'The doctor would like to talk to you, Mrs Hobson, before you see your husband.' She knocked at a door just off the entrance hall and popped her head inside. 'Mrs Hobson to see you, Dr Wilson.'

The doctor rose from behind a massive desk to greet Ellen. His handshake was powerful and Ellen knew, as she looked into his piercing grey eyes, that here was a man who would be honest with her. She also knew, instinctively, that what he was about to tell her was not good news.

'Do sit down, Mrs Hobson.' There was a little pause before he spoke again. 'We are very pleased with your husband's recovery, from the shoulder wound, that is. His hand and arm are still a little stiff, but that is only to be expected. He's had some trouble using his fingers...'

'Which is why he hasn't written, I suppose?' asked Ellen. She was trying, even now, to be hopeful.

'Quite so. *One* of the reasons. Yes, as I say, physically your husband is doing very nicely. But I'm afraid, Mrs Hobson, that I have some rather disturbing news for you.' Dr Wilson looked down for a moment, rearranging the stack of papers in front of him.

'Shell shock, is that what it is, Doctor?' asked Ellen. 'I had a feeling, you know, that there was something else.'

'Yes ... shell shock. That, of course, is what has caused it. A very loud explosion, we think. You see, Mrs Hobson, I'm afraid your husband has lost his memory.'

'What?' Ellen frowned. She couldn't under-

258

stand this at all. What was the doctor saying? 'You mean … he can't remember anything? Me, his family … the war? Nothing at all?'

The doctor shook his head. 'We're not sure. Ben seems to have retreated inside himself most of the time. We can't get him to say much at all. At first he didn't even know his own name – now he accepts that he's called Ben. Well, Benjamin. We assumed that you called him Ben?'

Ellen nodded.

'He chats now and again, when he feels like it. To us, or to the other patients, but it's just about general things. The weather, the food – you know.'

'No, I don't know. How could I know?' Ellen was feeling more than a little anxious. Why had she been kept in the dark for so long? It was June now, and Ben had been in this hospital for a few weeks. She wasn't sure how long; it had been quite a while before they even let her know. 'Why didn't you write to tell me what had happened? I'm his wife … I've a right to know.'

'Partly because we've been hoping it would be only a temporary thing. It usually is. There's no haemorrhage, you see, no bleeding around the brain area. The injury was just to his shoulder, but there must have been a severe explosion at the same time. He had concussion, and when he came round in the hospital in France, he just couldn't remember. The brain is a very complex organ, Mrs Hobson. There's so much about it that we don't understand.'

But that isn't helping me, thought Ellen, nor Ben. 'Can I see him?' she asked, far more peremptorily than was her usual manner. 'Now?'

'Of course.' Dr Wilson smiled. 'It might even do the trick. A sudden glimpse of someone he knows well and loves could trigger a return to normality.'

'Then why didn't you let me know before,' asked Ellen again, 'if you thought that might be the answer? He's been here quite a while, hasn't he?'

'We waited a fortnight, that was all. Like I said, we thought there was every chance he would recover. We are very busy. There are so many, so very many casualties. I'm afraid the communication side of things doesn't always work as well as it might. I'm sorry.' He stood up and Ellen did likewise. 'Come along, Mrs Hobson. Ben's in the garden.'

There was a more secluded lawn at the back of the house and there, seated in the shade of a spreading oak tree, clad in the distinctive blue jacket and trousers, was a familiar figure. Familiar ... and yet this man looked considerably older than the Ben Ellen remembered. His hair, once so bright, was now faded and grey at the temples and his face looked pale and drawn. He was still handsome though; he was still her beloved Ben, and Ellen felt her heart turn over as she looked at him. He hadn't heard them approaching across the grass and his head was bent towards the periodical on his lap.

The doctor moved forward and touched his arm. 'Someone to see you, Ben. I told you your wife was coming, didn't I? Here she is. Here's Ellen.'

Ellen stepped forward. She had been hanging back, half-afraid, but why did she ever need to be afraid of Ben?

'Hello, Ben,' she said, standing right in front of him. 'Hello, love.'

Ben glanced up. He smiled. He had always had such a radiant smile. 'Hello,' he said, quite cheerfully. But there was no light of recognition in his eyes.

Chapter Thirteen

Ellen stayed for only half an hour with Ben, although it seemed much longer. There was no point in remaining. He had no idea who she was; it was all so very, very heartbreaking.

'I'll leave you with him for a while,' the doctor had said, putting a comforting hand on her arm. 'If you want me for anything don't hesitate to ask. And I'll see you before you go.'

Ellen pulled up a nearby chair and sat down next to Ben. 'Now, how are you feeling?' she asked in what she hoped was a bright, normal sort of voice.

'Not so bad,' Ben answered. 'My shoulder's a bit stiff, and my hand.' He flexed his fingers once or twice. 'They said there was a bullet there, you see ... in my shoulder.' There was a silence, then, 'It's good of you to come and see me,' said Ben. 'It's very kind of you, Helen.'

'Ellen,' she corrected him quietly, her heart almost breaking. She leaned forward and gently touched his hand. 'My name's Ellen, and I'm your wife, Ben. I know you can't remember, but don't worry about it. You will ... soon. I'm going to ask the doctor if I can take you home in a little while – next week, maybe. Your shoulder's getting better now. They say you're doing very well.'

'Home?' said Ben, frowning a little. 'What do you mean, home?'

'Home to Blackpool, where we live. You and me, and Rachel and Georgie.' Georgie wasn't there at the moment, of course, but Ben couldn't know that. It would be no use either, to mention his parents, or his brother and sisters. *Oh Ben,* her heart cried out. *Come back to me!*

He shook his head perplexedly. 'I don't know...' he said. 'I'm all right here. They're looking after me very well, but I don't know why I'm here. It's good of you to take the trouble to come. Where did you say you'd come from?'

'Blackpool,' she said again, very patiently. 'That's where we live. And it's no trouble, Ben. How could it be any trouble?'

'I see ... Blackpool,' he repeated, but obviously the name meant nothing to him. They looked steadily at one another for several seconds. It was Ellen's eyes that were lowered first. Then, 'I'm sorry,' said Ben. 'I'm sorry I don't remember you.'

'You can recall nothing at all about us? About you and me?' asked Ellen gently.

'No.' Ben smiled shyly. 'But I think you're very pretty.'

Then there seemed to be nothing more to say. Ellen noticed that Ben's eyes kept returning to the periodical on his lap. From what she could see, it appeared to be a motor magazine with pictures of the latest models. Of course! Ben had long had an interest in motor cars although he had known that he couldn't possibly afford one, not at the beginning, that was. Ellen wondered if these pictures might awaken a flicker of recollection, but she didn't dare to ask. Maybe it could prove to be a way back, once she got him home. She was determined to do that.

She stood up. 'I'll leave you now, Ben. Take care of yourself, and I'll come and see you again soon. Goodbye.'

'Oh, all right then.' Ben glanced up from his magazine, not seeming to care whether she stayed or went. 'Goodbye, Helen.'

Dr Wilson was thoughtful for a few moments after Ellen had asked her a question. 'Mmmm...' He pursed his lips. 'I can't see that there would be any harm done if he were to go home. In fact, it might do a lot of good. There's very little wrong with him now physically, and we can certainly use the bed he'll vacate. The reason I hesitate, Mrs Hobson, is because I'm considering you, rather than Ben. If he was violent at all, or difficult, I wouldn't be too happy about it. Some are, you know. But he's not. Ben's a very amenable, co-operative sort of patient and I can't see him giving you much trouble. But I must insist that you bring someone with you when you come to take him home. Is there a man you could ask to accompany you? It's quite a long journey and it'll all be strange to Ben.'

Ellen started to think quickly. She couldn't possibly ask Ben's father, and most of the younger men were away. What about Arthur Broadbent, Bella's husband? He would probably be able to take a few hours off from his tram driving. 'Yes,' she said. 'My friend's husband... He's too old for the Army.' One always tried to excuse men who had not joined up. 'I'm sure he'll come with me.'

'Good, good.' The doctor nodded. 'I think it's safe to promise you that Ben will not be going back to the action, but you must get in touch with your own doctor at home, Mrs Hobson. He will still need a great deal of care and attention, of course.'

'Of course,' Ellen repeated. 'And you can be sure that he'll get it. I'll do all I possibly can.'

'I know that, my dear. Otherwise I wouldn't be letting him go.' The doctor's smile was sympathetic. 'Shall we say a week today? It'll give your husband time to get used to the idea that he's going home. I'll talk to him about it.'

Ellen watched anxiously as Ben stared round the bedroom, at the mahogany wardrobe, the matching dressing table and chest of drawers and the double bed with its eiderdown of blue quilted satin. So many tender and loving – often rapturous – moments they had spent together there, but now it was as though Ben were gazing into the room of a complete stranger.

'This is where I'm going to sleep?' he asked, tentatively touching the billowing eiderdown. Ellen remembered how, when she had first seen it in Donnelly's department store, she had gasped at the price. So expensive! But she had fallen in love with it and so she had bought it; the business had been doing well and they were beginning to afford a few luxuries. But now Ben was looking embarrassed at the thought of sleeping beneath it. 'But ... this is where you sleep, isn't it?'

Ellen realised how stupid she had been. Of

265

course Ben couldn't sleep here! Or she couldn't; not both of them. How could they possibly share a bed? 'Yes, I sleep here,' she answered brightly. 'Usually, but I'll move into the back room; the one where my mother used to sleep.' Ben looked at her questioningly. 'My mother lived with us when we first moved here,' she went on to explain, 'but she died.' Yes, that would be the answer, she thought, her heart positively aching with the anguish of it all. She would move into the spare room.

'No.' Ben frowned, shaking his head. 'Why should you? I'll go into the spare room. You've got all your pretty things in here.' He pointed towards the dressing table. There were her silver-backed brushes and mirror, a present from Ben on their tenth wedding anniversary; a cut-glass hair tidy and scent bottle; a china trinket tray decorated with flowers; and a photograph in a silver frame. Ben peered at this closely, then looked at Ellen, his face puzzled. 'The children … they're yours?'

'Yes, that's my daughter, Rachel, and my son, George. That was taken ages ago, of course. They're grown-up now.'

'Then they must be…' Ben stared at her confusedly. 'Are they…?'

'Are they your children, do you mean?' said Ellen, very gently. 'No, Ben. I was married before, you see. But we were all very happy together, you and me, Rachel and Georgie. Rachel will be home from work soon. She's looking forward to seeing you. And Georgie … he's in the Army; he's serving in France.'

266

'France.' Ben repeated now. 'Yes, I see.' But it was obvious that he didn't. How Ben would react on meeting the rest of the family she couldn't imagine. They would just have to take it one step at a time, but Ellen would be with him every step of the way.

He had behaved quite normally with Arthur Broadbent, who had been a pillar of strength to Ellen on the journey from York. Ben had treated him like a complete stranger, but he had appeared to trust him. Just as he is trusting me, thought Ellen. He has to take my word for it that I am his wife … and he is putting his complete faith in me. But then Ben had always had a trusting nature, an ability to see the best in people, and that characteristic was unchanged.

Ben followed Ellen out of the front bedroom, the one they had shared. 'And that's George's room,' she said, pushing open the next door.

This was most obviously a boy's room with its simple unadorned oak wardrobe and chest of drawers, and orange and brown striped eiderdown on the bed. George's battered old teddy bear still sat on the basket chair, his books and jigsaws from childhood days filled the shelves at the side of the bed, and on top of the chest stood a collection of toy motor cars and engines, and an automated tinplate clown which turned somersaults when you wound it up – George's favourite toy as a little boy, Ellen recalled.

Ben was peering into the room interestedly. 'I like that,' he said. 'That's a real lad's room, isn't it? You say that your son – George isn't it? – he's not here now?'

'No, not at the moment,' replied Ellen.

'Then can I sleep here?' asked Ben, rather like a child asking for a lollipop. 'I'd like that.'

'Of course you can,' said Ellen, turning her head away so that he wouldn't see the tears.

She really would have to try and keep a grip on her emotions, she thought as she went downstairs, leaving Ben to sort out the few belongings he had brought with him and to get acclimatised. There would be sure to be many, many incidents that would pull her heartstrings almost to breaking point, until such time as her beloved Ben regained his memory.

He settled down remarkably well, but it was as though he were a guest in the house, a punctual, polite, reliable guest who remained always on the fringe of the action. Ellen had talked things over with his parents and sisters – his brother, Alec, was still overseas – urging them to behave normally, just as though Ben knew perfectly well who they were. He would take them at their face value, she assured them; he had already looked at photographs of them.

'Hello, son. Good to see you again,' Dick Hobson had said gruffly the first time he had seen his son, putting an arm about his shoulders and giving him an awkward sort of hug. Dick was a different person altogether these days; his drinking bouts and wife beating were seemingly at an end.

Gertie Hobson, too, though finding it hard to stem her tears, had greeted Ben normally, kissing his cheek and briefly stroking his now faded hair. And Ben had smiled and nodded and said, 'Hello,' although he didn't use their names. It was very rarely that he used anyone's names, except Ellen's – he was managing to get it right now – and occasionally Rachel's. The young woman was very good with him and Ellen was grateful to her for the ordinary way she treated him, still calling him 'Dad' as though it was all the same as it used to be.

Conversation, though, was often difficult. What could there be to talk of, as a family, with no mutually remembered experiences? And the rock factory, which the Hobsons always tended to discuss when they got together – how could it be otherwise with all of them involved? – was a completely foreign notion to Ben.

'Where does your daughter work?' Ben had asked that first day of his return, as they awaited Rachel's homecoming.

'At the rock factory,' Ellen had replied easily. 'Our factory, Ben. She does the accounts there. I work there as well – I'm in charge, you see – but I'm having a few days off. We have a very good staff and they all work together very well. They can easily manage without me,' she laughed.

'Rock?' Ben had frowned. 'You make ... rock?'

'Yes, that's right.' Ellen went to the sideboard and took out a few sticks, a pink, an orange and a green. 'Like this, in different colours and flavours. Do you remember?'

'I know about rock,' Ben replied. 'Mint rock – that pink one – they sell it at the seaside. It tastes nice.'

Ellen's heart had skipped a beat. He was remembering! Thank God; it was all coming back to him.

But Ben had frowned again. 'You say you make it? You have a factory that makes that stuff?'

'Yes. So had you, Ben,' Ellen ventured very quietly, not knowing if she dared.

Ben gave a little laugh, but he also shook his head. 'Seems a funny sort of thing to do. Still, if you say so...' The smile faded from his face to be replaced by a blank expression as he stared into the fire.

Ellen found this very perplexing. She couldn't understand it at all. If he knew about rock – he even remembered that he liked the taste of it – why then could he not remember that he had made it, that he had been, in fact, one of the best rock-makers in Blackpool? She asked the doctor why it should be that some things were clear to him whilst others were a complete blank.

'I can't answer you, Mrs Hobson,' Dr Frobisher replied, in perfect honesty. 'There is so much about the human mind that is still a mystery to use. All I can do is reiterate what the doctor in the hospital has already told you; there is no brain damage, as far as we can tell, and his memory will come back. When? Well, we don't know that, but we have to go easy with him, not force him to recall things. One thing I *am* sure of... He was having a grim time over there in France until he was wounded. There will be a lot that his mind just doesn't want to recall. I'm speaking as a layman now, not as a doctor. I'm sorry, Mrs Hobson. You've a son out there, haven't you?'

'Yes, but I've no illusions, Doctor,' replied Ellen. 'I just keep on praying that George will come home safely. And that it won't go on much longer.'

The doctor nodded. 'It's beginning to look as though it might end fairly soon. Let's hope so. As far as Ben is concerned, you must try to give him as much freedom as he wants. You say you're worried if he goes out on his own? Well, try not to be. It's hard to get lost in Blackpool anyway; all roads lead to the sea, eventually. Just make sure he has his name and address somewhere on his person.'

Like a child going to school for the first time, thought Ellen, but she knew it made sense. She had hoped that the sight of his home town, some familiar feature – the Tower, North Pier, the Big Wheel, maybe? – might strike a chord in Ben's memory, but once again, her hopes were to prove fruitless. Ben appeared to like Blackpool, especially the promenade and the sea, but it was as though he was seeing it all for the first time, as a holidaymaker would do. He always wanted to cross over the tramtrack, away from the crowds, and walk on the sea side of the prom. He would stand stock still from time to time, staring out across the vast expanse of golden sand, or grey-green sea, if the tide happened to be in, towards the distant horizon.

Oh Ben, where are you, my darling? Ellen's heart cried out as she stood at his side, holding on to his arm. *Please, please come back to me.*

She couldn't always spare the time to accompany him on these walks he enjoyed so much. Ben realised this and it was he who suggested that he might sometimes go on his own.

'You have your work to go to, haven't you, Ellen?' he said. 'The rock factory?' His glance was quizzical, half-amused. 'Don't worry about me. I can find my way about Blackpool now. I like it – I'm glad I live here.'

Ellen was gratified that he seemed to like her, too, and to have accepted the fact that she was – once – his wife. The evidence was there anyway in the photographs she showed him, over which he would nod gravely and occasionally ask questions.

'And that one's Scarborough, did you say? Yes, it looks a nice place. And this is your sister, Mary, and her husband … Fred? And the twins, Charlie and … Tommy? You see, I'm remembering, aren't I, Ellen?'

'Yes, Ben.' Ellen would smile fondly at him. He was remembering, but only what she had told him. What had happened years ago, when he had known all these people and places, which were now just pictures to him, was still like a blank page in the book of his memory.

Ellen wondered what was going on in his mind. Might he fall in love with her all over again? Or was she just someone – a nurse, as it were – who was looking after him? He talked to her as a friend, but there was no intimacy, no loving glances, no tender touch of his hand on her arm or holding of hands. She longed to put her arms around him, to caress his head against her breast, but she knew that she couldn't do this. Ben had always been a reserved sort of person; it was possible that, now, he didn't even think of her in that way. She took his arm when they went out for walks – all couples who walked out together did so – but, apart from that, she kept her distance from him. And it hurt.

She thought that time might hang heavy for him, but it didn't appear to do so. She bought him some large jigsaws and these kept him engrossed for hours at a time. And motoring magazines; she sent away for catalogues of the latest models over which he pored avidly.

'Now that's a marvellous motor car,' he would exclaim from time to time. 'Supercharged engine – sixty-five horse power! Just think of that, Ellen!' Facts which still meant nothing to her, as they had meant nothing in the days before their marriage when the eager young man he had been then had enthused about his passion of his. He remembers about the motor cars, Ellen thought to herself. Why, then, can he not recall where and when he gained this knowledge, or that he has talked to me before in just this same way? But the mystery of Ben's mind and what was going on there was far too complex for her to understand; even the doctors couldn't understand it.

It would have been pointless for him to go to the factory and never once did he express a wish to do so. Nor did he want to go to chapel with her, although she still continued to attend most Sunday mornings. She invited him, tentatively, to go along with her, but she couldn't help but be somewhat relieved when he refused. Most folk at the chapel knew of Ben's homecoming and something of the state he was in – word quickly got around on parochial grapevines – but it could, nevertheless, prove embarrassing.

'No, thank you, I don't think so, Ellen,' he replied, quite cheerily. 'I don't think I want to go to chapel.' She wondered if he had any inkling what 'chapel' was; he certainly had no recollection of what a pillar of the community he had once been. 'I'm all right here. I'll read the newspaper and keep my eye on the roast beef. I think I can manage to do that. I must say you're a splendid cook, Ellen.'

He had told her so before; he seemed very appreciative of her homemaking skills. He ate well, she assumed he was sleeping well – he took, nightly, the tablets the doctor had prescribed; a type of sedative, Ellen supposed – and he seemed contented enough, secure in his own little world. He would read the newspaper, he had told her. He did so every day, but he never commented on what he read there.

The Russian Royal Family had been murdered in July; and now, at the beginning of August, a counter offensive had been launched on the Western Front. The British and French, helped by powerful tanks and with the aid of their American allies, were at long last driving the Germans back. It was reported that the German people at home were beginning to lose heart; the British Navy was stopping food from reaching them and many were starving; there were strikes and riots in many German cities. But what these things meant to Ben, whether he understood about them or even cared, Ellen had no idea.

Sometimes she feared he would be lost to her for ever.

Towards the end of August the weather was hot and sultry. Ben had gone to bed early, as he frequently did, and Rachel, too, had gone upstairs. She often read in her room at night and didn't go out much these days. There were no young men left to act as escorts to the young women and Rachel had never been much of a one for going about with a crowd of girls. Ellen was aware that letters occasionally arrived from Harry Balderstone. Each time she saw the envelope with the familiar bold writing lying on the mat the feeling of dread was rekindled in Ellen, but at least Rachel never mentioned him now. Ellen had the sense to know that that might not necessarily be a good sign. But anything could happen before this wretched war came to an end – look what had happened to Ben – and when, *if*, Harry came back, they might find they no longer cared for one another. So Ellen reasoned with herself, but most of the time her thoughts were not with Rachel and her ill-fated love affair. She had other worries, much closer to her heart.

Soon after eleven Ellen decided that she, also, would retire. She laid aside her magazine; she was unable to concentrate sufficiently well these days to read a book, as she had used to do, but *People's Friend* had such heartwarming stories; they helped to take her mind, though only momentarily, away from her problems. She could hear a distant rumble of thunder. She hadn't noticed the flash of lightning that must have preceded it; now she waited, alert, for the next one. She went to the window and peered out. Yes – there it was, a vivid flash of sheet lightning, illuminating briefly the houses and gardens opposite. Ellen began to count. One, two, three, four... However many she counted up to it meant that the heart of the storm was so many miles away. So her mother had told her when she was a little girl, and Ellen still held to the childish precept. Ten ... it was a fair distance away yet. It might even move away altogether in the other direction; all the same, she would go to bed and take refuge beneath the bedcovers. Ellen wasn't abnormally afraid of thunderstorms. Another thing her mother had told her, she recalled now, was that sheet lightning was not dangerous, only the forked variety which could fell you to the ground in an instant. But she always felt safer in bed and was always relieved when the storm had passed.

Ellen remembered, as she passed Ben's room, that he hadn't liked thunderstorms either. He had, in fact, been more scared of them than she was. She stood by the door which was slightly ajar and listened. He was breathing deeply, peacefully, it seemed, and she smiled to herself. She still loved him as much as ever.

To Ellen's dismay, the storm was getting nearer. She huddled beneath the blankets – even on a warm evening she was glad of the comfort of them – trying to blot out the sound. Suddenly, there came a flash so brilliant that the whole room was lit up for a few seconds, and, simultaneously, a tremendous crash which sounded as though the roof were caving in. The shock of it made Ellen sit bolt upright in bed; she could feel her heart pounding and the sweat beading on her forehead. Then it came again; a flood of light and a second almighty crash as the torrential rain battered against the window.

Then she heard another sound. 'Ellen, Ellen... Oh God, please help me! Ellen! *Where are you?*'

She sprang out of bed and raced into Ben's room. In the light from the landing window and in the faint glimmer filtering through the curtains she could see him sitting up in bed, a look of sheer terror on his face and his arms outstretched towards her. 'Ellen ... oh, Ellen,' he shouted as she rushed over to him. The words issued from his throat in a muffled cry. 'Ellen ... make it go away.' He covered his face with his hands, his shoulders shaking with convulsive sobs.

Ellen sat beside him and put her arms right round him. 'It's all right, Ben. It's all right, darling, I'm here,' she said, whilst in her heart she was whispering, *Oh thank You, thank You, God!* For she had known the moment she saw the look in his eyes – a look of terror, yes, but also one of reawakened perception – that he was back with her.

She cradled him in her arms, his head against her breast, as she had yearned to do ever since his return, whilst the storm gradually abated. There were several more loud crashes, and at each one Ben put his hands to his ears.

'Look out!' he cried. 'There's another one coming. Keep your head down, for God's sake, or

277

you'll be killed.'

He was back in the trenches of France, she realised, back with his mates who had shared in the horror of it all, and who, in all too many cases would not be returning. At that moment he seemed to have forgotten her again, but as the storm slowly died away he used her name more and more. It was as though he were in two places at once, back on the battlefield, and yet, at the same time home again, safe in his wife's loving arms.

'They're going, Ellen. I think it's over for now. We're all right. We're safe.' All the breath was expelled from his body in a convulsive sigh as he flung himself away from her, back against the pillows. He lay there, limp and exhausted, his face running with perspiration and his eyes tightly closed.

There was silence in the room for a few moments – the rain had ceased now – as Ellen took hold of his hand; then, gently, with a corner of the sheet she wiped the moisture from his forehead and cheeks. Slowly he opened his eyes and looked at her. She knew that she hadn't imagined it; his intense gaze was one of full recognition.

'Ellen. What's happened? Where am I?'

'You're home, Ben. You're safe home again,' she whispered, as he raised himself up and began to stare curiously round the room. 'You were wounded, you see.'

'But this is George's room, isn't it?' he said, a worried frown creasing his brow. 'What on earth am I doing in George's room?'

'We thought it was better, Ben,' said Ellen soothingly. 'You were ill, you see. You'd been wounded. And you seemed to want to ... to be on your own.' How on earth could she possibly explain to Ben that he had lost his memory, that she had been a complete stranger to him? She didn't know how to even begin to do so.

'You say I was wounded?' His eyes narrowed thoughtfully, then his left hand went to his right shoulder. 'Yes, my shoulder. I remember the terrible pain.' His fingers explored the region. 'It seems to be healed now. There's a scar there... Yes, that still hurts a bit.' He winced slightly as his fingers probed at the wound. Then he frowned again, shaking his head in puzzlement. He closed his eyes tightly and Ellen could tell that he was trying to remember. 'There was an explosion... Dear God, what an explosion. That was just after the bullet had hit me. Then ... nothing. I was in France, now I'm here.'

He opened his eyes again, staring at her intently. 'What day is it, Ellen? No, what date? What month?'

'It's August, Ben,' she answered calmly. 'Next week we'll be into September.'

'August!' he shouted, sitting bolt upright. 'But it was May, wasn't it? I'm sure it was May. Where have I been, Ellen? What the hell's been happening?'

Ellen thought, fleetingly, that it was the first time she had ever heard her husband use a swear word, even a mild one. She decided to be truthful. 'I'm afraid you lost your memory, Ben, for a while,' she said gently. 'You were in hospital over there, in France. Then they brought you back to England – near York, it was. I came to see you – then they said you could come home. You've been home for about two months now.'

'Two months!' Ben gaped at her in slowly dawning horror. 'But I can't remember any of it. York, you say?' he shook his head again in bewilderment. 'All I remember is being in that damn trench. Sam had just copped it. Oh God, yes. The blood was gushing out of his forehead, then his mouth.' Ben put his hand to his own mouth as the horror of it all returned. 'Then ... my shoulder ... and that almighty bang. Then the next I knew, I was here ... Ellen.' He stared at her in silence for a few seconds. 'Does that mean that I didn't know you? I've not been unconscious, have I?'

'No, darling. You've been perfectly normal in every way, except that you couldn't remember. Not me, not any of us.'

'Oh God, how simply dreadful!' Ben sighed. 'And how awful it must have been for you.'

'Yes, it was,' smiled Ellen. 'But everything's going to be fine now, isn't it? You're back with us, and maybe it'll soon be over. The war, I mean.'

Ben looked thoughtful. Then, 'What about our Georgie?' he asked suddenly. 'Have you heard from him lately?'

'Yes, he's still in France.' Ellen's smile faded for a moment. 'He writes, but he doesn't say very much.'

'No, he won't, poor devil,' breathed Ben, almost to himself. 'None of us did.' He shuddered. 'And what about Rachel? She's all right?'

'Yes, right as rain.' Ellen cocked her head in a listening stance. 'If I know Rachel she'll have slept through it all,' she chuckled. 'It takes more than a thunderstorm to wake our Rachel. Now...' She patted Ben's hand. 'I'm going down to make us a cup of tea, then we'd better try and get some sleep. No – stay where you are,' she remonstrated, as Ben made to get up. 'I'll do it.'

But Ben had jumped out of bed and was pulling on his dressing gown. 'No, I'm coming with you.' He followed her out on to the landing. 'I don't want to let you out of my sight, not ever again.' As he passed her bedroom door he tentatively peered inside. 'And then I'm coming to sleep in here, with you.' His glance was almost shy. 'This is where I belong, isn't it, Ellen?'

'Oh Ben, my darling, of course it is,' cried Ellen, as she flung herself into his arms.

Chapter Fourteen

Dr Frobisher was delighted to hear the news that Ben had regained his memory. He was able to allay Ellen's fears that her husband might now have to return to the conflict.

'Not a chance of it,' he said. 'Ben is home for good. Apart from the shoulder wound, which was quite a nasty one, he has suffered in other ways as well. You mustn't be surprised, Mrs Hobson, if he seems to be rather ... changed. Given to fits of depression, or moments of panic, sometimes for no apparent reason. It may not always be easy dealing with him, now his memory is returning.

'I've seen quite a few cases similar to your husband's; not the loss of memory, but the shell shock.' The doctor nodded his head reflectively. 'This war has done some strange things to our lads. If you ask me, those that are in charge – the top brass – have a lot to answer for. Maybe I'm speaking out of turn, but so be it.'

'There's no chance of it happening again, is there, Doctor?' asked Ellen. 'Ben losing his memory again, I mean.'

'It's not very likely,' the doctor reassured her. 'We can't completely rule it out, of course. The mind can play strange tricks, especially in wartime, as we've seen. But no, I shouldn't think so. There's every chance that Ben will make a complete recovery, given time. But these few months, the period since his injury, will always remain a blank to him. We can hardly expect him to remember the time when he lost his memory, can we? It just doesn't make sense.'

It soon became clear to Ellen that the doctor's warning that Ben might be somewhat changed was all too true. She had been overjoyed, that first night, when Ben had moved back into her room – *their* room – but she soon realised that what he wanted, more than anything else, was the comfort and reassurance of her presence; her protection, almost. He would snuggle close to her, burrowing beneath the blankets, nestling his head against her shoulder or her breast, more like a small boy seeking the affection of his mother than a husband showing his wife that he loved her. His kisses were tender and loving, but lacking in any passion whatsoever, and never did he attempt to make love to her.

'Give him time,' the doctor had said, not about this matter, of course – Ellen would never have dreamed of mentioning such an intimate subject to the doctor – but about his general state of health. And Ellen knew, now he was safely home, that they had all the time in the world.

'I don't want to let you out of my sight,' Ben had said to her on the night of the thunderstorm, 'not ever again.' Before long Ellen realised, somewhat ruefully, that he meant it, too, for he followed her everywhere. If she went into the kitchen to prepare the supper Ben went as well, leaning against the dresser and chatting to her, though not, she noticed, attempting to help as he had done in the past. Now, it seemed, he liked to have things done for him, as most husbands did. Ellen had known, before Ben joined up, that her husband was unique, in that he helped her about the house. Now, all that had changed. Ellen did have other help with the housework, though, as she had had for several years; a daily woman who came in and did most of the cleaning while Ellen was at work and then stayed to prepare an evening meal. Ellen was thankful now, more than ever, for the ministrations of this Mrs Cooke, because it would have been far too much for her to cope, single-handed, with her home and her job.

Ben had not yet returned to work, nor was he showing any inclination for so doing. This was reasonable enough, Ellen supposed; he was, after all, convalescent, and it might be considered by the powers that be that if he was well enough to work in the factory, he was well enough to fight. That, at all costs, must be avoided; but he resented Ellen's going to the factory, and this she found hard to understand.

'Oh no, you're not going there again, are you?' he had asked, a trifle peevishly, when he saw her putting on her coat one morning in mid-September. 'You were there yesterday. They were all managing very well, too, from what I could see. Everything was going very smoothly. I don't see why you have to be there all the time. Stay here ... with me.'

'I can't, Ben; you know I can't,' she tried to reason with him. 'I'm supposed to be the boss, the one in charge ... until you come back, at least,' she added. 'They may well resent it if I keep taking time off.' She didn't say that she had already had more than enough time away from the factory and shops when Ben had first come home.

'When will you be back then?' He had followed her to the front door, watching her petulantly as she adjusted her hat in the hall mirror. He reached out and held on to her arm. 'Don't be too long, will you, love?'

'I'll pop in at dinnertime and have a bite to eat with you, a sandwich or something.' Midday was still 'dinnertime' to Ellen, even though they now had their main meal in the evening. 'And then ... well, I'll see. I might be able to pinch an hour or two this afternoon.'

'Yes, do try Ellen.' Ben's limpid brown eyes looked at her imploringly. 'You said you'd go with me to buy some new shirts, you know.'

'Yes. I haven't forgotten, Ben,' said Ellen in what she hoped was a patient voice, leaning forward and kissing the side of his mouth. 'We'll get your shirts, don't worry.' Ben had lost weight whilst in France, and even with the substantial meals he had eaten since his return home, he hadn't regained much of it. He had always been of a slim build, but now his cheeks were hollowed and his clothes hung limply on his angular frame.

'I won't be long, I promise.' Ellen's finger lovingly traced his firm jawline. 'Mrs Cooke will be here in a little while; she'll be able to see to anything you need. See you soon, darling.'

Ellen's cheerfulness – she always tried to put on a brave face when she was with Ben – evaporated slightly when she left her husband. She was thoughtful as she walked to work. The doctor had warned her that it might not be easy, and most certainly it wasn't. In many ways, she thought, with a stab of guilt, it had been easier dealing with him before he had remembered who she was. At least during that period he had seemed to realise that she was a working woman who needed to spend time at her job; indeed, he had encouraged her to do so. Now, he appeared resentful about any time that she spent away from him.

He had been into the factory with her the previous day, the second time he had done so. Ellen had been relieved at the ordinary way in which he had greeted his former employees and also those who were not known to him. There had been quite a few new hands engaged and quite a turnover of staff since the start of the war. Ben had chatted easily enough to them all; they knew of his history, of course, and realised that they had to tread carefully. He had shown an interest – not a consuming one, admittedly, but more than a polite interest, nonetheless – in all the stages of rock-making, the processes in which he at one time had been so passionately involved. He had even, to Ellen's surprise, suggested to them that they might soon be using the red, white and blue colourings again and the Union Jack design for the end of the war.

'Let's hope so, Mr Hobson,' they had all agreed fervently, obviously pleased to have him in their midst again. Those who had worked for him had known him always to be a very fair and considerate employer; a hardworking one, too, who would not expect them to do any job he could not tackle himself. At the busiest times – the holiday season or Christmas – he had put on his white overall and worked away with the rest of them.

Now he was an observer, not a participant, and Ellen wondered if he would ever take his rightful place again as head of the company. She had tried to explain to him that she had taken charge only in his absence; all over Britain women were now undertaking the jobs formerly done by men. It was true that Ellen, with her mother, had started the sweet-making business when they had first come to Blackpool in 1904. Since their marriage, however, it had been Ben, with his enthusiasm and expertise who, more and more, had taken the lead and had become the undisputed head of the firm. Would he ever do so again? thought Ellen. But it was early days yet; she mustn't be despondent.

More disturbing than Ben's clinging dependence on her, though, was his flat refusal to attend chapel; his total rejection, or so it seemed, of the God who had once meant so much to him. The first Sunday after his return to normal – what Ellen had at first thought of as normal, although she was now beginning to wonder – she had reached into the wardrobe for her hat and coat. Ben, as usual, had followed her upstairs and he looked at her curiously.

'Where are you off to then?'

'To chapel, Ben,' she began. 'It's Sunday...' she went on hesitantly, as she could see a closed look coming over his face. 'You know that we always used to go to chapel on a Sunday morning.' Ben hadn't been since his return home. Now that things were ... different, she had hoped that he would accompany her, to give thanks that he had now returned to them, completely. She thanked God every night for this blessing of Ben's returning memory, even though she was realising, with every day that passed, that it was something of a mixed blessing. Now she wanted to show her thankfulness in the presence of others. She had been sure that Ben would want to do so as well. How wrong she had been.

'Never again, Ellen.' The look he gave her was a sorrowful one, but there was deep anger there, too, and the pain of remembered suffering. 'I shall never set foot in the place again, or in any place of worship. It's all a lie, Ellen.'

'But Ben...' Ellen was dumbfounded. She had no idea how to answer him. She just stared at him in astonishment, scarcely able to believe what she was hearing. His faith had been a fundamental part of his life for so long.

'Is it still the Reverend Patterson?' asked Ben. Joseph Patterson had been the minister until a couple of years ago. Ben had known him well and worked closely with him, then the minister had surprised everyone by suddenly joining up – he hadn't been a young man. Ellen supposed he was a padre now, somewhere in the thick of it all. She thought she had written to tell Ben about it.

'No,' she answered him warily. 'Mr Patterson joined up. Don't you remember?'

'Did he? Poor sod,' he breathed, surprising her with the strength of his language.

'No, we've a new minister now, the Reverend Davidson. An older man, about fiftyish, I'd say. I thought I'd told you.' She had told him; she was sure of it.

'Hmmm ... you might have done. Don't remember.' Ben sounded as though he didn't much care either. 'But you can tell him from me, this Davis, or whatever his name is...' Ben turned a belligerent eye on her again '...you can tell him that he's talking a load of clap-trap. God of love, indeed! Huh! That's all my eye and Betty Martin. He wants to get over there and see what men are doing to one another.'

'But, Ben, that isn't God, is it?' cried Ellen. 'It isn't God's fault. You've just said, "What men are doing to one another." It's man's fault, isn't it, all this dreadful war and what it's doing to people. You can't go blaming God.'

'I'm not blaming Him,' Ben shouted back. 'Can't you see? I'm telling you there isn't one. There *is* no God. There can't be. If there was, then he wouldn't allow it all to happen. What was it we used to sing? "Immortal, invisible, God only wise. Almighty, victorious..." and so on. Wasn't that what it said, that hymn? I'm telling you, Ellen, if He was all that wise and Almighty, then He couldn't sit back and let men kill one another like this. He doesn't care ... and the reason He doesn't care is because He doesn't exist.'

'Ben, I know how you must feel,' she ventured, taking a step towards him and putting a hand on his arm, but did she really know? How could anyone know if they hadn't been 'over there'? 'What I'm trying to say is, don't you think God

289

might be – well – limiting His own power?' This was difficult; she was no theologian, but she had listened to enough sermons in her time. 'He's given us free will, hasn't He?' She came out with the truism that she had heard expounded from the pulpit, time and time again. 'To choose between good and evil, and men so often choose evil.'

'I don't know, Ellen,' Ben said bleakly, shaking his head and staring down at the floor.

She hoped – she must believe – that this was only a temporary aberration. She remembered now how, on the night of the thunderstorm when Ben had recovered from his amnesia, he had called upon God to help him. 'Oh God, please help me,' he had been crying when she dashed into his room. It had been an automatic reaction for him to do so. Surely, deep down, it must still be a part of him. Ellen had felt a little annoyed that the Reverend Davidson had not been round to see Ben. Although the minister didn't know him Ben was, nevertheless, one of his flock. Now she was relieved that he hadn't done so. It could have proved embarrassing, although she was sure that 'men of the cloth' were used to coping with all sorts of situations.

Ellen knew that she had to stand up to Ben now. 'Very well then,' she said in a matter-of-fact voice. 'You've no objection to me going to chapel, I suppose, like I always do?' Until her marriage to Ben, Ellen had been a somewhat spasmodic church attender. Now it meant a great deal to her.

'S'pose not,' Ben mumbled. 'I'll read the newspaper.'

'And you can keep an eye on the Sunday joint for me,' said Ellen brightly. 'I've got a shoulder of lamb for today. I've just put it in the oven.'

Ben appeared somewhat disconcerted. 'What about Rachel? Can't she do that?'

'No, she's coming with me.'

'Tch, tch! I don't know! A couple of women in the house and now a fellow has to cook his own dinner.' Ellen didn't know whether or not he was joking. The old Ben would have been. There would have been a humorous glint in his warm brown eyes, but there was none evident there today.

He did apologise, though, later that day. Much later, it had been, when they were in bed together. The atmosphere in the meantime had been more than a little strained.

'I'm sorry, Ellen,' Ben said, snuggling close to her. 'About this morning, chapel and all that. I can't make any sense of it, you see – God, I mean – with all that I've seen over there. It doesn't add up. So don't ask me again, to go to chapel. I can't … not yet. Perhaps not ever.'

'All right, Ben, I won't.' Ellen squeezed his hand. 'Don't worry about it. Try to forget it. All of it.'

'I can't, love. I can't forget it. That's the trouble.' She was aware of Ben shuddering as he leaned against her and she drew him closer. 'It's all there, in my mind. Horrible pictures … the mud and the rats and the … the dead bodies. I can see them clearly when I close my eyes. Sometimes they give me no peace, no rest.'

But Ellen knew in spite of what he was saying,

that Ben was sleeping reasonably well. The sleeping draught the doctor had given him was helping, although he sometimes awoke suddenly, shouting out in alarm at some imagined menace. And when he did Ellen was there to soothe and reassure him. As she tried to do now.

'Dr Frobisher says this is bound to happen, now you're starting to remember again. But it'll pass, my love. In time these awful memories will fade. Would it help, do you think, to tell me about it? It isn't always good to bottle things up. Maybe if you talked it out of your system...'

'No, Ellen. No, my love, I can't do that.' For the moment Ben was speaking rationally, as he had always used to do, as though he were the one taking charge. 'There are things I couldn't tell you. Things that no woman – certainly no lady, like you are – should know about. I can't tell you, especially with our Georgie still out there. He'll have to go through his own personal hell, poor devil, like we all had to do ... till it's over.'

'If he survives,' Ellen murmured as a sudden spasm of fear gripped hold of her.

'Don't say that, my love.' Ben was the one doing the comforting now and he drew her head on to his shoulder. 'It won't be long now, and Georgie'll be all right, you'll see. We'll just have to keep our fingers crossed for him.'

At one time Ben would have said, 'We must trust... We must pray for him.' Had he been on the brink of saying it now? Ellen closed her eyes and whispered, in her mind, her own fervent prayer for her son's safety, as she did every night.

The end of the war seemed to come all of a sudden, to those at home, but to those who were fighting it was, no doubt, a different story.

'They'll hardly be able to believe it, poor devils, I can tell you,' said Ben. 'We all thought it'd go on for ever. Anyroad, that's the end of it, thank goodness. Now we can look forward to our Georgie coming home.'

'Thank God.' Ellen amended Ben's words in her mind. Not just 'Thank goodness.' Ben was still stubbornly sticking to his denial of the Almighty, although, in other ways, there were encouraging signs of a return to normality. He no longer clung to Ellen so dependently and didn't seem to mind as much about the hours she put in at the factory and shops. He went there himself from time to time although he had no set pattern for so doing. It was as though the rock factory was a hobby, rather than his life's work, as it had been in the past; and Ellen found this perplexing.

Now, Ben's chief concern seemed to be with himself rather than with others. His supreme passion was for motor-car magazines and catalogues. They had become his only reading matter and the house was littered with them.

Yes, Ben had changed; but there was no doubt about that, Ellen often thought regretfully. But was it to be wondered at after all he had been through?

George didn't arrive home until May 1919, some six months after the Armistice had been signed. His job back home was not considered important

293

enough for him to be given an early release – not like the Durham miners, for example, who were soon weeded out of the Army and sent home to ease the severe labour shortage in the north-east. Others were sent to Germany to become part of the Army of Occupation, whilst the majority, George included, kicked their heels in the barracks in France. They were thankful that the war was over, but at the same time many of them felt that they had lost their sense of direction and the purpose that the war, dreadful as it was, had given to them. For some, indeed, all they had to return home to was a dole queue. George, at least, had a steady job, a good position in the family business if he put his mind to it, and for that he was thankful.

Ellen found her son, also, had changed more than a little. George, since he had been in his teens, had grown very tall; now he looked taller than ever and heavily built, too, as though the meagre Army rations had done him little harm. It was only his face that seemed to have suffered. There were lines around his mouth and forehead which you wouldn't normally expect to see in a lad of nineteen, and a haunted look could now and again be glimpsed in his bright blue eyes when you caught him off his guard.

His eyes were just like his father, William's. Ellen had had quite a shock to see how closely he now resembled his father. It was almost like coming face to face with William again, and not a younger edition either. William had been only twenty-five when he died and this young man looked easily that. The same upright bearing, vivid blue eyes, dark wavy hair, ruddy cheeks. Even though his face looked somewhat haggard Ellen couldn't help but notice the ruddy cheeks.

George had matured, too. Ellen recalled how he had always used to trail along in the wake of his more dominant sister. This, she felt sure, would no longer be the case. He was soon chatting away to Ben as though they were mates much of an age, rather than stepfather and son. Ellen was glad about this. That was what Ben needed; another man with whom he could discuss the matters which women didn't concern themselves with overmuch. Ellen had heard them talking about Lloyd George and his promise to provide a land fit for heroes to live in. George seemed to think that the Prime Minister had made a pretty poor job of winding up the war effort, but it wasn't clear what Ben thought about it all. Ellen was only relieved that for a while at least, he had taken his head out of those blessed motoring magazines.

He did seem to agree with George that it was a step in the right direction to give the vote to all men over the age of twenty-one, not just householders. They both seemed unsure though, Ellen overheard with a twinkle in her eye, about the wisdom of letting women vote! (And at the moment, you had to bear in mind, it was only for women over thirty.) Ellen couldn't help thinking how Ben would have championed the cause of women at one time; not that she had ever been overly interested herself in the question of votes for women. Now, it seemed to her that it was, in Ben's eyes, very much a man's world.

All the same, as she sat with the pair of them by the fireside a couple of evenings after her son's return, she reflected that she was happy, so very happy, to have them back home safe and sound, even though they were both somewhat changed. It was far more than a lot of poor women could say. Many had lost both husbands and sons, she thought, as she knitted away quietly, listening to Ben and George – mostly George – putting the world to rights on the sofa opposite her. She had a great deal for which to be thankful.

It was about nine o'clock when George stood up and said that he was going out.

'But where?' asked Ellen in surprise. 'It's a bit late for going out, isn't it?' She wished immediately that she hadn't said that. After all, it was none of her business really, was it? George was no longer her little boy, he was a man who had just returned from serving his King and Country. 'Of course, it's up to you, dear,' she added. 'I just wondered.'

George grinned at her quite amiably. 'I met a lad I was at school with when I went downtown this morning. He's been over in France an' all, a different part though. We said we'd meet and have a natter.'

'Very well, dear.' Ellen had to bite off the admonition not to be late, just as she had learned to do when Rachel went out with her friends. She was out at this moment, but it was very rarely that Rachel came in late.

The young woman did, in fact, return home at eleven o'clock, flushed and obviously happy, although Ellen didn't enquire where she had been. Rachel went straight to bed and a few moments later Ellen, too, decided to call it a day. Ben had retired some while ago, and Ellen knew that it wouldn't do, with this new grown-up George, to have his mother waiting up for him.

She was disturbed, about half an hour later, by a loud hammering on the door. Ben gave a shout and sat bolt upright in alarm, as he often did at a sudden noise.

'What is it? Ellen … Ellen…' He reached out to her. 'Don't let it start again.' His eyes were filled with the panic she had seen there so many times.

'It's all right, Ben.' She stroked his brow. 'Calm down, love. It's nothing to worry about. It'll be our Georgie, I'll be bound; he must have forgotten his key.'

Ben gave a long shuddering sigh, collapsing back against the pillows. 'Don't know why I do this, Ellen. I feel such a fool afterwards. But it's as though I'm *back there*.'

'Don't worry about it, Ben.' Ellen smiled comfortingly at him. 'You're here, and you're safe. All right, all right, lad – I'm coming,' she cried, sliding her feet into her bedroom slippers as the banging started again. 'Won't be a minute, Ben. You go back to sleep.'

When Ellen opened the front door she was nearly knocked over by the staggering figure of George as he lurched across the threshold. 'Where the hell were you, Mam? It was like trying to raise the dead.' His speech was slurred and he put his hand against the wall for support.

'It should be me who's asking that, my lad,' retorted Ellen, her good intentions not to enquire

297

about his whereabouts fast disappearing. 'Where have you been till this time? No, you don't need to tell me. I know where you've been.' She stared at the sprawling figure of her son – by now he was slumped at the foot of the stairs – more in sorrow than anger. 'I know only too well where you've been. To a pub. You've been drinking.'

'Full marksh, Mummy. How ever did you guesh? Yesh, you could say we've been drinking, old Wally and me. We've gorra lot in common, Wally and me. He was over there an' all...'

'Never mind about all that now,' said Ellen brusquely. 'You'd better get yourself off to bed, and be quick about it, too.' She knew she was being hard on him, but she could feel little sympathy for this slouching figure, his collar and tie all awry and his eyes bleary and red-rimmed. As she looked down on him in distaste Ellen felt, also, the beginnings of fear; for now, in this drunken state, he reminded her more than ever of William. Oh no, please God, no... She found the prayer forming in her mind. *Please don't let him turn out like William.*

He resembled his father so much in other ways; she couldn't bear it if he were to take after William in this respect as well. It was the first time, though, she very quickly reminded herself. She had never seen Georgie like this before; and it was only in looks that he took after his father, not in nature. Georgie was nothing like the arrogant bombast that William had been ... or he had never used to be. But it had been the drink, of course, that had done that to William.

'Come on, lad. Up you get,' she said, with a

298

little more compassion now. She stooped down and pulled at his arm. 'Try to get yourself upstairs. Hang on to the banister.' She knew that if she tried to assist him it would probably end in them both tumbling down the stairs, and she didn't want to shout for Ben.

George silently did as she asked, hauling himself up one step at a time. He was certainly in a bad way.

'And don't you ever bang on the door like that again, d'you hear me?' she admonished him in a fierce whisper when they reached the landing. 'Next time you go out, remember to take your key. You gave your father a real nasty turn, all that crashing and banging!'

George looked at her then, his eyes almost steady for the moment, appearing more than a little shamefaced. 'Oh Lor... Yes, yes, of course. I'm sorry, Mam. I didn't think.'

'Get to bed, George, before you wake our Rachel up as well,' Ellen sighed. She gave him a shove towards his bedroom door. 'Good night. See you in the morning.'

'Yes. G'night, Mam.'

He did manage to get into the room without crashing into the furniture. She quietly closed his door and went back into her own room. Ben was still awake, as she thought he might be.

He turned to her as she slid into bed beside him. 'I gather our Georgie's had one over the eight?' To her amazement Ben seemed to be half-chuckling.

She raised herself on one elbow, staring down at her husband. Even in the semi-darkness she could see the glint of amusement in his eyes. 'He's drunk, Ben! There's no other word for it. He could hardly stand up, the stupid young fool! To think that a son of mine should come home in a state like that. I can't imagine what possessed him.'

'Can't you, Ellen? I can.' Ben wasn't smiling now.

'You can, Ben? You ... of all people? After the way that you–' She stopped, not wanting to mention the Band of Hope. She hardly ever mentioned chapel now, or anything to do with it.

Ben mentioned it, however. 'Yes, even after the way that I preached about abstinence at the Band of Hope meetings. I've not forgotten that, Ellen. But that was before I saw all that horror and filth and vileness. War's an obscenity, Ellen!' He was almost shouting now. 'And some fellows had to drink to help them to forget about it. I daresay George was one of them. And I can't say I blame him,' he added in a whisper.

'But you didn't, Ben?'

'No, I didn't, and I doubt if I ever will. I *know* I never will. But far be it from me, any more, to condemn those who do. And I'll tell you something else, Ellen. It was a damn close thing. I came near to it many a time. Don't be too hard on the lad, love.'

'All right, Ben, I won't.' Ellen leaned over and kissed his cheek. 'Now, we must try to get some sleep.'

Ellen lay wide awake for quite some time, listening to her husband's deep rhythmic breathing. This war had a lot to answer for, one hell of a lot. But she knew that her husband, in spite of being somewhat changed, in spite of denying the God he had once loved so much, was still, deep down, very strong-minded. Much more so than her son...

In the next bedroom Rachel, too, lay wide awake. Her brother hadn't woken her up because she hadn't yet been to sleep. Idly she fingered the ring which she wore, most of the time, on the chain round her neck. Only when she was with Harry did she slip it on to the third finger of her left hand. Soon, though, she knew she would have to wear it all the time. She couldn't put it off any longer, especially not now... She would have to tell her mother and stepfather that soon – very soon, she suspected – she and Harry were to be married.

Chapter Fifteen

It was in the April of 1919 that Harry Balderstone returned home. Some three weeks later Rachel, for the life of her, couldn't have explained why she hadn't yet told her mother about his return.

It was partly because the Hobson family had been awaiting George's arrival, and any news of someone else coming home before him seemed to upset Ellen, far more than it would have done at one time. Rachel knew that her mother had had so many worries, what with Ben losing his memory, and on top of that the running of the factory and shops.

Admittedly, Hobsons had a grand bunch of employees who all pulled their weight. Everyone who entered the firm seemed to want to work hard, and Rachel herself tried to cope with the book-keeping and accounts without worrying her mother unduly with the details. But it was Ellen, ultimately, who was in control. She was the kingpin around whom the whole company revolved, and Rachel knew that she wasn't finding it easy nowadays. Especially as Ben was showing little inclination to assume his former role.

Rachel had feared that any talk of Harry coming home might upset her mother even more. Ellen seemed to have taken against him suddenly, around the time he joined up.

Their first meeting at Blackpool Central Station was ecstatic and Rachel knew that she was more in love with him than ever. He appeared very little changed, unlike poor Ben, who was a shadow of his former self. There were possibly a few faint lines around his mouth and eyes that hadn't been there before, but his hair was still the same glossy dark brown and his greyish-blue eyes still shone with good humour and friendliness ... and with ardour, too, as he held her in his arms again and kissed her.

That first evening, a pleasant, balmy evening which held all the promise of spring, they had taken a tram ride to South Shore then wandered on to the sandhills. They had both known, without uttering the words, that they had to find somewhere where they could be completely alone. And there, with the soft sand and the prickly star-grass beneath them, Rachel had given herself, in complete willingness, to Harry. How could it have been otherwise, when they had been parted for so long? It wasn't the first time. They had made love, just once, before Harry went away to the war, but this time it seemed to set a seal on their relationship. Rachel knew that this was for ever.

'I love you,' murmured Harry, and she whispered the same words back to him. And the thought niggled at her that soon she would have to tell her mother.

Afterwards they sat for a while, watching the red ball of the sun sinking lower and lower in a roseate sky which was so beautiful that Rachel almost felt like crying at the wonder of it all. Then, as the evening turned chilly, they walked hand in hand over the sand dunes to the edge of the sea. The clouds were gold-tipped and the smooth expanse of water was translucent turquoise, here and there shimmering and dancing with thousands of dazzling golden sovereigns.

'Beautiful, isn't it?' said Harry in almost awed tones, as they walked northwards. 'You certainly get the most wonderful sunsets here.'

'It isn't always like this,' Rachel told him. 'You should see it when there's a ninety-mile-an-hour gale blowing and the waves are pounding over the sea wall. Blackpool's a place of many moods, I can tell you.'

'But you love it here, don't you?' Harry turned to smile at her.

'Yes, I do. It's been home to me since I was six years old. I hardly ever think about Preston now. It's funny that I was born there, and you were as well, and yet we didn't know one another.'

'Not really surprising, you silly chump.' Harry laughed as he put his arm round her shoulders and gave her a squeeze. 'You've just said you were only six when you left. Preston's all right, I suppose. My dad thinks there's no place like it – Proud Preston – but I'm hoping we can settle here, you and me, when we're married. Don't let's leave it too long, eh, Rachel? We've waited long enough.'

'No, we won't wait too long,' Rachel replied. 'We'll get married ... but we can't rush into it straight away, can we? I haven't told my parents yet.'

Harry looked at her curiously. 'But you're wearing my ring.' He drew her hand to his lips, gently kissing her fingers. 'I'll buy you another one soon, darling, like I promised. This was only meant to be a token thing. I'll get you one with real stones; diamonds and – what else would you like? Rubies? Emeralds? I've got my gratuity pay.'

Rachel laughed and shook her head. 'No. This one'll do fine. I love it. Don't waste your money, Harry. You'll need it, when we get married.' She looked down at her left hand, turning it this way and that. The truth was the ring felt strange, because most of the time it had remained on a chain round her neck. She couldn't tell Harry that; he might be hurt, but she knew that she had to be reasonably honest with him. 'I haven't been wearing it all the time,' she ventured.

'What do you mean? Why not?' Harry was staring at her in puzzlement. 'What's the matter, Rachel? You are sure, aren't you?'

'Of course I am!' she cried. 'You know I am. How could you doubt it? But … it's difficult to explain, Harry. It's my parents – well, my mother really.'

She had already told him, in letters, about Ben and about the effect it was all having on her mother. Now she tried to tell him how Ellen had changed in her attitude, how she didn't like the idea of Rachel 'going steady' with any young man, not just Harry. But Rachel knew, although she didn't admit it to him, that it was the mention of Harry that had, inexplicably, upset her mother, the sight of Harry's letters... Because of this Rachel had hidden them away, letting Ellen believe, if she so wished, that it was all over between them. But she couldn't tell this to Harry.

'It'll be different now I'm home,' he remarked casually. 'You're making a mountain out of a molehill, my love. It's understandable that your mother wouldn't want you getting serious about some young fellow who was quite likely to get himself killed. Oh yes,' he went on as she looked at him in horror. 'You know as well as I do how many chaps won't be coming home at all, poor devils. And it could easily have been me. Or your Georgie, or Ben.'

'George's still away,' Rachel remarked. 'That's one of the reasons I've said nothing. Mum misses him so much. She's had such a lot on her plate, poor love. And Ben's not the help to her that he used to be.'

'He's just another of the casualties of this blasted war,' replied Harry. 'Your mam'll be all right, you'll see. Maybe news of our engagement might cheer her up, you never know. Tell her, Rachel.' He nodded towards her decisively. 'I'm looking forward to seeing her again. And soon, d'you hear? I liked your mam. And I've never met your father yet, you know. I was hoping he might find me a job in the factory, when I come to live here ... when you and I get married. Do you think he might? I've mentioned it to you before, in one of my letters, but you didn't answer me.'

'Mmmm, I daresay.' Rachel nodded evasively. 'It would be up to Mam though, as far as I can see, not Ben. He doesn't seem to be up to making any decisions yet. What about the mill? Aren't

306

you going back there?'

'Yes, they've got a job for me at Horrockses; charge-hand over a few looms, same as I was doing before. I've got a week off to settle down, then I'll be going back there. But it's not the be all and end all to me, Rachel. I'd just as soon try my hand at something else – rock-making, for instance.' He gave a chuckle. 'My old man, now – I can't imagine *him* ever wanting to work anywhere but at the mill. He's a tackler – overseer, y'know, in charge of one of the weaving sheds. He's been there donkey's years – cotton's in his blood, he says. My mam works there an' all, just part-time. A lot of folk in Preston have some connection with one or another of the mills, 'specially with Horrockses.'

'Yes, I do remember that,' replied Rachel. 'My Uncle Fred still works at Horrockses, and my Aunt Mary did at one time, then she took over the sweet shop when we moved to Blackpool. And now the twins, Charlie and Tommy, are there as well. They were just too young for the war – Aunty Mary was jolly relieved about that.'

'I don't know 'em,' said Harry, 'but then the mill's a big place. I don't know everybody.'

'I doubt if they'd have been there when you joined up,' Rachel pointed out. 'They'd probably still be at school. And that reminds me, talking of relations ... I still haven't met yours.' She turned to grin at him, at the same time giving him a poke in the ribs. 'So it isn't just me, you see. When are you going to introduce me to your mam and dad?'

'Very soon, my love, very soon.' Harry stooped

307

to kiss the tip of her nose. 'Never fear. They've heard all about you, you know. Yes, I'm dying to show you off to Mam and Dad. And my two sisters, as well, eventually. Stepsisters they are, really, but they're not at home, of course; they're both married now.'

'Stepsisters, are they?' said Rachel. 'You haven't mentioned it before.'

'Haven't I? Well, I was brought up along with them, so they seem just like full sisters to me. My father had been married before, you see. His first wife died when Jane and Nora were still very small, so when he married my mam she brought them up as if they were her own.'

'Like Ben did with me and our Georgie,' said Rachel. 'He's been a wonderful father to us. I remember my real dad, of course, and I know that Mam was none too happy with him. Like she is with Ben, or was,' she added thoughtfully.

'I'm sure if you were to ask her she'd still say she was happy,' Harry commented. 'It sounds as though your dad's going through a rough patch, and your mam along with him … because she loves him. But they'll come through it, you'll see. That's what love's all about, taking the rough along with the smooth. I daresay we'll have our ups and downs, too, before we've finished, my love. But first of all you've got to tell your mam and dad about us. Promise me you will?'

'All right, Harry. I promise. But I'll have to choose the right moment. You don't understand how difficult it is.'

Lying wide awake at midnight some three weeks later, Rachel reflected that the right moment still hadn't come. When the news had arrived, at last, that George was coming home her mother had been so excited that her feet had hardly touched the ground. That might have been a good time to tell her, but Rachel had failed to do so. She had caught a bad cold – maybe it had been chillier on the sand-hills than she had realised! – and, confined to her room, she had been out of touch with everyone. She hadn't been able to meet Harry for several days; then he had been asked to work overtime at the mill to which he had recently returned. So, time had gone on and still Rachel hadn't said anything.

By this time Harry, understandably, was getting more than a little impatient with her. He wouldn't invite her to Preston to meet his folks, he told her, until he had first met Ben and until Rachel had told her parents that they were 'going steady'.

And now, to crown it all, George had arrived home the worse for drink. Rachel could have laughed at the to-do going on on the landing if she hadn't been so worried about other matters. I'll tell her tomorrow, Rachel decided, turning her hot pillow over and giving it a thump, and that is definite. At all events, it might help to divert Ellen's mind away from Georgie. As Harry had said, it might even cheer her up. But she wouldn't tell her everything, not all at once. She would just say, first of all, that Harry had come home and she had started seeing him again.

Ellen placed her cup on the saucer with a loud

clatter. Her hands were suddenly unsteady and she clenched them on her lap beneath the tablecloth. What on earth was she to do or to say? Fool that she was, she had thought it was all over between Rachel and Harry Balderstone ... or maybe she had only been trying to convince herself. How long had she been seeing him? Just how long had the lad been home, she wondered. Ellen had assumed that Rachel was out with her friends. Since the end of the war she had been going out a lot more, often with Ruth, the young woman who worked in the office with her. And Rachel had deceitfully let her go on thinking that that was what she was still doing. To think that all the time she had been seeing...

Ellen felt a cold prickle of fear run through her, but she must try to keep calm. She knew that she would have to tell her daughter, but not now. She couldn't face it now. Later today, perhaps, when she had talked it over with Ben. Her husband, as yet, knew nothing of the catastrophe, partly because Ellen had pushed the whole business to the back of her mind, and partly because, sadly, they no longer discussed things the way they used to do. But this time Ben would have to listen.

'You might have told me, our Rachel,' Ellen said now, as casually as she could.

'Well, I'm telling you now, Mam,' replied Rachel brightly. 'I didn't tell you before, mainly because it seemed to upset you, me talking about Harry – I never knew why.' Rachel was looking at her keenly and Ellen found it difficult to meet her glance. 'But now I thought you should know he's

310

home and I'm seeing him again and–'

'I had my reasons, Rachel,' replied Ellen, very quietly. She stared down at the tablecloth. 'In fact, there's something I've got to...' Her courage failed her; she felt sick at the thought of what she knew she ought to tell her daughter, and she needed Ben's moral support. 'I'll tell you about it some other time,' she said, hastily rising and starting to stack the breakfast pots together. The mundane task helped to steady her a little. 'I'll take this lot into the kitchen, and you'd best be getting off to work, hadn't you?'

'I'll help you to wash up.'

'No, it's all right. I'll do them. I'm not going in till later.' Ellen couldn't bear to be with her daughter a moment longer with this dreadful secret still undisclosed.

'Very well then. If you're sure.' Rachel gave her an odd look. 'I'll go and get ready.'

It was Saturday, a day that Mrs Cooke didn't come in to do the chores, and a day when Rachel worked only a few hours at the office, finishing at midday. Ben and George were still in bed. Goodness knows what time Georgie would surface, Ellen mused, considering the excesses of the night before. She decided to leave him to his own devices – George was one problem she could easily shelve at the moment – but she would take Ben some breakfast in bed. It was something he would never have dreamed of letting her do at one time, but now he liked to be spoiled a little.

He continued to eat his boiled egg, dipping the 'soldiers' into the runny yolk with all the

311

enthusiasm of a small boy, as she recounted her story. She wondered if he was listening, if he was taking in the enormity of what she was saying, but it appeared that he was. He wiped his mouth on his serviette, folded it carefully, then looked at her.

'So you think that this young man is her brother? Her half-brother?' he said, frowning a little. 'You can't be sure, Ellen. Not just because of the name – that's not enough to go on.'

'But it's such an uncommon name, isn't it?'

Ben nodded. 'I suppose so.'

'And he *looks* like William – well, a bit like him. He has the same colouring. And anyway ... I just know.'

'You've never mentioned it before, not to me at any rate. Why didn't you?'

'You were away, Ben, in France. I couldn't worry you with something like this. You'd enough to think about. I've not mentioned it to anyone ... no one at all.'

'I can't understand why you didn't tell Rachel what you suspected, right at the beginning. That's what you should have done.'

'I know, Ben. I was stupid, I realise that now. But I thought it might all come to nothing. It was wartime ... he might even have been killed. Not that I'd have wanted that,' she added quickly. 'I really thought it was all over between them. It gave me a real turn, I can tell you, when she mentioned him again.'

'You'd closed your mind to it, Ellen,' said Ben, showing much more perception than he had done of late. 'But you'll have to tell her now, you know. You can't wait any longer.'

'I will, Ben. You'll be with me, won't you, when I tell her?'

'Of course I will. We're in this together, my love.' Ben's eyes were warm with tenderness and Ellen felt that he was closer to her than he had been at any time since his return.

As it happened, it was Sunday morning before Rachel was confronted with the devastating news. She had seen Harry the night before and had been able to tell him that her mother now knew that she was seeing him again.

'It wasn't too bad after all,' she said, as they walked arm in arm along the promenade. 'I don't know why I was getting so worked up about it all. Mam was all right. She seemed a bit cagey though. She said she'd something she wanted to tell me. I can't imagine what. Maybe she feels she ought to tell me about the birds and the bees,' she giggled.

'It's a bit late for that, love,' said Harry, giving her a sideways glance.

'Yes, I know it is,' replied Rachel, a trifle primly. There was something she hadn't told him yet – her life, at the moment, seemed to be beset with secrets – but she knew she would have to do so soon. 'Anyway, I've decided that tomorrow I'm going to show them my ring. And I'm going to tell them that we're talking about getting married.'

'Good girl.' Harry beamed at her. 'But don't you think I should go and ask your father, formally, if I can have his daughter's hand in marriage? Isn't that what they do in all the books? You're not twenty-one yet, you know.'

'I will be in a few weeks. But, yes – I think Ben would like that. I know he likes to be thought of as my real father. It would please him. But I'll tell them that we're sort of … unofficially engaged, and that we want to make it official, as soon as we can.' And it may well be only a short engagement, Rachel added to herself. She wasn't sure, of course, not absolutely sure. She had missed only one period, when all was said and done, and she was sometimes late, especially when she'd had a dreadful cold like she'd had recently.

'And then, perhaps, I can come over to Preston and meet your parents?' she added.

'Yes, of course you can. I was only waiting for you to make the first move, you know. I'll come and see Ben … let's say Monday. No time like the present. Then you could come to Preston on your half-day – Wednesday, isn't it?'

Rachel nodded happily. Things were moving at last, and it was her own fault, entirely, that they hadn't done so earlier. She couldn't imagine now what she had been so worried about. If the worst came to the worst and she did turn out to be *pregnant* – she uttered the word to herself uneasily – her mother had never been the sort of person to throw a fit. Ellen would take it in her stride as she did most things. And Rachel knew that her beloved Harry would give her all the support she needed, if the worst came to the worst. But the worst turned out to be far more dreadful than Rachel could ever have anticipated.

After she had dressed on Sunday morning she boldly slipped the ring on to the third finger of her left hand, intending to tell them over the breakfast table. Her mother and father were already there – it was somewhat unusual for Ben to be down for breakfast early – and she fancied that they glanced uneasily at one another as she entered the room. But why should they? She must be imagining things.

She tucked into the bacon and eggs which her mother fetched from the kitchen, but her parents appeared to be eating very little. Ellen was toying with a piece of toast and Ben was reading the newspaper which was propped up against the teapot, something her mother usually frowned upon. It was a very silent meal and Rachel decided that the pair of them must have had a tiff of some sort. They hadn't noticed her ring. Well, maybe this would help to break the ice.

'Mam ... Dad,' she began, her voice seeming loud in the abnormally quiet room, 'I've something to tell you – about Harry and me.' Ellen and Ben, still unsmiling, immediately looked at one another before turning their grave glances upon Rachel. They made her feel uneasy. Nevertheless she lifted her hand from beneath the tablecover and waved it at them. 'See ... Harry gave me this ring before he went away, but I've only just started wearing it. We want you to know that we're thinking of getting married.'

'You can't, Rachel.' Ellen's voice was quiet, but very decisive and Rachel noticed that her mother was looking at Ben, rather than at her, as if for support.

'I don't mean yet,' Rachel continued, at the same time thinking that it might well have to be soon if what she suspected was true. 'I know I'm only twenty. Is that what you meant, Mam? Is that why you said I can't...?'

Ellen was shaking her head distractedly, opening and closing her mouth but the words would not come. 'Harry's going to come and see you both,' Rachel continued, 'to ask you if we can be engaged, officially, I mean. We didn't want to do anything without asking you.'

'It seems to me that you already have done,' Ellen replied sadly. 'You're wearing his ring, aren't you, and we didn't know a thing about it. But you can't marry him, Rachel; it's out of the question.'

'But why? You're being terribly unfair. I know I didn't say anything when he came home, but it's because you were so funny about it all. You didn't like me mentioning Harry, and so I stopped talking about him. But we love one another and—'

'Hold on a minute, Rachel.' Ben, speaking for the first time, raised his hand. 'There's a very good reason why you can't marry this lad and your mother isn't being unfair, truly she isn't. The only thing that's unfair is, she should have told you before.' He turned to look at his wife. 'Tell her now, Ellen. Go on, love. You know you must.'

Ellen looked down at her clenched hands, not at her daughter. 'You can't marry Henry Balderstone. You can't marry him...' she gave a deep, shuddering sigh '...because he's your brother.'

'What!' Rachel couldn't have been more

stunned if her mother had said that the young man was Jack the Ripper. 'What do you mean? What are you talking about? Of course he's not my brother... How can he be?'

Ellen looked steadily at her now, her brown eyes filled with sadness. 'Your father ... William – he had another woman. She was called Balderstone. Jessie Balderstone. And she had a child – William's child – a little boy, your age. He's the same age as you, isn't he, your Harry?'

'Yes,' Rachel breathed, almost inaudibly. 'Two months older than me. He's twenty-one. But that doesn't mean–'

'I met them, both of them, Jessie and her son, before we left Preston.' Ellen went on. 'The little boy's name was John Henry. You see? Henry – Harry...'

'But – but that's not Harry's name. He's not called John!' Yet Rachel knew that she wasn't really positive.

Ellen shook her head sorrowfully. 'He's obviously dropped the John. He might not have wanted to go through life as John Henry.'

Rachel was staring at her mother more in disbelief than horror; the full horror was to dawn on her later. It was all so ridiculous, so impossible. That was what she told her now. 'You're talking nonsense, Mam, absolute rubbish. Just because this woman's name was Balderstone, that doesn't mean a thing. Besides, Harry's got a father. He talks about his mam and dad and his ... sisters.' A dreadful thought suddenly struck her. Stepsisters, he had said. She tried to stifle it. 'I don't believe you.'

'But you haven't met them, have you, his mother and father?'

'No, but I'm going to, on Wednesday. After Harry's been to see you. He was coming tomorrow ... I don't believe a word of it, Mam.'

'You've got to believe me, Rachel,' Ellen implored. 'I know Jessie may well be married now. It's more than likely that she would be. The man he talks about could be his stepfather, like Ben is to you. You don't always mention it, do you?'

'But then Harry wouldn't be called Balderstone, would he?' Rachel could feel herself getting angrier and angrier. Never before had she felt so angry with her mother. She couldn't, in fact, remember ever feeling much animosity to her at all; they had always been such good friends. 'It seems to me, Mother, that you want it to be true,' she shouted. 'You want him to be my brother ... and I tell you he's not!'

'Of course I don't. Don't be silly, dear. That's the last thing I want. But it's too much of a coincidence. You must admit it, love. It's the name, mainly. It's such an unusual one ... and Harry may well have kept it when his mother remarried. And where they live, as well. Harry lives in Maudlands, doesn't he, near St Walburge's Church?' Rachel nodded unwillingly. 'That's where Jessie lived. Besides, he looks rather like your father, Rachel. I don't like to admit it, but he does. Same colour hair and eyes...'

'He's nothing like him!' Rachel leapt to her feet, the force of her movement making the chair

318

fall backwards. 'And if you were so sure, Mother, why didn't you tell me before, when I first met Harry? Why wait till now?'

'Your mother didn't know at first, Rachel,' said Ben calmly. 'It was only when she found out his surname and where he lived. And then, well, Harry went to France, and Ellen thought—'

'She thought he'd be killed! Yes, I know – she *hoped* he'd be killed!'

'Of course I didn't, Rachel love!' cried Ellen. 'I just thought it would fizzle out. These things often do. You'd had a lot of young men. I'm sorry, love, really I am. I realise I should have told you before. I know I've left it too late.'

'You're dead right it's too late! A hell of a lot too late, Mother!' Rachel had never felt so wounded in her life. At that moment she wanted to strike out at Ellen, to hurt her just as much as she herself had been hurt. 'And d'you know why? Because I'm having a baby, that's why. I'm expecting Harry Balderstone's child!'

Rachel burst into tears, then, sobbing uncontrollably, she stumbled over the fallen chair and dashed out into the hallway. By the time her stunned parents had followed her she had already pushed her arms into her weekday coat which hung on the hallstand and was ramming her straw hat on to her head.

'Rachel, come back, love. We'll talk about it. I didn't want to upset you like this. Come on, take your coat off,' Ellen pleaded.

'It's too late to talk about it, isn't it, Mam? Like you've just said, you've left it too late.'

'But where are you going? You can't go out in

that state.' Ellen reached out and took her arm. 'Come on, love. Be sensible.'

Rachel snatched her arm away as though her mother's touch were red-hot. 'Leave go of me! I'm going to find Harry, that's where I'm going. And he'll tell me ... he'll tell me it's not true. It's all a pack of lies!' She wrenched open the front door and the glass panel in it shook as she slammed it behind her.

'Leave her, Ellen,' said Ben consolingly, putting his arm round her. They listened to Rachel's frenzied footsteps on the path, then the sound of the iron gate opening and clanging shut behind her. 'It'll make things worse if we go after her. There's nothing else we can do for the moment.'

'No, I've already done more than enough.' Ellen buried her head against his shoulder. 'Oh Ben, whatever are we going to do?'

Chapter Sixteen

Rachel didn't often give way to tears and, whenever she did, they were of short duration. Her outburst now was due mainly to shock. She would be devastated if what her mother had said turned out to be true, but she didn't believe one word of it! It was all the most ridiculous nonsense, and Harry, when she found him, would be able to confirm this.

So Rachel told herself as she hurried along the quiet Sunday streets towards Central Station. There were a few early-season visitors out and about, taking a stroll after their boarding-house breakfast, but it was too early for church- and chapel-goers. Rachel took a peek at her fob watch; it was not yet ten o'clock. She didn't know the times of the trains to Preston, but she assumed there would be quite a few, even on a Sunday. She hadn't given that a thought when she had rushed out of the house. She had only known that she had to put as much distance as possible between herself and her mother, and that she couldn't possibly wait until the next day to see Harry. She had to find him right away; he would be able to banish her fears.

Fortunately there was a train waiting to leave at ten-fifteen and Rachel hurried aboard. She was worried that Ben might be chasing after her to beg her not to be so hasty and to come back home, but the train pulled out on time without her being pursued. There was no one else in the compartment, and she was thankful for that. Most holidaymakers, no doubt, would be going home later in the day, making the most of their precious time at the seaside; besides, the middle of May was rather early for visitors at all. Apart from a few days at Easter and Whitsuntide the Blackpool season didn't begin in earnest till June.

Rachel had collapsed gratefully on to the seat, more than a little out of breath; she had been almost running by the time she reached the station. Now, as the train pulled away, passing the gasworks, then the Big Dipper at South Shore Pleasure Beach, she rose to her feet and peered into the fly-blown mirror on the opposite wall. Anxious brown eyes – so like her mother's – stared back at her and she found that her legs were still shaking a little; her hands, too, as she lifted them to adjust her straw hat. She had rammed it on to her head without looking and it was somewhat askew. She straightened it, so that the spray of artificial pink roses was at the side, where it should be, and tucked some stray wisps of her fair hair under the brim. The collar, too, on her brown coat was crooked and she put it straight. She was most unsuitably dressed for a late spring day – apart from the hat – and a Sunday, at that, but she had come out in a terrible rush, giving little heed to her appearance. Now she realised she hadn't even got her gloves with her, without which someone as fastidious as Rachel didn't consider she was properly dressed.

Her mother, she mused, would tell her she looked like the wreck of the *Hesperus*. But she didn't want to think about her mother just now. It was all Ellen's fault that she was here at all, making this headlong dash to Preston.

Rachel sat down again, knowing full well that her titivating in the mirror was only a ruse she had invented to take her mind away from her real problems. Now as the train rattled along, the full enormity of the situation began to dawn on her. It was all very well for her to tell herself that it was not so, that Harry would set her mind at rest ... but supposing he was unable to do so? Supposing his mother *was* called Jessie; supposing the man he spoke of as Dad, or his 'old man', was only his stepfather. Supposing he were, after all, her *brother*... What then? The thought was too awful to even contemplate and Rachel took a firm grasp of the arms of the seat at each side of her to stop the fit of trembling that had begun. She took deep breaths, in and out, in and out, until she felt calmer, relieved at least that she still had the carriage to herself. No one else entered at Kirkham and then it seemed no time at all before the tall spire of St Walburge's Church came into view. She was almost there.

It was this church that Rachel knew she must head towards, for it was in that district, known as Maudlands, that Harry lived. She knew his address, Springfield Street, but it didn't mean very much to her. When she had lived in Preston as a child it had been at the other end of the town; and she couldn't remember ever venturing as far as that particular neighbourhood. She alighted from the train, and was immediately tempted to hop on one going in the opposite direction, back home to Blackpool; but she knew that she had to carry on with the task she had set herself ... to prove her mother wrong.

She climbed the steep cobbled incline that led from the station to the main thoroughfare of Fishergate. She was surprised how familiar this part of Preston still looked, even after so long an absence. They had lived a good half-mile from here, near where Fishergate merged into Church Street, and it was there that her Aunt Mary still managed the sweet shop. Walking quickly, Rachel crossed the main road, passed the Corn Exchange on Lune Street, then, keeping the spire of St Walburge's Church in view, she hurried up Friargate. It was when she reached the area near the gasworks that she realised she hadn't a clue where she was, or in which direction she should be heading. Because she hadn't seen them before, all these little streets of redbrick houses looked alike to Rachel.

She knew that she must ask the way, but there were very few people about. Many of them would be at Sunday morning worship; as she passed St Walburge's Church she could hear the faint sound of a congregation singing, but she doubted that Harry was among their number. As far as she knew he wasn't a Catholic ... or was he? She realised, with a sudden stab of fear, that there were many gaps in her knowledge of Harry. She had known him for a comparatively short time before he went away to the war, and now he was home, what did she really know about him? Panic threatened to overcome her as she wandered along yet another short street of terraced houses. Don't be such a fool, she admonished herself. You can't turn back now. You must be nearly there, and then you'll know. Even if it comes to the worst ... you'll know. For Rachel had discovered in these last panic-stricken couple of hours that uncertainty could be more destructive, even, than knowing the truth.

On the next corner there was a public house. Rachel could see two men approaching the swing door and she quickened her footsteps, but they had gone inside before she could speak to them. It was then that a young man crossed the road and walked on the pavement in front of her. She could see only his back view; he was of medium height and build and beneath his soft felt hat he had dark curly hair. Harry had a brown tweed jacket exactly like that. He had bought it since leaving the Army and he looked so handsome in it. Thank heaven! What a stroke of luck ... it must be him! Forgetting all her troubles for the moment, Rachel broke into a run.

'Harry! Harry ... wait!' She caught up with the young man and touched his arm.

The young man turned round. He was a complete stranger.

'Oh! I'm so sorry.' Rachel felt her face drop the proverbial mile and she quickly withdrew her hand. In the few seconds she looked at his face, Rachel perceived that this young man had bluish grey eyes, like Harry, and the same sort of dark curly hair. He was like him – quite a lot like him, in fact – but this man's nose was longer, his eyes were closer together and the set of his mouth was different; his lips were narrow and he looked as though he could be ill-tempered. 'I do beg your pardon,' she faltered. 'I thought you were...'

He had looked annoyed for a moment as he turned round, then, as his eyes alit on Rachel, his thin lips curved into a smile and his eyes glinted with wry amusement. 'You thought I was Harry. Don't apologise, sweetheart. Seems as though it might be my lucky day.'

'I'm sorry,' Rachel said again, quite matter-of-factly this time. 'I mistook you for someone else, that's all. Perhaps you could help me.' There was no reason after all why he should not do so. 'I'm looking for a friend of mine, a gentleman called Harry Balderstone. I know he lives in Springfield Street, but I'm not quite sure how to find it from here.'

'Well, well, well!' The young man burst out laughing. 'Harry Balderstone of all people! That's my name an' all ... Harry Balderstone. Well, sort of.'

'What on earth are you talking about?' Rachel frowned impatiently. 'What do you mean, it's your name? Do you know Harry or don't you?'

He didn't, at first, answer her last question. 'I'm called Balderstone anyroad,' he said, nodding towards her, his eyes seeming to take in every part of her, from head to toe. 'John Henry Balderstone, that's me. That's the name me daft old woman gave me anyway, and that's what she still calls me when she gets mad with me. "John Henry!" she says. So I suppose I could've called meself Harry if I wanted to, but I didn't. I'm Jack

... that's what everyone round here calls me. Jack Balderstone.' He held out his hand. 'Pleased to meet you, miss. And you are...?'

'Rachel,' she replied bemusedly, taking his hand a trifle unwillingly. 'Rachel Hobson. But I don't understand. Harry – my friend, Harry – you know him, do you?'

''Course I know him! He's Henry, me cousin, isn't he? Born within a few weeks of one another we were, Henry and me. Could've been a bit confusing like, us having nearly the same names, so he called himself Harry and I settled for Jack.'

Rachel was totally confused. Was it *her* Harry he was talking about? And this young man was Jack, short for ... John Henry? All of a sudden the realisation hit her like a thunderbolt. So this young man was John Henry! She still couldn't take it in. 'You say you're cousins?' she asked hesitantly. 'You and Harry – how are you cousins?'

'Because me mam and his old fellow are brother and sister. Mind you, me Uncle Joe doesn't approve much of me, nor our Jessie ... that's me mam. What's up, luv? You look as though you've seen a ghost. Is there summat wrong?'

He took hold of her arm, but Rachel didn't pull away. 'No, not at all,' she said wonderingly, looking into his puzzled bluish-grey eyes, so like Harry's, and yet not like them. 'No, there's nothing wrong.' She hadn't taken to this young fellow; instinctively, she had found herself disliking him. But now she couldn't stop the smile that she could feel spreading all over her

327

face. 'Nothing wrong at all, thank you.'

He must think she was no end of a fool, though. 'It was just that I was getting rather worried, thinking I'd never find my way. And it was a surprise, finding out that you and Harry are cousins. Do you think you could tell me, please, how to get to Springfield Street?'

'I'll do better than that – I'll take yer.' He gestured towards the public house. 'I was going in there, but that'll have to wait. Come on, luv. It's not very far. Just past the mill and round the next corner.'

Rachel fell into step next to him, still not quite able to comprehend what was happening. Jack pointed down the next street they passed. 'That's Gordon Street. That's where me and me mam live. Only a stone's throw from Harry's place – not that we see much of one another, mind. Relations aren't all that cordial between them and us. Joe doesn't care for me mam's goings-one.' He gave a snigger and nudged at Rachel's arm.

She felt herself recoiling, but tried to contain her feelings; after all, he was being helpful. 'Oh yes, I see,' she muttered.

'Shouldn't think you do, luv,' he chuckled, nudging her again. 'You wouldn't see at all, proper young lady like you. You're Harry's lady friend then, are you?'

Again Rachel felt his eyes scrutinising her from her straw hat to her pointed-toed shoes. 'Yes, I am,' she replied.

'Well, well – Harry's a lucky devil, isn't he? And where might you be from? Not from round here, that's for sure, or you'd know your way about.'

'I'm from Blackpool.' There was no point in going into further details, in telling him she had once lived here, for instance. She had the feeling that the less she told him the better it might be.

'Blackpool, eh? Oh, I do like to be beside the seaside...' He broke into song, though not at all musically. 'Didn't know old Harry had a lady friend in Blackpool, but then I don't know much about him, do I? Why didn't he meet you at the station? I should've thought that 'ud be the proper thing to do and our Harry usually knows his manners.'

'He's not expecting me,' Rachel answered. Really, this fellow was far too nosey!

'Oh, I see, surprise visit. Well, well, well – lucky old Harry, that's what I say. Tell you what, luv – if he's not there, then you come back and find me. Number fourteen Gordon Street. I'll be waiting.'

'I thought you were on your way to the pub?' Rachel couldn't help but grin at him. He was probably only trying to be friendly, and she had reason to be grateful to him, very grateful. 'Anyway, I expect he'll be at home.' She crossed her fingers tightly as she said this.

'Aye, I daresay he will. Anyroad, it's been nice meeting you, luv. Mebbe I'll see you again sometime, who knows.' He slowed his footsteps as they reached the next corner. 'Here we are – Springfield Street. It's just along there, number seventeen. I won't come any further – I've told you how it is.'

Rachel smiled at him. 'Thank you very much.

You've been very helpful.'

'Tara, luv. Be seeing you.' He winked at her then strolled away.

Number seventeen was similar to the other houses in the street in size and style; redbricked terraced dwellings with slated roofs, the front doors opening straight on to the pavement. Very much like the houses her gran and aunt had lived in on Sefton Street, Rachel recalled, although her Aunt Mary and family, thanks to the profits from the sweet shop and market stall, had now moved to a semi-detached house at Frenchwood. Number seventeen, however, appeared more spruce than some of its neighbours; it had fresh brown paintwork, clean and tidy lace curtains, and stone steps and window sills edged in white with a donkey stone.

She lifted the brass knocker, still feeling bewildered at the turn that events had taken and having little idea of how she was going to explain things to Harry – such a complicated tale it was turning out to be – always supposing that he was there. Fortunately he was; it was Harry who opened the door at her knock.

'Rachel, what a surprise! A nice one though,' he added quickly. 'There's nothing wrong, is there, love? I was coming over tomorrow you know; I haven't forgotten.'

'No, there's nothing wrong, Harry. At least, I thought there was something wrong, but now I know there isn't.'

'What do you mean? You're talking in riddles, my love.' He put his arm round her shoulders and gave her a squeeze. 'Anyway, come in and meet my mam and dad, then you can tell me all about it.'

He led the way into a homely room in which a huge fire was burning in the grate. Brass ornaments gleamed on the mantelpiece and on either side of the clipped rag rug were comfortable-looking chairs covered in flowered chintz. Just such a room as Rachel remembered from her gran's house, and not unlike Bella Broadbent's cosy parlour where her mother had used to take her when she was a little girl. She at once felt at home.

'Mam, Dad – where are you?' called out Harry. 'Surprise for you.'

A man who looked very much like Harry, but older, and a buxom woman with dark hair greying at the temples, came through the door which, Rachel assumed, led into the kitchen.

'This is Rachel.' Harry led her forward. 'You've been wanting to meet her, haven't you? Well – here she is.'

'How d'you do, dear?'

'Pleased to meet you. We've been wondering when our Harry was going to show you to us. We've heard a lot about you.'

The welcome from both of them was warm and sincere, though Rachel couldn't help but be aware of the slightly puzzled look in their eyes. After all, she had descended on them without any warning, and she was conscious, too, that the table at the back of the room was already laid for Sunday dinner, with three places.

'How do you do?' she greeted them, shaking their hands. 'I'm so glad to meet you at last. I'm

331

sorry I've come at such an awkward time.' She glanced at the table. 'But something happened at home, you see, something my mother told me ... and I had to come and tell Harry right away. It's difficult to explain,' she faltered. 'I don't know where to begin.'

'Begin at the beginning, lass. That's always best.' Joe Balderstone grinned at her, patting the seat of an easy chair. 'Sit down and make yerself at home. Give us your coat first, 'cause you'll be stopping and having your dinner with us, won't you? Oh yes,' he said, as Rachel made to protest. 'Susan's got a joint of beef in the oven and we can easily peel a few more spuds.' He hung her coat on a hook on the back of the door then drew up a dining chair and sat down. 'Now, what's the problem? Or is it summat you just want to tell Harry?'

'No, all of you,' said Rachel, looking up at Harry as he perched on the arm of her chair. Susan Balderstone quietly sat down in the easy chair opposite. Rachel felt a little discomfited as three pairs of eyes looked questioningly at her, but they were smiling encouragingly and Harry's arm around her shoulders seemed to give her confidence.

'Begin at the beginning, you said.' She smiled back hesitantly at Harry's father. 'Well, that would be when we lived in Preston, when I was a little girl. My mother was married then to a man called William Bamber...'

'Bamber!' Joe gave a start. 'That was the name of the cobbler, wasn't it? The one that–'

'Yes. He was my father,' said Rachel.

332

The three eager listeners said little as she told the story in her own way, but she was conscious of their sympathy and understanding and, once she got going, it was all quite easy.

Susan Balderstone shook her head ponderingly. 'Dearie me, your poor mam! I can understand how she must've felt when you took up with our Harry, and it was an easy enough mistake to make. I always said, didn't I Joe, that their names were too much alike, one called Henry and the other John Henry. Not that we've had much to do with Jessie lately. The less we see of her the better. She's an embarrassment to us, that one, especially with her having the same name. She's disgraced the name of Balderstone, hasn't she, Joe?'

'Aye, I reckon she has,' Joe replied quietly. 'But least said, soonest mended.'

'Jessie's your sister then?' asked Rachel, breaking into the momentary silence.

'Yes, and she still has the same name because she's never wed.'

'Huh! Never needed to,' interrupted Susan.

'Aye, I can see how the mix-up has occurred,' said Joe, frowning slightly at his wife. 'Our name's rather an unusual one. It's not surprising your mother thought what she did. Pity she didn't tell you right at the start, though. She could've saved herself a lot of worry and heartache, to say nowt of upsetting you like she did. You must've been in a rare old state, lass.'

'Yes, I was,' Rachel agreed. 'And then I met that young man... Oh!' She put her hand to her mouth as a thought suddenly struck her. 'That

333

man I was talking to – Jack – he must be … my brother!' Only now was the astonishing truth coming home to her.

''Fraid so, love.' Joe gave a rueful smile. 'It isn't our proudest boast I can tell you, that he's my nephew … or that she's my sister.'

Harry had said very little. Now he shook his head, giving a long, low whistle. 'Whew! This lot takes some swallowing. Rachel and that good-for-nothing scoundrel are brother and sister?'

'Half-sister, actually,' said Joe, 'like our Jane and Norah are to you.'

'Wait a minute,' Rachel interrupted, turning to Harry. 'You told me you had two stepsisters. That was one of the reasons I thought it might be true, what my mother said.'

'He meant half-sisters,' said Susan. 'He always gets it mixed up. Stepbrothers and sisters are when you have no parents in common. Jane and Norah are Joe's girls by his first wife, but he's father to all three of them.'

'I'm still a bit lost,' said Harry. 'I knew Jack was illegitimate, of course. I've always known that. He came in for a fair amount of stick when we were at school – you know what kids are like – about him having no dad.'

'Yes, I know he's not had it easy,' said Susan, sounding rather grudging.

'But I didn't realise that you knew all along who his father was,' Harry went on. 'Rachel's real father was a clogger, you say? And he was the chap Aunt Jessie took up with?'

'Among others,' said Susan drily.

'There was no reason for you to know, lad,' said

Joe. 'It's all history now, though it's come back, sure enough, to give poor old Rachel a slap in the face.'

Rachel smiled. 'Never mind; it's all sorted out now. It's the first I'd heard of William Bamber's carryings-on, too. I'd no idea until Mam told me this morning. I knew Mam and William weren't happy though. I can't call him Father,' she explained. 'Ben's my father now, you see.'

'Aye, it's a rum tale and no mistake,' said Joe. 'I knew that Bamber's widow had turned the place into a sweet shop. I even knew she'd moved to Blackpool to start a business there; it was quite a nine days' wonder at the time – you know how folks gossip. But I didn't make the connection, even when Harry told us your parents had a rock factory.'

'No, you wouldn't,' said Rachel. 'She was still called Bamber then. And when she married Ben our Georgie and I took his name. Georgie...' she went on thoughtfully. 'He's Jack's brother as well, then – half-brother. They're not all that much alike though, apart from the colour of their hair and eyes. Jack's more like you, Harry, isn't he? Well, something like you – in looks, I mean.'

'There's a family resemblance, certainly,' agreed Joe. 'Sure to be because Jessie and I are the most alike of any of our lot. But our Harry's nowt like that young layabout in disposition, I'm glad to say. Bone idle, that one is. But shifty with it.'

'Doesn't he work then?' enquired Rachel.

'When he has to. I think he's doing a spot of bricklaying at the moment. Lives by his wits,

335

y'might say. And he's certainly not witless. Crafty as a cartload of monkeys, is Jack Balderstone.'

'Was he in the war?' asked Rachel.

'No – trust Jack. Talked himself out of that very nicely. Flat feet, so he said, and a weak chest. Anyroad, he managed to pull the wool over their eyes – he usually does. You didn't tell him owt, did you?' Joe asked, turning to Rachel. 'About ... all this lot – what you've just been telling us?'

'No, of course I didn't,' replied Rachel. 'Only my name, and that I lived in Blackpool. He did most of the talking.'

'Aye, our Jessie was bitter about things for quite a while,' Joe went on musingly. 'She thought she should have been taken care of – in the will, like, but it seems there was no will and it all went to your mam, which was only right, in my opinion. Jessie was expecting another bairn an' all, but she lost it. Just as well, if you ask me.'

'Was it my ... was it William's?' asked Rachel.

'Aye, so she said. I know she used to go round touching your mother for all she could get. Anyroad, after she lost the baby she disappeared for a while, her and John Henry. We never knew where she'd been. Probably no further than Wigan or Chorley. Then she turned up again like a bad penny and settled a couple of streets away.'

'She didn't carry on pestering my mother, did she?' asked Rachel. 'After we moved to Blackpool?'

'Not as far as I know,' said Joe. 'No, I shouldn't think she did. She did a lot of talking, mind, about how she'd get her own back one day, how she'd been cast off without a penny an' all that.

But then she found … other interests.'

'Aye, outside the Old Dog Inn, or the Grey Horse and Seven Stars, that's where she used to hang out,' put in Susan, rising and going towards the kitchen. 'That was before the war. Now they know where to find her and come knocking at t'door. Well, if you'll excuse me, I'd best go and see to the veg. Sitting here chatting won't buy the baby a new bonnet.'

Rachel was conscious of the warning frown that Joe levelled at his wife and the imperceptible shake of his head as she spoke of Jessie's goings-on. Such things were hardly ever mentioned in Rachel's hearing, certainly never within her own family, but she knew what Susan was talking about. She was well aware that there were such women; she had seen them herself on occasions, hanging about outside Yates's Wine Lodge in Blackpool.

'Aye, it's a rum do, it is an' all,' said Joe again. 'Anyhow, there's no reason why it should affect you two all that much.' He leaned towards Rachel, his blue eyes twinkling. 'So will we be hearing wedding bells soon, eh? We've heard a whisper from Harry here that things might be heading that way.'

'I think so, Mr Balderstone, now we've sorted things out a bit.' Rachel smiled warmly at him. 'Harry was going to come and see my parents tomorrow. That was … before all this happened.'

'I'll come back with you today,' said Harry, squeezing her shoulder. 'I can't let you go all that way on your own.'

'It's only eighteen miles,' laughed Rachel. 'And

I'm a big girl, you know.'

'All the same, I'm coming with you. You've had a nasty shock, and I'll help you to explain it all to your mam and dad. Your poor mother ... no wonder she was looking askance at me. Not that I've seen her since I came back from France.'

'She'll be all right with you now,' said Rachel, though not very confidently. She was not at all sure, in fact, that she wanted Harry with her when she went back home. She had left in such a temper this morning and she would have preferred to sort things out in her own way. Besides, there was something that she still hadn't told Harry, and she didn't feel that she wanted to tell him, not today. Like a fool, though, she had gone and blurted it out to her mother and Ben, all because she'd been in such a rage. Now she was wishing she hadn't.

So much had happened that it was all feeling more like a dream than reality. She took hold of her wrist and pinched the flesh hard. Yes, she was wide awake all right, and the jumble in her mind was starting to sort itself out into coherent facts ... Jack was John Henry, the child that her mother remembered; he was half-brother to her and George, incredible though that seemed. He was also cousin to Harry. But she and Harry – thanks be to a most merciful God! – were not related at all.

It was the middle of the afternoon when Rachel and Harry climbed aboard a Blackpool-bound train.

'Your parents made me so welcome,' said Rachel, as the train pulled away. 'And that dinner

– goodness! I can't remember when I ate so much.' She patted her full stomach. 'This morning, when Mam told me that awful tale, I felt as though I'd never be able to eat another thing. I left most of my bacon and egg ... I've only just realised.'

'Then that's why you were so hungry,' smiled Harry. 'You've got a good appetite, I must say, for someone so slim and dainty. But then my mam's a good cook. I doubt if anybody'd be able to resist her treacle tart.'

'Mmm ... it was delicious,' agreed Rachel.

She was certainly full up, replete, as they would say in more elegant circles. She might be tempted to think she was 'eating for two', but she had always enjoyed her food. Besides, now she was not too sure. There was a niggling pain at the pit of her stomach which she didn't think could be due to indigestion, and it was getting worse. She leaned back in her seat and closed her eyes. After a few minutes she was in no doubt. The pain was severe now and there was something happening down below which was unmistakable. She was not pregnant, after all.

'Rachel? Rachel, love, are you all right?' Harry leaned forward and grasped hold of her hands. She hadn't spoken for several minutes.

She opened her eyes, staring blankly at him. The pain did this to her sometimes, made her insensible to everything except the grinding torment in her abdomen. 'Yes, I mean no, I'm not all right. But I will be, when I get home.' All she needed at times like this was a hot water bottle and a good dose of aspirin.

'Rachel, whatever is it?' Harry came and sat beside her, his arm encircling her. 'You've gone as white as a sheet. Oh, is it...?' He looked a trifle discomfited.

Propriety decreed that such things were not mentioned between young men and women, but they were, after all, soon to be married. 'Yes. It's the time of the month,' Rachel whispered, although there was no one to hear but Harry. 'It's painful sometimes, especially when I'm late.'

She clung tightly to his hand; she saw him wince at her grasp as a spasm of pain seized her. 'Harry,' she breathed, as it subsided a little, 'I've something to tell you. I was late – a few weeks late – and I thought ... I thought I was having a baby.'

'Whew!' Harry gave a low whistle. 'And now you know that you're not. Well, that's a relief, love. I'm sorry you're feeling poorly, but we'll soon have you home again.'

'But, Harry...' Rachel looked at him imploringly. 'The awful thing is I've already told my parents. I told them I was expecting your child.'

'Oh, Lor...' said Harry.

Chapter Seventeen

'You look beautiful, Rachel love, really beautiful.' Ellen smiled fondly at her daughter as she stood before her in her wedding dress of cream silk. The straight unfitted bodice – quite the latest style – and the ankle-length skirt, falling gently from a waist inset of silver-trimmed lace, suited her trim figure to perfection; and the headdress of silken and wax flowers, holding in position her long flowing veil, highlighted the delicacy of her complexion.

'It's more than you deserve though, you know,' Ellen went on, but the hint of a mischievous grin in her brown eyes told her daughter quite clearly that it was only mock disapproval and that she had forgiven her for her misconduct. 'A white wedding … you know what that's supposed to signify, don't you? And … well, you're not, are you?'

'It's cream, Mam, not white,' smiled Rachel, fingering the delicate material of the skirt, 'if that makes any difference. Anyway, Harry and I haven't, not since that time. I'd like you to know that. It was only because he'd just come home and we were so happy to be together again.' She looked down at the bedroom carpet, a faint blush tingeing her cheeks. 'We knew, after I'd had such a shock, that it would be all the better if we waited.

'I'm so glad you like him, Mam, you and Dad. And we can't thank you enough for letting us have this lovely wedding.' Rachel gave a little laugh. 'It hasn't happened yet, but it's going to be a lovely wedding, I just know it is.' Her brown eyes were alight with happiness and Ellen felt the trace of a tear in her own.

'It's what I wanted as well, darling,' she replied. 'You're my only daughter, and I've always dreamed of seeing you married in style to the man you love. And I know you love Harry and that you're going to be very happy together. Yes, Ben and I do like Harry, very much, and we couldn't have chosen anyone better for you. I'm sorry I put you through such an ordeal when I thought ... well, you know what I thought. But it's all turned out wonderfully well, thank God.'

'It's all right, Mam,' said Rachel. 'I can understand it now. But I always knew you'd like Harry once you got to know him.'

Ellen, over the last few months, had grown very fond of Harry Balderstone. Within a few weeks of that first meeting between Harry and his prospective in-laws, he found lodgings in Hornby Road, and Ellen and Ben hadn't needed much persuading to find him a job at the factory. Now, some five months later, Ellen was wondering how they had ever managed without him. He was a hard and enthusiastic worker – just as Ben used to be when she had first known him, Ellen thought wistfully.

Ellen had explained to Harry that the rock factory was not at all like a cotton mill. They employed relatively few staff and all the men they engaged, unless they were experienced workers from another factory, were obliged to start at the very bottom. Rock-making was a skill that had to be learned gradually.

Harry had quickly mastered the various procedures; the mixing and boiling, the colouring and flavouring; the pulling; and – most importantly – the lettering and assembling. Ellen could see, the way things were heading, that Harry Balderstone would very soon be regarded as the first hand at the factory rather than her own son, George. Sam, Ben's brother, who had been a skilled worker, had been killed in France. Bertie Shaw, his co-worker, also had not returned. The temporary staff they had employed had left for one reason or another, so the regular male staff now consisted of Amos Hardy (Ellen's protégé from Preston, who had never progressed much beyond the job of pan man), Harry, and George.

George, alas, was still drinking heavily. Ellen only prayed that he would try to keep sober for his sister's wedding. She had hoped that his intoxication, which had so dismayed her soon after he returned home, would prove to be an isolated incident. But her hopes had soon been shattered. Now, he arrived home the worse for drink several times a week, although he usually had enough sense to keep out of his mother's way and to hide the worst of his excesses. Ellen stoically tried to turn a blind eye. She didn't want to be thought of as a nagging mother, but if his drunkenness started to affect his work, then she would have to speak to him. Fortunately, like his father before him, he always seemed to be no worse for his intemperance the morning afterwards. But there might always be a first time. It was a blessing that Harry was now there to keep a watchful eye on George, because Ben was still seemingly oblivious to much that was going on at the factory.

'You and Ben were married in October, weren't you?' Rachel was saying now. 'I remember the flowers in the chapel, chrysanthemums and dahlias, how lovely they looked – all the glowing autumn colours – and the flowers you carried were golden, too, weren't they?'

'Yes, just a little spray on my Bible,' said Ellen. 'The one that Ben bought for me,' she added pensively. 'They were the same colour as the flowers you'll be carrying today, but yours is a much bigger bouquet, of course. You're a proper bride, but for me it was the second time so I couldn't really have all the trimmings.' She smiled reminiscently. 'It was a wonderful day though – fifteen years ago; 1904 it was – and Ben and I have been so very happy together. If you and Harry are only half as happy then you'll have a lot to be thankful for.'

'You can still say that, Mam? After all that has happened, that you are happy?' Rachel was looking at her concernedly, a trifle doubtfully.

'Of course we are, dear. I suppose contented is more the word now, rather than blissfully happy. I know how much Ben has changed – you know it too, Rachel – but that's the war. It's caused so much misery for so many people, and there are thousands who are worse off than me. I've just learned to be thankful that he came back at all. He might not have done ... one of this brothers didn't.'

'Yes, I know things are different,' she went on. 'Ben has become so much more ... self-centred, and that's a thing he never used to be, but I'm only glad that he's found something to occupy his mind, even if he does leave all the business of the factory to me. We still love one another, and – yes – we're still happy. I took him for better or worse. That's what you'll be saying too, Rachel, in an hour's time. You can't just turn your back and pretend you don't want to know when the going gets rough.'

'At least I'm glad he agreed to give me away,' said Rachel. 'It would have been dreadful if Dad had said he wouldn't walk down the aisle with me.'

It had been Ellen who had broached that subject with Ben; he was still sticking to his resolve not to enter a place of worship again. However, he had agreed without demur to give Rachel away, and for that Ellen was more thankful than she could say. 'Of course I will,' he had said. 'Did you really think I would refuse to be at our daughter's wedding? If she wants to ask a blessing on her marriage then that's between her and–' He had stopped abruptly. 'Yes, of course I'll give her away.'

Ellen was not sure whether Ben had been going to say 'between her and Harry' or 'between her and God'. The God he professed to have forsaken.

She had agonised deeply at first about the

change in Ben's personality and outlook. He did make love to her now, very occasionally, but he appeared preoccupied, even at such intimate moments, and the act no longer brought her the deep joy and satisfaction that it once had done. But gradually she had learned, as she had told Rachel, to accept things as they were and to be content. Even to live with Ben's obsession with his latest diversion, the motor car he had coveted for so long.

'It seems to me as though Ben has had to find something to fill up the emptiness in his life ... in his soul, if you like,' Bella Broadbent, in her wisdom, had suggested to Ellen. Ellen still found consolation and encouragement in her occasional chats with the older woman.

'Look at it this way,' Bella had said. 'His religion was everything to him, wasn't it? Well, nearly everything, apart from you and his happy home life, of course – and I know he still loves you, Ellen, in spite of the way he's changed. Well, now he's turned his back on God, or says he has, he has to have something to fill up the big space that's left; it stands to reason. And he's not showing much interest in the factory, so he's making this new motor car his god. At least, that's the way it seems to me. Let him have his way, Ellen, if it's keeping him happy. And go out with him in the blessed thing, even though it might not be quite your cup of tea. Anyroad, it might only be a phase. He may well return to the fold – like that lost lamb in the hymn we sing in chapel – after your Rachel's wedding.'

Ellen had been unable to disguise her

misgivings or her alarm when Ben had returned home a couple of months before with a brand new Austin Twenty motor car. She succumbed eventually to Ben's idea of buying a motor van for their deliveries, to replace the old horse and cart. It was one of the few suggestions he had made and she was beginning to see that it made sense; although it had meant that they also had to employ a delivery man to drive the van. But a motor car for their own personal use? Ellen couldn't see the sense in that at all. There were perfectly good trams and omnibuses in Blackpool, and trains if they wished to travel further afield. Besides, what was wrong with Shanks's pony? Ellen had always walked; to work, to chapel, to visit friends and relations, and she couldn't see that she would ever want to do any different.

'But can we afford it?' she had asked, looking dubiously at the gleaming vehicle standing at the kerbside near their front gate. She didn't want to throw cold water all over Ben's new toy, which was, if she were honest, how she regarded it. His golden-brown eyes were alight with an enthusiasm which she knew she should be pleased to see there – he often looked so apathetic – but she couldn't with any sincerity share his excitement. 'I mean, it must have cost quite a lot.'

'Not all that much,' said Ben evasively. 'And of course we can afford it, Ellen. The factory and the shops are doing really well, you know they are.'

Yes, I know they are doing reasonably well,

347

thought Ellen. But how do you know, Ben? You hardly ever go there. But she didn't say anything like this. Only: 'Well, if you think we can afford it, then that's all right.' She gingerly touched the shining dark green bonnet. 'It's … very nice.'

'Very nice! Is that all you can say? She's a beauty, she is that! We're going to have some rare old times in this, I can tell you. We can drive out on a Sunday, to Morecambe or Southport. Perhaps to Scarborough, even. You'd like that, wouldn't you, Ellen?'

'We couldn't get to Scarborough in one day, Ben,' said Ellen, aware that she sounded somewhat curt. A thought suddenly struck her. 'You don't know how to drive it, do you?'

'No, but I shall learn. Nothing easier. I've been studying motor-car manuals for years, Ellen; you know I have. I know all about the mechanics of driving; I know just what to do.'

'How did you get it home?'

'A chap from the saleroom drove it. He gave me a few pointers as we were going along. And he's promised to go out with me again until I get the hang of it. Don't look so scared, Ellen. The motor car's here to stay, you take it from me. The days have gone, you know, when a man with a red flag had to walk in front of it. I bet this little beauty could do forty miles an hour.'

'Forty miles an hour!' Ellen was horrified. 'Good gracious, Ben, don't even think of it. Don't ever try it… Promise me you won't.'

'Of course I won't,' Ben chuckled. 'I wish you could see your face, Ellen. I only said that's what it could do … but I won't. At least not when you're with me.'

'Ben!' Ellen's voice was ominous.

'All right, all right, dear – only joking. But you'll come to love it, I know you will.'

Ellen was not so convinced. 'Where will you keep it?' she asked prosaically.

'Out here on the street – where else? They're even building houses with places to keep cars now. Motor stables, they called them at first; now they're calling them garages. But we haven't got one, unless we have one built in the yard at the back.'

Ellen, albeit reluctantly, had taken Bella's advice and tried to go along with Ben's obsession. She had to admit that he had mastered the mechanics of driving quite quickly and easily, and had driven her to such places as St Annes, Fleetwood and St Michael's on Wyre. She had seen parts of the Fylde countryside she had never viewed before, but it was hard to disguise her aversion to this modern mode of travel. Some people had called the motor car an invention of the Devil when it first appeared on the roads, and Ellen was inclined to agree. She could foresee a time when roads would be jam-packed with the infernal things, causing all manner of havoc and congestion, just as the vast numbers of horse-drawn vehicles had used to do in the big towns.

Ben's Austin Twenty was an open-top tourer. There was a hood which could be fastened over in inclement weather, but Ellen hated the smell of petrol and leather which built up in the enclosed space; so most of the time they drove with the top down, the wind playing havoc with Ellen's hair and blowing smuts into her face. She even bought a motoring costume, to show Ben how eager she was to please him; a cavalry twill coat with a large cape collar, and a hat with a gauze veil to tie under her chin or to pull over her face if needs be.

At least it was keeping Ben happy and occupied, she often told herself, and that was always Ellen's chief concern; to keep her husband happy. She had put her foot down, though, about the wedding. On no account would they be using their own motor car. She, Ellen, and the bridesmaids, would be driven to chapel in a hired limousine, as befitted the mother of the bride. And Rachel would arrive, five minutes later, in a separate motor car with Ben.

'It's been the happiest day of my life,' Rachel told Harry as they sat in the Morecambe-bound train.

'Glad to hear it, love.' Harry peered beneath the wide brim of her elegant hat, pulled low over her forehead, and tenderly kissed the tip of her nose. 'Let's hope there'll be many more happy days. A whole lifetime of them.'

There was silence for a few moments, save for the clattering of the train wheels, as Harry's arms encircled her and they kissed passionately. Rachel's large straw hat fell off and tumbled to the floor.

'Hey ... my best hat!' Laughingly she retrieved it and dusted it down.

'Leave it, darling,' said Harry, as she made to put it on again. 'You look nicer without it.' He stroked her fairish hair which waved softly around her cheeks and the nape of her neck, contrary to the current short fashion. 'Don't ever cut your hair, will you? I hate to see women looking like shorn lambs, and certainly not you.'

'I will if I want,' she answered pertly. 'Don't you try to tell me what to do with my own hair, Harry Balderstone!' She was laughing though, so he would know there was no animosity in her words. All the same, Rachel intended to start the way she meant to go on.

'All right ... Mrs Balderstone,' Harry grinned. 'I'm not going to be a domineering husband. Doubt if I'd get away with it with you, would I?'

'Mrs Balderstone,' Rachel repeated. 'Fancy that! Yes, that's who I am, isn't it? Mrs Balderstone.'

'I don't think your mother has ever really forgiven me for my name, has she?' Harry remarked. 'And I can't do anything about it. It's something I'm stuck with.'

'Mmm...' Rachel nodded thoughtfully. 'She says it brings back bad memories. At least, that's what she said at first, but I think she's getting more used to it now. She'll have to; as you say, we're stuck with it. It was nice to meet your relations, Harry,' she went on. 'And Susie and Sally behaved really well, didn't they?' Two of Harry's small nieces had acted as bridesmaids, whilst Ruth, Rachel's friend from the office, had been the chief attendant.

Rachel had met several of Harry's relatives for the first time that day. It was, however, such a large family, that it had proved impossible to invite all of them. Even so, there had been more than forty people who had gathered at Jenkinson's Café in Talbot Square to partake of the wedding breakfast.

'My mam's been concerned, I must admit, about not inviting your Aunt Jessie and your cousin, Jack. She was frightened there might be repercussions. Jessie threatened her once, you see, and she can't seem to forget it. But I've kept telling her not to worry about it. It's ages ago, and they don't even know who we are, do they?'

'No,' said Harry. 'They don't know about the connection with your father. Jack knew I was getting married though. I met him a few weeks back and I told him. He wasn't surprised... He remembered you. But they wouldn't expect an invitation. We didn't invite any of my dad's brothers and sisters, did we? Apart from Uncle Albert – he's always been a favourite of mine – so they can't say they've been left out. Anyway, never mind them. They're best forgotten. We're living in Blackpool now, so our paths won't cross, will they? And I hope it won't be long before we have a little place of our own.'

When they returned from their honeymoon in Morecambe they were to commence their married life at the Hobson home in King Street. It was a big house with ample room for all of them, but they hoped to have their own home before many months had passed. Rachel intended to carry on working in the office, so with two wages coming in it shouldn't take them long to save enough money.

'I met Harry in the pub the other night,' Jack Balderstone told his mother, one evening in the early autumn of 1919. 'He's getting wed.'

'Oh, is he indeed?' Jessie carried on painting her fingernails as though she were not the slightest bit interested. 'What our Joe's lot do or what they don't do it doesn't matter a tinker's cuss to us, John Henry. He's shown me all too clearly what he thinks of me, has our Joe, so as far as I am concerned he can go and jump in the bloody river. To hell with him, and his son an' all. Toffee-nosed little pipsqueak he is, looking down his nose at me as though I'm a bit of muck.' She paused with the tiny red-covered brush held between her finger and thumb. 'Who's he marrying anyroad?'

'That lass from Blackpool. I told you – I met her in the street a few months back. Rachel Hobson, she's called.'

Jessie looked at her son sharply. 'You never told me her name. Rachel ... Hobson, you say?'

'Aye, that's it. I'm sure I told you though, Mam. What the hell does it matter, whatever his bit of fluff's called? She's a good-looking lass, though. Harry's a lucky sod, I must say. I wouldn't mind–'

'Hobson...' Jessie was staring into space, an unfathomable look on her face. 'You never told me she was called Hobson. Do you know, that was the name of the fellow she married – Hobson. And I know she had a daughter called Rachel. Two kiddies they had, her and William; Georgie and Rachel. Good God! I don't believe it.' A wild look had come into her grey eyes and the nail-varnish brush fell unheeded from her fingers on to the table top.

'Who, Mam? What the hell are you going on about? Do you know her then, this lass of Harry's?'

'No, but I knew her mother, damn her to hell and back! And I knew her father – at least, if she's who I think she is.' Jessie's eyes narrowed as she looked at her son. 'I've got a funny feeling – right in my gut I can feel it – that that lass you're telling me about, the one your Cousin Harry's going to marry, may very well be William Bamber's kid. Your sister.'

'*What!!*'

'You heard me, John Henry. Your sister ... well, half-sister. I'm sure I'm right.'

'But my father was called Bamber. You've told me often enough about William Bamber, the clogger. You've made no bones about it. I remember him an' all ... very vaguely.'

'But I've not told you much about her, have I? Nellie Bamber, his stuck-up cow of a wife. You met her when you were a little lad, on the market stall, her and her mother. She used to give you ha'penny lollipops as though she were handing out the bloody crown jewels. You remember that, don't you?'

'Aye, I think I remember the lollipops,' said Jack. 'And that woman, she was...?'

'That was Nellie Bamber. I haven't mentioned her much lately, though, not since she took herself off to Blackpool.'

'Blackpool?'

'Yes, she moved there years ago. Good riddance

to bad rubbish, I thought. I could manage without her anyroad. I was getting on my feet again. But I didn't forget about her, not me. I don't forget somebody that's done the dirty on me, like that stuck-up cow did. I kept my ear to the ground, didn't I? It's surprising what you learn when you keep your ears open. And I knew she'd got married again, to a fellow called Hobson. And I know they've got a rock factory, used to have, at any rate. But I've not heard anything of her for ages.'

'It might not be the same girl, Mam.'

'But I've a feeling it is, Jack. Find out for me. I want to know.'

'What for? You've just said you couldn't care less about Joe and his friggin' family, so why the sudden interest?'

'It might be useful information, that's why. Go on – find out, it shouldn't be hard. He'll have done some swanking in the pubs, will Flash Harry. Don't go asking him owt, though. Least said...'

'Give me credit for a bit of sense, Mam, can't you? Aye, I'll do a bit of sniffin' around.'

Jack was able to report back, before many days had passed, that in all probability it was the same Rachel Hobson. Her parents had a rock factory and two shops in Blackpool as well as a few seasonal stalls. In fact, theirs was one of the big names in the Blackpool rock fraternity; they seemed to be very well thought of.

'Huh! She's done all right for herself, hasn't she, Lady Muck!' Jessie tugged a comb through her wavy hair with more force than was necessary. It was now cut in a short, fashionable style, but was still as dark as it always had been. Jessie made sure of that.

'You've not done so badly yerself, Mam,' said Jack mildly. 'We're not exactly on the bread line, are we?'

'No, but it's no thanks to her.' Jessie looked at her son through the mirror over the mantelpiece. 'If it'd been up to her we'd have been in the workhouse, both of us, John Henry. I know our house is a little palace now, compared with a lot of 'em round here, but what I've got I've had to work bloody hard for, and don't you forget it. I haven't noticed you getting off your backside so much, you lazy sod.'

'Aw, come on, Mam. That's not fair. I pay me way, you know I do. I just have to wait for the right … opportunities.'

There were no secrets between the pair of them about how they each made their money; Jack by dodgy dealings of one sort and another, and his mother from payments from her various gentlemen 'friends'. Jessie's house was now sumptuously appointed with new carpets and furniture and, what was more, she owned the property, which was more than a lot of her neighbours could boast. Jack had stayed with his mother because he knew on which side his bread was buttered and because, in spite of their frequent squabbles, they understood one another; they could be said to be fond of one another.

'Have you never thought of moving, Mam?' Jack asked now. 'I know you've made it posh an' all that, but we could afford summat a bit better, couldn't we – a bit classier, like?'

'Oh, I don't know about that, Jack. The folks round here know me. Ignore me for the most part, I admit, but at least they leave me alone. I couldn't live in a swanky area. I might run into all sorts of bother.'

Jack watched his mother in silence for a few moments as she applied her lipstick. A calculating gleam came into his eyes. 'How would you fancy living in Blackpool, Mam?' he asked.

'Blackpool?' Jessie appeared startled for a moment. Then, 'You mean because of...?' she faltered.

'Yes. I thought that was maybe what you had in mind, when you told me to find out.'

'Yes, happen I did.' Jessie nodded thoughtfully. 'I don't know though. I've got me own ... customers here, Jack.'

'You can easily find some more. Rich pickings in Blackpool, Mam, I shouldn't wonder.'

'And what about you? What'll you do in Blackpool?'

'Same as I do here. This and that ... you know. I'll go and have a scout round soon, see what I can find out.'

A week later, when Jessie discovered that her brother, Albert, and his wife had been invited to Harry's wedding, and she and John Henry hadn't, her fury knew no bounds. 'We're being victimised, Jack,' she stormed. 'We're not good enough.'

'Aw, come off it, Mam. You didn't really expect

an invite, did you? I didn't. And you know damn well you wouldn't have gone. You don't want that Hobson lot knowing who you are, do you?'

'That's not the point. I *might* have gone. Nellie Bamber's probably put two and two together already. I bet she's having kittens at the thought of her precious daughter marrying a Balderstone. Hey, that'd be a turn-up for the book, wouldn't it, if I barged in on their fancy wedding? She'd be wetting her drawers.' Jessie gave a coarse laugh. 'But happen it's best if we keep 'em guessing a while. Yes, I think I like the idea of living in Blackpool. I like it very much.'

Chapter Eighteen

George was fed up with being bossed around. Damn it all, the fellow wasn't even a Hobson, and there he was throwing his weight about as though he owned the place. His mother kept insisting that Harry was one of the family now, since he had married Rachel. Even before that, George recalled, Ellen had fussed around him as though he were the Prince of Wales but, when all was said and done, he didn't have the family name. Hobson's Rock (The Only Choice) – *that* was the name of the firm and, as far as George was concerned, so it would always be. Anybody who wasn't called Hobson was just an outsider.

There were four of them now, engaged in the first stages of the rock-making process; George, Harry, Amos Hardy, and a new young pan man called Sidney. Amos, though keen and strong and seemingly tireless – there was no one more able than Amos at hauling the 'lump' around – still could not be trusted with the lettering and assembling. He was the first to admit that he got in a 'right flummox' when faced with words, reading and writing being skills he had never mastered. Until Harry Balderstone arrived on the scene it had been George who was mainly responsible for putting the letters in the rock, an intricate procedure involving the utmost care and expertise. Now it seemed as though Harry was regarding it as his province. And when George complained to his mother, all she did was reprimand him for being childish!

'Do act your age, George,' said Ellen, in what he considered to be a very snappy tone of voice. 'You should be pleased that you've got someone to share the workload with you. I bless the day that Harry joined us, I really do. He's just what we needed, someone to put his back into the job and get things moving.'

'Meaning that I don't, I suppose?' said George sullenly.

'Of course I don't mean that! You know very well I don't. As a matter of fact, I was referring to Ben. You know I never like to criticise him, but – well – he has been inclined to take a back seat since he returned from the war. I suppose he thinks he may as well leave it to the younger ones … and to me,' Ellen added quietly. 'I was hoping you and Harry would be a good team. And I'm grateful to you, Georgie, for showing him the ropes.'

'Yes, I did. I taught him all I know. It was me that showed him, Mam, not anybody else; and now he's damn well taking over. I don't need somebody standing over me, watching me like a blasted hawk when I'm doing the lettering. Anybody'd think I wasn't capable. He's going to be boss of the whole show before long if we don't watch out.'

'Oh, don't be so silly, George! Here, sit down.' Ellen patted the sofa cushion next to her. 'I can't talk to you while you're towering above me like a volcano about to erupt. Sit down, and calm down as well.' She placed her hand briefly over George's larger one as he sat down next to her. 'You know that has never been the way we've worked at Hobson's, one person ruling the roost over all the others, and I can assure you that it won't happen now. Harry's not trying to take over. He's very keen, that's all. He wants to prove to us that we were right to take him on.'

'You'd no choice, had you, seeing as how he married my sister!'

'You have to have an aptitude for rock-making, same as for any other job,' replied Ellen reasonably. 'You know that, Georgie, don't you? And if Harry hadn't had a flair for it he wouldn't have been any use. But he is good. You've got to admit it. He's turning out to be very good indeed.'

George nodded because he knew it was true and it would be stupid to deny it. His brother-in-law had mastered all the skills very quickly and was fast becoming an expert in the field of rock-making. So much so that the other workers, not only the pan men, but the women rollers and wrappers as well, were beginning to regard him as the boss. Harry Balderstone – the gaffer – instead of him, George, the son of the family. Not the out and out boss, of course. His mother, Ellen, was that, indisputably, especially since Ben had opted out of his responsibilities. But if she didn't watch herself, Harry would be nudging her out of her position as head of the business. At least, that was the way that George saw it, but Ellen didn't agree.

'Yes, I know he's good,' George admitted now.

'And he damn well knows it an' all. You can't tell him anything! He's far too bossy for my liking.'

'Assertive, I would say, not bossy,' replied Ellen. 'I've watched him at work and that's what I think. The others look up to him because he's got that certain air of authority. And I suppose that's what's niggling away at you, isn't it?' His mother was looking at him more sympathetically now. George didn't nod in agreement. There was no need to; she seemed to know him very well.

'Try not to let it worry you, Georgie. This confident manner – like Harry has – it's something that some people have, and some haven't. You can't always do a lot about it. Anyway,' she smiled, 'we're paying you both the same wages, you and Harry, so you've nothing to complain about really.'

'Except that he's a partner ... and I'm not.'

Ellen sighed. 'Only because he's married to Rachel. Your turn will come, Georgie. You're not twenty-one yet, you know.'

'I will be, next March.'

'Yes, so you will. That's in about...' she made a quick calculation '...nine months' time. Very well, if that will make you feel happier we'll regard you as a full partner, as from March next year. Then you can start taking a small share of the profits as well as your wage; like Ben and I do, and Rachel. She had to wait till she was twenty-one, you know.'

'And now Harry's a partner as well...'

'Oh, for heaven's sake, George, why do you keep harping on about partners? You know very well that it's always been a very simple sort of arrangement at Hobson's. We don't go in for shareholders and board meetings and all that sort of thing. It's a family business, always has been and always will be. Nobody outside of the family makes any decisions. And because Harry's married to Rachel he's family now, and if he comes up with any good ideas – as he has done already – then of course we listen to him! Being a partner will mean you have to take your share of the responsibility as well, George, not just the profits. And if you have any new schemes – ways of developing Hobson's Rock – then we will be only too happy to consider them, when the time comes.'

George hadn't any ideas. He only wanted to make sure of his rightful place as son – and heir – of Hobson's Rock. But that wasn't what he told his mother. 'Yes, I'm sure I will,' he said, rising to his feet now. 'I'll have lots of ideas. But you'll have to wait till next March to hear them, won't you? I can't go divulging them now and let somebody else take the credit. Anyway, I'm off now, Mam.' He walked towards the door, turning before he went out. 'I just thought I'd let you know how I felt. You always say, don't you, that you don't like us to harbour grudges. So you can tell Harry from me that I don't need any help with the lettering. It was always my job until he came ... and it's still my job. All right?'

'Very well, dear. We'll work something out,' said Ellen patiently. 'Er ... meeting Wally, are you?'

'Yes, I'm meeting Wally.' George's reply was curt. He would have liked to say, 'What the hell has it to do with you?' but he had never been in the habit of answering his mother rudely. Deep down, he thought too much about her. 'See you later, Mam.'

George knew that that was unlikely. Ellen and Ben were usually in bed when he returned home. He had to admit that neither of them had reprimanded him too severely about his frequent drinking bouts. His mother turned her soulful brown eyes on him from time to time and he did, then, feel a trifle discomfited. He didn't like to displease his mother. All the same, there were times when he was damned annoyed with her. He wouldn't be at all surprised if it was Ellen who had asked Harry to keep an eye on him at work. Well, his meddlesome brother-in-law would be told to get lost the next time he started watching him like a bloody policeman.

As George strolled down Clifton Street, heading for Yates's Wine Lodge, he nodded confidently to himself. Yes, he'd tell him where to get off all right! Ben, good old Ben, seemed to have the best idea, George mused as he pushed open the swing doors of the pub. Tinkering with his motor car and zooming off into the wide open spaces whenever the fancy took him. The goings-on at Hobson's Rock didn't worry Ben at all and perhaps that was the best way to be. But George knew, in the heart of him, that Ben was a casualty of the war, just as he, himself, was. They had both suffered ... and they were both, in their different ways, seeking for a means of forgetting. But such high-flown thoughts didn't trouble George overmuch. There was Wally at the bar with a pint glass, already half-empty, in front of him. And plenty more where that came from...

Ellen was thoughtful after George had left. She must warn Harry not to make his vigilance too obvious. It had been Harry who had warned her that George's hand, once or twice, had been a mite shaky. Rock-making required steady hands and an equally steady mind or goodness knows what might happen. And so Ellen had asked her son-in-law to keep an eye on her son. Now it was causing friction, something Ellen had always taken great pains to avoid in her factory. She had found, over the years, that happy and contented workers were usually keen and willing workers. And George, at the moment, seemed far from happy.

He had always worked to the best of his ability, coping competently with all the skills involved. But he had never shown the flair – that extra something – that Ben had had, and which Harry was now revealing. Harry was a leader, too ... and poor Georgie was not. George was a couple of inches taller than his brother-in-law, broader, too, and fuller of face, altogether what might be termed 'a fine figure of a man'. But it was Harry, the son-in-law, whom the rest of the employees looked up to, as George had already noted and commented upon, not the son of the firm. Dark-haired and blue-eyed they both were, too; although, here again, it was George who had the more arresting colouring. Why then was it Harry that people noticed? At least they had turned out to be unrelated, merely brothers-in-law and not brothers as she had once feared. Ellen never ceased to be thankful for that. As for that other dark-haired, blue-eyed young man, somewhere in Preston, Ellen prayed that he would never cross their path.

Harry Balderstone was turning out to be just the man that Ellen would have chosen for her daughter, and anyone seeing them together couldn't fail to notice how happy they were and how well matched. They were now, in the summer of 1920, living in Dickson Road, in the flat above the shop that Hobson's owned. This little shop had been a going concern for several years, in addition to the first shop in Euston Street, where the factory was situated. The Dickson Road premises had been leased as a lock-up shop; but when, earlier that year, the rooms above the shop had become vacant, as well as the premises next door, Harry had suggested that Hobson's should buy the lot. He and Rachel, who were looking for their own place, would live above the shop which would be expanded into a more extensive business.

It had been Harry's idea to diversify by stocking toys, novelties and postcards – anything a holidaymaker might need – in addition to Hobson's usual lines of lettered rock, toffees, sweets and fudges.

'We'll attract the passing trade, Mother-in-law,' Harry had said. That was what he always called her, and Ellen found that she liked it. She got on well with Harry. 'Just think about it. All the visitors going home from the North Shore area have to pass our shop on Dickson Road, just before they get to the station. Well, I'm going to

366

make sure we stay open long enough to attract every one of 'em. I shall find out the times of the excursion trains and we won't close till the last one has gone.'

'But won't they have done all their shopping by then?' Ellen was dubious at first. 'Presents to take home and all that. Visitors usually get them earlier in the week.'

'Not always. The day-trippers won't, at any rate. There's always a last-minute souvenir that folks'll want to buy, and if we have a good selection ... well, they won't be able to help themselves, you'll see. Folks coming to Blackpool have to spend every last penny, you know.'

Ellen smiled. 'Yes, I know that. Mill folks think it's a crime to take any money back home with them. They've saved it, and they're going to bloomin' well spend it; that's what they say. But don't forget that Hobson's is a rock firm, Harry, first and foremost. That's what we've always sold – rock, and sweets, toffees, fudges – that's how my mother and I started all those years ago, and I wouldn't want to see that diminished in any way.'

'Don't worry, it won't be. Rock and sweets will still be the main stock. The other'll be just sidelines.'

Very profitable sidelines they were proving to be, too, and Hobson's second shop, in its newly extended form, was turning out to be a little gold mine. It was now double-fronted, with confectionery in one window and souvenirs of various kinds in the other. China ornaments emblazoned with *A Present from Blackpool* and the coat-of-arms of the town; pottery vases, glass dishes and ashtrays; tin toys and celluloid dolls; inexpensive tokens to take home to show those left behind that they were not forgotten. Outside on the pavement, as it was now summertime and the holiday season was in full swing, was a rack of postcards; sepia views of Blackpool, and some of the rather saucy cards which were now becoming popular, featuring fat wives and tiny hen-pecked husband, and battle-axes of seaside landladies. Another stand held buckets and spades, fishing nets, paper flags, sun hats and sand shoes; all the requisites for a day at the beach.

Ever since the season had started in earnest a few weeks ago, the shop had stayed open from nine o'clock in the morning until late at night, closing time being governed by the departure times of the holiday excursion trains leaving North Station. And as long as there were visitors passing along Dickson Road, there was Hobson's with the door wide open and all the lights blazing, ready to sell a last-minute souvenir or a stick of rock. Ellen had gone along there one Saturday evening, just out of curiosity – although she had done her share of serving whilst she was there – and had been amazed to see the shop packed solid with customers for about half an hour. Then a lull … before another mass of visitors arrived some twenty minutes later, just before the next excursion train was due to pull out.

And this shop had been Harry's brain-child. Ben's sister, Dora, had been in charge of the shop when it was only a small concern. Now they needed more staff, and so, in addition to Dora, two young girls had been engaged on a seasonal basis, and Rachel, whose home was in the flat above, worked there also when extra help was required. She had given up her full-time office job because she and Harry were now expecting their first child; it was to be a Christmas baby, they had announced in great joy. And Harry himself put in several hours each week in the new shop; serving, shelf-stacking, helping with accounts – anything that was required of him – in addition to his full-time job at the factory. Ellen only wished that her son had half the enthusiasm for the business.

George looked his brother-in-law straight in the eye. 'I can manage,' he said, adding curtly, 'thank you.' He knew it would be better to be polite; his mother would be angry if she found out he'd been rude. 'It's Blackpool rock today, nothing complicated, so it doesn't need two of us. Go and give Amos a hand with the next boiling and let me get on with this.' If Harry could throw his weight about then so could he. It wouldn't do any harm to let Rachel's precious husband see that he wasn't the only one who could give orders, without being too arrogant or doing too much shouting.

It seemed as though Harry had got the message. To George's surprise he gave a slight shrug, raising his eyebrows only fractionally. 'All right,' he said. 'Fair enough. There's plenty for me to be doing over there.'

George had made sure that he kept himself well

369

away from the boiling this morning. Although his eye had been steady enough when he stared at Harry – he had made sure of that – his hands were definitely not so. And George had enough sense to know that to attempt to lift the huge copper pan, full of the boiling sugar and glucose mixture, would be foolish to say the least. He had already suffered, as had many sugar boilers, from blisters on his hands where the liquid had splashed them. There was no point in courting disaster. Besides, in an hour or so he would be as right as rain again. He always was. He went across to the heated table where the lumps of white and red mixture were being kept warm and pliable. He started to cut and shape the letters, blinking and shaking his head from time to time as the colours blurred in front of him. B … L … A … K…

'Well! That's marvellous, isn't it? Bl … bloomin' marvellous!' Ellen, to her consternation, had very nearly uttered a swear word, something she had never done in her life. But this son of hers was enough to make a saint swear. She stared at the ruination of a few hours' work on the table in front of her, to say nothing of the waste of all that sugar and glucose. Hundreds of sticks of Blackpool rock, all emblazoned through with the words, BLAKPOLO ROCK.

'I can't believe this, George,' she spluttered. She couldn't remember when she had felt so angry. 'You have the nerve to say you don't want anyone watching you, then when Harry leaves you on your own for half an hour, this is the mess

370

you make! He warned me that you'd been unsteady once or twice, but I never thought–'

'Oh, he did, did he?' George sounded like a petulant little boy as he glared at his mother. 'I might've known. An' I suppose it was you that told him to watch me like a bloody hawk.'

'And with good reason, it seems! Really, George!' Ellen was fast running out of words to express her annoyance. She took a handful of pink sticks of rock and waved them in front of her son's face. 'What are we going to do about this lot? Tell me. How can we sell rubbish like this?'

'Anybody can make a mistake, Mam. 'Tisn't the first time somebody's made a cock-up, I'll bet.'

'Yes, mistakes have been made,' said Ellen. 'Ben and I made a few when we were starting out, little ones, but nothing like this. Well, it's the last one you'll make, my lad, with the lettering at any rate. Like it or not you'll have somebody watching you from now on. Or else you'll leave this job to those who know what they're doing.'

'Harry, I suppose.'

'Yes, Harry. It's a good job we've got him, isn't it, or this place would be going to rack and ruin. You and your confounded drinking!' She stopped speaking for a moment then, looking at him plaintively, 'Why do you do it, Georgie?' she asked. 'Why? There's no need.'

'Don't know, Mam.' George looked contrite for a moment. 'Can't seem to stop now, but it's the first time I've done anything wrong. I don't know why you're making all this fuss.'

'We've a reputation to keep up, that's why.

371

Hobson's have a good name in this town.'

Harry walked across and joined them now. He had kept well out of the way whilst the argument was going on between George and his mother. It was only when several of the sticks had been wrapped that the mistake had been discovered, and Ellen had chosen that moment to pay her daily visit to the factory. If Harry had known what was going to happen he would never have left George on his own, but perhaps it was just as well. Maybe the lad would have learned his lesson, and it wasn't as if everything was lost.

'There's worse troubles at sea, Mother-in-law,' he said, casting a rueful smile in George's direction, and just the suggestion of a wink. 'We can sell this lot as rejects.'

'What? Rejects – from Hobson's!' Ellen sounded indignant. 'That won't do us any good, will it, when this story gets around.'

'No. What I mean is, we can chop it into small pieces and sell it in quarter-pound bags,' explained Harry. 'No one'll notice the spelling if we do that. It'll go like hot cakes in the Dickson Road shop.'

'Oh, all right then, if you say so,' said Ellen, a trifle unsurely. 'But not a word to anyone outside these four walls. We'd be a laughing stock if it got out. We'll just have to try and salvage what we can out of the disaster.'

'Disaster! Don't be so melodramatic, Mam.' George gave a scornful laugh. 'It's a mistake, that's all, and I've said I'm sorry,' he added in a mumble.

'I haven't heard you,' said Ellen, 'not till now. I

372

didn't hear any apology.'

'All right then, I'm sorry,' said George, raising his voice. 'It won't happen again.'

'You're darned right it won't!' Ellen's voice was still ominous and Harry chose that moment to take his leave of them.

'Don't worry,' he said to George, placing a consoling hand on his arm. 'It'll all come out in the wash, as they say. And I know you won't make the same mistake again.'

'You won't get the chance,' added Ellen as Harry walked away. 'And you'll have to watch your step, my lad, if you've still got ideas about becoming a partner when you're twenty-one. Because at the moment that's not in the cards at all. Definitely not!'

He'd show them – the whole lot of them, George seethed as his mother also walked away, leaving him with the results of his blunder scattered on the table in front of him. What a blooming fuss and palaver, all over a little mistake such as anyone could make. His mother had no right to raise her voice at him, the son of the firm, like that, especially with those lasses at the next table with their ears out on stalks. He'd heard their furtive giggles and had seen a few amused glances cast in his direction, before his baleful stare made them turn again to their rock-wrapping.

And his brother-in-law, too; condescending prig that he was! *Don't worry,* he'd said, with that self-satisfied smirk on his face, as if he owned the bloody place. *There's worse troubles at sea...* What the hell had it got to do with him anyway? He'd show them though. One of these days George Hobson would get the better of them all.

It was nothing unusual, Ellen thought regretfully, for Ben to be absent when she wanted to confide in him. As it was such a lovely summer morning he had zoomed off somewhere taking a packed lunch with him. Not exactly zoomed, Ellen supposed. Ben always kept to a reasonable speed, especially when she was with him, and he had been driving quite slowly and sedately when she waved goodbye to him; but there was no knowing what he did when he was on his own. He was like a small boy seeking adventure when he set off on these excursions, his brown eyes alight with enthusiasm and a spring in his step as he walked down the path.

'Too nice for work,' he had declared that morning. 'Who on earth wants to work on a day like this?'

Some of us have to, Ben. But Ellen's thoughts had not been spoken out loud.

'Sure you don't want to come with me, love?' The question was phrased in such a way that Ellen suspected Ben would rather be on his own.

'No, I don't think so, darling.' The idea had been tempting though. A day away from all the worry of the factory and shops, problems that Ben seemed to be able to set aside so easily. Maybe she was working too hard, Ellen had pondered; maybe, this once, she should go with him. But she had promised Agnes, in the Euston Street shop, that she would go and give her a hand this morning. The young woman was new to the job, and though she was coping well she sometimes needed advice with the ordering and general management.

'I tell you what, Ben.' Ellen had decided to compromise. 'We'll have a day out on Sunday, a whole day. How about that?' She would give chapel a miss for once. 'What about going to Morecambe? It's ages since I was there.'

'Good idea, darling.' Ben clasped his leather-gauntleted hands together, obviously ready to be off. Although it was a warm day Ben, as at all times, was dressed in the appropriate clothing. He pulled on his flat tweed hat with the large peak and his goggles. 'I'll look forward to that, Ellen. I'm glad you suggested it.' One hand already on the front door knob, he turned and kissed her cheek. 'Cheerio, love. See you later, about teatime.'

'Where are you off to then?' He hadn't told her. Often he didn't know, when he set off, where he was bound.

'Oh, I'm not sure. I might head for Scorton and Abbeystead; take her towards the Trough of Bowland, maybe. I've never been there.'

Neither had Ellen; it was wild and beautiful countryside, she had heard. 'All right – don't get lost.' She grinned at him so he would know she was only teasing, omitting to tell him to drive carefully. It only served to annoy him when she did so.

She had watched him drive away with a cheery wave before setting off for her day's work. And what a day it had proved to be! It was a good job she had been here, with Georgie making such a mess-up of things this morning. He would have made the same mess, of course, whether she had been in town or not, but at least she had been there to show him her displeasure. George could be in no doubt as to how angry she was with him. Silly young fool! But Ben had not been around to add weight to her words. Neither was he here now, at the end of a tiresome and tiring day when what Ellen needed more than anything else was a confidant.

He had said he would be back by teatime. Five o'clock or thereabouts, Ellen had supposed; it was now half-past five and there was still no sign of him. Ellen, watching for him from the front window, had felt no premonition of disaster. Even when, a few moments later, she opened the front door to see a policeman standing there, she still couldn't allow the thought to take shape that something awful might have happened to Ben. Afterwards, she felt that she should have known. She and Ben had always been so close, like one person they had been at times; why then, she asked herself, had she not been given some premonition of what was happening to him?

'Mrs Hobson? May I come in for a moment?' The policeman removed his helmet and his tone was polite, but regretful, as he followed Ellen into the living room. 'Benjamin Hobson – he's your husband? And he drives an Austin Twenty motor car?'

Ellen nodded dumbly. She knew what was coming now, although her mind couldn't grasp the enormity of it.

'I'm afraid there's been an accident...'

376

Ben was not dead, but his injuries were very severe. There was no other vehicle involved, the policeman told her. From what they could gather he had taken a corner too fast on a country road near Chipping; the car had collided with a tree and ended up in a ditch. It was a lonely road and it must have been several hours, they guessed, before another motorist came upon the accident. By that time, Ben had lost a lot of blood.

When Ellen arrived at the hospital on Whitegate Drive she was shown into a small room off a main ward. Ben, his head and one of his arms bandaged, was lying on a high bed; his face was almost as stark white as the clinically stiff sheets and his eyes were closed.

'I'll leave you for a few moments.' The kindly nurse touched Ellen's arm briefly. 'We've done all we can, Mrs Hobson. I'll be over there, if you need me.'

At the touch of her fingertips on his face Ben opened his eyes. 'Hello, Ellen,' he said softly. 'I'm a silly chump, aren't I?' She could hardly hear him, but he seemed to be perfectly aware of where he was, and who he was. Ellen had feared that his memory might have gone again, or that, by the time she arrived, Ben might have gone altogether. But as she smiled back at him Ellen knew that she wouldn't have him for very long.

She bent to kiss him. 'Never mind, Ben. I'm here now. I'll always be here.'

'You were … always here.' Ben's voice was gruff, almost inaudible. 'I … love you … Ellen.'

She leaned forward, taking his cold, still hand between her own. 'And I love you, Ben. Thank you, my darling, for making me so very happy.' She could hardly speak for the tears, but Ben couldn't see them as he had closed his eyes again.

They remained closed for several moments and Ellen, gently releasing his hand, sat down on the chair at his bedside. She sat for a while, just watching him, the dear, dear face of the only man she had ever loved ... and now, he was leaving her. How ever would she be able to face life without her beloved Ben?

Suddenly his eyes opened and he stared at Ellen, a rapt expression coming over his face, a radiance she hadn't seen there for a long, long while. 'He's there, Ellen,' he whispered, his brown eyes positively glowing. 'I can ... see Him.'

'Who, my darling?' She leaned towards him. 'Who can you see?'

'Jesus.' Ben closed his eyes again. 'He's ... here.' His head slumped sideways against the pillow and his mouth dropped open a little.

Ellen gently tried to close his lips, then she kissed his forehead and his gaunt cheek for the last time, all the while feeling desperately for the pulse at his wrist, but she knew that she wouldn't find one. Ben had left her.

'Goodbye, my darling,' she breathed. Then she turned and tiptoed to the doorway. 'Nurse,' she called softly. 'I think he's gone.'

Ellen, without hesitation, chose one of Sankey's gospel hymns to be sung at Ben's funeral. It told the story of the lost sheep, poignantly paraphrased, and she felt that the last two lines were particularly apt.

And the angels echoed around the throne;
Rejoice, for the Lord brings back His own.

She managed to join in with the singing with the rest of the congregation, even thought her heart was breaking; because there was a certain joy that shone through the sadness – 'the rainbow through the rain', as it was expressed so beautifully in the second hymn that Ellen had chosen. For Ellen knew that at the moment of his death Ben had found his Saviour again.

'Ellen, tell me something,' said Bella Broadbent, the day after the funeral. She was regarding the younger woman affectionately but very concernedly. 'You surely can't believe that God would have shut Ben out of His kingdom, if he hadn't – as you've told me – come to believe in Him again?'

'Of course not,' replied Ellen, 'even though it's what some hell-fire preachers would have us believe. I think there's room for all of us – at least, I hope so,' she added simply. 'I'm just glad that Ben died happy, and that what he saw – or thought he saw – was able to help him ... made it easier. Oh Bella...' Ellen covered her face with her hands, giving way once more to the grief she had been trying desperately to overcome. 'I find it so hard to understand. Why has he been taken from me so suddenly? It's too much to bear. And sometimes I feel so afraid of what will happen. Death ... it's so frightening. And yet Ben seemed to slip away so peacefully.' She looked imploringly at her friend between fingers wet with her tears. 'I don't know what I'm going to do without him.'

'I know you don't, lovey,' said Bella. 'And how can I tell you that time heals when you're feeling like this? It's always seemed a cruel sort of cliché to me, but I suppose it comes true … in time. Most of your memories are happy ones, Ellen, and that's more than a lot of women can say. Ben never made you unhappy, did he? Or he never meant to. The way he changed – that was only because of what had happened to him. He couldn't help it.'

Ellen nodded. 'We were happy together; happier, at times, than anyone has a right to expect. And another cruel cliché is that life has to go on. And I suppose it will, even without Ben.' She smiled sadly, more composed now. 'I like life, Bella. I always have. I find it exciting. And that's what I meant when I said I was sometimes afraid. I don't want it all to end … and yet I know it must, eventually, for all of us. I'm angry that it's ended so soon for Ben. I know I said I was glad, about what he saw, but I can't help feeling angry too. He was forty-one, Bella, that's all, the same age as I am. He was too young.'

'Aye, we can't choose our time, that's for sure,' sighed Bella. 'And it's quite understandable that you should fear the unknown. That's what death is, a step into the unknown. But as you get older it becomes a little less fearsome, you take it from me. You'll survive, Ellen. You've to look ahead now. You've got your business to run and your family to see to. And there's a new grandchild on the way, isn't there? You mustn't forget that.'

'Yes, of course.' Ellen smiled gratefully at the woman who had, over the years, become like a second mother to her. 'I'll be a grandmother soon, won't I? I wonder what it will be? A son, perhaps, to come into the business, like his father has done.' In spite of her deep sadness, Ellen knew that she must try very hard to look to the future.

Chapter Nineteen

It was, however, a daughter who was born to Rachel and Harry, on Christmas Day, as her parents had predicted. The child had been born in the early hours of Christmas morning, and Ellen, bending over the cradle a few hours later, thought she was just too perfect for words. A pink and white baby, giving lie to the fallacy that all newborn infants are red and wrinkled, with just the softest covering of fair hair over a perfectly shaped head. Her eyes were closed, but Ellen guessed that when they lost the cloudy blue colour common to all babies' eyes, they would be brown as hers and Rachel's were. And like Lydia, her great-grandmother's, had been. Another fair-haired, brown-eyed child, like all the females in her family.

But whoever she resembled, this little baby would be loved and cherished. For the first time since Ben's death, Ellen began to feel that she had something to live for. She had put on a brave face and tried to look forward, as she had vowed to Bella she would do, but there had been times when it had been difficult to carry on. Life without Ben seemed to have lost all meaning. But now ... Ellen placed her finger in the baby's curled-up fist, then smiled with delight and wonder as the tiny fingers grasped at her own. Tiny little fingers, each of them less than an inch long, and each of them tipped with a delicate pale pink pearl of a fingernail. Every newborn baby was a miracle, thought Ellen, so wonderfully formed in every way.

She turned to her daughter, tired, but smiling radiantly in the bed at the side of her. 'She's beautiful, darling. And her little hands ... I can't get over it. Yours must have been the same when you were born, but I'd forgotten how tiny they are. And look at her fingernails, like little pearls.'

'That's what we're going to call her, Mum,' said Rachel. 'Pearl ... we've already decided.'

'Pearl,' repeated Ellen. 'Yes, that's a lovely name. Unusual in our family at any rate – I've never known anyone called Pearl – but very nice. And very appropriate. I know she's going to be precious to all of us.'

The firm of Hobson's Rock (The Only Choice) had come on by leaps and bounds since the end of the war. The factory, the two shops and the seasonal stalls had kept going throughout the war years, although at times very little profit had been made and only a skeleton staff had been kept on. Hobson's had always prided themselves on keeping going all through the year, unlike many of the rock firms which laid the staff off during the winter months, re-employing them only when the busy holiday season started again. Hobson's, however, because they manufactured other lines as well as rock – a wide variety of sweets, toffees and now chocolates – had never needed to close down completely; and the smaller amount of rock they made during the

383

winter months sold well in their own shops.

By the beginning of 1921, some six months after Ben's death, Ellen knew that Hobson's was considered to be one of the most enterprising rock firms in the town; and that she herself was thought of as a highly successful businesswoman. The idea amused her at times. It had come from such small beginnings – Tucker's Tasty Toffee, the market stall started by her mother. And now it seemed to Ellen that it was growing into a veritable empire. The Dickson Road shop was making money hand over fist; more so in the summer months, although Christmas, also, had proved to be profitable, with people buying not only confectionery, but toys and ornaments that Harry had stocked, believing they would be good sellers. He had proved to be right, as he usually was.

The Euston Street shop, though smaller, was no less successful. It was here that Ellen had introduced, a few months ago, her new line of luxury hand-made chocolates. Distraught and at a very low ebb following Ben's death, she had known that she must find a new challenge to take her mind away from her depressing thoughts. If she had gone with him in the motor car that day, as she had considered doing, it would never have happened. This was the thought that kept returning to haunt her, but in her more rational moments Ellen knew it was foolish and futile. Ben had gone, and though she would never forget him or stop loving the memory of him, she was still here and life had to go on. And so, in her own kitchen at home, she had started experimenting.

Hobson's Chocolates (The Only Choice) had been the outcome. Truffles, fondants, caramels, fudges, fruit creams ... all hand-dipped in the smoothest chocolate, both milk and plain, and packed in elegant boxes. Nothing too fancy, Ellen had decided, rejecting the colourful, often gaudy kind of packaging used by such firms as Cadbury and Rowntrees in favour of plain cardboard boxes, like those they used for their toffees and fudges, in dull gold or silver instead of white, tied with a fine tinsel thread and sealed with their own label. The new venture had been very popular in both shops over the Christmas period, and now that the new year had started, sales were still keeping up very creditably. Ellen didn't, however, envisage selling these luxury chocolates on the promenade stalls. These had always been, and always would be, mainly rock stalls where the visitors were the chief customers.

Ben's mother, Gertie, was now in her mid-sixties. She was still reasonably spry and alert, but the rheumatism in her hands prevented her from making as much toffee as she had done in the past. Her daughter, Millie, had now taken over the bulk of this job, though her mother still helped. Ellen had always made the fudges, coconut ice and marshmallows, but as the business had grown she had engaged other helpers. Mrs Cooke, the woman who cleaned for Ellen each day, and her married daughter were now responsible for much of the softer sweetmeats, leaving Ellen with more time to concentrate on the new chocolate lines.

Ellen didn't consider that she was wealthy, not

when compared with some of the big businesses in Blackpool, but she was what she termed 'comfortably off'. Hobson's was still, by and large, a family firm, and that was what Ellen wished it to remain. George was still pestering her about being made a partner in March, when he would be twenty-one, but Ellen was making no promises. He did seem to be working a little harder though, and had made no more disastrous mistakes, probably because he hadn't been given the chance. Ellen knew that Harry was more watchful of him than ever.

But the two young men appeared to be getting along reasonably well, working together on ideas for new lines of rock. The original ideas had, of course, been Harry's. Rock made into fruit shapes – bananas, apples, pears, oranges – instead of ordinary sticks, then coated in the appropriate colours. At the moment they were experimenting and perfecting a few lines ready to sell on their own stalls and to other retailers when the season started.

George seemed happier, too, maybe because he now had a lady friend. Nothing serious, he had assured them, but Ellen was glad that he had started seeing Ruth, Rachel's friend from the office, outside of working hours. She was a year or so older than George which was perhaps no bad thing because she did seem to be a steadying influence on him. Ellen thought that his drinking was now on the wane, at least there were no obvious signs of his intemperance, but you couldn't be sure with George. He took Ruth out only a couple of times a week. Where he was on the other evenings Ellen didn't know and she didn't ask. But George knew that if he blotted his copy-book again he would have to wait a long time for his partnership in Hobson's.

The first intimation that all was not well came in the March of 1921 when Agnes, the young woman in charge of the Euston Street shop, announced that she was leaving. Ellen was surprised because Agnes had seemed to be very happy and was coping admirably with the work. All she would say was that she had the chance of a better job – a more highly-paid one, Ellen presumed – although she wouldn't say what it was. Ellen didn't offer to raise her wage, which she considered to be more than adequate already, and had no choice but to let her go.

'Right on Eastertime, too,' Ellen grumbled to Rachel and Harry. 'Really, I do think it's inconsiderate, but some young people have no sense of loyalty. That's one of the reasons I want to keep Hobson's as a family firm. Your own family, at least, are dependable. What on earth am I going to do now?'

She engaged, in desperation, the first applicant, a middle-aged woman who saw the advert in the window. An older woman, Ellen told herself, might turn out to be more reliable. But she soon regretted her decision. Mrs Bennett was slow and became muddled with the prices, and Ellen found that she was doing most of the work herself. She had, in fact, been working in the shop since Agnes left. She wasn't sorry when, in May, Mrs Bennett decided it was all too much for her.

There was no shortage of seasonal labour in the town and very soon, in time for the start of the holiday season, she employed a young woman whom she hoped would prove suitable. May Barrowcliff, aged nineteen, earnest-looking and seemingly very competent, came with good references and Ellen breathed a sigh of relief. Now she could concentrate on the rest of the business and, hopefully, have just a little time to herself. Time, also, to spend with her new grandchild. Pearl, at five months, was getting to the more interesting stage; she was no longer asleep most of the time, but was now staring around with eyes that were, as Ellen had predicted, deep brown and alert. Ellen was more and more captivated by the little girl each time she saw her.

It was at the end of May that Harry noticed a significant decrease in the amount of rock that they were selling to the street hawkers, and he remarked on it to Ellen. It was Wednesday teatime, the afternoon Ellen always took as her half-day, and Harry had called in to see her on his way home.

'Goodness knows what's happened to them,' he said. 'I haven't counted up properly, but I'll bet there's six or eight of our regulars who haven't turned up. They used to be there as regular as clockwork on a Friday teatime, stocking up for the weekend, but I've seen neither hide nor hair of them for the last few weeks. And the ones that are still coming are saying nowt.'

'Hmm ... honour among thieves, I suppose,'

388

Ellen remarked. She had to admit she was still a mite prejudiced about the hawkers, although Hobson's sold a fair amount of rock to these sometimes shady characters.

'Oh, they're not all tarred with the same brush, Mother-in-law,' Harry replied, defending the hawkers, just as Ben had done in the past. 'Some of them are very honest traders, same as we are – not all, I must admit – but that's hardly our concern, is it, so long as they've paid us the price we want for the rock. How they sell it is up to them.'

'They must be getting it somewhere else then, is that what you mean?' asked Ellen. 'One of the other rock firms is undercutting us?'

'Seems like it,' said Harry. 'Although we've always given them a very fair deal. And I thought our competitors had their own clients, anyway. It's an underwritten rule, isn't it, that you don't poach on someone else's patch?'

Ellen shook her head. 'Not everybody looks at it like that, not any more. There have been a few new firms started up since the war ended, as you know, Harry. I should imagine some of them'll be "here today and gone tomorrow", especially if the products they turn out are inferior; but it seems as though some of our regulars have gone to try their luck with these new boys. They no doubt think they'll be getting a better deal.'

'It's never a good deal to buy poor quality produce, is it?' said Harry. 'You get what you pay for.'

'Quite so, but that's something they'll have to find out for themselves, won't they? Roger

Redman sold out last year,' Ellen went on thoughtfully, 'round about the time Ben died. He was Ben's uncle, you know – of course, I must have told you that before – and Ben worked for him before we started up on our own. I always felt a bit guilty about Ben leaving him. It did cause something of a stir in the family, as you can imagine. But Redman's managed to keep going, just about, thanks mainly to Ben's Aunt Myrtle. I've never bothered to find out much about the person who took it over, for fear they'd think I was being nosey. All I know is that it's a fellow called Edwards. Have you heard anything about him?'

'Not much,' replied Harry. 'Exchange Street, isn't it, behind the station? I'm too busy with our own affairs, I must admit, to bother too much about what other firms are doing. Why? D'you think they might have pinched our customers?'

'I don't know, Harry. It's just a thought. Somebody has, that's for sure. But it won't affect us much, surely? What we sell to the hawkers must be only a small percentage of our total sales.'

'Yes...' Harry pursed his lips. 'But I'll bet that on a good weekend those six or eight hawkers – the ones we've lost – could sell a couple of tons of rock. That's at the height of the season, of course, and they're at it till after midnight sometimes.'

'Rather them than me,' remarked Ellen. 'And I should imagine that most of what they earn goes on drink and fines ... some of them,' she added, trying to be fair. 'Anyway, if they've gone elsewhere that's that, and we'll have to manage without their custom. I don't think it will harm Hobson's very much in the long run. We'll have to try and concentrate on our new lines. Almost ready, are they?'

'Yes,' Harry nodded. 'It's like a greengrocer's shop in the warehouse, all ready for the Whit weekend. Apples, oranges, pears, bananas, peaches ... I've even tried my hand at carrots with a bunch of green leaves at the top. They'll be in our shops and on the stalls in time for the season.'

'What about our other customers?' asked Ellen. 'I don't mean the hawkers, I mean the shops we sell to in Blackpool and elsewhere. Are they buying them?'

'They haven't had the chance yet, Mother-in-law,' Harry told her. 'I thought we'd try in our own shops first, to see how they go. Then Cedric can have a try at selling them further afield.'

Cedric Butler was the young man whom Hobson's employed as a commercial traveller, advertising their wares not only locally, but as far away as North Wales and Yorkshire.

'I see. I thought you might have already got some orders,' Ellen observed. She had left a good deal of the organisation, of late, to Harry. She had been too stunned for a while after Ben's death to take as much notice as she should have done of what was going on, and since then she had been concentrating on her chocolate production.

'All in good time,' Harry replied. 'The orders'll come; I've no fear of that. Cedric's been promoting your chocolates, hasn't he? And they're going extremely well. I thought we'd better wait a little while before we introduced yet another of Hobson's new lines.'

'You're right, of course, lad,' said Ellen, smiling at him. When he had gone she thought again how fortunate she was that the firm had fallen into such good hands. She was relying on Harry more and more, just as she had once relied on Ben.

It wouldn't matter two hoots about the hawkers, she told herself as she set the table for the meal that Mrs Cooke had half-prepared for her. She had always wished that they could manage without these dubious characters, but it had been Ben who had convinced her, when they first started out, that they would be foolish to turn their backs on the street-traders. They always had been and always would be part of the Blackpool scene.

Now, on hearing Harry's news, she was a little apprehensive although she tried to convince Harry – and herself – otherwise. It was the second odd thing to happen recently at Hobson's. First there was Agnes's hasty departure and now this. Ellen's mother, Lydia, always used to say that trouble came in threes. Ellen didn't really believe that; it was an old wives' tale. All the same, she couldn't help but wonder if something else was going to happen.

She didn't have long to wait. It was a few days later when she was shopping on Bank Hey Street that her eyes were drawn to a display in Pearson's sweet-shop window. Mr Pearson was one of their customers; the shop was only a hundred yards or so from their own Euston Street premises, but that didn't matter. There were enough visitors in Blackpool during the season to keep any number of sweet shops going. But now Ellen stopped in her tracks and gaped, for there, right in the front of the window, was a display of rock, and not just ordinary rock; these were rock novelties – oranges, apples and bananas – such as Harry had been perfecting recently, but which had not yet reached the retailers. Besides, hadn't Harry told her that they were to be sold only in Hobson's shops at first? What on earth was going on?

Ellen marched resolutely towards the door, then, with her hand already on the latch, she stopped. It wasn't wise to be hasty and she might make herself look a fool if she went in without knowing the true facts. She would have a word with Harry first. But when she saw another similar display in a shop at the top of Victoria Street – another of their customers – she was convinced that something funny was happening.

Harry was as flabbergasted as she was. 'What!?' he exclaimed. 'But they can't be. The stuff's not due out till next week. It's all ready and waiting as it happens, but it's only for our shops at first, like I told you.'

'Are you telling me I'm seeing things, Harry?' Ellen was more than a little indignant.

'No, of course not.' He shook his head bemusedly. 'What the hell's going on?'

'Somebody's pinched your ideas, that's what,' said Ellen.

'I'll get to the bottom of this,' Harry's tone was grim; neither was he so reticent as Ellen had been

393

about tackling the vendors of the produce. He had a quick scout around the town. To his dismay he found another couple of shops with similar displays in the windows; one was a customer of Hobson's and the other was not. But at each of the three shops he entered he found the assistants, and in one case the owner of the shop, uncommunicative. They refused to say where they had bought the produce; Harry got the distinct impression that they had been warned to keep mum.

'It's not really my job,' he said, when he reported back to his mother-in-law, 'going round touting for custom. Maybe I shouldn't have gone in myself, but I was so angry – I still am. It's Cedric Butler's job, he's the commercial traveller. Perhaps he'll be able to salvage something out of this misfortune, get us some orders elsewhere. I should have listened to you, Mother-in-law, and got in quickly with the rock novelties. Now somebody else has beaten us to it.'

'It's hardly your fault, Harry,' Ellen tried to console him. 'We'd better get the novelty fruits into our own shops right away though and cut our losses a bit.'

'Yes, we will. They'll be there tomorrow,' said Harry, sounding very dispirited. 'I've no doubt at all that they'll be good sellers. But it's taken the gilt off the gingerbread all right, somebody pinching my ideas. Who the hell...?' A puzzled frown creased his brow.

'Never mind. I daresay you've some more good ideas up your sleeve, haven't you?' said Ellen. 'Weren't you telling me something about baskets of strawberries? And pebbles and shells made of mint rock?'

'What? Oh, yes,' Harry sounded preoccupied. 'I'm working on them. And I was wondering about plates of bacon and eggs – rock ones, I mean – or black puddings. How about that? Things that visitors like to eat for their breakfasts.'

'Sounds good.' Ellen tried to smile. 'I'm sure we'll get over this, Harry. It's only a drop in the ocean. Hobson's have scores of contacts, and not only in Blackpool. We'll just have to make sure that no one gets wind of our ideas in future. Or maybe it's just coincidence. Do you think it might be? Perhaps somebody else had the same idea as you. Rock fruit ... I know it's a novel idea, but if *you* thought of it, maybe someone else did as well?'

'Maybe,' said Harry, but he did not believe that at all. As he left Ellen and walked home to Dickson Road he was more thoughtful than ever. What Ellen had failed to grasp was that there must be someone at Hobson's who was passing on his ideas to a rival firm. Ellen was a very astute woman, but she was sometimes too nice, too trusting for her own good. Harry had no idea at all which firm it was that was guilty of poaching, but he could make a shrewd guess as to who had leaked the information.

George ... it must be George. Who else could it be? Although the young man hadn't said anything and though he appeared to be working amicably along with his brother-in-law, Harry knew that George was angry that his mother still hadn't made him a partner in the firm. Ellen was biding her time; it was only three months or so since his twenty-first birthday, but to George, no doubt, it must seem unfair. Why should he have to wait? Harry thought he could understand how the young man's mind was working, but what did he have to gain, for heaven's sake, from divulging Hobson's secrets?

Harry's mind shifted to Ruth, the young woman in the office. She was friendly with George now, but he would have thought that she was beyond reproach. Harry wracked his brains, unwilling, at the heart of him, to suspect his brother-in-law. Maybe it was just that George had unwittingly said too much, in the hearing of someone who was quick to seize an opportunity. Drink made him garrulous and Harry knew, in spite of what Ellen was trying to believe, that George was still drinking heavily. And Harry had noticed him more than once, recently, chatting with – almost flirting with – Lily, one of the rock-wrappers. Harry was determined to keep his eyes and his ears well open.

The rock fruit novelties sold well throughout the summer in Hobson's shops and stalls, and Cedric Butler managed to procure several orders, not nearly so many, however, as Ellen and Harry would have liked. Orders for all their produce were, on the whole, much lower than they had been since the war ended. It was mainly the Blackpool shops and stalls that were failing to renew their contracts, telling Cedric that they were now getting a much better deal elsewhere.

But they all refused to say which factory – or factories – was now supplying them.

Cedric was deeply distressed, but both Ellen and Harry assured him that he was not to blame. Someone was trying to do them damage. Even Ellen had to admit that now. Cedric began to travel further afield, as far as Skegness, Great Yarmouth and Lowestoft, and the orders began to pick up again. But their takings, as the summer advanced, were rapidly decreasing as several more of the regular hawkers and seasonal stall-holders took their custom elsewhere.

Harry, to his relief, managed to get in first with his baskets of strawberries; bright pink, luscious-looking fruits which resembled the real thing, and tasted, too, of a strawberry flavour that was quite authentic. And seaside pebbles and shells, mint-flavoured, coloured in realistic hues from pale fawn, through all the shades of brown, to black. He was not surprised, however, when the selfsame products, though not made by Hobson's, appeared in some of the shops that had now deserted them. Harry grimly decided that, with his next idea, he would apply for a patent, something he hadn't thought of doing before. And all the time he was keeping an eagle eye on George, and Ruth, and Lily, but he could find no evidence for his suspicions.

It was the end of August when he noticed a familiar figure crossing Church Street. At first, from the back view, he had thought it was George; it looked like George's jaunty walk, but he had just left his brother-in-law busily working in the factory while he slipped out on an errand.

When the young man reached the opposite pavement Harry realised, to his astonishment, that it was Jack – John Henry. What on earth was *he* doing here, in Blackpool? Harry half-lifted his hand to attract his cousin's attention, then, just as quickly, he dropped it. A curious thought had entered his mind. Almost too fanciful to be true, surely? All the same, Harry couldn't help but be suspicious...

Chapter Twenty

Jack Balderstone couldn't, at first, have explained rationally, even to himself, why the idea of moving to Blackpool was so appealing. But once the thought had taken root in his mind, and his mother had agreed to fall in with his plans, Jack didn't waste much time. In the spring of 1920 he paid a few visits to the resort to have a 'sniff around', as he put it, to find out how, when they moved there, he could best earn a good living without having to work too hard.

He wanted to know, also, how his Cousin Harry was faring. That, of course, was the chief motivation for the move to Blackpool; to get even with Harry Balderstone, as well as his mother's old adversary, Ellen Bamber (that was) although Jack didn't, at the outset, fully admit this. It wasn't as if he had any scores to settle with Harry, not really. The two of them had never fallen out, apart from one or two minor scraps when they were kids, but Jack had always resented his cousin. Harry had loving parents – two of them – and two big sisters who fussed around him as though he were Little Lord Fauntleroy; whereas Jack had been frequently neglected as a child. It had upset him very much when his gran died; he had loved her in a way that he hadn't loved anyone else, before or since. It wasn't that Jack's mother was unkind to him;

Jessie didn't knock him about like the mothers of some of the kids he knew, but a lot of the time she just wasn't there. Jack would oftentimes come home from school to a cold, empty house, and sometimes in the evenings she would disappear again, leaving the child alone in his bed. He had never told her how afraid he was of the dark.

As he grew older he had come to understand that Jessie was a woman on her own – a woman who had been badly wronged – and needs must earn a living. That was what she had told him often enough, and Jack, brought up with this way of life, had never thought there was anything questionable about the way Jessie Balderstone made her money. An affection of sorts had developed between them. Jack admired his mother. She was a good-looking woman. Even in her mid-forties, which was her age when they moved to Blackpool, she was still very attractive with her short black hair, slim figure and stylish clothes. She hadn't let herself go like some of the slovenly women you saw around the neighbourhood, clogs on their feet and shawls covering their drab clothing. Their lives had always been hard, Jack knew that; but if they hadn't the gumption to find other ways of earning a few extra bob, as Jessie had done, then Jack considered they only had themselves to blame if they were poor. A lot of these honest, hard-working, shabby women looked down on his mother. The nerve of it! They wouldn't even give her the time of day when they saw her in the street. Even her own brother, Joe, and his fat, boring wife refused to have anything to do with her, and their uncompromising attitude had rubbed off on their son, Harry. He, also, stuck his nose in the air when he saw her, Jessie had reported to Jack.

Not any more, though, because Harry was now in Blackpool; and doing all right for himself as well, thought Jack, as he scouted around the streets of the town. Surreptitious questioning in a few pubs had given him the initial information he needed. Hobson's, the rock people, he was told, were well known and well respected in the town. Ben Hobson didn't take much part in the business now. He had been invalided out of the Army and had been behaving a bit strangely since then, but his wife, Ellen, she was the one who was the driving force. And there was another fellow working there now, a young chap called Harry. He had married the daughter and seemed to be working his way in very well.

Very well indeed! Jack's resentment, which had long been building up inside him, grew steadily as he saw with his own eyes, throughout the town, the evidence of Hobson's prosperity. And now Harry, seemingly, was an important part of this set-up. Jack discovered, first of all, the little shop on Euston Street and the factory next door to it. This was where they had started out and where most of the produce was made. Jack took only a cursory glance at the attractive well-stocked shop and the clean and tidy whitewashed building next door. He didn't want to linger and to risk being recognised. There was only Harry, of course, who would know him. Harry, and maybe that stunning-looking bird he had married; she might recognise him if she saw him again. Jack forgot from time to time that this girl was his half-sister, or so his mam said. He kept his head down and continued his quest.

There were several stalls on the promenade bearing the slogan, *Hobson's Rock – The Only Choice*, and there was another stall, Jack had been told, at the South Shore Pleasure Beach, but there wasn't time to go down there that day. At the site of the second shop on Dickson Road there was a lot of activity. Building work was in progress and though it was 'business as usual' at the little shop, it seemed as though they were about to expand and take over the premises next door. The animosity which Jack had not, until recently, fully acknowledged, now began to bubble up inside him. And it was intensified on his next visit to Blackpool, by which time the double-fronted shop was open and bustling with holidaymakers.

The sight of it filled Jack with a white-hot rage. The woman who owned all this, Ellen Hobson, she was the one who had done the dirty on his mother all those years ago! Jessie had, of late, told him the tale time and time again. And his Cousin Harry – smug, too-good-to-be-true Harry – who had always, in Jack's mind, considered himself a cut above him and his mother, he was a part of it all. Jack made up his mind there and then that he would do his damnedest to make life as unpleasant as possible for this self-satisfied family. He'd ruin them if he could...

But first, they had to move to Blackpool, and

he, Jack, had to get some sort of a job.

They lived in lodgings at first whilst looking around for a suitable house, not too big and not too small. Jessie eventually found what she wanted on Ashburton Road, in the North Shore area, a nice house with a neat little garden at the front; Jessie had never had a garden before. It didn't matter that the yard at the back overlooked the railway sidings; the house was convenient for North Station and the shops, but far enough away from where Ellen Hobson lived – or Nellie Bamber, as Jessie always called her. Jack had insisted that they must keep their heads down. The Hobson family had not to be given any inkling of their proximity, not until they were ready to reveal themselves. Eager as he was for revenge, Jack was well aware that his scheme for retribution, not yet fully planned, might take a while to get under way and even longer to achieve results. But they would get there in the end. He was sure of that.

Jack was very soon savouring the delights of Blackpool, mingling with the holidaymakers on the promenade and chatting with the locals in the public houses. There would be time enough to find a job, he told himself, when he had weighed up the scene. He soon came to the conclusion that it would be as well to avoid Yates's Wine Lodge as it was a regular haunt of one of the Hobsons.

'See that young chap over there?' one of his drinking companions had said to Jack soon after he had made the move to the town. 'The dark young fellow – that's George, the son of the

Hobson family. You were asking about 'em, weren't you, the last time I saw you?'

'Yes,' Jack admitted. 'Only a casual enquiry, like. I'd heard summat about 'em, that's all.'

He cast a curious glance in the direction his companion had indicated. He saw that George Hobson was a well-set-up young man, quite striking-looking with dark curly hair and a florid face, though Jack wondered if that could be due to the liquor he knocked back. He looked as though he enjoyed his pint. Jack suddenly realised, with a jolt, that this young chap he was scrutinising was his own half-brother, if his mother was to be believed, and sister to that stunning lass, Rachel. Yes ... the fellow did have a look of him, just a slight one, although Jack knew that he, himself, resembled his mother, Jessie. He and this lad, though, had the same father, so there was sure to be a certain likeness. Jack wondered if George Hobson had blue eyes as well; he couldn't tell from this distance. Uneasily he looked away. It was an odd thought. All the same, he was getting the gossip on the Hobson clan, which was what he wanted.

'Looks a bit sorry for himself,' Jack remarked, for George Hobson seemed very morose, staring sullenly into space and not answering the remarks of the lad next to him who was obviously his mate. 'Looks as though he's lost an 'alf crown and found a tanner.'

'Aye, happen that's because there's been a death in the family. He lost his father not long ago – well, I believe he was his stepfather really,' Jack's companion remarked. 'I've heard he thought a lot about his old man. I was telling you about him, wasn't I? Ben Hobson – he went a bit funny-like, when he came out of the Army. Anyroad, he was killed a couple of weeks back. His motor car went off the road, out in t'country somewhere, and that was that. Poor old Ben.'

'You mean the chap that was married to Ellen?' asked Jack. 'He's dead?'

'Aye, I've just said so.' The man looked at Jack curiously. 'Why, what's it to you?'

'Nothing … nothing at all,' replied Jack, but he realised he was seeming too inquisitive. He would have to find another drinking place in future.

'Serves her bloody well right,' remarked Jessie maliciously when Jack reported back to her what he had heard about Ben Hobson. 'Now she'll know what it's like to be on her own, same as I've been all me life.'

But Jack knew that was not strictly true. His mother could have company as and when she chose; moreover, she relished her times of solitude. Sometimes she even admitted that she wouldn't have a husband given her, even if he came 'with a gold clock'. Her friendships over the years had borne rich fruit and she could now live in comparative ease. Her days of standing on street corners were well and truly over, she had informed Jack. Jessie Balderstone now wanted a little more class.

When Jack changed his drinking venue, to the more salubrious Clifton Hotel in Talbot Square, and sometimes the Manchester, further south along the promenade, he took his mother along with him on a few occasions. It wasn't long before she struck up an acquaintance with a local businessman, then a town councillor. Jessie had developed a nose for likely clients.

Jack knew that he, too, must find employment, ultimately, of course, in the rock business, but first he had to feel his way. His hunting ground was the Central Beach area of Blackpool, where he worked for a week or two as a deckchair attendant. Then he turned his sights on the Golden Mile. This colourful, raucous, more seamy part of Blackpool, often shunned by locals or by the more discriminating holidaymakers, was just up Jack's street. It consisted of a mile or so of stalls and sideshows, many of an unsavoury nature.

There was a tribe of Africans with discs protruding from their lips, billed as 'The Plate-lipped Savages from Darkest Africa'; and another group of 'Giraffe-necked Women' wearing brass rings round their necks, stretching them to unbelievable lengths. There was the fattest woman in the world, and another poor woman who was billed as the ugliest one. Then there was the lobster-clawed man who had no arms, just two small claw-like hands protruding from his shoulders; he was able to perform great feats of juggling and balancing with them.

Jack sampled all these pleasures before getting a job with a horse-racing game. He was at first employed as a 'gee', and his job was to mingle with the crowds around the stall in order to 'gee-up' the custom. Twelve players sat in a circle with an electric button in front of them and the name of a well-known race horse. A panel above the stall lit up the names of the horses as a small model horse galloped around. Wherever the horse stopped, that player would receive a prize. Jack was soon promoted to looking after the game while the owner had his breaks; but he didn't stay there more than a couple of weeks. He knew that he had to wheedle himself into the rock business.

There were many respectable stalls along the Golden Mile as well; vendors of tea and sandwiches, ice creams, shellfish, candy floss ... and rock. Hobson's was just one of them. Rock was also sold on the sands and Jack soon learned that rock-sellers were only allowed to sell their produce there when the tide had gone out beyond a certain point on Central Pier. There were always a few horses and carts at the ready belonging to various rock firms, all making an effort to be the first to set up their pitch and draw a crowd. There were also vendors who seemed to work on their own, wandering amongst the crowds, selling their goods from big wickerwork baskets.

Jack could be very personable when he so wished, and it didn't take him long to get chatting with one of these men, after first ingratiating himself by buying half a dozen sticks of rock. He was informed that working for yourself could be quite a lucrative business if you stuck at it. Most of the rock-makers in the town sold to hawkers; it was part of their livelihood. Hobson's did, and so did Edwards's, where Jack's confidant bought his stock. Luke Edwards was new to the business and gave quite a good deal. Yes, there was always room for one more. No, Jack was assured that he wouldn't be queering anyone's pitch, provided he didn't try to pull any fast ones and kept to his own patch. It would be up to him to sort out his own stamping ground.

Jack was surprised to discover that Luke Edwards's rock factory, in Exchange Street, immediately behind North Station, was only a stone's throw from his and Jessie's home on Ashburton Road. What Jack didn't know – and it would have been of little significance to him anyway – was that this was where Ben Hobson had once worked and where Ellen had first been given the idea for her move to Blackpool. Roger Redman, in fact, had sold out to Luke Edwards only a few weeks ago.

The new owner was only too pleased to welcome another customer and Jack knew that the fellow was impressed by his courteous greeting, charming smile and neat and tidy appearance. Jack was aware when he bought his first basket of rock that not only must he make a success of this venture, but he must also endeavour to keep his nose clean. This was an unusual decision for someone who had delighted in operating on the wrong side of the law, but that had been back in Preston. From now on, Jack could afford to take no chances. He couldn't risk a conviction for illegal trading, and so he obtained the required licence. And, as the chap on the sands had warned him he must do, he kept to his own patch and didn't try to pull any clever tricks.

He had watched a few unscrupulous salesmen operating on the sands, their object being to persuade the crowd that they were getting something for nothing, 'summat for nowt', as they said round here. Some of them chucked the rock around for the crowd to catch, others promised a present for whoever bought a stick of rock, the present being their money back. This generosity didn't last long, the 'present' rapidly diminishing to a tiny stick of rock, whilst the rock being sold was getting larger and more expensive. Jack noticed that not all the folk in the crowd were gullible, not by any means, and he soon found that his own ready charm and persuasive patter – for he soon worked out a routine – brought him as much custom as he needed. So much so that his basket was soon empty and he was going back for a fresh supply.

By the time he had found his feet, however, and established his procedure it was September and nearing the end of the season. He decided it was time to ingratiate himself further with Luke Edwards. Luke was a pleasant, easygoing, middle-aged fellow, eager to see the best in people, rather than the worst. At least, that was the impression that Jack had formed of him as soon as he met him, and on further acquaintance Jack discovered that Luke, new to the rock business and feeling his way around was, in reality, as green as grass.

'Come in and have a look round my factory,' Luke said to him, with obvious pride, one morning in mid-September. Jack had, till then, been no further than the door, but this was the chance he had been waiting for. He listened with keen interest as Luke explained about the various processes involved, but he decided there and then that the actual making of the rock – all that kneading and pulling and rolling – was too much like hard work, although he didn't say so. There were a couple of pretty girls wrapping the rock and Jack gave them one of his winning smiles.

'Nice girls,' Luke Edwards remarked as he led Jack into the office, a cubbyhole partitioned off from the main building. 'Good workers, too. They're all good workers, the sugar boilers an' all. Most of them worked for Roger Redman before me, and they've shown me the hang of things. It's a pity I'll have to lay 'em all off soon.'

'Oh, why's that?' asked Jack, surprised.

'End of season, mate,' said Luke briefly. He sat down on a bentwood chair and motioned to Jack to do the same. 'There's not much rock sold during the winter, so we'll have to close down and re-open in the spring, and just hope that the staff come back to us; apparently they usually do.'

'But don't some of the firms stay open all the year?' enquired Jack.

'Yes, some of 'em do. Those that are in a big way, like Hobson's, for instance. They've got shops, you see, as well as stalls, and from what I can make out they sell rock all the year round, not to mention all their other lines. So they manage to keep a few staff on during the winter months. But as for me...' Luke shrugged his shoulders '...all I've got at the moment is a stall on the prom, and half a dozen hawkers, like yourself. Not nearly enough to keep going all year round.'

'But don't you make rock for other resorts?' asked Jack. 'You know – Morecambe and Southport and so on?'

'Yes, we do. I inherited some of the orders from Roger Redman, but they only want the stuff during the summer. And I doubt if some of them will re-order. To tell the truth, he'd let it go quite a lot over the years, had Mr Redman. I think he was glad to get out.'

Jack nodded, looking around at the untidy office, at the accumulation of bills, letters, files and ledgers littering the top of the desk. He had thought there might have been an office girl working away busily in here, but there was no sign of one.

Luke noticed his scrutinising glance. 'This is my province,' he said, 'at the moment, at any rate, but I'll have to find somebody to take it in hand for me before next season starts – all the orders and bills and suchlike. I've not got much of a head for figures, I must admit, but I've managed to get by so far, just about. It's all new to me, you see, Jack. To be quite honest, I came into a bit of money when my old fellow died recently, and it was the wife's idea that I should buy my own business. She runs a boarding house in High Street, next street to this one.'

'And what did you do before?' asked Jack.

'Oh, this and that. I've been a plumber's mate and I've been a coal man … Jack of all trades, me, but I wanted something a bit different.'

Jack smiled. 'This is different all right.'

411

'It is an' all, mate,' Luke chuckled. 'The wife wanted me to help her in the boarding house, but I said "No fear!". Then she heard this place was up for sale and she persuaded me to go for it.'

'You're not having regrets, are you?' Jack's glance was, he hoped convincingly sympathetic.

'No, it's early days yet. I can't see anything for it but to close down soon – just for a few months – but I've got my eye on a little shop on Topping Street. It's to let at the moment, so if I go for that, then happen we'd be able to keep the factory open all year. Make our own toffees and suchlike as well as rock. It's just a thought.'

'And an excellent thought, too,' said Jack, clasping his hands together in a decisive gesture. 'Luke...' He leaned forward deferentially. 'You don't mind me calling you Luke, do you? I've noticed a lot of people do.'

'No, not at all.' Luke seemed pleased. ''Course I don't.'

'Well, Luke, it seems to me that it's up to you to do all you can to make a go of this, and I'm sure you will.' Jack hesitated, as if an idea had just occurred to him, although he had been mulling it over in his mind for several moments. 'This office work – you said you wanted someone to take it over for you?'

'That's the idea.'

'Well, I wouldn't mind having a go at it, if you'd let me. This is my line of business really,' said Jack, not at all boastfully. 'I'm quite new to Blackpool, as I think I told you. My mother and I moved here only recently, and I'm looking for a permanent job. I've only been filling in, doing the hawking job, while I found something more suitable.'

Luke Edwards looked at him steadily. Maybe the fellow wasn't quite as green as he seemed, thought Jack, meeting his gaze unflinchingly. 'Mmm ... you say you've done this sort of work before? You can provide references?'

'Of course,' Jack smiled. 'I worked in the office at Horrockses for a while, and then I was at one of the big shops in Preston.'

This much was true. One thing that Jack had excelled at, at school, had been sums. He had been able to tot up a column of figures as fast as anyone in the class. When he left school at thirteen he had been taken on as an office lad at the mill. They never discovered who had been fiddling the petty cash, and Jack had moved on before things became too hot for him. Likewise at the department store on Fishergate. He had done a variety of jobs since then; it could be said that he would try his hand at most things, provided not too much effort was involved. Rows of figures had always had an appeal for him. They could quite easily be manipulated, if you had the mind to do it. And references would be no problem, not to Jack Balderstone.

'My previous employers can vouch for me,' he said, nodding convincingly. 'I just hope you'll give me a try.'

'Done!' Luke Edwards held out his hand and Jack shook it eagerly. 'It might be a few months, Jack, before the business with the shop is all sorted out. I'm definitely going to try for it – you've convinced me it's the right move – then

413

you and I will get together. Leave me your address and I'll be in touch.'

A good morning's work, thought Jack, as he sauntered home. An excellent morning's work, in fact. He couldn't wait to tell his mother. In the meantime, though, there was the winter to get through. He could perhaps get casual work as a barman – Blackpool abounded with public houses – or, if not, then his mother was well able to provide for him. After all, he would very soon be able to give her what she had wanted for years; to see Ellen Hobson and her family get what they deserved.

Blackpool was a big place, and a busy place, too; therefore it was quite easy for Jack to go about his business, keeping his eye on the Hobsons and their doings whilst remaining, as it were, invisible. It amused him to think that his Cousin Harry had no knowledge of his proximity, and yet here he was, working away at all sorts of plans to get the better of the Hobson clan, and they hadn't the foggiest idea. Soon they would begin to feel the draught, but they still wouldn't know who was causing it, not until Jack chose to reveal himself.

Luke Edwards got in touch with him, as he had promised, early in 1921. He had procured the lease of the shop on Topping Street and he hoped that it would open in time for the Easter weekend. Luke had re-engaged the staff – fortunately, most of them had been willing to return – and soon Jack was established in his little office, in charge of all the finance. He wasn't as conversant with book-keeping as he had pretended to Luke, and as his excellent references had proclaimed, but Jack was not unintelligent and he quite quickly got the hang of it. He was responsible not only for settling the bills for the raw materials used in the rock-making, but also for sending out accounts to the various shops and stalls that 'Edwards Rock' supplied; and for dealing with the staff wage packets at the end of each week. There should be quite a few opportunities here for 'cooking the books', thought Jack, but not yet. At the moment all that he did in the office must be absolutely above board, and must be seen to be so.

When Luke mentioned that he needed staff for the Topping Street shop, Jack told him, 'Leave it to me…' Jack also told him that he would need to pay good wages, rather more than the going rate, if possible, if he was to secure the best applicants; Luke agreed that that sounded like sensible advice. It was Jack who put the advertisement in the local paper, realising it would look odd if they didn't advertise; but it was Jack, also, who persuaded Agnes, the girl from Hobson's shop, to apply for the job. He had gone boldly into the shop in Euston Street, even though it was in enemy territory, in order to get friendly with the girl.

Agnes was plain and unprepossessing, unused to flattery, and it hadn't taken long for her to fall for Jack's persuasive charm and to agree to have a try for the job. He had had quite a laugh to himself to see the adoring smile which lit up her ugly mug when she was told she had been successful. (It had been Jack, of course, who had arranged the interviews.) Silly cow! He wouldn't be wasting any time there, although it was a feather in his cap when the girl, in spite of her mouselike appearance, turned out to be an excellent saleswoman.

Far more to Jack's taste was May Barrowcliff, the darkly mysterious barmaid he had met when he was pulling pints at the Talbot Hotel. She didn't ask any awkward questions when he persuaded her to apply for the job at Hobson's Euston Street shop. He guessed that she was as enigmatic as he was himself. She was also very entertaining between the sheets and didn't seem to mind that she was not the only pebble on Jack's beach.

But even before Jack had placed his spy in the enemy camp he had convinced Luke Edwards that he needed to step up his production and widen his range of contacts.

'Make 'em an offer they can't refuse,' said Jack. 'It stands to reason – if your rock is the cheapest on the market, then retailers'll go for it. They'd be fools if they didn't.'

Luke had at first seemed doubtful. 'Under-cutting, you mean?'

'Yes, if you want to call it that,' Jack sighed. 'It seems to me that it's the only way, Luke. You're new in the business, aren't you, and you've got to make your mark.'

'It's not right, though, is it?' Luke argued. 'Other folks have their livings to make as well.'

'And so have you. It's every man for himself in business, and there's nothing illegal about it.'

416

'No, not illegal. Unethical, though.'

'Depends which way you look at it,' Jack smiled. 'How do you think the other rock-makers got started, eh? Not by hemming and hawing and being high-principled, I'll bet.'

'No, perhaps you're right... We can't afford to sell it too cheaply though, Jack. We've got to make a decent profit.'

'And the more we sell the more profit we'll make.' Jack was soon able to convince his boss that what he said made sense.

By the end of May there was a queue of hawkers at Edwards's door, rather than at Hobson's or at some of the other factories; although Jack wasn't concerned about the others. Word had got around that Luke Edwards was giving a very good deal; but amongst themselves the hawkers were tight-lipped and not a word leaked back to the manufacturers as to which firm was the one guilty of pricecutting.

It was the same with the orders from the local shops and stalls. Jack made it his business to find out which retailers ordered from Hobson's ... and then he moved in for the kill. When Luke saw his order book rapidly filling up he put his scruples behind him and began to give Jack the encouragement he had been waiting for. Luke's next move was to employ a young man to obtain orders for rock and toffees, not only in Blackpool, but further afield. Until then it had been Jack who had obtained the orders, but Luke believed that his right-hand man already had his hands full with the office work, and with the new ideas he was launching.

Rock fruits resembling the real thing; that was a novel idea if ever there was one! Luke was thrilled to bits when Jack suggested it and agreed wholeheartedly that they must forge ahead with the production before someone else had the same idea. Yes, Luke had nodded sagely. You couldn't be too careful. He was already learning that rock manufacturing was a cut-throat business.

Knowing that he was dicing with danger, Jack had hung around the Euston Street area in the early spring of that year, watching the Hobson's employees leaving their workplace. At just about half-past five each day they came out of the factory – three, sometimes four young men, including George, Jack's half-brother, who had been pointed out to him in the pub; and the same number of young women. There had been no sign of Harry, on the two occasions he had kept watch, or of Ellen Hobson. Jack had seen Ellen in the shop, however, or a woman he had assumed to be Ellen, instructing the shop girl, Agnes. Jack surmised, as he waited at the corner of the street, his eyes fixed with feigned interest on a window display of pipes and tobacco, that Harry – conscientious, nose-to-the-grindstone Harry – would still be hard at work in the office. Jack didn't intend to hang around long enough to see him. It was the young women on whom he had set his sights. Particularly, after his second day of vigilance, on the plump and pert ginger-haired one.

She was with a friend, but Jack followed them,

keeping a safe distance behind. The friend had gone her own way at the corner of Abingdon Street, leaving the ginger-haired one to walk past the Winter Gardens on her own. Jack quickened his footsteps.

'Excuse me, miss.' As he touched her arm the girl turned surprised green eyes upon him. 'I'm sorry, I didn't mean to startle you, but I think you've dropped this.' Jack held out a lace handkerchief. 'I think I saw it fall out of your pocket.'

'No, it's not mine.' The girl shook her head. 'Never seen it before.' If she had hurried away, as she might well have done, that would have been that. But Jack was self-confident enough to believe that she would linger ... and he was right. She gave him an appraising look and a half-smile.

'Oh dear, I really am sorry, miss,' he went on. 'I can assure you I'm not in the habit of accosting young ladies in the street, but I was so sure...' He shook his head in a bewildered manner. 'It must have been the girl walking the other way who dropped it. And I can't do anything about that.'

The ginger-haired girl started to laugh. 'Whatcher worriting about? 'S only a hanky, in't it? Not exactly the Crown Jools.'

Jack smiled at her, just a friendly smile with not a hint of flirtatiousness. 'As you say, it's only a hanky.' It was actually one of his mother's. 'Don't let me detain you. Which way are you walking?'

'Up there.' The girl pointed up Church Street. 'I live on Park Road; in digs, I mean.'

Jack fell into step beside her. 'That's the way I'm going, so I'll walk with you, if you don't

419

mind. I've an errand to do on Caunce Street.'

'All right; suits me.' The girl grinned at him.

'Just going home from work, are you?' Jack asked casually. 'Are you a shop assistant?'

'No, am I heck as like.' The girl laughed. 'I work in a rock factory. I'm a roller and wrapper.'

Jack stopped dead in his tracks, staring at her, and the girl stopped too. 'What's up then? Have I said summat funny?'

'No, not at all. It's just the most amazing coincidence.' Jack gave an incredulous little laugh as they resumed their walk. 'It's a small world, as they say. That's what I do as well. I work at a rock factory. I'm in charge of the office at Edwards's, on Exchange Street.'

'Is that a rock factory an' all?' The girl gave a sniff. 'Never 'eard of it. But then I wouldn't. I'm only interested in Hobson's, that's where I work.'

She told him that her name was Lily Jessop and that she was nineteen. He introduced himself as Jack Baldwin, which was the name he had also given to Luke Edwards. He couldn't be too careful, not when there was someone else with the unusual name of Balderstone working in the rock business. Lily said that she had left her home in Blackburn because she was the eldest of eight and she wanted a bit of privacy. And Blackpool was the best place in the world, Lily thought. So many exciting things to do. You could go dancing or to the pictures or the Music Hall, if you had the money, of course. She couldn't always afford it because she had to pay for her digs and she tried to send a bit home to her mam as well; but Mrs Banks, her landlady, wasn't a bad old stick and she didn't charge the earth.

She eagerly agreed to let Jack take her to the Music Hall the following night, and it wasn't long before she was seeing him a couple of nights a week … and telling him all the gossip about Hobson's. Jack learned that George Hobson was a bit of a fool really, although she liked him. He'd made such a mess last summer as you wouldn't believe. Spelling Blackpool wrong, all through the bloomin' rock! Talk about laugh! His mam hadn't been laughing though…

'She didn't half give George what for about that rock,' Lily chuckled. 'And, would you believe it? That was the very day that Mr Ben was killed. Poor lady. She did have her troubles.' Lily shook her head feelingly.

She'll have more before much longer, thought Jack, leading Lily on. What a gossip the girl was. She would tell him anything – and do almost anything as well – for a box of chocolates.

'So you like George Hobson, do you?' he asked her teasingly soon after they met. 'And does he like you an' all?'

'Oh yes, I think so,' she giggled. 'He's always winking at me. 'S matter of fact he asked me to go the pictures with him once, not long ago,' she added coyly, her luminous green eyes twinkling up at Jack.

'Oh, he did, did he? And did you go?'

'No. I told him I had to wash me hair,' Lily laughed.

'Well, you certainly won't go out with him, d'you hear? You're mine now, aren't you?' he said

421

coaxingly, leaning across the pub table to grasp her hand tightly in his. 'Er, Lily,' he went on, 'you remember what I said, don't you? It might be as well if you don't tell anyone we're going around together, with me being a boss at one of the other factories, I mean. They might think you were giving away secrets.'

'But I'm not, am I, Jack?' Lily's wide-eyed stare seemed completely guileless. 'When I told you about them rock fruits we were making, you said you'd already thought of that. You said that Mr Harry's idea hadn't been all that clever.'

'Yes, that's right,' replied Jack. 'We'd already gone into production with the fruit novelties at Edwards's some time before. In fact they're ready to go out to the shops next week,' he added nonchalantly. 'But not a word, do you hear?' He playfully tapped the tip of her turned-up nose. 'You can tell me what they say, though, when they find out. And what are you making now? Has your Mr Harry got any more bright ideas up his sleeve?'

Jack listened intently to Lily's description of the baskets of strawberries. 'You can hardly tell 'em from real 'uns, Jack...' and the peppermint pebbles and shells. Yes, his Cousin Harry was, indeed, an innovative blighter, but it wouldn't do him an 'aporth of good.

Chapter Twenty-One

Lily Jessop was having a whale of a time that spring and summer of 1921. Two young men were dancing attendance on her and, so far, she had managed to keep each of them in the dark about the other. She hadn't, however, been able to resist telling Jack that George Hobson had asked her out, revelling in the look of angry jealousy that had suffused his face. But what she had then gone on to tell him had been a lie. She hadn't told George that she was washing her hair; she had gone to the cinema with him, to see a lovely film starring Rudolph Valentino, her favourite. And she had been out with George on several occasions since then; to the pictures and the Music Hall and once to the Winter Gardens, dancing in the wonderful Empress Ballroom. George knew how to treat a girl, and, though she had heard many times that he enjoyed his pint – it had been said that he was the worse for drink that time he made a mess of the rock – he never took Lily into a public house.

She knew, of course, that nothing could come of it. George was one of the bosses, wasn't he? His mother owned the business whilst she, Lily, was only a rock-wrapper. George had never taken her to his home, which he would have done if they were courting properly. Lily liked him, though; she liked him a lot, even though she knew that he was also seeing Ruth Bishop, the girl who worked in the office. George hadn't told her about this ... but she knew. There was very little, in fact, that Lily *didn't* know, and her look of wide-eyed innocence was often assumed. She guessed that he would have taken Ruth to his home. Ruth, who was already a friend of his sister, Rachel, would be a much more acceptable young lady for the son of the firm.

George had been to Lily's home though, her digs on Park Road at Mrs Banks's lodging house. It had been Amos Hardy, the slow-witted fellow who worked at Hobson's, who had recommended the place to Lily. Amos was reckoned by some of the workers to be 'only eleven-pence in the shilling', but Lily liked him and got on well with him. She had never regretted her decision to take a room at Mrs Banks's, where Amos also lodged. Lily wasn't altogether sure that Mrs Banks would approve of her having male visitors in her room. She was an old-fashioned soul, well turned sixty, Lily guessed, who liked to keep a motherly eye on her lodgers. So Lily always made sure the coast was clear before inviting George – or Jack – up for a cup of tea.

And that was almost all it amounted to with George – a cup of tea. George was shy, too slow to catch a cold, and apart from a few inexpert kisses he had made no amorous moves towards Lily.

Jack Baldwin, however, was quite a different kettle of fish. Lily knew as soon as she met him that he was something of a villain and that life with him might prove to be very exciting. That was what Lily craved; excitement and the thrill of leading a fellow on. She couldn't do that with George – he was too nice, was dear old George – nor had she really had the opportunity as yet to try out her charms on many men. But Jack's roguish allure struck a chord in Lily. It would be fun to see if she could get, and keep, a handsome devil like this in her clutches.

She didn't believe all he said though, not by any means. All that business with the handkerchief; that was an old wheeze if ever there was one. He must have thought she was born yesterday. But she had felt flattered that he had followed her, and she believed wholeheartedly, at first, in the coincidence of them both working in the rock trade. After all, quite a few folk in Blackpool did, and he couldn't possibly have known before he met her that she was employed by Hobson's.

All the same, she realised after a while that he was pumping her, encouraging her to divulge trade secrets. But it was no skin off Lily's nose to let him know what was going on at Hobson's. Why shouldn't she? Jack was generous with her, always giving her little presents like chocolates and silk stockings, and paying for the best seats at the cinema. Loyalty was something that didn't occur to Lily. Why should such as she be loyal to Hobson's? She worked for them, that was all, but she didn't owe them anything. She liked George very much, but she would think even more about him if he were honest enough to tell his family that he was seeing her outside of working hours. Lily wasn't, in fact, fully aware of how much this somewhat insulting behaviour of George's influenced her tendency to gossip.

Jack hadn't taken her to his home either, but he had told her that he had an elderly mother who was bedridden and didn't like visitors. This was another story that Lily had taken at face value. It didn't matter because Lily's digs were very comfortable, affording her much more freedom than she would have had if she were still living in Blackburn. It had been a few weeks before Jack had suggested that she should take him into her bed, as a little thank you, he said, for all the nice presents he had given her. Lily hadn't demurred, and once she had experienced his love-making she was only too eager to repeat the experience. By the time she had known him a few months, however, she was beginning to find his demands rather excessive … and perplexing. She had had little idea, before meeting Jack, about what went on in bed, apart from the basic principles. Surprisingly enough, she had been a virgin when she met him. Her coquettish looks and manner concealed a certain naivety, as far as the wiles of men were concerned, but now she was no longer quite so innocent as she had been. Jack had soon taught her what she needed to know … but Lily wondered what next might be expected of her.

She had learned, very soon, that he had a jealous nature. The anger he had shown when he heard that George had asked her out he had managed to subdue fairly quickly; but that was the case no longer. On subsequent occasions when Lily, knowing full well she was playing with fire, had tried to make him jealous by mentioning George, his rage had been almost uncontrollable.

On one occasion he had seized her by the throat. It was only her frightened scream and the look of terror that must have spread over her face that had made him come to his senses. He had flung her away from him on to the bed. But his love-making, in the aftermath had been so thrilling that she had forgiven him. On another occasion, again because of his jealousy, he had beaten her; half in jest, or so he reckoned. But Lily had been scared and unwilling to participate in his wild demands.

Most of the time, though, he was a pleasant enough companion, good fun to be with and with plenty of money to lavish on her. Lily felt she would be a fool to give him up now; so long as he didn't find out that she was seeing George. She wasn't fully aware of how dangerous the game was that she was playing. She had known for some time that his questions about Hobson's were not as random and innocent as he would have her believe. All the same, she had had the shock of her life that day in September when he had walked into the factory looking for Mr Harry, and when it was revealed that he was none other than Harry Balderstone's cousin, well! You could have knocked her down with a feather!

Jack had been unable to contain himself any longer. He knew that he would have to make his presence in Blackpool known to his adversaries. By the September of 1921 he had done them a great deal of damage, or so he imagined. He had pinched their shop assistant from Euston Street and conveniently placed there one of his own lady friends. (Just what he had in mind for May Barrowcliff he wasn't exactly sure, but it was useful to keep her there. She kept him informed as to how well – or how badly – certain lines were going.) He had drastically undercut Hobson's prices, resulting in the loss of several of their hawkers, and cancellation of orders from many of their usual outlets; and he had blatantly copied their ideas for rock fruits and other novelties. These were now selling well, not only in Topping Street, where Agnes was proving to be extremely competent, but also in various other shops (formerly Hobson's customers) throughout Blackpool.

Yes, it was high time he called on Cousin Harry and surprised him with the news that he, Jack Balderstone, was now a successful businessman … in exactly the same line as himself. He wouldn't admit outright that he was the one who was causing Hobson's business to founder – as he was sure it was doing – but if Harry chose to put two and two together, well, Jack would be highly delighted.

He knocked on the office door of the Euston Street factory, then opened it as a voice told him to, 'Come in.' An attractive-looking young woman with dark hair was sitting at a desk behind a typewriting machine.

'Excuse me, miss, I wonder if it would be possible to see Mr Harry Balderstone?' Jack's voice oozed gratuitous charm.

The young woman, however, didn't seem to be impressed. 'Just a minute.' She turned away to study a paper on her desk, then, 'I'll see if I can

428

find him,' she said casually, after a moment or two. 'Who shall I say is wanting him?'

'Er, Jack Balderstone.' Jack smiled, a little less fatuously. 'As a matter of fact, I'm his cousin. Is he in there?' He motioned towards the large working area he had glimpsed on entering the factory. 'I'll go and find him myself, if you like – give him a surprise. It's ages since I saw our Harry. I'm sure you must have plenty of work to be getting on with.'

'All right then.' The young woman still looked a mite suspicious. 'Seeing that you're one of the family I don't suppose he'll mind. As far as I know he's doing the lettering, up at the top end. Mind how you go,' she added, as Jack turned towards the door. 'There might be some sugar boiling going on and it gets pretty hot in there.'

'I know … I'm in the same line of business myself.' Jack couldn't resist telling her, the snooty cow! 'I know all about the dangers in a rock factory, thank you very much, miss.' He nodded curtly, not smiling now.

He was surprised when he entered the workplace to see how large it was – larger, he estimated, than Luke Edwards's premises; and, at a first glance, easily as efficient, if not more, although Jack didn't at first admit this. He wasn't sure how he could tell so quickly, but there was an air of sparkling cleanliness – spotless work tables, gleaming utensils and pristine white overalls and headgear of the workers – and a general ambience of busyness and … prosperity. Yes, in spite of all he had done to them there was no hint here of their misfortune. Still, this was only on the surface. Goodness knows what damage he had done them underneath all this semblance of success. Jack tried to quell his annoyance as he looked around.

A pair of green eyes in a familiar face stared at him in amazement across the work-bench. But he had expected this, and looked forward to it as well. He frowned at Lily, shaking his head and forming his lips into a silent 'Shhh...' as she opened her mouth to exclaim 'Jack!' Fortunately she didn't utter the word, and her two colleagues were too busy staring at the handsome visitor, or so Jack imagined, to notice Lily's surprise.

He took a deep sniff as he walked up the room. From the smell he guessed they were making aniseed rock today; and when he reached the table where Harry was busily engaged he knew he was right, for there was the lump of orangey-brown mixture, ready to form the outer coating of the rock. His cousin didn't look up immediately, and when he did he didn't seem half as amazed as Jack had expected. In fact, he hardly seemed surprised at all.

'Jack...' He nodded at him, half-smiling, as though he had seen him only yesterday. 'Thought you'd pay us a visit, did you? Excuse me, would you, just a few moments, while I finish this ... then I'll show you round.'

'Good to see you again,' Jack mumbled, as his cousin deftly rolled the orangey-brown mass around the white centre. From what Jack could make out, the letters spelled RHYL ROCK. That was a place that Edwards didn't supply, not yet. 'Aren't you surprised to see me?' he asked, already feeling deflated, although he was damned if he would let it show.

'Not particularly.' Harry's tone was casual in the extreme. 'Here … Amos, I think you could take over now.' He broke off to speak to a gangling, somewhat simple-looking fellow who was standing nearby. 'I want to show my cousin around the factory. No, I wasn't all that surprised to see you,' Harry went on, motioning to Jack to follow him. 'As a matter of fact, I caught sight of you a while ago, crossing Church Street, and then I saw you again in Talbot Road, although you didn't see me. And my parents told me that you and Aunt Jessie had disappeared, almost overnight … so I put two and two together. Living in Blackpool, are you?'

'Yes, we are. We've got a nice little place in North Shore, the select area, you know.' This wasn't going at all as Jack had intended. 'And wait till I tell you, Harry! I'm in the same line of business as you.' At that, Harry did raise his eyebrows.

'Yes, I'm in the rock business, would you believe? I'm in charge of the office – the manager, you know – at Luke Edwards's place on Exchange Street. You'll have heard of it, won't you? We're in quite a big way, and expanding rapidly.' Jack's eyes narrowed as he looked meaningfully at his cousin.

'Yes, I've heard of Luke Edwards. Quite new, isn't he? Well, there's plenty of room for all of us.' Harry shrugged his shoulders, and Jack seethed. Surely the fellow couldn't be as nonchalant as he seemed? 'Come along. I'll show you round our

431

place. That's what you've come for, isn't it?'

'Well...' Jack was nonplussed. 'Not exactly. Just thought I'd look you up, you know.'

Harry levelled an appraising glance at him and there was a few seconds' silence before he repeated, 'Come along then.'

Jack looked with resentment at the work going on, although he tried to show avid interest in the mixing and boiling, the pulling, the colouring, flavouring and lettering processes. He recognised George Hobson, who was now assisting the chap called Amos in the first stage of rolling. Harry called to him.

'George, you haven't met my cousin, have you? This is Jack, Jack Balderstone. You may have heard me mention him. Jack – this is my brother-in-law, George Hobson.'

The two young men looked steadily at one another, both of them mumbling, 'How d'you do?' George didn't hold out his hand, but that was hardly to be expected as both his hands were occupied and also they would be very sticky. Jack knew full well who this young man was, but did George know, he wondered, that he was looking at his half-brother? It was not apparent from his bland stare.

Jack was aware, however, of Lily goggling at him from across the nearby work bench – Harry's words could easily be heard – and when he half-turned towards her he could see that her eyes were wide and her mouth open in astonishment. He frowned at her again. He had seen more than enough now and as Harry wasn't showing any signs of further hospitality, such as inviting him into the office for tea and a chat, Jack made his excuses without, he hoped, too much loss of face.

'Ta very much, Harry. I've enjoyed looking round. Nice little place you've got here. I'll be seeing you again I daresay. Sure to, seeing as we're in the same line.'

'Yes. As you say, we're sure to,' Harry repeated. Were his words significant, Jack wondered. There was nothing to be learned from his even tone, but he was certainly not smiling. 'Cheerio, Jack. If you'll excuse me, there's work to be done.' Harry turned abruptly and walked away leaving Jack to see himself out.

That's put the wind up him all right, Jack tried to convince himself as he walked back through the town. And I've not finished with him yet, not by a long chalk. The summer season was almost over, but both firms, Hobson's and Edwards, would be staying open during the winter. It would be up to Jack to ensure that Edwards's shop on Topping Street was the one that attracted the custom. And if he couldn't do it by fair means – what he had done so far, in Jack's view, was only shrewd business tactics – he would do by foul. For his longtime bitterness against his cousin had been rekindled on seeing his competence and the obvious respect he engendered in his staff.

It might not be a bad idea, either, to pay a visit to his cousin's wife, Rachel. How on earth Harry – dull-as-ditchwater Harry – had managed to get a ravishing bird like that was beyond him. Good-looking she might be, but she was no doubt tarred with the same brush as her mother; a

433

stuck-up bitch, too big for her britches. Well, Jack Balderstone was the right one to take her down a peg or two. But before that, he had to contend with Lily. He had arranged to see her that evening outside the Raikes Hotel where they sometimes went for a drink.

'Here ... why did yer tell me yer name was Jack Baldwin?' It was her opening remark, as he had guessed it might be. 'I heard Mr Harry as clear as anything. He called you Jack Balderstone. Whatcher think you're playing at?'

'Nothing! I'm playing at nothing.' Jack seized hold of her arm, almost spitting into her face. 'Baldwin's what I call meself. Have you never heard of a business name, you stupid woman? Well, that's what it is. And it's nowt to do with Harry Balderstone, so you don't let on, do you hear?'

'But he said you were his cousin. I heard him.' She really was a persistent little cow. 'Why didn't you tell me, Jack? You pretended you didn't know him.'

It was quiet on Leamington Road, a fair distance from the bustle of the town centre, and Jack pulled Lily away from the pub doorway, propelling her towards a nearby garden wall. He seized her roughly by the shoulders. 'Because it's none of your bloody business, that's why. And you keep your bloody trap shut, do you hear? You don't let on that you know me, not to anyone.'

'But why, Jack? What does it matter?'

'Because you'll get yerself the sack, won't you, if they find out you've been telling me tales!

434

Right little gas-bag, aren't you? Well, you'd best remember, keep that buttoned.' He caught hold of her lips between his finger and thumb and squeezed hard until he could see tears springing to her eyes. Then he pulled her towards him and kissed her savagely. 'Just think on … or it'll be worse for you. And keep away from that George Hobson, d'you hear?'

He pushed her towards the pub door. 'Now I'm ready for a drink. C'mon, cheer up.' He nudged her, grinning playfully now. 'You look a right miseryguts tonight. Folks'll be thinking we've had a row or summat.' He held open the swing door for her to enter, which she did in silence, not even glancing at him.

She was very poor company that night and she didn't invite him back to her digs afterwards. Not that Jack would have waited for an invitation if he had been anxious to get her between the sheets. But he wasn't, not tonight, not with that moody cow. There were plenty more fish in the sea. Besides, she would come round… She always did.

Harry called to see Ellen after he had finished work. She was working at home today, as she often did, at her chocolate making. It was a blessing, he thought to himself, that she had not been at the factory when Jack paid his visit. In spite of the cool impression he had tried to give his cousin, it had been something of a shock to find that the blighter was involved in the rock business. Ellen would have to know of the encounter. It was only fair to tell her, as head of the firm. Besides, Harry felt that his vague suspicions, which had started when he caught sight of his cousin in the street, were now substantiated.

Ellen blanched visibly when Harry told her that Jack – or John Henry, which was how she had known him – was now living in Blackpool and working in the rock trade. And that wasn't all; his mother was with him.

'Jessie … here?' She put her hand to her mouth and her eyes were wide with alarm as she sat down heavily in an easy chair. 'Oh no, oh no … not that.' She glanced around fearfully, as though her enemy were about to walk through the door at any moment.

'Steady on, Mother-in-law.' Harry hurried across to her and put an arm round her shoulders. 'It's all right. I'm sure Aunt Jessie won't be bothering you. It's him, Jack, that I'm concerned about. I'm sorry if I gave you a shock, but I felt you had to know.'

He sat down opposite her. 'You see, I know it sounds incredible, but I'm sure he's at the bottom of all the trouble we've been having. Losing our trade, and our staff … and our ideas. I don't know how or why he's done it, but the more I think about it, the more convinced I am. Well, I do know why,' he added. 'I know only too well why he's doing it. He's always been jealous of me, ever since we were kids.'

'And then there's Jessie,' said Ellen, speaking slowly. 'She'd be only too pleased to find a way of getting back at me. Are you sure though, Harry? As you say, it sounds incredible.'

'Not all that incredible,' replied Harry, his voice and his expression grim. 'Not when you know Jack like I do, and the shady dealings he's been involved in over the years. It's a miracle he's escaped gaol, I'll tell you. Well, he did serve a short sentence once, a good while ago.'

'So ... what are you going to do? What do you think we should do?'

'At the moment, nothing. If we give him enough rope he might hang himself, and we're wise to him now, aren't we? We can try to be one jump ahead.'

'*If* it's him.' Ellen sounded a trifle dubious. 'We can't be sure. If he was plotting against us, surely he wouldn't advertise it, would he, by putting in an appearance? It doesn't make sense.'

'It's just the sort of thing he would do.' Harry gave a wry laugh. 'All mouth and trousers, that one. He wouldn't be able to resist letting me know he'd got one up on me ... or thought he had.'

'But we're not doing all that badly after all, are we?' Ellen remarked. 'If John Henry – or someone else – is trying to do us harm, then they're not succeeding all that well.'

'And that's mainly due to you and your chocolates.' Harry smiled at her. 'That was a real brainwave of yours, you know. We could have been in Queer Street right enough if it hadn't been for the chocolates.'

Orders for rock had, indeed, slumped badly during the spring and summer, but they were now picking up again as Cedric Butler had obtained several orders further afield. Ellen

437

pointed this out to Harry now, modestly playing down her own achievements, as was her way.

'We'll make out,' she said with quiet confidence. 'Hobson's always does. I was worried earlier this year, I'll admit it. Profits were well down. But we seem to be gaining a little ground now, in spite of your cousin.' The look of fear suddenly came into her eyes again. 'Harry, do you think you're right in doing nothing? If it *is* him.'

Harry nodded. 'Trust me, Mother-in-law. I would need more proof anyway, and it isn't as if he's done anything criminal.' Not yet, he added to himself. He knew John Henry only too well. 'And now, well – I'm ready for him, aren't I?'

'And you don't think that Jessie…?'

'If I know Aunt Jessie she'll have other fish to fry.' Harry smiled meaningfully. 'No, I don't think for one moment that you'll see anything of her.'

All the same, he was thoughtful as he walked home, and more than a little worried. He was convinced that Jack Balderstone would have a few more tricks up his sleeve.

Jack had been keeping his eye on the shop in Dickson Road and he knew that there were times when Rachel looked after it on her own. Several lunchtimes, between one and two o'clock, he had seen her there when the other assistants had gone for their midday break. He guessed that Harry would take a packed lunch to work as he himself sometimes did, and that Rachel, who lived on the premises, kept the shop open throughout the lunch-hour to catch the passing trade. Good position, that, near to North Station, he thought enviously, but he hadn't finished with the Hobsons yet.

She was there again one lunchtime in mid-September, the week following Jack's surprise visit to Harry. Jack watched her for a moment or two from the doorway, her shapely ankles visible as she climbed a stepladder at the back of the shop, reaching up to push a few boxes on to a shelf. Her dainty curves, however, which he remembered from the first and only time he had met her were well hidden by the shapeless white overall she was wearing. He waited until she came down from the ladder before entering the shop. He wasn't sure, even when he pressed down the latch and heard the ping of the bell, just why he was paying a visit on Rachel Hobson – Rachel Balderstone, as she now was. But he never could resist a pretty face, and she certainly had that. Besides, the girl was his sister, wasn't she?

He adroitly turned the notice on the door to *Closed* as he stepped into the shop, unobtrusively pressing a catch so that the door couldn't be opened from the outside. Rachel's surprise, a look of disbelief, almost, registered on her face as soon as she set eyes on him. It was obvious that she had recognised him.

'Hello there. Remember me?' Jack's greeting was cheery, but Rachel didn't return his dazzling smile.

'Yes, I remember you.' Her voice was cool.

439

'You're my husband's cousin. We met in Preston.'

'Aye, we did that, luv. A fair old flummox you were in that day, weren't you, looking for old Harry. You found him then? Well, you must have done. I heard you'd got wed.'

'Yes, we have a little girl now,' said Rachel, more confidently than she was feeling. 'She's nine months old. Were you wanting something, Mr Balderstone? Did you want serving?'

'Mr Balderstone? What the heck...? It's Jack to you. Don't tell me you've forgotten me name. And you're ... Rachel.' He moved closer to her, bringing his face to within a few inches of hers. 'I don't forget, you see. Jack Balderstone never forgets anything.'

Rachel was scared, though she tried not to show it. She wasn't sure why this fellow's cold grey-blue eyes should instil such fear in her. They had done so when she had met him that day in Preston, although she had to admit he had been quite helpful to her afterwards. And he was her half-brother; almost impossible to believe, but he was. Surely he couldn't want to do her any harm. But maybe he was unaware of the relationship. These thoughts flitted through her mind as she tried to edge her way round to the back of the counter. If she had three feet of mahogany between them she would feel safer, but Jack was barring the way. Every time she moved a few inches, so did he.

'Went to see your husband the other day ... our Harry.' Jack grinned at her. 'Did he tell yer?' He had taken a step away from her now, to her relief, but he was standing in the space between the two

440

counters, preventing her from getting through.

'Yes, he told me,' Rachel answered, as casually as she was able. Harry had also told her of his suspicions; another reason, apart from the malevolent gleam in his eyes, to be very wary of Jack Balderstone. 'He said you were in the rock business too. I hope you're doing well,' she added, but with no conviction.

'Very well, darling. Very well indeed. But I'm always ready to pick up a few hints – know what I mean? Your husband's got a nice little business there.'

'We think so.' Rachel's tone was icy now. 'It's my mother's business, actually. We work along with her. Now, if you'll excuse me, I have work to do.' She turned around, starting to walk away, but Jack's hand was on her arm.

'Hey, not so fast. What work? I can't see any customers.'

Rachel glanced towards the door, praying that someone would come in. It was only then that she noticed that the sign had been turned round. *Open* was what she read from inside the shop. She felt her stomach turn over in alarm and she opened her mouth to protest, but Jack interrupted her. 'No, there won't be any customers, not yet awhile. You're closed, aren't you? It says so on the door. And d'you know what else? The door's locked.'

'How dare you?' Rachel pulled away, but the grip on her arm tightened. 'Let go of me. Let go!' Jack had hold of both her arms now and was pushing her back against the counter. She kicked out with her foot, then tried to bring her knee up

441

between his legs, but he was too strong for her. He pushed himself closer to her and to her horror she could feel the vital part of him pressing against her. Rachel was angry now, as well as frightened.

'Let me go, you stupid fool!' she yelled, her only hope being that a passer-by might look through the door, or hear her and call for assistance. But the back of the shop was in shadow and it was doubtful that her voice could carry so far. She was on her own, with only baby Pearl asleep in the room at the back; and it could be half an hour or more before Dora and the other assistant returned from lunch.

'Stop struggling, darling.' Jack was laughing at her, all the while rubbing himself against her. 'It won't do any good. I'll let you go when I've had a kiss. That's all I want, a nice little kiss. You're my cousin's wife, aren't you? Surely I deserve a kiss.'

'Get away from me.' Rachel turned her head away in distaste. 'You're disgusting! I know you're Harry's cousin, but you're more than that. Damn it all, you're my—'

'Yesss,' Jack hissed in her ear. 'I'm your brother, aren't I? Did you think I didn't know? Your long-lost brother... So I'm disgusting, am I?' He cupped her face savagely between his hands. 'Well, let's see if you find *this* disgusting.' His open mouth came down on hers, his teeth bruising her lips and his tongue forcing its way between her teeth. But her arms were free now; and a thought had occurred to her. If only she dared... It was risky, but it was a chance she had to take.

442

Trying not to make her movements too obvious, she stretched her arm backwards, feeling desperately along the counter top. There was a pair of scissors there, somewhere near the till, which they used for cutting string. Yes, there they were. But just as her fingers curved round the blades Jack became aware of her movements.

'What the hell? What are you doing, you bitch?' He lunged out at her with one arm, the other hand seizing hold of her hair and pulling her head backwards. The hair pulled at her scalp, bringing tears to her eyes, but the scissors were in her grasp now. She managed to slide her fingers up the blades, gripping hold of the handles. She raised the implement high in the air, then turned the points, like a dagger, towards Jack.

'Get away from me. Get away, before I kill you!' she yelled, sounding far, far braver than she felt. In truth, she was terrified and she knew, too, that she would never be able to carry out her threat.

'Give over, you stupid bitch! You wouldn't dare.' Jack gave a careless laugh, but he had let go of her and a half-fearful look had come into his steely blue eyes.

'Don't come any nearer … or I will, I'll kill you!' She held the scissors rigid, staring him out.

'All right, all right.' He was backing away from her now. 'Anyroad, what's all the fuss about? I told you, I just wanted a kiss.'

'Get out. Now – before I call the police.'

'And what would you tell them, eh?' Jack sniggered again, but Rachel knew she had no more to fear from him, at least not in this encounter. He was all bluff and bluster now.

'That I kissed you? Me cousin's wife that I hadn't seen for ages…'

'Just go – now.' Rachel's voice was calmer now, but she still continued to point the scissors at him. 'And don't ever come back. *Not ever,* do you hear?'

'All right, all right, I'm going. Don't know why I ever came here in the first place, you frigid cow!' He turned his back on her and sauntered out of the shop.

The scissors fell to the floor with a clatter as Rachel let out a shuddering sob of relief. Her arms and legs were trembling as she staggered to the back of the counter and flopped on to a chair. When Dora – Ben's sister, who was in charge of the shop – returned from her lunch break she found Rachel collapsed in a pathetic heap behind the counter, her face as white as death. The pains in her abdomen had been too severe for her to even drag herself upstairs, as she lost the child she had been carrying for the past three months.

Harry's fury knew no bounds as he heard about what had happened. Fortunately, the family doctor was soon called to the scene and he did what he could for Rachel. There was no need for her to go into hospital, and a few days' rest in bed should put her right again.

'Never mind, darling,' Harry tried to comfort her, later that day. She had had a good cry and a sleep, and was sitting up in bed, more composed, but still white-faced and looking so very, very sad. Harry's heart ached for her. She had been so thrilled, as he had, about the coming baby. 'We have plenty of time. All the time in the world. And we've got our Pearl, haven't we? Our precious little Pearl.'

Harry knew that he must act calmly in front of Rachel, but in reality he was bubbling up inside like the pans of boiling sugar in the factory. It was Jack who had caused this; there was no doubt in his mind about that. He hadn't yet heard the full story from Rachel's lips, but she had managed to tell Dora, in spite of all her pain, the gist of what had happened, and Dora had told Harry.

Later that night Rachel astounded him with her account of how she had threatened Jack with a pair of scissors.

'What!' Harry stared at her in disbelief. 'You mean, you would have stabbed him?' He was horrified, but at the same time so very proud of her.

Rachel shook her head sadly. 'I don't suppose so. I doubt if I'd have had the guts. But he would have forced me, Harry, to ... you know.' She hung her head, her voice almost inaudible. 'I'm certain he would. I could feel him...' She gave a shudder and he could see the loathing in her eyes. 'He'd have done it, I know he would ... to his own sister.'

'Perhaps he doesn't know,' said Harry ponderingly. 'Not that that excuses him, not one scrap. I'd like to kill the bastard myself. I'd have stabbed him all right! But he might not know.'

'He knows ... he told me,' Rachel muttered, almost as though she were talking to herself. '"I'm your long-lost brother", he said.'

'Right, that settles it.' Harry gripped hard at the

445

sides of the bedroom chair. 'Jack bloody Balderstone can take what's coming to him. I'm going to see Luke Edwards tomorrow. It's time he knew what sort of tricks his so-called manager is getting up to.' He also wanted to find out Jack's address so that he could go and sort him out, but he didn't tell Rachel this. 'How anyone can trust him at all beats me. You've only to look at him to see what a deceitful so and so he is.'

'That's because you know him, Harry. He may not seem like that to other people. We can all give a good impression when we want to. Anyway, what he's done … it's nothing to do with Luke Edwards, is it?'

'What! When he's tried to rape my wife?' Harry's eyes blazed with fury. Then a little more rationally, 'No, I suppose you're right,' he said. 'That's my affair and mine alone – and I'll get even with him if it's the last thing I do. But as for all his other tricks – and I'm more sure than ever now that it was him – if Luke Edwards is an honourable businessman he won't like it at all. My mind is made up, Rachel love. I'll be paying him a visit tomorrow.'

And Jack Balderstone, too, he added to himself. He kissed her gently. 'Now, you snuggle down and go to sleep and try to forget all about it. I'll be up in a little while.' Harry was more angry than he had ever been in his life. But there was worse to come…

Jack knew that he had made a mistake in going so far – or trying to – with Rachel. It had given him the shock of his life when the silly bitch had turned on him; he wasn't used to women spurning his advances, and as for threatening to kill him... Jack had been scared at the time, he was ashamed to realise, but now, later that day, he had recovered from his fright and he was simply furious. She'd be made to suffer for this... He still wasn't sure why he had gone to the shop in the first place, but sometimes there seemed to be a demon inside him luring him on ... and on.

It was all that cow Lily's fault. She had been playing fast and loose with him for the last week or so, ever since he had spoken a bit harshly to her following his visit to Hobson's factory. She had hardly let him touch her since then and it was driving him wild. That was why he had got so carried away with Rachel; and the fact that she was his sister had made it all the more exciting. Forbidden fruits ... they were far more tempting than the ones you were entitled to.

And, to crown it all, May Barrowcliff, his other bit of fluff, who was usually more than willing to oblige him, had coyly told him that it was 'the wrong time of the month'. Still, he had got something from May. He had had it for a long time now, waiting for what he thought was the right moment. Jack fingered the key, deep in his trouser pocket, a duplicate to the one that May had borrowed for him. Tonight, after the pubs had closed and the streets were quiet, he would make use of it. He'd show that bitch, Rachel Hobson, what came of threatening him. Nobody in this wide world got the better of Jack Balderstone.

Chapter Twenty-Two

Ellen and Harry stared in horror at the devastation that confronted them in the Euston Street Shop. It was Ellen who had made the shocking discovery, it being one of the mornings when she helped out there. She had arrived rather earlier than usual, having spent a sleepless night worrying over Rachel, and had decided that she might as well be up and doing as lying in bed brooding.

Harry had arrived at work a few moments later, but had gone into the shop rather than the factory on seeing the smashed pane of glass and the chaotic jumble in the window. There, the eye-catching displays of chocolate boxes – mostly dummy ones as a safeguard against the sun – sticks of rock, jars of sweets and trays of toffee had been flung around, mostly coming to rest in a topsy-turvy heap in the centre of the window.

Inside the shop the destruction was far, far worse. Large jars of sweets – pear drops, aniseed balls, dolly mixtures, humbugs and the like – the only items that Hobson's bought from other wholesalers – had been tipped upside down, their contents scattered far and wide across the floor and the glass jars smashed into smithereens. Dozens of Ellen's boxes of luxury chocolates had been opened and the sweetmeats ground into the floor, as had several trays of marshmallow and fudge. Ellen experienced a moment of *déjà vu* as, horror-stricken, she gazed down on the un-believable mess. Marshmallow and fudge stamped into the floor by a savage boot, just as it had been all those years ago back in their Stonygate home in Preston, when William had come home unawares and, in his drunken fury, had created havoc.

It was this sight that upset Ellen more than any other and, to her consternation, she began to weep. At first she had felt only anger and disbelief, but now she was frightened. 'Why ... why?' she sobbed, putting her hands to her face to try to stem the flow of tears. 'Whoever would want to do this to us? Who can hate us so much? What have we ever done to deserve this?'

Harry came quickly to her side, putting both arms around her. 'Shhh ... Ellen, hush.' It was the first time he had ever called her Ellen. 'It's just a bit of stock. We'll soon replace this lot. I'll pull the blind down, then I'll send a couple of the girls in to help May to clear up. Where is May, by the way? She should be here by now. We'll soon get this lot sorted out, don't you worry. And I'll be telling the police,' he added grimly.

Ellen looked at him in alarm. 'The police?'

'Oh yes. He's not going to get away with this, is he? Because we know who's responsible. We know damn well who it is, and you can bet he's left his fingerprints all over the place. No, on second thoughts...' Harry nodded slowly, 'we'll leave things just as they are. We'll inform the police first, then tidy up afterwards. Don't you worry, Ellen, we'll get Jack Balderstone for this.

One thing beats me though. How the devil did he get in? The glass in the door's not broken, only the window. Looks as though he might have had a key...'

It was at that moment that May Barrowcliff arrived. 'What's happened. Oh no! Who's done this?' Her reaction was one of alarm, as might be expected, but Harry, watching her closely, thought he could see a glimmer of fear in her dark eyes.

'We've had visitors,' he replied ominously. 'Or, rather, one visitor, if my suspicions are correct. Nobody's borrowed a key off you, have they, May? Or you haven't mislaid it, and then found it again, by any chance?'

'No.' Her reply came almost too quickly. 'Of course I haven't – not that I can remember,' she added.

Harry continued to look at her searchingly, but after that first flicker of unease she didn't appear to be unduly worried. And, after all, they had no reason to suspect May. Ellen always said what a good worker she was; a little secretive, maybe, and uncommunicative about her private life, but very conscientious and reliable.

Harry nodded briefly. 'Very well. There's nothing much you can do here for the moment. Mrs Hobson and I have decided to leave things as they are until the police have been, but you'll have to stay. I expect they'll want to see you as well.' The girl still looked unperturbed, even at the mention of the police. 'The best thing you can do right now, May, is to go and make a strong cup of tea for Mrs Hobson. Plenty of sugar; she's had a nasty shock.'

'Yes, Mr Harry.' May's eyes were unfathomable as she hurried away into the cubbyhole at the back of the shop where there was a small gas stove.

'What do you think? You trust her, do you?' Harry whispered, when she was out of hearing.

'Yes.' Ellen nodded numbly. 'I've had no reason not to.' She still seemed dazed, more than willing to let Harry take control of the situation. 'Harry, if it's him, John Henry, they'll get him, won't they?' she asked fearfully.

Harry assured her that, of course, they would. But when the police came, very soon afterwards, they drew a blank. There were no fingerprints anywhere in the shop that didn't belong to the staff, they informed Ellen and Harry later that day. The culprit must have worn gloves. Ellen, Harry and May had all had their fingerprints taken – for Ellen a most intimidating experience, despite her innocence – and, after quite rigorous questioning, May was unable to provide them with any clues.

Suspicions were not enough, the Police Sergeant told Harry. You couldn't go along and start questioning someone when there was no evidence against them.

'You've mentioned your cousin more than once,' he said, 'a Mr Jack Balderstone, but the gentleman's not known to us.' Harry fumed inwardly at the word 'gentleman'. 'If he was, then it would be a different matter. But what you've been telling me about pinching your ideas and your orders and all that, surely that's only part of

451

the cut and thrust of business? Somewhat unprincipled, I agree, but not criminal. And you've no real evidence to accuse him of this, have you?' The Sergeant glanced round at the shop which had been almost cleared of the debris now; it would remain closed for the rest of the day whilst a glazier came to fit a new window.

'Only in here.' Harry tapped at his forehead. 'I know it's him. I know him only too well, you see. He's waging a vendetta against us – family reasons; it goes back a long way.' There was no point in telling the policeman all about Ellen and Jessie and the connection with Rachel – it was all too complicated – just so long as he understood how serious it was. 'And he called round to see my wife at the other shop yesterday. Made ... suggestions to her; upset her so much that she lost the baby we were expecting. So you can imagine how I feel.'

'I can indeed, sir. I'm sorry to hear that,' said the Police Sergeant, quite sympathetically. 'But – again – it's not really our business.'

Harry was beginning to feel exasperated. He was getting nowhere. 'I'd be obliged if you could keep your eye on him all the same,' he said. 'I tell you, he's dangerous.'

'Difficult, sir.' The policeman pursed his lips. 'If we watched everybody that a member of the public's got a grievance against we'd run out of coppers. I'll tell you what we can do, though. We'll keep a close eye on this place, be extra vigilant, like. I reckon the fellow that did this was damn lucky to get away with it. The bobby on this patch neither heard nor saw a thing; must've been right at the other end of his beat.

'We'll get him though, sir,' he went on, 'you rest assured – or them. It's my guess that it's a bunch of young hooligans that goes on the rampage every now and again. We've had trouble with 'em in the Central Drive area. This is a bit far away from their usual haunts, but it's got their hallmark all right. Brick through the window as a parting shot, you might say, and causing a nuisance rather than any serious theft. Yes, I reckon it's them.'

But Harry knew differently. He wondered how the news of this latest calamity would affect Rachel, but she appeared to take it in her stride. Noting he could tell her now could make her feel any worse than she did already, she told him. She was still very distressed over the loss of the child, making Harry keener than ever to get even with his rat of a cousin. He decided to visit Luke Edwards at his home on High Street, rather than at his place of work, and this he did that same evening.

It was the first time Harry had met Luke Edwards, although he knew him by sight; a pleasant-seeming, middle-aged man, insignificant and slightly balding, the sort of chap you might pass in the street and not notice. He greeted Harry affably, though he appeared somewhat surprised, showing him into the private sitting room at the rear of the boarding house.

'Mr Balderstone, isn't it?' he said, shaking his hand and looking quizzically at Harry. 'I know you by sight, of course, but it's the first time I've had the pleasure of meeting you. I was sorry to hear about your bit of bother at your shop by the way – what a shock it must have been for you.'

'More so for my mother-in-law, Mrs Hobson,' replied Harry. 'She was the one who discovered it. You heard about it then? News travels fast.'

Luke nodded ruefully. 'I'm afraid so. Bad news always does. I've no doubt you'll be able to claim on your insurance, but it's the nuisance of it all, isn't it? I would be devastated if anything like that happened to me. Now, sit down, Mr Balderstone, and tell me, what can I do for you?' He leaned forward, his elbows on his knees.

Harry looked steadily back at him. 'That's partly what I've come about – the break-in at the shop.'

'What!' Luke Edwards looked startled. 'Surely you don't think *I* had anything to do with it?'

'No, of course not,' Harry was quick to reassure him. This was a straightforward, trusting chap if ever there was one. Harry could tell that even now, when he had only just met him. It was easy to see how Jack had managed to pull the wool over his eyes. 'But I wanted to ask you about one of your employees. You have my cousin working for you, I believe. A Mr Jack ... Balderstone?'

Luke stared at him blankly, then he shook his head. 'No, I haven't. No one of that name. I would have been curious about someone with the same name as yourself; an unusual one, if you don't mind me saying so. No, I've nobody called Balderstone.'

Harry raised his eyebrows. 'The young fellow who looks after your accounts? Your ... manager?

454

At least, that's what he says he is.'

'Jack Baldwin?' Luke frowned. 'I don't know as I'd call him my manager, but I've a chap called Jack Baldwin in charge of the office.' He stared confusedly at Harry. 'Why, do you mean…?'

Harry looked steadily back at him with some concern. This fellow had been led along the garden path all right. 'Oh, so that's what he's calling himself, is it?' He nodded meaningfully. 'I'm afraid, Mr Edwards, that that's not his real name. He's Jack Balderstone … he's my cousin. And – I'm sorry to say this – but I have reason to believe that he's doing us, Hobson's, a lot of damage.'

Luke Edwards closed his eyes, sighing deeply. 'Good God! I might have known … I must admit I was a little dubious about him, but he seemed so plausible. And he had references, too – excellent ones – made out to Jack Baldwin.'

'Did he, by Jove? Yes, I'll bet he did! Written by himself, no doubt.'

Luke was shaking his head bemusedly. 'I'm finding all this very hard to take in. He was so good at his job, you see. The accounts were in perfect order, until just recently,' he added thoughtfully. 'I did wonder… There have been one or two discrepancies, but he explained them all to me.'

'Aye, he would. I've no doubt he would.' Harry's tone was ominous.

Luke was regarding him curiously. 'And you say he's been doing you damage, Mr Balderstone. What do you mean?'

Harry went on to tell about the loss of staff, and

455

orders, and ideas; and all the while Luke Edwards stared down at the floor, from time to time shaking his head disbelievingly.

Eventually he looked up. 'I knew, of course, about the hawkers, but I didn't realise they'd all been taken away from you. And I knew that our shop assistant, Agnes, used to work for Hobson's. But he – Jack – said it was every man for himself in business. I was just starting out and so...' He spread his hands wide. 'I went along with him. But all the new orders – I didn't know they were all poached from you. I find that despicable. And the fruit novelties; you say it was your idea? I must admit we've been making them, but I thought we were the first.'

Harry nodded. 'At the beginning, yes, I like to think they were my idea.' He had only just had his suspicions confirmed that the idea had been pinched by Luke Edwards's firm. 'But that's not to say that someone else may not have had a similar idea. And there's no patent on them, unfortunately.'

'Jack said he'd thought of it. He couldn't make 'em himself, of course – he's never had anything to do with the manufacturing side – but he drew us some diagrams, quite good ones, they were, and our chief sugar boiler had a go at them. Very successful they were, too. I'm sorry, Mr Balderstone. What more can I say except ... I'm very sorry for all this.'

'That's all right,' replied Harry evenly. 'Hobson's have survived all that – the loss of the orders and the ideas – mainly because we've gone into chocolate production as well. And these things happen in business. My cousin was right, in a sense, in saying that it's every man for himself. I wouldn't care so much, except that it's a personal vendetta that he's waging against our family. And this break-in last night at the shop; well, that's just put the tin hat on it.'

'You surely don't think Jack Baldwin had anything to do with that?' Luke seemed really alarmed now.

'I'm afraid that's exactly what I do think. I know it in here,' said Harry, tapping his forehead, just as he had done with the Police Sergeant. 'But the police can't nab him. He left no fingerprints, the crafty devil, and they've nothing on him so they can't even question him. And that's not all.' Harry went on to tell Luke about Jack's visit to Rachel and its disastrous consequences.

'So you can imagine how I feel, Mr Edwards. Completely frustrated at every turn. That's why I've come to you. I thought you should know what a bastard you have working for you.'

'Yes, thanks for telling me. Believe me, I'm grateful.' Luke Edwards sounded bemused. 'And for heaven's sake, call me Luke. Everybody does, and that cousin of yours didn't need inviting to do so, the smarmy devil! I can still hardly believe... And you're Harry, aren't you?' he asked.

Harry nodded. 'That's right.'

'I'm glad you've come to me, Harry, but considering all you've told me I'm only surprised you didn't come round earlier today, to the factory, I mean, to give your cousin a damn good hiding.'

457

'I thought of it, believe me,' said Harry. 'And it's what I intend to do, but I couldn't leave Rachel yesterday. Nor would it have been fair on you to cause a commotion at your place of work. Anyway, I've no idea where Jack lives, except that it's in North Shore.'

'I can tell you that,' said Luke quickly. 'Ashburton Road. I'm not sure of the number, but I'll look it up before you go. Lives with his mother, doesn't he?'

'Yes, my Aunt Jessie.' Again, Harry didn't go into the ins and outs of the complicated affair, except to say, 'This family feud goes back a long way, I'm afraid.'

'They often do, lad,' said Luke kindly. 'But it isn't often that folks behave as despicably as that one's done. I'd go and give him a black eye if I were you. But as for my part in all this ... I'm not sure. I can't very well sack him, not yet.' He gazed into space, frowning deeply.

'You say your books didn't balance?' enquired Harry. 'And it's Jack that looks after all the accounts?'

'Aye, that's right. They balanced when he explained it all to me, but I was still a bit suspicious. I wondered if there'd been some jiggery-pokery. Now I'm sure.'

'If I were you I'd get an accountant to look at the books,' said Harry quietly, wondering how anyone could be quite so gullible. 'Without telling him, of course.'

'That's just what I intend to do, Harry. I'm not all that stupid, you know. I have an accountant in every so often, like my predecessor used to do.

458

And the last time – in the spring – it was all fine and dandy.'

'What's the betting it won't be now?' Harry raised his eyebrows.

'Quite.' Luke nodded decisively. 'I'd almost decided to tell him I'd found out his real name and all about his shady dealings with Hobson's, but now I'm thinking it's best not to say anything. I won't breathe a word about you coming here. Let him think I'm still completely in the dark, eh?'

'I think that's the best plan,' said Harry. 'Let's keep you out of it, for the moment. But we're both wise to him … and I'm going round now to give him what for, if you'll just let me have the number of his house.'

Harry refused Luke's offer of a drink of beer, or even a cup of tea. 'Fisticuffs' was not normally his line, and he knew that if he lingered he might well get cold feet. 'By the way,' he said, as he was leaving, 'you've not heard Jack mention any girlfriends, have you? I've a feeling there must be someone who leaked the information to him, about the rock fruits, for instance. And we don't know how he got into the shop. I don't like being suspicious of people, but you haven't heard him mention a girl called May, have you?'

Luke shook his head. 'No, he's never mentioned any young women.' It was just as Harry thought. Jack played his cards very close to his chest.

Jack was obviously taken completely unawares by Harry's appearance at his door. He blinked

459

confusedly when he saw Harry, taking a step back into the hallway. Harry didn't waste a second. Seizing him by his shirt-front he dragged him down off the step so that they stood on a level. Then, quick as a flash, he struck out with his right fist, landing a hefty punch on his cousin's jaw.

'That one's for Rachel,' he said, his anger giving him a strength he hadn't realised he possessed. Before Jack had time to recover Harry struck out again, this time catching him on his left temple, a blow that sent him reeling. 'And that's for Rachel's mother!'

Jack staggered back from the garden wall where Harry's punch had landed him. Feebly he thrust his fist out in his cousin's direction, but he seemed too dazed to offer any real resistance. Harry guessed he had had a skinful and it was rendering him insensible. Besides, Harry was too quick for him. He darted away down the garden path, only stopping to shout back, 'And you keep away from my family, do you hear? If you come near any of us, ever again, you won't live to tell the tale.'

Harry found himself trembling, partly as a reaction to his boldness in going for Jack like that. He never thought he would have had the courage, and if Jack had not been befuddled by drink Harry knew it might have been a different story. But he was also trembling with the feeling of elation that the encounter had given him. He knew he had to protect his womenfolk from the likes of Jack Balderstone, and he would do the same again if needs be. But he believed, now, that they had seen the last of that bastard.

Harry, however, was to be proved wrong...

Jack was livid about his black eye and bruised jaw, both of them noticeable enough to provoke a few comments. He brushed these off by saying that he had walked into a lamppost, having had, admittedly, 'one over the eight'. To his mother, however, he had been forced to tell the truth as she had been in the living room at the time. She had given him an odd look, saying very little. To Jack's surprise, and consternation, too, Jessie seemed to have become far more respectable since their move to Blackpool. She had only a couple of steady gentlemen visitors and she didn't appear to be very interested any longer in Jack's feud with the Hobson family. Jack couldn't understand her at all.

It was his opinion that Harry had played a dirty trick on him. He could have given as good as he got – and more – in a clean fight, but the way Harry had crept up on him was sneaky. And Jack hadn't been feeling well either. That was why he had gone home early from the pub, because he had a splitting headache. His cousin had taken him unawares – but then Harry had always been a self-righteous sneak, even as a lad, Jack told himself now. This was not true, but Jack's memory, over the years, had played tricks with him, painting people much blacker than they actually were. He wouldn't be at all surprised if Harry hadn't told tales about him to Luke Edwards, but it seemed as though he hadn't. Luke, the credulous fool, was still as un-

461

suspecting as ever, placing implicit trust in his manager and never interfering in the running of things. He was the only one who had shown anything like sympathy over Jack's black eye, swallowing completely the story of the lamppost and advising him to rub it with some raw steak.

May Barrowcliff, whom Jack met the night following the skirmish, raised her shapely eyebrows and half-smiled in that supercilious way she had. 'So he's sorted you out, has he?'

'Who? What d'you mean? Walked into a cupboard door, didn't I? Me mam will keep leaving 'em open.' But Jack didn't turn on her as aggressively as he would have done with Lily. May wasn't the sort of girl to be trampled all over and used as a doormat, like you could with some.

'Pull the other one, Jack. It's got bells on it,' she said, before taking a nonchalant sip of her port and lemon. 'It was Harry Balderstone, wasn't it? You can't kid me.'

'Why, what's he said?'

'Nothing. You don't think he'd say anything to me, do you? But I know ... and I'm telling you now, Jack, I'm having nothing more to do with it. I told lies for you when the police came. It was you, wasn't it, that messed up the shop?'

'Who else would it be?' Jack sneered. 'What d'you think I wanted the key for?'

'Well, I'm not going to be dragged into it, not any more. I've got a good job at Hobson's – I like Mrs H – and I don't want to lose it. So I've decided, Jack, I'm not seeing you again, not ever. I don't want them making any connections between us. I'm surprised they haven't done so already – Mr Harry's a shrewd devil. And if you try any funny business I'll land you right in it, good and proper, just you see if I don't.'

Jack could feel the rage flooding through him, reddening his face and neck. He rose to his feet, knocking the stool to the floor. His fists clenched into balls and he felt like striking out at her, but even Jack knew better than to do that in the middle of a crowded pub. Leaving his tankard half-full on the table, he turned and stormed out of the door. If that was the way she wanted it, he certainly didn't intend seeing the snooty bitch again. Getting pally with the Hobsons, indeed!

But there was always Lily. She was still trying to play hard to get, but he could sweettalk her. He'd go round now to her digs on Park Road and see if she wanted to go for a drink. The night was still young.

Lily came to the house door in answer to Jack's ring of her bell, clad in a woolly dressing gown and with her head draped in a towel. 'What are you doing here?' she said in an angry whisper.

Jack shrugged. 'Just thought you might like to come for a drink.'

'I've told you, haven't I, not to come calling, not unless I invite you in? Mrs Banks doesn't like her lady guests having men in their rooms, not at night, and not unless they're engaged or summat. And we're not, are we, Jack Baldwin, or whatever you call yourself. Anyroad, I'm washing me hair.'

Jack, for once, was at a loss for words, but it was mainly his anger that was making him thus. The bloody bitch! Here was another of them

463

answering him back. How dare she? He felt like forcing his way in, dragging her upstairs and beating her till she was black and blue, but he knew she'd scream blue murder if he tried. He struggled to contain his wrath. It was hard, but he managed it after a moment.

'Suit yerself,' he shrugged again. 'Just thought you might like to come out with me. But I can see you're washing your hair. Some other time then.' He knew he wouldn't get invited in tonight.

'All right then – tomorrow,' said Lily, somewhat to his surprise. But she was not smiling and she was still keeping her foot firmly in the door. 'Raikes Hotel, eight o'clock. Will that do yer?' She peered at him more closely. 'Somebody been blacking yer eye, Jack?' Her green eyes looked faintly amused.

'Don't you start!' snapped Jack, turning his back on her and walking away. 'All right. See yer tomorrow,' he called back, not even looking at her. 'Eight o'clock.'

Lily was thoughtful after Jack had gone and she felt more than a little proud of herself for sticking up to him like that. She hadn't been to bed with him for a couple of weeks now; she hadn't even invited him up to her room, not since that time he had been so rough with her outside the pub. She'd had enough of Jack Baldwin ... or Balderstone or whatever his name was. She had only said she would meet him the following night so that she could tell him she didn't want to see him again, not ever. She quaked at the thought – he had such a temper – but she knew it had to be done.

She didn't trust him now and, what was more, she wondered how she could ever have believed anything he said. She was sure he had had something to do with that awful incident at the shop; it had happened not long after his visit to the factory. Lily had been terrified when she saw the police there; she had felt certain it was only a matter of time before they started asking her questions. But they hadn't. Jack had told her time and time again that she wasn't to breathe a word to anyone about them being friendly, and she never had done. Well, they were not going to be friendly from now on. Lily had quite made her mind up about that.

Besides, there was George. He was getting much keener now and he had even invited her to go with him to a big dance at the Tower Ballroom next month. He had hinted that he would like to 'go steady' with her and had even promised, at Lily's persistence, that he would tell his mother they were friendly. Ruth, he had told Lily, had never been more than a friend, but she, Lily, was different. In the privacy of her room his kisses had become more passionate, though she knew he was still very inexperienced. Once she had got rid of Jack she would take him in hand, teach him everything she knew.

She had been obliged to tell George that she had another young man. There were occasions when George had wanted to see her and she had another 'date'; but he had no idea at all who his rival was. Jack had been so insistent that she mustn't tell. But she had promised George faithfully that she would send the other one packing, so that she could keep herself just for him.

What she had told Jack tonight about Mrs Banks's scruples was not strictly correct. The woman kept a watchful eye on her lady lodgers, that was true, but she had shown no opposition when, on a couple of occasions recently, she had seen Lily inviting George Hobson into the house. Rather, she had smiled encouragingly. She knew he was a gentleman from a highly respected family, and she had even had his stepfather lodging there at one time. Her knowing nod seemed to say that she thought Lily was on to a good thing.

But when the next evening, Friday, had been and gone, Lily still hadn't told Jack she wasn't going to see him again. He had been morose and irritable and she just hadn't been able to pluck up courage. To her relief, though, he didn't ask her to see him the following evening. On Saturday night she was going to the pictures with George.

Lily loved Douglas Fairbanks in *The Three Musketeers* almost as much, she enthused to George afterwards, as she had loved Rudolph Valentino as the sheik. But George was disinclined to chatter. He was, in fact, more than a little angry with her. She had confessed to him, foolishly – Lily was, at times, too blatantly truthful for her own good – that she still hadn't told her other boyfriend that she wouldn't see him again.

To her surprise, George turned on her, his blue

466

eyes blazing with an annoyance she had seldom seen there, making him look, in that instant, uncannily like Jack Baldwin. How very odd, she thought; she had never noticed that before. He seized her by the shoulders and shook her. Not all that roughly, but it gave her a shock. 'You promised me you'd tell him, whoever he is. You've got to tell him, d'you hear me, Lily?'

He let go of her then, his hands hanging limply between his knees as he sat at her side on the bed settee. 'It's not fair of you to go on seeing another fellow,' he muttered gruffly. 'Not now, not when I've told you I want to see more of you. I won't play second fiddle, not to anyone. And I'm not seeing Ruth any more. I told her I couldn't, 'cause I knew you didn't like it.'

'I bet you didn't tell her about us though, did you?' said Lily slyly.

'As a matter of fact I did. But Ruth won't say anything.'

'And why shouldn't she say anything, may I ask?' retorted Lily. 'What's the big secret, George Hobson? I'll bet you haven't told your mother, like you promised.'

George hung his head. 'It's not all that easy. But I will do, when you've finished with that chap.'

'All right, Georgie Porgie.' She put her hand on his knee, stroking his leg in an upwards direction. 'I will, I promise. Come on, luv. Don't let's quarrel.'

His kisses soon showed her that she was forgiven, for the moment, just as she had forgiven him; but Lily knew that she couldn't prevaricate much longer.

'Where's Lily?' asked Harry of her two work-mates at about nine-thirty on Monday morning. 'It isn't like her to be so late. In fact, I don't ever remember her being late at all.'

The two young women, Madge and Connie, looked at one another and shrugged.

'Search me.'

'Don't know, Mr Harry. P'raps she's a bit under the weather.'

'She seemed all right on Saturday though.' Madge, of the two of them, seemed the more concerned. 'And if she was ill she'd have sent a message with Amos Hardy, wouldn't she? She did once before, d'you remember, when she'd got that stomach upset?'

'Mmm ... unless she's too ill to get out of bed.'

'All right, thank you.' Harry nodded at them. 'I don't suppose it's anything to worry about. I'll have a word with Amos Hardy.'

But Amos declared he hadn't seen Lily since the previous day. He'd caught sight of her on the landing in the early afternoon and she had seemed as right as rain then.

By midday, when she still hadn't put in an appearance, her colleague, Madge, was more than a little worried. 'It's not like her, Mr Harry,' she told him. 'She'd have let you know if she was ill, I'm sure she would. Look, I'm going round to her digs to see what's up. I can get there and back in me dinner-hour.'

'Right. I'll come with you.' Harry was never to know why he made this decision. Later, he thought it might have been a premonition that made him accompany Madge. It was not usual for one of the bosses to be so concerned about a young woman employee, but Lily had been with the firm for quite a while – longer than the other girls – and Harry, like Madge, felt unusually anxious about her.

'I'm going round to Lily's digs to see what's the matter,' Harry told his brother-in-law. 'Hold the fort here, would you? I won't be long.'

George gave him an odd look, mumbled that he didn't know what all the fuss was about; she'd probably only got a cold. Harry looked keenly at him. He had suspected, at one time, that George and Lily Jessop might be getting friendly, but he hadn't seen much evidence of it recently; and George didn't seem all that bothered about her now. He seemed ill at ease, though, as he turned back to his task of adding the colour to the 'lump'.

Mrs Banks shook her head. 'No, I haven't set eyes on Lily, not since yesterday. She had her Sunday dinner with us – I cook a roast for my lodgers, you know, Mr Balderstone – and she tucked into it like she always does. There wasn't much wrong with her then. But you can never tell, 'specially with young women. Come on, let's go up and have a look-see. I've got my own key, if the door's locked.'

Lily's door was not locked. It was Mrs Banks who opened it and stepped inside, after knocking and receiving no answer. At her terrified scream, Harry and Madge quickly followed her into the room.

'Oh my God … no!' Harry breathed, as Madge

put her hand to her mouth and turned away in horror, and Mrs Banks collapsed, sobbing with fright, against the door jamb.

Lily was lying spread-eagled on the bed settee, which had not been made up for the night, her sightless eyes staring at the ceiling and one arm hanging limply at her side. Her face was suffused with a reddish-purple hue and there was a livid bruise on her throat. There was no sign of any struggle. Everything in the room looked, not exactly neat and tidy, but as one would expect a young woman's room to look, homely and lived-in. On a small table there were two cups and saucers and two plates, all showing signs of recent use, a teapot and a half-empty plate of biscuits.

She'd had a visitor, thought Harry, and it looked as though it was someone she knew and trusted.

'Come along.' Gently and firmly he ushered Madge and Mrs Banks out of the room. 'There's nothing we can do for her … I'll ring the police.'

Chapter Twenty-Three

Harry could scarcely believe what was happening. It was all like a horrible nightmare. George, his brother-in-law, taken to the police station for questioning; George, accused of ... murder? The police had come to the factory in the late afternoon and taken him away. There was no way that Harry could hide the truth from Rachel, although Ellen would not need to be told until the following day. She had gone to Preston early that morning to see her sister, Mary, and intended staying overnight.

'But it can't possibly be George,' Rachel kept insisting. 'Why pick on George? It's ridiculous. He couldn't have had anything to do with it.'

'I've told you – he was friendly with her,' Harry explained. 'He'd been taking her out. It seems that one or two of Lily's friends knew about it ... and Ruth knew as well.' He sighed. 'It seems as though everyone knew, except the family.'

'Poor Mam. Goodness knows what this will do to her. She's had so much trouble. It could kill her. Do you think we should send a telegram to Aunty Mary's and tell her to come home?'

'No, I don't think so,' Harry replied. 'She'll be home tomorrow and it's not an easy thing to explain in a telegram. She'll know soon enough. I wouldn't worry too much about your mother, Rachel, love. I think she's made of sterner stuff than any of us realise. She'll cope.' He gave his wife a gentle hug.

'He's only been taken in for questioning, you know. We must try to get things into proportion. George only has to prove that Lily was alive when he left her yesterday, and he'll be in the clear.' So Harry tried to convince his wife, but he had to admit to himself that things looked very black for poor old Georgie.

Harry hadn't been very surprised to learn that George had been friendly with Lily Jessop. He had suspected as much, but he'd had no idea of the extent of their romance, if that was what it was. It was beginning to look that way. He had felt the first tinge of alarm when Mrs Banks had told him that George had visited Lily's digs, and not just the once. She had seen him there on a few occasions recently. Not that the woman had told him in a gossiping way; she had seemed to assume that he would know. And she didn't appear to believe that George had anything to do with the tragedy.

What she had said was, 'Oh, deary me! This'll upset young Mr George, won't it? I've seen them together, him and Lily, and he was that fond of her, I could tell.'

And so it had all come out, with Harry not admitting by so much as a raised eyebrow that it was all news to him. There was worse to follow. Mrs Banks had seen George there on Sunday afternoon; she had noticed him leave at about four-thirty ... and she hadn't seen Lily after that time. Harry had no doubt at all that she would have been forced to tell the police the same thing.

She could hardly have denied it, having already blurted it out – no doubt unthinkingly – in front of himself and Madge.

George had been devastated on hearing the news of Lily's murder. Harry didn't believe that such distress could be feigned; but he couldn't help but remember the strange look George had given him earlier on learning that he was going to Lily's digs. And he knew that his brother-in-law could be very hot-headed, particularly when he had been drinking. These thoughts Harry immediately repressed. They were shameful thoughts. As Rachel said, how could George possibly have anything to do with this?

'Can't you find out what's going on, Harry?' Rachel begged him now. 'Ring the police station. They'll have to tell you what's happening. He's my brother, for God's sake! They might even have let him go by now.'

But the police would say little except that Mr Hobson was being detained overnight for further questioning, and that he had requested to have a solicitor present with him the following morning.

'A solicitor? That looks bad, doesn't it?' Rachel seemed alarmed, but Harry was surprised at how well she was bearing up on the whole. He had thought she might go to pieces, but she was calmer than he had dared to hope.

'Not necessarily,' he tried to reassure her, although he had felt severe misgivings on hearing that George was still in custody. 'I think it's just that our George is insisting on his rights. He's quite a sensible young man when he wants to be, and he knows what's what.'

Harry had a sudden thought. 'Listen, love, will you be all right if I slip round and see Mrs Banks? The poor woman was distraught, as you can imagine, when we found Lily. She came round a bit afterwards, but I feel I must go and see her, make sure she's all right. Besides, I want to find out about something. I'm sure Lily must have had some other ... visitors. There couldn't have been just our George. In fact, George told me himself she'd been seeing someone else.'

Rachel assured him that she would be fine. She was going back to bed soon anyway, it being the first day she had been up for any length of time after losing the baby. That catastrophe, for the moment, had taken second place in their thoughts, overshadowed by today's terrible events.

Mrs Banks was still very distressed, especially, she kept saying, as she felt it was all her fault that they had taken poor Mr George in for questioning.

'I'm so sorry, so sorry, Mr Balderstone,' she kept repeating, alternately chewing at her finger ends or clasping and unclasping her hands. 'But what could I do? I had to tell the police that I'd seen him here. They drag it out of you, you know. They tie you in knots, them policemen.'

'Don't worry, Mrs Banks,' Harry tried to console her. 'You told the truth, and that's as much as anyone can do.'

'I keep telling her that.' Her husband, sitting at her side on the sofa, joined in. He took hold of her restless hands and stroked them. 'And I keep telling her that young Mr George'll be all right. They'll let him go when they find out it's not him. They can't keep innocent folks locked up.'

Harry nodded, although he doubted the truth of that. 'Mrs Banks, I wanted to ask you something, although I'm sure the police will already have asked you. Did you ever see anyone else, any other young men visiting Lily, apart from George?'

Mrs Banks shook her head. 'I keep wracking my brains to think, but no, I didn't. And yet there must have been someone else here yesterday, after Mr George left, because it couldn't have been him. Daft of the police, if you ask me, to even think it could be him, respectable young fellow like that. There was just once...' She hesitated. 'Not so long ago, I saw a young chap walking away down the path, and I had a feeling he'd been to see Lily. Dark-haired chap; I thought it was Mr George at first, but when he turned out of the gate I saw that it was somebody else. Somebody a bit like him ... but I only saw him the once.'

Harry felt his pulse quicken. 'You're sure? You didn't see this chap here yesterday?'

'No. I'm sorry, I wish I could say I had, but I can't. I didn't see him yesterday.'

'Would you know him again?' Harry persisted.

'I doubt it, Mr Balderstone. It was just a fleeting glimpse, you see.'

An unbelievable thought had just occurred to Harry, but he immediately told himself not to be ridiculous. There was nothing whatsoever, as far as he knew, to connect his Cousin Jack with Lily

Jessop. He was becoming paranoid about the fellow. And yet the idea persisted. A dark-haired young man, something like George ... and there must have been someone who had passed on all that information to Jack. Harry had suspected that it might be May, but now he was beginning to think it could very well have been Lily. If only he could make a connection between her and Jack Balderstone!

'It wasn't me. I swear to God it wasn't me,' George had kept insisting to Harry earlier that day, after he had broken down, sobbing alarmingly. There were just the two of them in the office. 'Yes, all right – I was there, Sunday afternoon.' He had at first denied seeing Lily at all on Sunday, although he had admitted he had taken her to the pictures on Saturday evening. 'I went round, middle of the afternoon it'd be, and we had a cup of tea. And then I left – and she was all right then, I tell you. But she had another fellow, you know. As a matter of fact, we'd had words about it. She kept saying she'd finish with him – I told her she had to – but she kept putting it off. It must've been him that killed her. He must've come round after I'd gone, the swine.' Tears had filled George's eyes again and he covered his face with his hands, rocking backwards and forwards.

'Who, George? Who was it?' Harry put a solicitous hand on his arm. 'Have you any idea at all who this fellow was?'

George shook his head bleakly. 'She would never say. And I don't know if he knew about me. Seems as though she was playing us both along.'

The two-timing little minx, Harry thought, but he couldn't go so far as to think she'd had it coming to her. Nobody deserved that.

'Just stick to your story when the police come here,' Harry warned his brother-in-law. 'They're sure to come, you know.' George had looked frightened to death, as well he might. He was bound to be the primary suspect. And, as Harry had feared, the police had seemed to think so as well.

Later that night, walking back from Mrs Banks's house, Harry hoped fervently that the police would be able to unearth some evidence about Lily's mystery caller ... if, indeed, there had been one. Because if there hadn't, then it all came back to George. And that was beyond belief.

It was Harry who intercepted Ellen at Central Station the following morning, Tuesday, to tell her the shocking news about Lily, and about George's arrest. She had left Preston on an early train as Mary had her business to attend to at the shop in Church Street, and Ellen, too, had plenty of work to do, especially after last week's disastrous happenings at her own shop. That had been her main reason for going to Preston, to get away from all her problems for a day or so and to have a good old chinwag with her sister. Now, on returning, the news was worse than ever.

Ellen categorically refuted the idea that George could have had anything to do with the murder. She was very shocked, of course, and had turned deathly pale when Harry told her. He had led her into the waiting room which, fortunately, was empty.

'But he was with me,' she said, her deep-brown eyes perplexed, not seeming, at first, to understand the enormity of the situation. 'He was with me all Sunday evening. He came in for tea – about five o'clock, it was – and he didn't go out again. You say he had been with *Lily?*' She shook her head in bewilderment. 'He didn't tell me that, but he was perfectly normal and happy when he came in. He's seemed a lot happier lately, our Georgie. And you say he'd been taking Lily Jessop out... Perhaps that's why he was happy. Poor George. He should have told me – I wouldn't have minded. And now the poor girl's dead... Anyway, George was with me. I'll go and tell the police. I can give him an alibi – that's what they call it, don't they? They'll have to let me see him, won't they, if I go to the police station. He's my son.'

'Yes, I should think so, Mum,' said Harry. 'We'll go there now, unless you want to go home first?' Ellen shook her head.

Harry didn't tell her that the alibi she could give Harry was as good as useless, the way things stood at the moment. Lily had not been seen alive after four-thirty. He would leave that for the police to tell her, as no doubt they would; unless she had managed to think it through for herself by then.

Ellen had, indeed, come to that same realisation. She knew that she hadn't been thinking straight when Harry had first broken the news, but by the time they arrived at the police station on Lower King Street, not far from Ellen's home, the whole awful truth was beginning to dawn on her. Supposing nobody had seen Lily after Sunday afternoon? That would mean that George was the last one to see her alive. Wasn't that what they always said in detective stories? Then came a thought so shocking, so shameful, that she immediately pushed it away; the memory of William, her first husband, in one of his drunken rages, and how he had beaten her so savagely ... and of how like his father George sometimes seemed, when he was the worse for drink. But George hadn't been drinking when he came home on that Sunday afternoon; Ellen was certain of that. All the same, things looked none too good for him.

'All right, Ellen?' Harry whispered, holding on tightly to her arm, as they turned into the police station.

'Yes, thank you. I'm all right,' Ellen nodded, but she knew she was *not* all right, and she never would be again, unless they released George.

They were about to go up to the policeman on duty at the desk when Ellen noticed a familiar figure sitting on a bench at the side of the room. At least, the woman had been very familiar at one time, although Ellen hadn't seen her for a good many years. But Ellen was sure it was her ... Lucy Banks. Her old rival for Ben's affections, she couldn't help but remember. She looked quite a lot older, considerably plumper and just as smartly turned out. Lucy was married now, of course, but Ellen had never known her married name.

The light of recognition dawned in the eyes of both women at the same time. Lucy got up and hurried across the room. 'Ellen.' Her blue eyes, still as bright as ever, were full of concern. 'I was so sorry to hear about your George. I couldn't believe it when Mam told me they'd brought him in here. In fact, that's why I've come.'

'What do you mean, Lucy?' Ellen frowned slightly. 'Why have you come?'

'To tell them it wasn't him.' Lucy's eyes opened wide. 'It couldn't have been. Ma said nobody had seen Lily after half-past four, but I had. So had my husband, Bert, and our two kids. We arrived for Sunday tea at Mam's, y'see, at five o'clock, and Lily was just going out to post a letter. She said hello to us as cheerful as anything. Of course, I didn't mention it to Mam, not then; why should I? I didn't know the poor lass was going to go and get herself murdered.'

Tears of relief filled Ellen's eyes as she gazed at Lucy in astonishment, scarcely able to believe what she was hearing. She caught hold of her arm. 'Lucy, this is wonderful! You don't know what it means to me to hear you say this.' She turned to Harry. 'Did you hear that, Harry? Isn't it amazing? You say you saw Lily at five o'clock? Well, by that time George was back home with me, and he never went out again. I can swear to that. Come on, what are we waiting for? Let's go and tell that policeman.'

And on hearing this new, irrefutable evidence the police were obliged to let George go free.

Ellen was overjoyed that her son had been

released and she thanked Lucy over and over again for what she had done. How providential it was that Lucy and her family had arrived at the house just at the moment when Lily was leaving. But Ellen's elation died down very quickly as she remembered the reason for George's arrest – that poor dead girl – to be replaced by an over-whelming sadness. This young woman, barely twenty years old, had been one of Hobson's employees, a lively, popular girl with all her life ahead of her, apart from the fact that she had been, apparently, more than a little friendly with George.

'But why, Georgie?' Ellen asked him, in the safety of their home, when he had recovered a little from the ordeal. 'Why didn't you tell me that you were friendly with Lily?'

'Don't know, Mum.' George sounded dazed, as was only to be expected. 'I was going to tell you, but it was difficult. I suppose I thought you might not approve.'

'Oh George, surely you know me better than that?' said Ellen, feeling unutterably sad. 'I'm no snob. I never have been and, please God, I never will be. You mean, because she worked in our factory, because she was a rock-wrapper? That doesn't matter at all. Why should it, if you loved the girl? Did you love her, George?'

'I don't know, Mam,' said George again. 'I wasn't sure. Perhaps that's why I didn't tell you. I thought I did … I was fond of her. She was good fun, and she made me laugh. That's what I needed – somebody to make me laugh. She was good for me, Mam. She helped me to forget all

481

the awful memories – you know.'

It was very rarely that George mentioned his war experiences, but now: 'That terrible time … it all seemed very far away, when I was with Lily. And I haven't been drinking as much, Mam, not since I met Lily. We didn't go into pubs. I know you never thought it was very nice to take a young lady into a pub…' His voice broke again and his eyes filled up with tears. 'And now she's dead and I won't ever see her again. I don't know if I loved her, but I needed her. Oh Mam, what am I going to do?'

Ellen put her arms round him, but she didn't reply to his anguished plea. How could she? It would be useless, surely, to tell him that she, his mother, was here, when what he wanted was a young woman's arms around him and the sound of her merry laughter. She guessed that Ruth Bishop, Rachel's friend from the office, though an admirably suitable and very pleasant young woman, might be a mite serious for the fun-loving George. At least, he had been fun-loving until that wretched war had wrought such a change in him. And she couldn't tell him at this moment, that in time he would meet someone else.

'I don't know, George,' was all she could say. 'It's dreadful. It's been a terrible shock for all of us. But we must be thankful that the police have let you go. Thank God that Lucy Banks was there, just at the right moment, although they would have released you eventually, of course.'

But Ellen was not at all sure, in truth, that George would have been freed, not unless further evidence had come to light. The consequences could have been too horrific even to contemplate. Murderers, with very few exceptions, were hanged. It was very seldom, even though they were now two decades into the twentieth century, that juries would accept any pleas of mitigating circumstances. Surely, by now, Ellen thought, the police must have found some clue about the person who had called on Lily, the fiend who had strangled her. It was unthinkable that he might go free.

'Let's just hope that they catch the devil, and soon,' said Ellen. 'Poor Lily ... and her poor parents. How ever must they be feeling? I expect the police will have been to break the awful news to them. George...' She looked steadily at her son. 'I think you'll have to try and face up to the fact that Lily may have been a bit of a ... well, a flirt. She probably had a few young men, you know. She was a pretty girl. And in the long run...' she was trying to offer him a crumb of comfort, '...she may not have been the right girl for you.'

George nodded blankly. 'There was somebody else. I know that. She told me. And if I could get my hands on him, I'd kill him!' His eyes were a cold, steely blue, glinting dangerously with the intensity of his rage, just as William's had used to do. And Ellen felt a tremor of fear and foreboding.

It was in the middle of Tuesday afternoon that Amos Hardy approached Harry. 'Mr Balderstone, could I have a word with you, like?' He was shuffling awkwardly from one foot to the other, his pale blue eyes troubled. That, however, was not unusual; small problems that other workers could surmount often assumed gigantic proportions to Amos.

'Yes, Amos, what is it?' Harry tried to answer patiently, but he was far too preoccupied to be involved in petty little disputes.

'It's about Lily.' Amos gave a loud sniff. 'I've been thinking about it ever since yesterday, when they took Mr George in. But they've let him go now, haven't they? I'm glad about that. I knew it weren't him what did it. Y'see ... I've seen another chap there.'

'What? At Lily's digs? At Mrs Banks's?' Amos, of course, had a room at the same house. Harry hadn't forgotten this, but he hadn't thought to question Amos any further, well aware that one couldn't always place full credence in all he said. But this could be important. 'Come into the office, Amos,' he said, 'and tell me all about it.'

'Who was it, Amos?' Harry spoke quietly, the suspense making his skin tingle and the hairs of his body stand up on end. 'Who did you see?'

'Why, it were that fellow what came here, weren't it? You know, you showed him round t'factory a couple of weeks back. You said he was yer cousin.'

Harry struggled hard to control himself. He had felt that it might be Jack whom Mrs Banks had seen and now his suspicions were confirmed. 'And you're sure it was my cousin, Jack Balderstone, that you saw visiting Lily?'

Amos nodded. 'Aye, I'm sure.'

484

'When, Amos? Can you remember just when you've seen him?'

'Don't rightly know, Mr Balderstone.' Amos scratched his head. 'I've seen him a few times. One day last week … at night, I mean. It were dark. I heard Lily go downstairs, but he didn't come in that time. I saw him walking away down t'path. I thought he looked proper mad, like.'

'And Sunday? This Sunday?' Harry prompted him again. 'Did you see my cousin at Mrs Banks's house on Sunday evening? Think, Amos. It's very important.'

'No, I didn't see him Sunday.' Amos shook his head quite definitely and Harry felt his heart sink. 'I couldn't have seen him Sunday, 'cause I weren't there, see? Me brother and his wife came over from Preston. Took me out for a slap-up tea, they did, at one of them big posh hotels, then we had a few drinks in a pub. It were quite late when they went to get their train and I didn't get back home till – oh, I dunno – I bet it were eleven o'clock at night. So I didn't see owt on Sunday. Not after I'd seen Lily early in th' afternoon, that was when I was going to meet our Frank. But I told you that afore, that I'd seen her, and I told the police.'

'Then why didn't you tell them what you've just told me, about my cousin?'

'Dunno, Mr Harry,' Amos shrugged. ''Cause they didn't ask me, I suppose. They was only asking about Sunday, and I'd seen nothing Sunday. But I've told you now, haven't I?'

'Indeed you have, Amos.' Harry smiled warmly at him. 'Thank you very much for telling me.'

Amos shuffled his feet again. 'Not that I want to get that chap into trouble, mind. He's your cousin … you told me he was your cousin, but I thought I'd best tell you about it. Just in case… Well, it's evidence, in't it.' His guileless blue eyes opened wide as he looked plaintively at Harry.

'Indeed it is,' replied Harry, adding quietly, almost to himself, 'And let's hope the police think so, even though it's not quite the evidence we want.'

Harry wished so much that he could embroider the evidence, to give the impression to the police that Jack had been seen at Lily's digs on the Sunday evening. But he knew that this would not be possible – he didn't really consider that it might be unethical – because Amos had stressed most vehemently that he wasn't at home on Sunday at the crucial time. That was not to assume, however, that Jack had not been there. Harry was convinced that he had, and now it was up to the police to prove it. He presented them with such evidence as he had.

To his relief they took him seriously, the Police Sergeant who interviewed him being the same one he had encountered over the break-in at the shop. 'Mr Jack Balderstone … again,' he said thoughtfully. 'Yes, I remember you mentioned him before. Your cousin, you said? You don't like him much, do you?' He gave Harry a searching look.

'Well, no, I must admit he's not my favourite person,' replied Harry, a little cagily. 'But there's nothing personal in this, you understand. I've found out he'd been visiting the girl who was murdered, and I thought you should know.'

'Yes.' The Sergeant nodded. 'We will certainly go and have a word with this Jack Balderstone, after we've verified your story with Mr Amos Hardy, you say? Yes, I remember him.' It sounded as though the Sergeant was dubious about attaching too much importance to anything Amos might say. 'There are some fingerprints in the girl's room we've not identified yet, but what we really want is evidence of a visitor on Sunday evening, after your brother-in-law left: he's in the clear, of course, now. But this is a start, certainly. Thank you, Mr Balderstone. We're grateful to you.'

Jack was not surprised to see the policemen on his doorstep late on Tuesday evening. It was what he had feared. He didn't know how they had got on to him; he had taken such pains that nobody should know about him and Lily. All the same, he had guessed that they might sniff him out. Now all he could do was to bluff his way through it. Perhaps it might be as well, though, to admit that he had known the girl. They obviously had found that much out... His stomach was turning somersaults, he badly wanted to visit the lavatory and his skin felt cold and clammy, but he smiled brightly as he greeted his unwelcome visitors.

'Yes, officers, what can I do for you?'

'We'd like to ask you a few questions, sir. You are Mr Jack Balderstone, I take it?' Jack nodded. 'Well, then, do you mind if we come in?'

Jack ushered them into the living room, where

his mother was reading in an easy chair. The two policemen briefly acknowledged her then sat down on two of the dining chairs, without so much as a by your leave. Jack seated himself opposite them, placing his hands squarely on the table in front of him. 'Now, what can I do for you?' he asked again, half-smiling at them.

'Did you know a young lady by the name of Lily Jessop, sir?' The Police Sergeant was not smiling back at him; rather, Jack found the fellow's steady gaze somewhat alarming, but he met it unflinchingly.

'Yes, I did know Lily. Terrible business, isn't it?' He shook his head sorrowfully, lowering his eyes.

'Oh, so you knew she'd been found murdered ... strangled?' The Constable was speaking now. 'And how did you know, sir, may I ask?'

'Well...' Jack spread his hands wide, shrugging his shoulders. 'News gets around, you know. It was in the local paper tonight, but I knew before that. I'm in the same line of business – I work at Edwards's rock factory, in charge of the office – and we heard about it this morning. It was a terrible shock. I couldn't believe it.'

'You knew her well then, sir?'

Jack, pursed his lips. 'Quite well. We were ... friendly at one time, but I haven't seen her so much of late.'

'Oh, and why is that, sir?'

'Let's say she had other fish to fry.' Jack smiled easily. 'I wasn't her only ... friend, not by a long chalk. Lily was a pretty girl, officer. When I took her out, which wasn't very often, I used to see the other fellows looking at her.'

'And that made you jealous, did it, Mr Balderstone?'

'No, of course not.' Jack gave a careless laugh. 'Why should it? I knew she met other young men. She told me. There was one in particular, Mr George Hobson...'

'Yes, we've met Mr Hobson,' said the Sergeant evenly. His grey eyes were shrewd as he stared at Jack. Jack was tempted to look away, but he knew he mustn't. 'We've had him in for questioning. I expect you knew about that, too, didn't you, sir?' Jack half-nodded, not knowing now what to give away and what to conceal. He could feel the sweat running down the back of his neck. 'And we've let him go again. Watertight alibi, you see, Mr Balderstone. What we're looking for now is the person who visited Lily Jessop soon after Mr George Hobson left.'

'When did you last see Lily?' It was the Constable's turn now.

Jack frowned, drumming his fingers casually on the table top, his eyes cast towards the ceiling. 'Let me see ... Thursday, last week – no, it was Friday. I called round on Thursday night to see if she wanted to come out for a drink, but she was washing her hair. She said she'd go out with me on the Friday, and she did. That was the last time I saw her.'

'You often visited her, didn't you, Mr Balderstone?'

'I wouldn't call it often, officer.'

'I would. You've been seen entering the house and leaving the house ... and you've been heard as well, in Lily's room.'

Jack was panic-stricken now. Who the devil had seen him … and heard him? That interfering old biddy, Mrs Banks, he supposed. But he was certain nobody had seen him on Sunday. He frowned perplexedly, guilelessly, he hoped. 'Who told you all this, officer?'

'A gentleman who lodges there, on the same floor as Lily, as a matter of fact. A Mr Amos Hardy.'

Jack frowned again, for real this time. Who the hell was Amos Hardy? Then he remembered. Yes, it must be that half-baked fellow that worked at Hobson's. He was called Amos. He relaxed fractionally. 'Well, really.' He smiled now, shaking his head as though the idea was just too incredulous. 'Amos Hardy? Surely you're not attaching any importance to anything *he* says?'

'He knows what he's seen, Mr Balderstone, and we believe him. And he recognised you, too. Saw you at Hobson's factory, didn't he?' The Sergeant's tone was grim. 'What's more, he's seen you several times in Park Road.'

'He may well have seen me. I've made no secret of it, have I?' Jack gave the policemen what he hoped was a blameless look. 'I've told you, I did know Lily … but I didn't murder her. Good God, what d'you take me for? Why should I want to do that?'

'We don't know, sir, but somebody did.' The Police Constable leaned back in his chair and the Sergeant took over again.

'What would you say if I told you you'd be seen leaving the house in Park Road … on Sunday evening?'

490

Jack felt his bowels move, but he sat tightly in his chair, staring impassively at the Police Sergeant. 'I'd say whoever told you that is a liar. It's a barefaced lie.' He spoke loudly, convincingly. 'I wasn't there. I didn't see Lily on Sunday. It's *just not true.*'

'I can vouch for that, officer.' The three men turned to look at Jessie who had been sitting quietly in the corner of the room. She had not spoken except to acknowledge the policemen as they entered the house. She had put her book on the arm of the chair and now held some knitting in her lap, the very picture of cosy domesticity. 'Sunday evening you're talking about? Jack was here, with me, all Sunday evening. Neither of us went out. He'd been out in the afternoon, then he came in for his tea – about half-past four, wasn't it, Jack?' Jack nodded. 'And he didn't go out again, not till he went to work on Monday morning.'

'Unusual, madam, isn't it, for a young man to stay in with his mother ... all evening?'

'Not really.' Jessie smiled charmingly. 'He's always out on a Saturday – lads' night out, you know. But Sunday nights, well, he usually spends them with me.'

'Doing what, madam?'

'Oh, listening to the gramophone.' Jessie motioned towards the box with the large horn atop of it. 'We both like music. Brass bands, that's our favourite. And we had a game of cards, I remember. Then we made some tea and went to bed about ... eleven o'clock, I suppose.'

'Hmmm. Very nice. Very cosy.' The Sergeant

sounded as though he didn't believe a word of it. 'All the same, we'll have to ask you to come down to the station. There are some fingerprints in Lily's room that we can't identify.'

'What – now?' Jack glanced at the clock. 'It's half-past ten.'

'Yes, now, if you don't mind, sir. The night's still young.'

'I won't be long, Mam.' Jack glanced towards his mother, meeting her worried look with a broad smile, albeit a forced one; he was finding it hard to move the muscles of his mouth. 'I'm sure we'll soon be able to sort this little matter out. Yes...' He turned to the policemen. 'My fingerprints may well be in Lily's room. I've told you; I did see her, from time to time. But I wasn't there on Sunday.'

'Very well, sir. We'll discuss it later ... at the station, shall we?'

Jack knew that he had no choice but to go, to all appearances, willingly. He had been so sure that nobody had seen him there on Sunday evening. If someone had, well, he was in it right up to his neck. His hands went involuntarily to his throat and as he followed the policemen out to the waiting motor car he could feel the bile rising and filling his mouth.

'He did it. I know damn well he did it ... but we can't prove it.' The Police Sergeant flung down his pad and pencil, staring gloomily at his colleague. 'We had to let him go, Bill. We had no choice. Watertight alibi, damn it, just like George Hobson had. And his fingerprints weren't on the cups and saucers, nor on the door-handle neither. Only George Hobson's, and we know it wasn't him.'

They had found only one or two indistinct fingerprints that could have belonged to Jack, and, after all, he did admit to having been there.

'He's a clever bastard, I'll say that for him, Sarge,' remarked Bill. 'That was a crafty move, pretending to come clean with us, admitting that he'd been using her to get information about Hobson's. All in the line of business, he said, and what's more, he's right. We can't touch him for it. It's every man for himself in business, and he was only trying to get his boss's firm off to a flying start.'

'Aye, and I'm pretty sure now that he was behind that break-in at Hobson's shop,' the Sergeant remarked. 'Harry Balderstone vowed all along that it was him, but there was no proof. Just like there's none now.' He stared despondently into space. 'We could be wrong, of course. It seems as though Miss Lily Jessop was a bit free with her favours.'

'No, I think we're right. It was him. And if he did it, then we'll nail him, don't you worry. But if we don't ... well, they never caught Jack the Ripper, did they, Sarge?'

Chapter Twenty-Four

'You killed her, John Henry, didn't you? You killed that poor lass.' Jessie stared coldly at her son, feeling, at that moment, almost pure hatred for him.

She had always known that he was what folks generally called 'a bad lot', but then, what chance had he had in the beginning? Admittedly, she had never been the best of mothers, so it was little wonder that he had turned out the way he had. She had known full well about his lying and cheating and his dubious dealings as he grew up, turning a blind eye and, at times, actively encouraging him. But Jessie drew the line at murder.

'Didn't mean to, Mam.' Jack stared back at her sullenly. 'It wasn't really what you could call murder.'

'You killed her,' Jessie repeated. 'I knew what you'd done as soon as the police walked through that door. I'd had my suspicions before, when you told me to say you'd been here all Sunday evening. I knew you'd been up to summat shady, as usual, but I never dreamed it could be ... *murder.*'

'It weren't, Mam. It weren't, I tell you. One minute she was alive, and the next minute ... she'd gone all limp.'

'Because you strangled her.' Jessie's eyes

narrowed as she looked with revulsion at her son. 'You've done some awful things in your time, John Henry, and so have I – I'm the first to admit it. I'm no saint, God knows, and I've always had my eye on the main chance. I suppose I've brought you up to be the same, grasping and self-centred. But murder...' She looked down at her open hands, as though they were the ones that had done the deed, shaking her head sadly, disbelievingly.

'You told 'em I was here, though, didn't you, Mam? You gave me an alibi.'

'What else could I do? You're my son, aren't you? I've lied and cheated along with you for most of your life. I couldn't let them hang you.' She saw Jack blanch and put his hands to his throat. 'Oh yes, that's what they'd have done, if I hadn't lied for you. You'd have been hanged by the neck until you were dead ... like that poor girl.' And you would have deserved it an' all, she added, but only to herself. Even now, in the midst of her near hatred and loathing of him, Jessie could feel a stirring of pity and a need to protect him.

'She laughed at me, Mam,' Jack mumbled, staring down at his feet 'She shouldn't have laughed at me. Taunting me, she was. Said she didn't want to see me again, 'cause she'd gone and got friendly with him, George flamin' Hobson. She said he was taking her to a big posh dance, with all the nobs, an' he'd told her she hadn't to have any other fellows, only him. After all I'd done for her. Buying her chocolates and scent and silk stockings an' all that, and making

495

such a bloody fuss of her.'

'And after all she'd done for *you*, John Henry,' said Jessie quietly. 'She was the lass that told you all that stuff about Hobson's, wasn't she? Put her job on the line for you, I shouldn't wonder. She'd have been in trouble if they'd found out what she was doing, giving away their secrets. And what thanks did she get? You killed her.'

'I've told you, I keep telling you, I didn't mean to! I was mad with her – anybody would have been mad, I can tell you – and I got hold of her and I shook her. And she started to shout, so I slapped her face, then I got hold of her mouth and her neck, just to shut her up, Mam, that's all. And the next minute she'd gone all funny and limp and she wouldn't answer me. I tried to bring her round, I did, honest. But I couldn't, so I put her on the settee and then I … I came away. It weren't my fault, Mam. I didn't want her to die.'

Jessie continued to look at him coldly. It was frightening how much her feelings towards him had changed over the last twenty-four hours as the realisation dawned on her that her son was guilty of the ultimate crime. It was because of her evidence – false evidence – that they had finally let him come home after keeping him at the police station overnight. When he had failed to return by the early hours of the morning she had feared that the worst had happened, that he had been charged with the girl's murder. Then, when he had appeared, she had felt relief, of a sort; but self-reproach, too, that she had lied over such a heinous crime as murder. Lies had not worried Jessie overmuch in the past, but this was different. But what else could she have done, she asked herself. Told the truth and let him hang? She had had no choice.

Jack seemed to be recovering from his ordeal now. He stood up, stretching his arms above his head. 'I'll make a cup of tea, Mam, then go and snatch a few hours' shut-eye. Didn't get a wink on that hard bunk.' Jessie didn't respond to his half-laugh. 'And I'd best go and ring Luke; tell him I'm a bit under the weather and I'll be in this afternoon. It'll be all right, Mam.' He looked uneasily at Jessie's impassive face. 'The police haven't got anything on me. They've let me go, haven't they? Thanks to you,' he added in a mumble.

Jessie still didn't answer, so Jack sat down again on the chair opposite her, leaning forward. 'Look here, Mam, it was because of you that I got friendly with Lily in the first place. It weren't just my idea, you know, to get even with the Hobsons and to get one over on that stuck-up cousin of mine. You were just as keen as I was to pay that Ellen Bamber back for what she'd done to you.'

'That's ages ago, John Henry...' Jessie gazed thoughtfully into the dead ashes of the fire. She hadn't had the heart, yet, to re-lay and light it this morning. 'Aye, I'll admit I wanted revenge, or thought I did. Revenge is sweet – isn't that what they say? But it's all gone sour on us now. It doesn't seem to matter any more, getting even with that lot. What matters now is what you've done, and how I've got to live with that for the rest of my days ... and so have you.' She looked up, turning sad and reproachful eyes upon her son, and even he was forced to look away at the condemnation he saw there.

Even before this dreadful matter had come to light, however, Jessie had been undergoing a change of heart. She had found, somewhat to her amazement, that she was very happy in Blackpool; and with this new-found contentment there had come a change of emphasis in her outlook. She liked the people here, she liked the town itself and her comfortable little home; and, even more to her surprise, she was growing increasingly fond of Archie Prendergast, the middle-aged local businessman with whom she had become friendly soon after they had moved to the town. She had had two such 'friendships' at first. Now there was only the one, Archie, who owned a string of seafood stalls, selling cockles, mussels, shrimps, oysters and the like, along Blackpool's promenade. He was a widower, very 'well-heeled', and he wanted her to marry him and go to live in his large house in South Shore, right at the other end of the town. Jessie had demurred. She had always drawn the line at marriage, never having seen the necessity for it. But Archie was persuasive. He knew something of her past – not all of it by any means, but quite enough – and, seemingly, it made little difference to him. He was sure that he wanted to marry her.

Now, as she sat in the chill October gloom of her little room, the idea of a change suddenly seemed very appealing to Jessie. Much as she had come to love her new home in the eighteen months or so she had lived there, nevertheless, she now felt that she would like a fresh start ...

away from Jack. She made a snap decision.

'There's something I've got to tell you, John Henry, and now's as good a time as any. You'll have to find yourself somewhere else to live. Archie wants me to move in with him; he's been asking me for a while, and now I've decided – that's what I'm going to do. So you'd best start looking for some digs or a flat or summat.'

'Hey, hold on a minute, Mam.' Jack's tone was petulant and he scowled angrily at his mother. 'I helped to pay for this house; you know damn well I did. So the way I see it, half of it belongs to me.'

'Very well, you shall have your half when I sell it,' said Jessie evenly, still not smiling. She was feeling as though she would never smile again, leastways not at this son of hers. 'I'm not arguing about that. As you say, you helped to pay for it. But it's high time you were on your own. We've been together too long, John Henry.'

'It's suited you well enough till now,' Jack glowered. 'Yes, I know; you just want me out of the road, so you can go and live over the brush with yer fancy man.'

'There'll be no living over the brush.' Jessie looked fixedly at her son. 'Archie has asked me to marry him.'

'Marry him! Huh!' Jack threw back his head with a derisive laugh. 'That's a turn-up for the book, I must say. I've heard everything now. You getting wed! What've you told him, Mam? Does Archie know how you used to hang around outside the Black Horse? Does he know how you used to leave me on my own in the dark while you went touting for custom? Does he know–'

'That's enough, John Henry!' In a few quick strides Jessie had crossed the room and given Jack two stinging slaps, one on each cheek. He held up his arms to shield himself from the blows.

'Give over, Mam! I've only said what's true. You know it's true. You're nawt but a whore...'

'And don't you ever call me names like that again. How dare you!' Jessie's anger was giving her strength, both mentally and physically. She seized hold of Jack's shoulders, forcing him back in the chair. 'I've not been the best of mothers, I know that only too well. But neither have you been the best of sons. And after what you've just done, I'm finished with you, John Henry. You just watch what you're saying to me, or I'll be down to see those coppers before you can say "Jack Robinson". I'm warning you ... I'll shop you if you don't watch your step, just see if I don't.'

'You wouldn't... They wouldn't believe you anyroad, not after what you've told them.' Stark fear showed in Jack's eyes and his lip was trembling. Still sickened at what he had done, Jessie let go of him and turned away.

'Go and make yourself some tea,' she muttered, 'then get up to bed. I'll get in touch with Luke Edwards and make your excuses.' Even now, it was second nature to her to tell lies for him.

'So they've had to let him go ... again. Would you believe it?' Harry bemoaned to Luke Edwards. He had called to see Luke at his home a couple of days after he had been to talk to the police about Jack. 'That Sergeant came to tell me, the

500

same one that I saw about the break-in. Jack's mother – that's my Aunt Jessie – gave him an alibi for Sunday evening, and they couldn't find enough evidence to hold him. It was him, though, I'm damn sure it was, and I think the police know it as well.'

'I should be careful if I were you, Harry lad,' said Luke, sounding somewhat worried. 'You can't go around accusing folks of murder. Breaking and entering's one thing – and, like you say, they can't even get him for that – but murder's something else. If he was to find out what you've been saying…'

'Don't worry. He'll be steering clear of me, will our Jack. And I can assure you I haven't said anything to anyone else. I didn't even tell the police I thought he'd done it; I just told them he'd been seeing Lily, which was perfectly true. I'm only telling you because … well, I think you should know. He works for you and–'

'Not for much longer, Harry, not if things work out the way I think they will.' Luke gave a grim smile. 'I've got an accountant going through the books even now. I let him have them at night, when Jack's gone, and then I get 'em back in the office early in the morning. Jack's not the most punctual of workers, believe me. And he's in for a nasty shock before long, all the nastier for it being a complete surprise. Thinks he's too clever for us, y'see. My accountant's coming across some surprising things. Anyway, Mum's the word for the moment.' Luke put his finger to his lips.

'And how's your family then, Harry? You've had some setbacks just recently, one way and another, haven't you?'

Harry nodded. 'I'll say. But Rachel and Ellen, both of them, seem to be coping pretty well. It was such a relief when George was released that nothing else seemed to matter. No, that's not true,' he amended. 'Of course it matters. We're all still very distressed about Lily. George and I are going over to Blackburn on Wednesday, for the funeral. That's where her family live. It's the very least we can do. No, what I mean is, we're trying hard to get back to normal; and our little Pearl helps, of course – we have to try to keep cheerful for her sake. Rachel's coming to terms with losing the baby and Ellen's getting the shop back on its feet again. But this business with Lily – d'you know, Luke, I find it hard to say the word "murder"; it's all too unbelievable, the sort of thing you don't ever imagine will happen to you. It'll take us a while to come to terms with it all.'

'Mmm. It gives me a funny feeling an' all, to think I might be working alongside a murderer,' Luke remarked. 'You can't be sure though, Harry. You don't know definitely it was him. I'm finding out he's a crafty, lying so and so ... but murder?'

'No, I don't know for sure,' Harry admitted. 'But it's what I believe, especially after the way he went for Rachel. My mother-in-law is of the same opinion, too, but we haven't let on to George about our suspicions. From what Ellen was saying, he was all for going and killing the swine that did it; that's what he said. He's inclined to be hot-headed, our George, and we can't risk him getting arrested for murder *again*. There'd be no mercy for him. You can't just take the law into your own hands and kill somebody, however much you may think they deserve it. So we're keeping our mouths shut about Jack, just hoping the police'll get him eventually.'

'Aye, well, they'll be arresting him before long for embezzlement,' said Luke, 'if not for murder. And that should put him away for a while.'

A few months later, in January 1922, Jack Balderstone was sent for trial at Preston Assizes and sentenced to eighteen months imprisonment. He had been found guilty of embezzlement and mis-appropriating the firm's funds for his own use. He had cleverly covered his tracks for a while, but had been found out when he became too ambitious. He had tried to form a company of his own, asking the clients – just some, very craftily, not all of them – to make their payments to *Rock Exchange* instead of to *Luke Edwards,* saying that it was a subsidiary branch of the same firm.

'Thank God for that,' said Harry when he heard the news. 'The only trouble, of course, is that eighteen months is not long enough, not for what he's done.' The police, as Harry had predicted, had still not found Lily's killer.

But Rachel and Harry already had other matters to occupy their minds. They now knew that their second child would be born in July. Rachel was taking no chances at all this time. At Harry's insistence, she was resting as much as she could and working only a couple of hours each day in the shop.

503

Harry, however, was working, it seemed to his wife, all the hours that God gave, sometimes not arriving home until very late in the evening. Rachel was beginning to feel just the tiniest bit neglected…

Ellen put her head to one side, frowning slightly as she fingered first one, then the other of the skeins of wool that the assistant showed her. They were all such pretty pastel shades – pale blue, oyster pink, lemon, and a delicate leaf green, as well as the ordinary white – and all very soft and smooth, just right for a baby's tender skin. Ellen didn't consider herself to be the greatest of knitters, but she wanted to be a proper grandma and make a few things for the coming baby; a matinée jacket and maybe some bonnets and bootees. It was such a thrill that Rachel was expecting again.

'This pink is lovely,' she remarked. The delicate shade reminded her of the tiny fingers and toes of little Pearl, now some sixteen months old. 'But I don't know … it might be tempting fate.' She smiled at the assistant. 'Pink is suitable only for a girl, isn't it? Whereas blue will do for either, or lemon.' Secretly, she was hoping that Rachel would have another little girl. Pearl was such a treasure, but she had to be sensible.

'I'll take the blue,' she said, 'and the lemon as well. And these patterns, please.' She had chosen a whole array of leaflets from which she would make her choice. 'You can give me four skeins of each colour. It'll always come in.'

Ellen turned away from the counter, dangling

the neatly wrapped parcel by its string, well pleased with her purchases. Donnelly's assistants were always so polite and obliging. She would treat herself to a cup of coffee, she decided, in the upstairs tea-room, but, before that, she would have a quick look at the materials. Donnelly's had recently started a dressmaking service and rumour had it that it was very good.

Idly she stroked the bolts of material displayed on the stands. That was a pretty cornflower blue in light wool; it would make up into a lovely two-piece, although Ellen had never considered blue to be really her colour. Or that heavy silk in the dark golden shade; it would be just right for what they called an 'afternoon' dress. Almost the same shade as her wedding dress had been, Ellen mused. Abruptly she turned away. She wasn't in the mood today, after all, for thinking about new clothes for herself.

If she had had more warning she might well have pretended she hadn't seen her, but it all happened too quickly. Ellen practically collided with the woman coming along between the display stands and they both stopped, muttering, 'Sorry.' Then their glances met.

Ellen saw a pair of luminous grey eyes – beautiful eyes – now darkly shadowed, in which recognition was just dawning, as it was in her own. The woman's hair was cut short now, in a fashionable style, but what showed of it beneath her close-fitting hat was still black. Her face was deeply lined around the forehead and mouth, showing the ravages of time, as well it might, thought Ellen, although she knew that this

505

person was not much different in age to herself – they were both in their mid-forties. It was Jessie Balderstone, her once dreaded adversary, but as Ellen looked at her for the first time in some twenty years, she knew instinctively that she needed to fear her no longer.

Jessie, for her part, saw the warm brown eyes of the woman she had almost knocked over cloud for a moment with alarm, to be replaced almost at once with what she recognised as empathy. Yes, the years had brought troubles to both of them. Jessie knew that Ellen had lost a dearly loved – second – husband, and that her recent problems had been manifold ... mainly due to John Henry, she found herself thinking. She no longer felt any animosity towards this woman whom she had once hated so intensely, or had thought she did. Ellen, too, looked older, possibly older than her years. Her face was unlined, but her once bright hair was streaked with grey and she appeared to have lost weight, although she had always been of a slender build.

They both spoke at once. 'Jessie...' 'Ellen...'

Not Nellie, thought Ellen with a pleasant surprise. She remembered how the last time she had encountered Jessie the woman had taunted her with, 'I'll get even with you, Nellie Bamber...' It was Ellen who spoke next.

'I heard you were living in Blackpool,' she said, a little hesitantly. 'My son-in-law, you know, Harry ... he's your nephew, I believe?'

Jessie gave a wry smile. 'Yes – small world, isn't it, Ellen? I was sorry to hear about your husband,' she went on. 'I've heard tell that you and Mr Hobson were very happy.'

'We were.' Ellen looked down for a moment. 'Very happy. I've a lot of good memories.' She glanced up again, meeting Jessie's uncertain look. They were still very wary of one another. 'You've had your troubles too. John Henry ... we've heard, of course.' Ellen couldn't bring herself to say she was sorry about the young man's imprisonment. That would be a lie; he deserved all he had got, and more.

'Aye, the least said about that the better,' replied Jessie implacably. 'He's had it coming to him. And when he comes out it won't be to me. As a matter of fact,' she gave what was almost a coy smile, 'I'm getting married – this week. That's why I'm here. I've come to collect my dress.'

'Oh, I see.' Ellen was at a loss for words. She was, in truth, dumbfounded, but she managed to recover sufficiently to say, 'I'm pleased for you. I hope you'll be happy.'

'I've moved in with him already,' said Jessie, with a touch of the old bravado, 'but we're making it all legal, come Saturday, Archie and me. Archie Prendergast. P'raps you've heard of him?'

'Yes, I think so.' Ellen pondered for a moment; the name sounded familiar to her. 'It's the chap that owns the seafood stalls, isn't it?'

'That's the one.'

'Yes, I know of him, but I've never met him. Anyway, all the best to you, Jessie.' Ellen hesitated, just for a moment, then she held out her hand.

Jessie, too, hesitated, then she took Ellen's hand. 'Ta very much. No hard feelings, eh?'

'No, no hard feelings,' replied Ellen.

There was tacit understanding in the look they exchanged. Ellen knew as she walked away that, although they could never be friends, their enmity was now at an end. She no longer needed to fear Jessie Balderstone. But as for her son, that was an entirely different matter. Ellen felt a tremor of unease at the thought of Jack; but, for the moment, he was safely locked away. Leaving Ellen and her family to get on with their lives.

Rachel and Harry's second child was another girl. She was as different in looks from her sister, Pearl, as it was possible to be. Pearl had been a pink and white, almost ethereal-looking baby, with just a covering of silky golden hair on her head. Her sister was robust and rosy – at eight pounds two ounces she had weighed over a pound more than Pearl – with ruddy cheeks and lips of a bright ruby red. Her hair, and there was such a mass of it, was black, showing a tendency to curl. She was obviously to take after the Balderstone side of the family, thought her mother, looking down at the hour-old infant in her arms with some awe.

'She's perfect, isn't she?' Rachel whispered to Harry. 'Not a bit like Pearl ... but still perfect. They're like Snow White and Rose Red,' she added whimsically. 'D'you remember the story?'

Harry nodded. 'Mmmm... A pearl and a ruby, I was thinking. How about that, my love? Shall we call her Ruby?'

'That's a lovely idea.' Rachel smiled up at him, before looking down, reverently, at her daughter. 'Another little jewel. She's so precious, isn't she, Harry?'

'Yes. We'll have a whole necklace of them before long,' he grinned, with a roguish gleam in his eyes.

'Not just yet.' Rachel didn't smile back at him. Enough was enough for the time being. Giving birth to baby Ruby had been an ordeal. Childbirth always was, and anyone who said any different, to Rachel's mind, was not speaking the truth. You forgot the labour pains after a while, admittedly, but at the moment it was all too fresh in Rachel's memory. She was tired and she wanted to rest.

It soon became obvious that little Ruby was very different from her placid, sunny-natured sister in temperament as well as in looks. There was little rest for either Rachel or Harry during the first few weeks. She was reasonably quiet during the daytime – it was easy enough, then, to pop her into her pram and push her round the block until the rhythmic motion sent her to sleep – but nighttime was a different matter. As soon as she was put down in her cot, dry and well-fed – and, one would have thought, with nothing to cry about – she would open her mouth wide in a gaping round O, bawling until she was picked up again.

And this, to Rachel, seemed to go on all night, although there must have been times, possibly an hour or two at a stretch, when she did manage to sleep. But Rachel was the one who was the most tired in the mornings. It was she who had to sit up feeding the child or pacing the floor with her. Harry, who had his work to attend to each day, needed to get his rest. Rachel tried to understand this, even when he moved into the spare room to get away from the screaming infant. If she were honest, though, she was not too worried about this; the way she was feeling at the moment there would be no more precious gemstones to add to their collection.

By the time Ruby was six months old, however, at the beginning of 1923, things had sorted themselves out a little. Rachel had weaned the child on to a bottle; she had been sore with the demands of the ever-hungry infant and unable to satisfy her. They had also hired a nursemaid, a couple of months previously, who lived on the premises; to help mainly with the baby and little Pearl, but also to give a hand with some of the housework as well. A sort of nanny, Rachel supposed, but she didn't use this term to her mother. Ellen seemed to be mildly disapproving, maintaining that she had always looked after her children herself – and gone out to work as well. Rachel refuted this claim, well remembering the long hours she and George had spent with their Aunt Mary, but she didn't argue. It was very rarely that Rachel and her mother argued. Besides, Rachel was satisfied in her own mind that she was doing the right thing. They were able to afford a helper as the business was now doing well again.

And it had meant that Harry could now move back into his own bed. The spare room was needed anyway by Amy, the nursemaid, and Ruby slept in a cot in her room. Harry, however, was still working long hours at the factory. Rachel wondered, at times, what he could possibly find to do to keep him there, sometimes until nine or ten o'clock of an evening. She never even entertained the thought that he might not be where he said he was. She trusted him implicitly, and she was right to do so.

When he said he was working at the factory Harry was doing just that. He had not had many girlfriends before he met Rachel, and in her he had found all that he had ever wanted. Now, with two little girls to care for as well, he knew that he must work extra hard to make life pleasant for them. And if it meant that some of the magic and romance of their early days together had to be sacrificed, well then, Harry considered it a small price to pay. This was part and parcel of marriage. He still loved his Rachel as much as ever and would work his fingers to the bone for her if needs be.

Rachel was the one who had once been something of a butterfly, flitting from one young man to the other ... until she met Harry. She had no regrets about marrying him. She loved him as much as ever; she was sure of that. But could it be possible that all this work was making him just a teeny bit ... *boring?*

'You need to get out and about more,' Ruth Bishop said to Rachel, soon after the beginning of the new year. 'There's no problem for you, is there, now you've got this Amy? She'll see to the

511

children, won't she, if you want to go out of an evening?'

Rachel agreed that she was sure Amy would do so; she was, indeed, very competent. The girl had her own day off each week, plus a couple of evenings, when she saw her young man or her family. The arrangement with the live-in help was working very well and Rachel had no cause to complain. Neither, she was sure, would Harry object to her going out with Ruth. Her friend was a serious-minded young woman, which was probably the reason that the friendship with George had come to nothing, Rachel mused. Ruth had suggested to Rachel that she might like to accompany her to the Literary Society she had joined the previous autumn.

'We meet once a fortnight at the Grammar School on Church Street,' she said, 'and we sometimes meet between-times at one another's houses. They're a grand crowd. Some of them are quite a bit older than us, but there are some young ones as well. You'd love it, Rachel. You've been doing more reading, haven't you, since Amy came to work for you?'

'Yes, I've more time to myself now,' replied Rachel, 'and I'm certainly not as tired as I was. Believe me, Ruth, I couldn't have considered going out at all a couple of months ago. I was worn to a shadow with that blessed goddaughter of yours yelling all the time.' She grinned at her friend. 'Yes, it'll do me good to get out more, as you say. Harry won't mind. It isn't as if we're going dancing or to a pub, is it? And he wouldn't want to come with me, not to a Literary Society.

Harry's not much of a one for reading,' she added thoughtfully. 'Only the newspaper.'

'I don't suppose he has much time,' said Ruth, staunchly supporting him, as Rachel had noticed she invariably did. 'He's always working, isn't he?'

'Yes, but I don't think he'd be interested anyway,' replied Rachel.

It was only over the last couple of years that Rachel had discovered the joys of reading. During her pregnancies, especially the second one, when she had rested more, she had been awakened to the delights of literature. She had started by reading light romantic novels, by such authors as Ethel M. Dell or Dodie Smith, and had then progressed, with Ruth as her mentor, to the works of Dickens and Trollope, Thomas Hardy, Jane Austen and the Brontë sisters.

Harry would look at her bemusedly from time to time, commenting that she always had her head stuck in a book. She sometimes reflected, rather to her disquiet, that the two of them hadn't as much in common as she had once supposed. They had their family, of course, but very little else. Rachel had left school when she was fifteen and had started work immediately in the office at Hobson's. There had been little opportunity for her to become acquainted with what she now thought of as the highbrow side of life; literature, poetry, music... Or so she told herself, forgetting that very often she had been out having a good time. She had also started buying gramophone records of classical composers – Mozart, Beethoven and Brahms –

instead of the brass band music or the Gilbert and Sullivan songs that Harry liked so much. And which she, too, had enjoyed when they first bought their gramophone.

Rachel knew that Harry had left school even earlier than she had done and had worked long hours at the cotton mill. There had been little chance for him, either, to educate himself. Rachel now believed that one should try to do this in order to make oneself a well-balanced, interesting person. If Harry wanted to set his sights no higher than the rock factory, with occasional forays into the pages of the *Daily Express* or the *Blackpool Gazette and Herald,* then that was his affair. But Rachel wanted a little more from life. Reading about characters in books was all very well, but she also needed to go out and meet people.

'Now ... we'll read together the closing pages of *Great Expectations,*' said Toby Meredith. 'I take it you've all done your homework? You've read the rest of the book?' The twenty or so people in the classroom at the Grammar School, squeezed into the desks normally used by the boys, smiled and nodded their agreement. 'Good – most of you had probably read it before; it's one of Dickens's most popular works. I'll read the part of Pip – he, of course, is the narrator – and Rachel, would you like to read Estella, please?'

Rachel felt herself blushing slightly with pleasure. She was aware, too, of the glances of the rest of the group. It wasn't the first time that Toby had chosen her to read opposite him. They

514

began to read…

'Estella!'

'I am greatly changed. I wonder you know me.'

The freshness of her beauty was indeed gone, but its indescribable majesty and its indescribable charm remained. The silvery mist was touched with the first rays of the moonlight, and the same rays touched the tears that dropped from her eyes.

'I have often thought of you.'

'Have you?'

'Of late, very often.'

'You have always held your place in my heart.'

Rachel felt herself moved almost to tears at the beauty of the prose, especially at the way it was spoken in Toby Meredith's mellifluous tones. He had such a wonderful voice, what she termed to herself as a golden voice, reminding her of sunlight on the sea, ripe corn, or deep yellow daffodils; with no trace of the northern accent one was so accustomed to hearing in these parts. Toby, of course, was a southerner and had moved up to Blackpool to take the post of English master at the local Grammar School.

'…the evening mists were rising now, and in all the broad expanse of tranquil light they showed to me, I saw no shadow of another parting from her.'

Toby closed the book and looked across at Rachel, smiling in that intimate, enigmatic way he had. With his soulful brown eyes, very much the colour of Rachel's own, and his rather longish brown hair, receding slightly at the temples, he reminded her of what she imagined one of the

Romantic poets might have looked like; Shelley maybe, or Byron. She smiled back at him.

Oh dear, thought Ruth, surreptitiously watching the two of them, and not for the first time. She wondered if she should warn Rachel about his reputation. Ruth knew that her friend must have come across men like this before. She was not one to gossip, and Rachel had her head screwed on the right way, when all was said and done. She must have had, to have married Harry; but Ruth sometimes thought that her friend didn't realise what a good husband she had.

Chapter Twenty-Five

It wasn't that she wanted to be unfaithful to Harry; not at all. Rachel certainly didn't want to risk losing her husband or her two dear little girls, but she did want to get better acquainted with Toby Meredith. She was sure, too, that the feeling was mutual. He hadn't chosen her again to read opposite him since that evening in April when she had been Estella to his Pip. He had perhaps been aware, as she had, of the slightly jealous looks of some of the other young women. But he always listened most attentively when she gave her opinions, about a novelist's style or characterisation or some such topic, and he nearly always agreed with her.

Yes, they were kindred spirits, Rachel was convinced of it, and although she knew there could never be anything physical between them – because she was a happily married lady – there could be no harm in furthering their friendship. (Although Rachel did, to her slight shame, sometimes have daydreams about stroking Toby's longish hair, or about how his rather full lips would feel pressed close to her own; fancies she would quickly try to banish.)

All these thoughts flitted through her mind, like moths in the twilight, as she hurried through the streets on this evening in early May. There were quite a few visitors about as the holiday season had started, and on hoardings and in shop windows there were advertisements telling of the forthcoming Blackpool Carnival. It would be, according to the notices, *The Greatest Show ever to be seen in Blackpool!* Harry was busy working on ideas for this, which was keeping him late at the factory, as usual.

Yes, Harry was neglecting her, Rachel told herself. He could hardly blame her if she formed other friendships. It might not do him any harm to know there were other young men who found her attractive. Harry, in fact, didn't seem to notice her any more; he was taking her for granted. All the same, she felt the nerves in her stomach tightening a little in apprehension. Would her reason for arriving early – a full half-hour early – for the meeting seem somewhat feeble?

The meeting tonight was to be held at Toby Meredith's home, not at the Grammar School, and when Rachel heard this she realised it was an opportunity too good to be missed. She had planned to arrive with ample time to show him a book she was sure he would appreciate, a very early edition of *Alice's Adventures in Wonderland* which had been presented to her grandmother, Lydia, for regular attendance at Sunday School and had now come into Rachel's possession. Toby was very interested in first editions and they had discussed the works of Lewis Carroll at one of their meetings.

Rachel had told her friend, Ruth, that instead of calling for her she would meet her there, at Toby's home, making the excuse that it was simpler to go straight to this new venue than to go out of her way to Ruth's house. She had tried to ignore the odd look that Ruth gave her, a look she had noticed on her friend's face a few times, whenever Rachel mentioned Toby Meredith.

Toby lived in a street off Raikes Road, quite near to the Grammar School where he taught. Rachel hurried up the short path and knocked, somewhat timidly, on the door. There was no answer, and it was then that she began to have second thoughts. Would he think her a fool? Was her excuse altogether too transparent? She pushed away the thought of Harry working late at the factory and her two little girls fast asleep in bed. No, she decided; she had come so far and she would not turn back now. Summoning up all her courage, but very much aware of the butterflies fluttering in her stomach, she knocked again, louder this time.

After a few moments the door opened and there was Toby. He looked at her in surprise, then he smiled, his deep brown eyes lighting up with interest and ... could it be a touch of amusement? Rachel hoped not. Oh dear! She didn't want him to think she was a silly impressionable female. But he was greeting her very warmly.

'Rachel... This is a surprise, but a very pleasant one, I must add. Come in, come in...' he added as she stood uncertainly on the doorstep, her mouth half open, unable to form any coherent words. 'You'll have to excuse the mess. I'm not quite ready.'

'No, of course not. I'm sorry; I know I'm early.

It's because I want to … I've brought something to show you.' Rachel knew she was stumbling over her words; she could have kicked herself.

'Ooh, that sounds interesting. I wonder what that might be?' Toby's eyes opened wide and he squeezed her arm as he ushered her into a room at the back of the house. 'And please don't apologise. As I said, it's a pleasant surprise.'

The room was not in a mess, as Toby had suggested. It was remarkably tidy, in fact, with just a pile of exercise books on one chair, which Toby quickly placed on the sideboard, and some newspapers on the chair opposite. He shoved them into a rack at the side then beamed at her. 'Now, as you're such an early bird I wonder if you could help me carry the cups and saucers in from the kitchen? I like to have everything ready and it'll be quicker if we both do it. Then it'll leave you more time to show me whatever it is you want to show me!'

He moved quickly towards her, then his hands were on her shoulder. 'Your coat, Rachel,' he laughed, as she gave a small start. 'Let me take your coat.'

'Oh yes … yes, of course.' Quickly, with Toby's assistance, she removed her coat, but kept on her little straw hat.

'I'll hang it out here.' He disappeared into the hallway, but was back almost at once. 'Now, cups and saucers…'

Rachel was glad to absorb herself in this mundane task for the next few minutes. It helped to calm her down but, to her annoyance, she was still unsure just what to say to Toby as they set out the willow pattern crockery on the brown chenille table cover in the living room.

'Is this your house, Toby?' she began, 'or do you just... I mean do you...'

'Do I own it or do I just lodge here?' He grinned at her. 'No, I don't own it, unfortunately, but I have very nice rooms here as you see.' He spread out his hands expansively and Rachel nodded in agreement.

'Yes, they are. I mean ... it is. Very nice.'

'I'm very lucky,' he went on. 'Not just a pokey bed-sitting room, like some lodgers have. No, I have the use of this room and a bedroom upstairs, and we share the kitchen and bathroom. I'm the only lodger, you see. There's only myself here and my ... my landlady, Mrs Jeffreys.'

'Oh, I see. And do you look after yourself? Cook your own meals, I mean, and all that?'

'Some of the time.' He smiled at her, that slow enigmatic smile she had noticed before. He sat down on the large settee – it was a very large room, containing a three-piece suite as well as dining furniture, and a few extra chairs, brought in, no doubt, for tonight's guests – and patted the cushion at his side. 'Now then, come and sit down, Rachel, and show me ... what is in that big bag.'

She sat down and opened her handbag, taking out the red leather-bound copy of *Alice's Adventures in Wonderland* which was in as almost perfect condition as it had been the day it was bought. 'This was my grandmother's and now it's mine. I thought you might like to see it.' Rachel was no longer stumbling over her words now she had something more definite to talk about. 'I think it's a first edition.'

There was no mistaking the pure delight on Toby's face as he reverently handled the copy. 'Oh yes … indeed it is a first edition. And a very fine one.' He turned over the pages and with heads bent closely together they looked at the coloured plates depicting the Cheshire Cat, The Mad Hatter's Tea-party and the Lobster Quadrille.

'I'm so pleased you brought it to show me. I'm sure you must treasure it very much.' Toby's eyes looked deep into her own as he placed his hand on top of hers. He left it there a moment before he took it away again.

'Oh yes, I do.' Rachel's heart had given a leap at the touch of his hand, but now she felt herself edging away a little. She hadn't intended that she should… At least, she didn't think that was what she had intended. 'I do treasure it,' she went on, speaking quickly, 'especially as it belonged to my grandma. She died when I was a little girl. I was very fond of her.'

'Yes, I miss my grandmother too,' said Toby, shaking his head sadly. 'I have no grandparents left now. They're all dead; and my parents are down in Surrey. Still…' He looked sideways at her from beneath half-closed eyelids. 'I have plenty of friends here.' He edged a little closer. 'I'm so glad you came early, Rachel. It's given us a chance to get to know one another … a little better.'

'Yes, that's what I thought,' said Rachel, greatly daring. 'We don't get a chance to … to chat very much, do we, at the ordinary meetings? To find out very much about each other, I mean.'

'No, we don't. And I've often thought I would like to get to know you better, Rachel, my dear.' His hand was resting upon hers again and this time she did not draw away. 'I don't know very much about you even though you've been coming to the meetings for – what is it? – four or five months now. Someone told me you have two little girls? Really, I would never have thought it possible.'

'Yes … yes, I have,' replied Rachel, feeling uncomfortable at the thought of Pearl and Ruby. 'But my … my husband doesn't mind me coming here; coming to the meetings, I mean. He likes me to go out, to do what … what I'm interested in.'

'I'm sure he does.' There was no doubting the amusement in Toby's eyes as he leaned towards her. They looked at one another intently for a few seconds. Then there was a knock at the front door.

'Damn!' said Toby under his breath, so quietly that Rachel scarcely heard him. The sudden – very loud – hammering on the door brought her to her senses. Whatever had she been thinking of? Another moment and she might have been … Toby might have… She had often fantasised about Toby's arms around her, his lips upon hers, but now she realised what a fool she was being.

'Excuse me.' Toby, his face grim, rose to his feet, squeezing her shoulder meaningfully. Then he went to answer the door. He came back almost immediately with Ruth.

Rachel's mouth dropped open with alarm when she saw her friend enter the room. Ruth's expression was unfathomable. 'Ruth...' she cried, her voice shrill. 'You're early. You didn't expect me to call for you, did you? I told you...' Her voice petered out.

'Not half as early as you, it seems,' said Ruth briskly. She quickly divested herself of her coat, handing it peremptorily to Toby. 'Thank you, Toby.' Her tone, to Rachel's guilty ears, sounded reproachful.

'Yes, I came early to show Toby a book. This book.' Rachel held out the red leather-bound copy. 'He's interested, you see. I don't think you've seen it, have you, Ruth? It was my grandma's.'

Ruth nodded, giving her friend a sharp glance, half reproving, but with a tinge of understanding, as she took the book from her. 'All right, let's have a look at it then.' She sat down on the settee, busying herself in the pages of *Alice's Adventures in Wonderland*.

The other members of the group, a dozen or so of them, soon arrived and Toby was kept busy answering the door. Rachel tried to enjoy the rest of the evening. *The Forsyte Saga* was new to her. She had read the first book, *The Man of Property* and was looking forward to reading the rest of the trilogy. But her mind kept wandering and she took little part in the discussion. Toby hardly spoke to her again and another young woman helped him to pour out the tea and hand round the biscuits. Rachel was more than a little apprehensive; she knew that Ruth would be asking some pertinent questions on the way home.

'What on earth do you think you were playing at?' Ruth started on at her as soon as they left Toby's house. 'Honestly, Rachel, I could shake you sometimes. Flirting with Toby Meredith like that!'

'We weren't flirting,' Rachel retorted. 'We were just ... talking.'

'Oh, pull the other one, Rachel. It's got bells on it! Of course you were flirting. It was written all over your faces, both of you. I knew as soon as I walked in that you were up to something.'

'Oh, you did, did you? Well, I can tell you, Ruth Bishop, we weren't "up to" anything, as you put it, so there. What's it got to do with you, anyway?' A sudden thought struck Rachel. 'And why were you so early yourself, eh?' Rachel's eyes narrowed suspiciously as she glared at her friend. 'Tell me that.'

'To stop you making a fool of yourself, that's why,' Ruth almost shouted back. 'I had a good idea what you were up to; telling me some tale about meeting me there because it would be nearer. You must think I was born yesterday. Listen, Rachel...' Ruth's voice was quieter now, more reasonable. 'I just didn't want you to get involved with Toby Meredith, can't you see?'

'Can't I see what? And I'm not involved with him. Anyroad, what's it to you?' Rachel knew that she sounded petulant, but she was vexed – with herself, with Toby, and now with Ruth.

'What's it to me?' Ruth stood stock still in the street and Rachel was forced to stop walking too.

Until then Ruth had been striding along so quickly that she could scarcely keep up with her. 'I'll tell you what it is to me. It's about time you realised, Rachel Balderstone, what a good husband you've got.'

'I do realise,' Rachel protested. 'Of course I do. And I would never have... Surely you don't think Toby and I would have...'

'I wouldn't be surprised at anything Toby Meredith would do,' said Ruth darkly. 'Don't tell me you haven't heard about him?'

'Heard what?' Rachel's tone was sulky.

'Well ... all the rumours. I've heard he came up north because he got a girl into trouble down in Surrey.'

'I don't listen to gossip,' Rachel set her mouth in a determined line, then, after giving her friend a baleful glance, she started to walk on again. 'And I didn't think you did either.'

'I don't as a rule,' said Ruth holding on to her arm. 'You know I don't. Here, steady on love. You must realise I'm only concerned about you. All right, it might only be a rumour, but I've heard it more than once. And you must admit there's talk about him living in that house, just him and Mrs Jeffreys. She's not much older than you and me, Rachel, and she's only been a widow for a year or so. There's a lot of talk.'

'Folks should mind their own business,' said Rachel, but not as forcefully as she had spoken at first. 'It's the first I've heard of it anyway.' But she had wondered; she had to admit to herself she had been a mite suspicious when Toby spoke about his landlady. Oh heck! She felt the colour flushing her cheeks as she realised what a fool she might have made of herself. 'We didn't do any-thing … honestly we didn't,' she added lamely.

'I'm sure you didn't.' Ruth tucked her arm through Rachel's. 'But perhaps it's as well I arrived when I did, eh?'

Rachel nodded silently.

'You might have been in hot water, you know,' Ruth went on, 'a married lady alone with an attractive young man. And I'll grant you he is very attractive. But there's many a young woman, I can tell you, who would give their eye teeth to change places with you, with your Harry and your two lovely little girls. You're very lucky, you know.'

Rachel, noticing the two spots of colour burning on her friend's cheeks, knew that she was looking at one of these young women. 'I do know,' she said. 'I know Harry's a good husband, but…' She gave a deep sigh. 'Just lately he thinks of nothing but that blessed rock factory. Sometimes he's so … boring. That's why I started going out; and it was you that asked me, Ruth.'

'That's true,' Ruth agreed. 'And I suppose I can see what you mean. I work with Harry, remember? I've tried to tell him about all work and no play. Look here, Rachel, you're his wife; it's up to you. Can't you persuade him to ease off a bit, to take you to the pictures now and again, or go dancing like you used to do?'

Rachel didn't answer at first.

'And if I were you,' Ruth continued, 'I'd try to take a bit more interest in what he's doing at Hobson's. It's your family's firm when all's said and done and Harry's doing it for you. He's got all sorts of good ideas for this Carnival that's coming up. Hasn't he told you?'

'He's told me a bit,' replied Rachel, still rather sulkily. She didn't like being told what she should do – she never had – even though it made sense. 'I might ask Harry to take me to the cinema,' she said grudgingly *Four Horsemen of the Apocalypse* is on this week, and I do like Rudolph Valentino. But I'm not sure Harry does...'

They had now reached the end of the street where Ruth lived and Rachel was glad to take leave of her. 'I'll think about what you've said.' She looked somewhat sheepishly at her friend. 'I do love Harry, you know, really I do.'

'I'm glad to hear it,' replied Ruth sharply. ''Bye, Rachel. See you soon.' She hurried away without stopping to chatter on the corner as they usually did.

Rachel was thoughtful as she walked the rest of the way home. She had learned a bitter lesson tonight. She realised now that she must try to spend more time with her husband. When Ruth had pointed this out she had felt resentful. She considered that Harry was as much to blame as she was, if not more so, for the apathy between them, but she was gradually coming to the conclusion that it was up to her to make the first move. If she didn't, then there could well be others who might succumb to the charms of her not unattractive – though somewhat staid – husband. Ruth, she knew, was an honourable young woman, but by no means all were so.

When she arrived home, however, she found Harry in a not very responsive mood.

'Hello, love,' she greeted him cheerily as she entered the living room, determined to put all thoughts of the early part of the evening behind her. 'I'm not late, am I? I said I wouldn't be. It's a lovely evening, really mild. What's the matter, Harry?' She stopped suddenly, for Harry was staring into space, his eyes out of focus, as though he didn't know she was there.

'What?' He came to with a start. 'Oh ... nothing, love. There's nothing the matter. Sorry, I hadn't heard you come in. Have you had a nice evening?'

'Yes, it was all right,' Rachel answered shortly. 'Come on, what is it, Harry?' She could tell there was something troubling him.

'Nothing,' he said again, a trifle irritably. 'I'm a bit tired, that's all. I was late getting in.' Then, as she continued to look at him, frowning a little, he went on: 'Well ... there is something. I wasn't going to tell you, not yet, but I suppose I would have to tell you eventually.'

'What is it?' Still wearing her hat and coat, she knelt on the hearthrug at the side of his chair.

'It's Jack.' Harry gave a deep sigh. 'I've heard today – they're letting him out, next week.'

'Oh no, not so soon!' Rachel felt all her other worries pale into insignificance. 'But it's not eighteen months yet, surely?'

'No, about six weeks less, I think. He's being let out early for good conduct.' Harry gave a bitter laugh. 'Have you ever heard the likes of that? Jack flamin' Balderstone, good conduct!'

'Hmmm ... I daresay he kept his nose clean in there,' Rachel commented.

'Aye, no doubt he would, the crafty devil. He didn't get long enough, anyroad, for what he'd done. I always thought so. By rights he should have hanged,' Harry added in an undertone.

'We don't know that, Harry. It's never been proved. And I suppose eighteen months was fair enough if he was in for embezzlement. We always knew, didn't we, that he'd be coming out again? I suppose it's been a case of "out of sight, out of mind".'

'Yes, I reckon we've tried to put him to the back of our minds. We've had other things to think about. But he'll be turning up again, sure enough, like a bad penny.'

'He won't be troubling us, though?' Rachel looked fearfully at her husband. 'Surely he wouldn't.'

'Not if he's any sense.'

'How do you know he's coming out, anyway?'

'Luke Edwards told me. Don't ask me how he knows; I haven't the foggiest. But Jack'll be out next week, and needless to say, he won't have a job at Luke's place any more.'

'Nor any home to go to either,' said Rachel, 'according to what my mother was saying, with your Aunt Jessie getting married.'

'Well, we're certainly not going to waste any sympathy on him. Even his own mother said he'd got what was coming to him. She probably knows a lot more than we do.' Harry narrowed his eyes thoughtfully. 'We're only guessing that he killed Lily.'

'Jessie gave him an alibi though, didn't she?'

'Well, she would.' Harry gave a grim nod. 'He's her son, even if he is an out-and-out bastard. Luke says the house in Ashburton Road is up for sale, but they don't seem to have got a buyer yet. So maybe Jack'll be living there for the time being. I don't know, and I don't much care, so long as he keeps out of our way.' He smiled at his wife, a little soberly. 'I thought you might have been much more upset than you are, darling. That's why I hesitated to tell you, but you don't seem too worried.'

'No, I don't think I'm all that worried,' Rachel smiled back at him. 'He can't hurt us any more, can he, Harry?' She took hold of her husband's hand, looking deep into his eyes. 'He tried to, but he couldn't. Except for Lily – that was dreadful, if it was him... And I know I lost the baby, but we've got our little Ruby now. Harry...' Her voice was uncertain. 'We are happy, aren't we, you and me?'

'Of course we are, darling.' Harry leaned forward, kissing her gently on the lips. 'Whatever made you say that?'

'Oh, nothing really. I just don't want anything to come between us.'

'Jack Balderstone won't, don't you worry. Just let him try!'

'No, I'm sure he won't.' But Rachel hadn't been thinking just of Jack. 'But I don't want you to work too hard, Harry. It's not worth it, not if it means we don't have time for each other.'

Harry looked at her in surprise. 'Of course we have time for each other! You are a silly girl.'

Obviously he hadn't noticed that they had been drifting apart of late. 'I realise I've been busy, but that's nothing fresh, is it? Work's my middle name; you know that. And you've got your new friends at that Literary thing. I thought you were all right. You are, aren't you, love?'

'Yes, I'm all right.' Rachel squeezed his hand, then she rose abruptly. 'I'll go and put the kettle on.'

At least she had made a move in trying to make him ease off work a little. Whether she would succeed was another matter. That was bad news about Jack, even though she had known he would be out of prison eventually. She did feel a tremor of unease, in spite of what she had said to Harry. The fellow was her half-brother, but she felt no sense of kinship with him whatsoever. She wished that she need never set eyes on him again; and she hoped that if he had killed Lily, he would get his just desserts, although it seemed very unlikely.

'Let's forget about Jack,' she said, as she carried their bedtime drinks into the living room. 'Tell me about the carnival thing, darling. Ruth says you've got all sorts of ideas for it.'

Harry blinked, then opened his eyes wide in surprise. 'I didn't think you'd be interested – well, not all that much. Since you stopped working there you've not taken much interest, have you? I'm not blaming you, of course. I know you've been busy with the children.'

'Well, I'm interested now.' Rachel smiled brightly at him. 'Tell me.'

'Goodness, where shall I start?' Harry laughed.

'There's the rock; probably that's the most important thing, with BLACKPOOL CARNIVAL running through it. And we're making some carnival bonbons, and your mother's busy with some new chocolates – she'll have told you about that, I expect. And we're trying to organise a float to put in the Trades Procession.'

Rachel tried to stifle a yawn, then took a sip of her cocoa. She was very tired – what with Toby, and then Jack, it had seemed an endless evening – but it looked as though she might be here till midnight.

Plans for the first Blackpool Carnival were going on apace. It was to be held from the ninth to the sixteenth of June and already there was an air of excitement in the town as they looked forward to the great event.

The staff at Hobson's, with Harry and George at the helm – George was now a full partner in the firm – were busy making festive items for the occasion. The special rock was gaily striped in rainbow colours – red, blue, green, yellow and orange – the most ambitious casing that Hobson's had ever attempted. Harry at first had thought of red, white and blue, then had amended his idea as it was a local, not a national occasion. The bonbons in reality were just rock sweets, in the same bright colours as the sticks of rock, but in their gaily striped carnival boxes they made an eye-catching display in the sweet-shop windows of the town. Ellen's famous chocolates, too, were packed in boxes specially made for the event. With the addition of a few more delicious centres – praline, rum truffle, and cherries coated in brandy-marzipan – the product was proving more popular than ever with residents and visitors alike.

'Let's just hope the weather's kind to us,' Rachel remarked to Harry as they walked arm-in-arm along the promenade, a couple of nights before the start of the carnival. 'You can't say that it feels much like June, as yet, but there's time for it to improve, I suppose.' There was a chilly wind blowing in from the sea, with the threat of rain, and Rachel was glad of her warm coat and closely-fitting cloche hat.

'That's one thing we can't guarantee, my love,' said Harry, 'especially in Blackpool. So long as it doesn't rain for the Trades Procession; I certainly don't want Hobson's float to get soaked after all the hard work we're putting into it, or is that too selfish of me?'

'No, why should it be?' Rachel grinned up at him. 'I expect all the other firms are thinking just the same as you.'

'I must say the decorations are quite spectacular,' remarked Harry as they walked northwards from Talbot Square. 'Blackpool has certainly gone to town with this lot.'

They had come out specially this evening to take a preview of Blackpool in its carnival attire, before the expected crowds arrived at the weekend. A floral arch had been erected at North Station to welcome the visitors. Talbot Square, the civic centre of the town, sported a huge Imperial crown, topping the tram shelter in the middle; and from there to Gynn Square the tram standards were decorated with national flags and gold and purple streaming banners bearing heraldic arms.

Rachel felt a glow of contentment such as she hadn't experienced for ages. She was looking forward to this week of revelry, hoping that she and Harry, together with their daughters, would be able to join in some of the celebrations. No doubt Amy, the children's nursemaid, would also want to take part in the fun. Rachel had never seen Blackpool look so festive; not even for the Victory celebrations had it looked as bright and colourful as this.

She had tried to put her worries to the back of her mind and, in the main, had succeeded. Harry was still, in her opinion, working far too hard. It seemed as though he couldn't help himself, but maybe after the carnival his workload would decrease a little. She was trying so hard to concentrate on her husband's good points, telling herself how fortunate she was. She never allowed herself to think about Toby Meredith. She felt guilty whenever she did so and quickly suppressed her thoughts. Ruth, good friend that she was, had not referred to the incident again.

Rachel's chief anxiety, which she never mentioned to Harry, was about her half-brother, Jack. He must be out there somewhere, wandering the streets of Blackpool, or working, maybe in a pub, or a shop, or a sea-front stall. How did she know that she might not suddenly come face to face with him? The thought of his unseen presence frightened her and she had to make a determined effort at times not to keep looking over her shoulder. Since that evening when Harry had told her about Jack's imminent release he had scarcely been mentioned. And if Harry had, by any chance, set eyes on him, he hadn't referred to it.

Forget him, put him out of your mind, she urged herself, clinging tightly to Harry's arm as they walked back along Dickson Road. Think about nice, happy things; your little girls, your home and your good husband. And about what a splendid time would be had in Blackpool next week ... if only the rain would keep off.

Chapter Twenty-Six

The rain, unfortunately, didn't keep off. Saturday, the ninth of June, was a day of heavy rain and dark lowering clouds. George was the only member of the Hobson family to brave the weather for the start of the week's festivities. He stood on the sands with hundreds of other dripping spectators, gazing up into the grey sky, awaiting the arrival, by aeroplane from Manchester, of King Carnival and his consort.

'Grand weather for ducks, eh?' remarked a cheerful voice in the crowd next to him.

'I'll say!' Tipping his large black umbrella slightly to one side, George met the merry blue eyes of a young lady. A very bonny young lady, too, with a round face and a wide mouth which was half-open in a smile, revealing teeth which were just the tiniest bit uneven.

'Oh look, you're getting soaked,' said George in concern. Even though the girl was wearing a raincoat and a sou'wester hat they were insufficient protection in such a deluge and the rain was dripping from the end of her nose; a very attractive, slightly turned-up nose, George noted. 'Come under my umbrella; there's plenty of room.'

'I'm right enough,' the girl laughed. 'I don't mind the rain. But thanks, I think I will.'

They stood waiting in silence, companionable

enough, but George, for the moment, couldn't think of anything to say. He was always a little tongue tied when he first met a strange young lady. The crowd around them was getting fidgety and impatient, but fortunately it wasn't long before the awaited aeroplane came to land on the wide stretch of sand and King Carnival and his consort stepped down. The cheer that greeted them was rather less than enthusiastic.

'D'you know who he is, the King?' George said, turning to his companion. He didn't wait for an answer; in all probability she didn't know. 'It's Doodles, the clown from the Tower Circus. He's been chosen to be King of Fun for the week. I don't know who his Queen is, though.'

'Well, fancy that!' The girl laughed. 'You learn something every day, don't you? Whoever they are, they're getting wet, like us.' The ermine cloaks and gold crowns of the royal pair, as they made their way to the waiting motor car, were incongruous garments in such a downpour.

'I think I've seen enough,' she went on. 'I just wanted to see them land, but I'm ready for off now. I can watch them again in the procession on Monday. Thanks for the loan of your umbrella.'

'Oh, don't dash away, please.' George tentatively held out a restraining arm. 'I mean, I'm going as well now. I'll walk up to the promenade with you, if you don't mind.'

''Course I don't,' the girl grinned. 'I tell you what – let's go and have a cup of tea, shall we? It might warm us up a bit.'

It was exactly what George was about to suggest himself; he had just been plucking up courage to do so.

They found a tea-shop near Talbot Square which was not too crowded. 'I don't make a habit of this, you know,' said the girl, taking off her long coat and hat and hanging them on the coat-stand by the door. She ran her hands through her hair which had been flattened by the restraining hat. Her hair was auburn – like Lily's had been, George recalled, but of a much darker shade; shorter, too, and more curly. 'Talking to strange men, I mean,' she explained. 'But I could see that you were all right. I can always tell.'

'Thanks.' George smiled a little ruefully. 'Yes, you're safe enough with me. I'm a bit on the shy side. At least, that's what girls always tell me.'

Over tea and toasted muffins they became better acquainted. George learned that the girl was Sally Heathcote from Oldham. Her parents owned a newsagent's shop there, where Sally worked, also selling sweets and tobacco. They had all come to Blackpool especially for Carnival week and were staying in a boarding house in Albert Road. But her parents hadn't wanted to get drenched, so they were busy unpacking whilst Sally familiarised herself with the town.

'Your first visit here?' George asked.

'No, not at all,' she replied. 'We often used to come here for family holidays when we were kids, my mum and dad and my brother and I. But we haven't been since the war ended. Our Billy was killed, you see, and we haven't felt like it.'

'No, you wouldn't,' said George, feeling an immediate affinity with her. 'I understand. I was there, too.'

Sally nodded solemnly. 'I guessed you might have been. Anyway, I managed to persuade them to come for the Carnival. It isn't actually Oldham holiday week – Dad was undecided at first because he didn't want to close – but we've some good friends who offered to look after the shop for us.'

'It's a small world,' George told her, well aware that it was not a very original remark. 'You say you sell sweets ... I'm in that line as well.'

Sally seemed fascinated to hear that he was in the rock business, and by the end of the hour or so they spent together he felt as though he had known her for ages. He asked her if she would meet him to watch the Carnival procession on Monday and, to his delight, she agreed.

'Shouldn't you be working?' Sally asked, as they stood together on the promenade, near to the Royal Hotel. 'You really mustn't neglect your duties to be with me. But I'm glad you are,' she added, smiling at him.

'Oh, I reckon I can please myself. I'm a partner in the firm now,' said George, with more than a little pride. He had waited long enough for this position. 'To be quite honest, I don't think there'll be much work done at our place this week. We're making sure everyone has some time off to join in the fun. And on Wednesday we're all taking part in the Trades Procession. Hobson's are entering a float, so you'll be able to wave to me from the crowd. Look – they're coming now.'

The Carnival procession was led by the King and Queen in their state coach. Then followed so many different displays – brass bands, Morris dancers, decorated floats and landaus, representatives of the armed forces – that the spectators began to feel quite bewildered. There was a bevy of bathing belles, accompanied by a replica of the new South Shore baths (which had been opened on Saturday in the pouring rain). Much admired were the grotesque figures with huge papier-mâché heads, three hundred of them, it was reported, made by artists specially brought from Nice.

The outlying villages of the Fylde were also represented; Thornton-le-Fylde with a tableau of Windmill Lane, featuring a model of their own Marsh Mill; and a Poulton with a facsimile of their village, complete with stocks and whipping post. As George remarked to Sally, this was fair enough because, at one time, Poulton had been the Mother village, of much more importance than the insignificant hamlet of Blackpool. But that was a couple of hundred years ago, of course.

At the rear of the procession was an all-too-familiar scene which brought back unpleasant memories for George; and for many others, too, he could tell by the murmurings in the crowd. For there was Tommy Atkins in his khaki uniform, in fighting position with a fixed bayonet, crouching behind a sand-bag trench. At the back of the lorry was a placard on which was written the significant word, WIPERS.

'That was unnecessary, in my opinion,' Sally remarked later, as they sat drinking coffee in Jenkinson's café. 'We're trying to forget about the war. Well, I know we can never entirely forget – we wouldn't want to forget our Billy – but what I mean is we're trying to come to terms with it. I can't see that it does any good to rake up unhappy memories. Surely, now, we should try to look to the future ... and happier times?'

George, who was in complete agreement, found himself telling his new friend about his own experiences, something he had never before discussed with anyone, not even Lily. Lily had been good fun; she had made him laugh and had taken him out of himself, but she wouldn't have wanted to listen to his troubles. He told Sally about his drinking and how, for a long while, it had got the upper hand. And about his stepfather Ben, who, even though he had died in a motor accident, had been a casualty of the war. He even told her about Lily...

'That was what made me come to my senses,' he said. 'Don't ask me how, but it did. I realised, you see, that I'd been using her ... to try to forget my own problems. It could have been any girl, but it happened to be Lily. And then, when she was ... murdered, I can't begin to tell you how awful I felt. Even though I didn't kill her, I still feel, in some way, that I was responsible. If it hadn't been for me, she might still be alive.'

'Don't say that. Of course you're not responsible,' cried Sally. She took hold of his hand, briefly, in a sympathetic grasp, then let it go again. 'How could it have anything to do with you? They proved you weren't there.' He had already told her about his arrest and subsequent alibi.

'No, but it was jealousy that caused it, more than likely, wasn't it? This other chap ... he must have been jealous of me. That's probably why he killed her. Perhaps he didn't even mean to,' he added.

'And they never caught him? You've no idea who it was?'

George was silent for a moment. 'They've never caught him, no. Lack of evidence, I suppose, but ... I know who it was. At least, I've a damn good idea. My family guessed, and they tried to keep it from me. I know jolly well they did; they were scared of what I might do, you see. I didn't know at first who it was, then I put two and two together. It all seemed to fit. He's caused havoc in our family, this fellow. He went to prison for something else, and now, all the desire I had for revenge seems to have ... gone.' He spread his hands wide. 'Whatever I do, it wouldn't bring Lily back.' What George didn't tell Sally was that the fellow was his half-brother. He had never known him nor did he want to, but the fact remained that they had had the same father.

'This Lily, did you love her?' asked Sally.

George shook his head. Looking into the candid blue eyes of Sally Heathcote he knew that he had never really loved Lily. 'No, I didn't. But I liked her, a lot. And she helped me, in her own way. I'm grateful for that.'

'And you're over it now, the drinking and all that? And the awful war memories?'

'Yes, I've got it under control. I know I'll be able to cope ... now.' George placed his hand over Sally's as it rested on the table top.

'I'm sure you will,' she smiled, returning his steady gaze.

Ellen, as she watched the Trades Procession on Wednesday morning with her daughter and her two granddaughters, began to realise that Hobson's float would probably not be one of the prizewinners. There were so many fantastic displays put on by the various Blackpool businesses.

There was a model of the Tower, constructed wholly from biscuits, made by the Blackpool Biscuit Company; a tableau of the Queen of Sheba and her hand-maidens, featuring Lawrence Wright's Music Company; and a most charming model of an old village inn, the entry of the C and S Brewery, famed throughout Blackpool and the Fylde for their ales. As well as coal merchants, plumbers, painters and decorators, butchers and bakers and confectioners...

Ellen was reminded, as the various floats passed by, of a similar occasion almost twenty-one years ago; the Preston Guild Procession of 1902 when her husband, William, had taken an active part on the Cordwainer's float. So had Amos Hardy, she recalled: he was still working at their rock factory, whereas William had died at the close of Guild Week. There had been another Preston Guild only last year, 1922, but Ellen had had no desire to go and watch the procession, knowing that it would evoke too many unhappy memories.

Such a lot had happened since that day more than twenty years ago. At that time she hadn't even met Ben; now she was a widow again. And in the meantime the country had been involved in the bloodiest war of all time. It was just as well – one of God's blessings, in fact – that we couldn't see into the future, she found herself thinking. If we could, we would never be able to face it.

Today, however, a joyous day in the middle of Blackpool Carnival week, was no time for introspection. Blackpool was doing its utmost to make it a memorable, fun-packed week for both visitors and residents. But it would have helped if the sun had shone. Wednesday, again, was dull and overcast, as it had been for the Battle of Flowers the previous day. There was a cool wind blowing too, and Ellen turned up her coat collar as she peered along the promenade.

'They're coming!' She turned excitedly to Rachel. 'There's our float. I can see the banner. Look – Hobson's Rock (the Only Choice). Very eyecatching, isn't it? Come on, Pearl. Grandma'll lift you up, then you can wave to Daddy and Uncle George.'

Hobson's float, near the tail end of the procession, proved to be worth waiting for. The main feature, in the centre, was an enormous stick of rock, some five feet in length and nine inches in diameter, gaily striped in the colours that Hobson's had chosen for the Carnival; red, blue, green, yellow and orange. The girls from the factory – the rock-rollers and wrappers, and Ruth, from the office – wore their own pretty summer dresses, with striped aprons and mobcaps which copied almost exactly the colours in

545

the rock. (Ellen had searched at the local markets until she had found a near-enough match.) The men, too, sported waistcoats of the same material and straw boaters with a striped ribbon. And the same bright colours were echoed in the hundreds of paper flowers that decorated the float.

'Look, there's Daddy. Wave to Daddy,' said Rachel. 'And Uncle George.'

Harry looked as pleased as Punch as he smiled and waved at his little daughters. George seemed happy enough too, but slightly ill at ease. He fiddled self-consciously with his bow tie as he smilingly acknowledged his family. Pearl, aged two and a half, recognised them and shouted with delight, whilst Ruby, who would be one year old the following month, stared uncomprehendingly from her pram at the unfamiliar scene.

'Well, that's that,' declared Ellen as the last tableau passed by. 'I think Hobson's float looked as nice as any. I don't suppose we'll win a prize, but they did us proud.' She beamed at Pearl. 'I think we deserve an ice cream, don't you? Let's go and see if we can find a "Stop Me and Buy One".'

Rarely had Blackpool witnessed such scenes of wild excitement as there were on the Saturday night of 16 June, at the close of Carnival week. Rachel and Harry joined the crowds in Talbot Square and watched as King Carnival was toppled unceremoniously from his throne, then carried, shoulder-high, on to the sands where he was to be set alight and burned. Not the real King Carnival, of course – alias Doodles, the clown – but a life-size effigy of the King.

'It's a bit callous, isn't it?' remarked Rachel, as they followed the crowd on to the beach. 'Bloodthirsty, you might say, burning the poor old King's effigy after they've been fêting him all week.'

'Symbolic, I suppose,' replied Harry. 'He's had his day, you see. He's reigned supreme all week. Now Blackpool has to get back to reality; to what it's best at doing ... making money,' he added, a little cynically.

They stood arm-in-arm on the fringe of the crowd. The huge bonfire soon caught alight. Even from a distance they could hear the spit and crackle of the flames and see the sparks flying into the darkening sky.

'Look, there he goes,' cried Harry, as the limp figure of the rejected King was swallowed up by the tongues of flame. His head lolled sideways, then he fell in a crumpled heap into the middle of the conflagration. 'Poor old King Carnival; that's him gone.'

Then there followed a firework display, a fitting climax to the week's celebrations. Roman candles, Catherine wheels and rockets fizzed and sparkled all around as the bonfire consumed its victim. It was a pretty sight, although it was really no different from the displays witnessed on Guy Fawkes' night, but Blackpool was determined to enjoy itself right to the end. Whoever had planned the festivities, however, had paid little heed to the sea and its movements. It was often said that 'Time and tide wait for no man', and already, as the firework display was at its height, the tide was advancing, lapping round the feet of the folk in the crowd. They shouted and laughed, jumping out of the way, then making regretfully for the promenade as the sea continued its relentless march.

'Ironic, isn't it?' said Harry. 'King Neptune has won after all, as he always will in Blackpool. The sands have been well-nigh deserted this week, there's been so much going on in the town, but King Neptune's the ruler now – look at him! Blackpool wouldn't be Blackpool without the sea.'

But Rachel was paying little heed to her husband's philosophising. She was staring at a figure some distance away on the other side of the bonfire. 'Harry, look ... over there.' She clutched at her husband's arm. 'Isn't that Jack?'

Harry looked; sure enough it was his cousin. Shoulders hunched, his hands shoved deep in his pockets, Jack was staring moodily in the direction of the leaping flames. 'It's all right,' whispered Harry, as Rachel drew closer to him, half-hiding her head against his shoulder. 'He hasn't seen us. Look; he's going now.'

The shambling figure, kicking disconsolately at piles of churned-up sand in his path, made his way across the promenade. This was certainly not the jaunty, devil-may-care person they remembered, but the very picture of misery.

'All right, darling?' Harry put a protective arm round his wife. 'We knew, didn't we, that we'd probably encounter him sooner or later. I wonder what he's doing with himself these days? I haven't heard. He doesn't look very happy.' He

548

continued to stare after the retreating figure as he mounted the steps and turned northwards.

'Anyway, we're not going to let him spoil our evening, are we? Let's find a café and have a cuppa. Your mother said she didn't mind if we were late.'

They followed the departing crowds off the sands. The sea was advancing rapidly now, washing round the base of the bonfire. Very soon the flames would be totally extinguished. The Carnival had come to an end.

Rachel was very quiet. She moved closer to her husband, in need of his protection, feeling a dreadful sense of premonition. But Harry, she knew, would tell her she was being fanciful, so she kept her fears to herself.

Jack, in fact, had seen his cousin and his wife ... his own half-sister. He had been watching them, unobserved, for several minutes, and as he saw them talking and laughing together as though they hadn't a care in the world, the bitter feelings that had never been quenched resurged with more intensity than ever. He looked away from them, towards the bonfire, where the flames were consuming their prey. The sight of the blaze inflamed Jack's anger and hatred. His resentment had long been a smouldering, tormenting glow within him; now it became a raging inferno.

He turned abruptly and walked away, a plan forming in his deranged mind. He'd pay them back all right; he would show the whole damn lot of them that Jack Balderstone wasn't to be trifled with. Even his own mother didn't want to know him now. He had seen her only once since his release from prison, three weeks ago, and she had been so taken up with her fancy man – now her husband – that she could hardly give her son the time of day. He had no home, not what you could call a home, because the house was now sold and the new occupants were moving in next week. He had got his share of the profits, though – Jack had made sure of that – but at the moment he was living in miserable digs in Bonny Street, behind the Golden Mile, all he had been able to find with the summer season now getting into its swing. He was working as a deckchair attendant – a comedown, he knew, for the talented Jack Balderstone. But he'd make a comeback. He'd show them. He would get even with the whole bloody lot of them. First of all, the Hobsons...

Reaching the promenade, he walked quickly, dodging and elbowing his way between the crowds, towards his former home on Ashburton Road. The shed in the backyard was never locked and he should be able to find there what he needed to carry out his plan. No one saw him as he entered the yard, then hunted around in the semi-darkness of the shed amongst the few rejected gardening tools and household debris. He had guessed that his mother wouldn't have moved this junk along with her good furniture. Yes, there it was. His eyes gleamed as he seized the petrol can that Jessie had used to rekindle a dying fire. He shook it, then nodded. It was half-full; with a bit of luck, there should be enough.

His target this time was not the shop on Euston Street, but the factory. He had no key, of course, as he had had for the shop, but the little street was deserted and the windows were at waist-height. He took out the hammer that he had put in the hold-all, along with the petrol can, and bashed it against the pane of glass. It seemed to make a deafening crash in the silence, but no one was near enough to hear. Jack put his hand inside and found the catch. It was so easy to open the window and climb in. What fools the Hobsons were, not to be better protected.

Jack wasted no time. He made for the back of the workplace where, he had noticed on his one and only visit, the sacks of sugar were stored. That was the obvious place to start a good blaze. He sprinkled them with the petrol, then struck and threw the matches – one, two, three – one for each sack. He smiled, then laughed out loud with glee as they set alight. He stood for a moment or two watching, to make sure he had achieved what he intended. Yes ... he knew that soon after he had gone the blaze would become an inferno, consuming everything in its path, reducing to ashes, in minutes, the industrious labour of many years. But it would serve them right, his toffee-nosed cousin and Ellen Bamber and all her sodding family. His mother didn't seem to care any more, but he, Jack, would show them that pride came before a fall. And they would certainly fall. The Hobsons would find them-selves right at the bottom of the muck heap, grovelling in the mire.

He turned now, hurrying away through the steadily thickening smoke. There was no time to lose, but the window where he had made his entry was still clear, open to the night air which was already fanning the flames. In his haste Jack failed to notice the large metal hook on the wall, the hook on which the clear toffee mixture was hung, to be pulled and pulled until it became opaque. As he took a step back, in readiness for his vault up to the narrow windowsill, the hook caught on to his coat, between the shoulder blades, tearing into the woollen fabric.

'What the hell...?' Jack pulled away, trying to free himself, but his sudden movement only made the hook dig deeper, holding him in its relentless grip. The more he struggled, the more entangled he became. Cursing out loud, blinking his smarting and watering eyes – the smoke was increasing in density with every second – he undid the buttons of his jacket and managed, with difficulty, to free one arm. But by now he was engulfed in a thick black haze and as he strained to free his other arm the smoke entered his nostrils and his mouth, choking him and making him cry out in terror.

'Help! Help! Somebody help me. For God's sake, help me!' he yelled, his cry drifting out into the darkness of the night. But there was no one near enough to hear.

He shouted only the once, for by now the thick smoke had completely overwhelmed him. His head dropped forward and his arms drooped limply at his sides as he hung there, imprisoned by the hook on the wall.

'Harry, let's have a look down Euston Street and make sure the shop and factory are all right, shall we?' Rachel had been persuaded, by her husband, to make the most of their evening of freedom. They had enjoyed a cup of tea at a sea-front café, but now the vague fears which had haunted her since seeing Jack earlier in the evening had returned.

Harry smiled indulgently at her. 'If you like, darling, but I'm sure there's nothing to worry about. It's seeing Jack, isn't it, that's upset you? I've told you; he wouldn't dare start anything again. But we'll go and make sure, just to put your mind at rest. Look, isn't that our George?' he said, as they turned off the promenade into Church Street. 'Yes, it is – see – just by the Grand Theatre, and that must be Sally with him. She looks like a nice girl, I must say.'

The family had already heard about George's new friend, but hadn't yet met her. Sally and her parents were to go home to Oldham the next day, but George had assured them she would be coming to Blackpool again. He had imparted this news with a decided gleam in his eye which boded well, they thought, for his future.

'We've been to the pictures,' George told his sister and brother-in-law, after introductions had been made, 'and we were just going for a walk on the prom. But – yes, we'll come with you and make sure that everything's as it should be. There may well be some hooligans around tonight, and it's as well to make sure.'

Rachel and Sally had walked on ahead and as they turned off Market Street, with the two young men following closely behind them, it soon became obvious that Rachel's fears had not

553

been groundless. Already a small crowd was gathering outside the factory and one man was running towards them along the narrow cobbled street.

'Fire!' he was yelling. 'There's a fire! I'm going to get the Fire Brigade!'

'Oh no, no, not that,' Rachel murmured, as the four of them started to run. 'I *knew* something was going to happen.'

Smoke was eddying out from a broken window and from beneath the somewhat ill-fitting door, and a red glow was visible inside, at the back of the large room. Harry drew out his set of keys which he always carried and fumbled around, trying to find the right one.

'For God's sake, Harry, you mustn't go in!' cried George. 'Don't open the door! It's the worst thing you can do.'

'Aye, he's right, lad,' agreed a bystander. 'You'll make it worse if the air gets hold of it. Just keep away. Someone's gone for t'Fire Brigade.'

'It's my factory, and I'm going in,' Harry shouted back. 'Don't tell me my business. I know what I've got to do.'

'Harry ... no, you mustn't!' Rachel was yelling, but he paid no heed to her. 'Just look after the girls,' he said to George, adding, in an undertone, 'It seems that Rachel was right, after all.'

He flung open the door, ignoring all the warnings shouted at him, peering through the thick grey fog that confronted him. The back of the room was well alight, the wooden beams and window frames cracking and splintering as the tongues of flame leaped towards the ceiling. And, through the haze, Harry could dimly make out the shape of a figure, slumped forwards, as though he were ... hanging.

'Oh, my God. No!' he cried, instinctively dashing across to the inert form. Only when he reached it did he realise that it was Jack, although he might have guessed that it would be. He tugged at him, then tugged again, and there was a ripping sound as Jack was freed from the grip of the hook. Then holding him under the arms Harry dragged him through the swirling smoke towards the door.

'We'll need ... an ambulance ... as well,' gasped Harry, coughing and spluttering, struggling to get his breath, as Rachel flung her arms around him and George knelt at the side of the motionless figure on the ground.

'Harry... Oh Harry, I thought you were going to be killed.' Rachel cradled his head against her shoulder as Harry leaned on her, his eyes smarting and streaming, blinded by the smoke, the acrid taste filling his throat and his nostrils. A few more moments in there and he, too, would have been rendered unconscious, just like his cousin. Then they would both have perished in the consuming flames.

'It's Jack, isn't it?' Rachel whispered. 'We've got proof now ... all the evidence we need. But it was so brave of you, darling, to save him. After all he's done.'

George looked up, his face grim. 'It's too late for an ambulance,' he said, his hand still holding the limp wrist of the man on the ground, the man who was his half-brother. Never once, throughout their lives, had they exchanged so much as a word. Now, at the moment of his death, George, for the first and last time, touched the hand of his half-brother, the man who had created such havoc in all their lives. 'He's gone. I'm afraid John Henry's ... dead.'

There was nothing more to be done for Jack. The police came, and an ambulance to take away his body. The Fire Brigade came, too, and the blaze was soon extinguished; but not before the flames had done their worst and almost the whole of the factory had been gutted. Part of the roof had fallen in, all the equipment was ruined, and the small office, too, had been partially destroyed. Only the adjoining premises had been spared. The shop, mercifully, and all the stock in it had survived intact. Now all that remained was to break the news to Ellen.

It was Ellen who gave them the heart, the next day, to pick up the pieces and carry on. She was overwhelmed for a time as she stood in the cobbled street with her family – Rachel, George and Harry – at her side, gazing on the sight of such devastation. This was the second time she had looked at the destruction of her property; first the vandalising of the shop, and now this. But this time it was far, far worse. The windows had all broken with the force of the blaze and inside the building was a scene of total blackness. The walls and ceiling – what remained of it, for part of the roof had gone – the work tables, the timber framework and the equipment were all charred or burned beyond recognition.

Ellen stood in silence for several moments, the tears welling into her eyes. The sadness she felt was not just for the dreadful scene confronting her, but the thought of such wanton wickedness. How that young man must have hated them, to do this. To think that the desire for revenge could go to such lengths, or last so long, more than twenty years. She spared a thought then for Jessie, with whom, thankfully, she had made her peace, albeit an uneasy one. Her old adversary must be feeling saddened beyond belief today. Jessie had said that she and Jack had parted company, but he was her son, for all that.

Ellen blinked back her tears. She mustn't give way in front of her family. They were feeling just as angry and upset as she was. But there was a glimmer of hope in that the shop was left, and the second shop on Dickson Road where Rachel and Harry lived.

'Heartbreaking, isn't it, Mum?' It was George who spoke first. 'Years and years of work, mainly your work, and Ben's, all come to this ... to nothing. All our equipment, our raw materials. It doesn't bear thinking of.'

'At least we're insured,' said Harry, though very dispiritedly. 'We'd have to be, of course, in a business like this. I suppose it's some consolation, but it'll be the very devil of a job to start again.'

Ellen looked at their three dejected faces and it seemed to her, fanciful though it might be, that at that moment Ben spoke to her. *You haven't lost everything*, said a voice within her. *You've got your health and strength, you've got your family, and above all, your determination not to be beaten.*

'Why should it be so difficult?' Ellen spoke with such resolution that they all turned to stare at her. 'Why should it be so hard to start again, tell me? What equipment do we need, for goodness sake?'

And as they all continued to look at her, dumbfounded, Ellen smiled at them, a little sadly. 'Ben and I started off with hardly anything. Yes, I know I had the shop in Preston, and the market stall – that was a good start – but when I decided to make rock we started from scratch. And, I say again, what equipment do we need? Rock is still made largely by hand – you know that as well as I do – so all we need are the pans and sugar and glucose ... and our own two hands.' She spread her own hands wide, looking down at them. 'Well, I'm right, aren't I?'

'Yes, you're right, Mam.' It was Rachel who replied. 'Of course you're right. And let me tell you something – I'm going to be working with you all.' She turned to smile at her husband, then she drew closer to him, holding on to his arm. 'I've plenty of time, now that Amy is looking after the children, so I've decided I'm coming back to work at Hobson's. I was wrong, Harry,' she added, speaking just to her husband, although the others overheard her words. 'I shouldn't have criticised you for working too hard. I'm sorry ... and from now on, I'll be working along with you.'

'That goes for me too,' said George. 'We'll make Hobson's "The Only Choice!" again, if it's the last thing we do. And before long there might be someone else in the family to help us,' he added shyly, unable to suppress a grin.

Harry and Ellen exchanged knowing glances. 'Yes, I reckon we'll come through this, Mother-in-law,' said Harry, speaking very quietly. 'Perhaps not here...' he pointed to the burned-out shell of the building in front of them, '...but somewhere. We'll start again.'

'Of course we will. There's nothing more certain.' Ellen turned and smiled at them, her chin uplifted and her eyes alight with conviction. 'We'll begin again. It's what Ben would have wanted.'

This Large Print Book for the partially sighted, who cannot read normal print, is published under the auspices of

THE ULVERSCROFT FOUNDATION